el hair sleeps with a boy in my head

angel hair sleeps with a boy in my head

the
ANGEL
HAIR anthology

edited by
anne waldman
and **lewis warsh**

granary books   **new york city** 2001

Library of Congress
Cataloging-in-Publication Data

Angel hair sleeps with a boy in my head :
the Angel hair anthology / edited by Anne
Waldman and Lewis Warsh.
    p. cm.
    Includes index.
    ISBN 1-887123-50-4 (cloth : alk. paper)
    -- ISBN 1-887123-49-0 (pbk. : alk. paper)
    1. American poetry--20th century. I.
Waldman, Anne, 1945- II. Warsh,
Lewis. III. Angel hair.

    PS536.2 .A48 2001
    811'.5408--dc21
                                2001040258

    Special thanks to Steve Clay, Amber
Phillips and Aaron Fischer for their devo-
tion to this project; to Don Byrd, who initi-
ated the idea to do this book in this form;
to Mary Burke, who worked on the book
from the start; to Bernadette Mayer, who
co-edited many of the last Angel Hair
books; to Reed Bye for keeping the Angel
Hair flame going; to Gerard Malanga and
Larry Fagin for the use of their photo-
graphs; to Linda P. O'Brien and Emily Y. Ho
for proofreading and indexing; and to Katt
Lissard and Andrew Schelling for their
ongoing support.

Book design by Amber Phillips

Printed on acid-free paper

Printed and bound in
The United States of America

Granary Books, Inc.
www.granarybooks.com

Distributed to the trade by D.A.P.
    Distributed Art Publishers
    155 Avenue of the Americas
    Second Floor
    New York, NY 10013-1508

    Orders: (800) 338-BOOK
    Tel.: (212) 627-1999
    Fax: (212) 627-9484

for Frances LeFevre Waldman & Ray Warsh

*

Hold to the future. With firm hands. The future of each afterlife, or each ghost, of each word that is about to be mentioned.

—Jack Spicer
from "A Textbook of Poetry"

CONTENTS

ANGEL HAIR 6

ANGEL HAIR BOOKS

HE DREAMS WHAT IS GOING ON INSIDE HIS HEAD

Angel Hair sleeps with a boy in my head.
She says: School is a drawing of your body,
and she paints lectures on paradox when she screws.
The boy has blue eyes but looks like me.
He says my beauty comes from lectures—
especially when they are boring.
In fact, this love of theirs is boring,
and sometimes I cover them with mist to feel
"this true fair world of things, a sea reflecting love."
Below, there is an island where thousands of white balloons
float above a class of high school girls learning grammar.
Earl-Jean sings after supper to the envying nightingales.
And when Angel Hair wakes up even she looks lovely,
and she spends time with me.
The boy is nice, too, and I like him to adore me.
Sometimes I let him in to walk with me by the fountains
and skyscrapers and listen to "Sexy Ways."
He pays to court me, but I am distant every time.
Then when I tell him about our Lord Tennyson,
wrapped round with a cloak while dying in the moonlight,
he has Angel Hair to turn to for his mad yearnings.
But I am jealous when they kiss her and I hear their breathings.
They surround me in their sad bliss,
and I watch how the ideas of my legs make them move.
My arms are homework and my blood runs for thoughts.
Still, when I sleep, they watch me, and once
they slept next to me.
They even got used to the smoke in my lungs,
and my heart does not wear them out.
When I read books, they take part in all of it,
and when I want to be alone, they go out for a walk.
They can never leave me, and I hope I will never go away.

—Jonathan Cott, *City of Earthly Love*

INTRODUCTION

ANNE WALDMAN

I met Lewis Warsh at the Berkeley Poetry Conference and will always forever after think we founded Angel Hair within that auspicious moment. Conflation of time triggered by romance adjacent to the glamorous history-making events of the conference seems a reasonable explanation. Perhaps Angel Hair was what we made together in our brief substantive marriage that lasted and had repercussions. And sped us on our way as writers. Aspirations to be a poet were rising, the ante grew higher at Berkeley surrounded by heroic figures of the New American Poetry. Here was a fellow New Yorker, same age, who had also written novels, was resolute, erudite about contemporary poetry. Mutual recognition lit us up. Don't I know you?

Summer before last year at Bennington where I'd been editing *SILO* magazine under tutalage of printer-poet Claude Fredericks, studying literature and poetry with Howard Nemerov and other literary and creative faculty, I was encouraged by Jonathan Cott—comrade I'd known since high school—to visit radical Berkeley and check out the poetry convention. It was certainly going to be more experimental than what I was exposed to at Bennington. A few students had been making queries about why no one taught Williams, Pound or Gertrude Stein, let alone H.D. I was trying to get the school to invite Allen Ginsberg to read. Jon and I had been exchanging work, he'd sent copies of Ted Berrigan's "C" magazine jamming my little rustic p.o. box. He'd known Ron Padgett at Columbia University. We were on to the New American Poetry and the poetry net was widening, inviting.

INTRODUCTION

LEWIS WARSH

Anne Waldman and I met in the earliest stages of our becoming poets. Possibly editing a magazine is a tricky idea under these circumstances. Possibly it's the best idea—to test one's ideas before you even have them, or when they're pre-embryonic. In a sense doing a magazine at this early moment was our way of giving birth—as much to the actual magazine and books as to our selves as poets. We were going on nerve, all of twenty years old, but trusting in our love, which was less tricky and in the moment defied all uncertainty.

The fact that we were growing up through the editing of the magazine and writing our own poems at the same time was a complicated process and gave us a lot of permission to make mistakes, stumble and recover. It was by making mistakes, as in every endeavor, that we learned. From the start, the contents of the magazine mirrored our social encounters as much as any fixed aesthetic. Yet we also had a point of departure and context—the poets included in *The New American Poetry* anthology edited by Donald Allen, which first appeared in 1960.

My mother's connection to poet Anghelos Sikelianos—he was her father-in-law over a decade—had decidedly informed my upbringing and aspirations to poetry. Frances was part of the utopian Delphic Ideal community in Greece in the 1930s spearheaded by Eva Palmer Sikelianos with links to Isadora Duncan, Jose Clemente Orozco, others, that had a humanistic brave notion that art, and Greek drama in particular, could "save mankind." There was encouragement in our bohemian household towards any act of poetry. I wrote stories and plays and e.e. cummingsesque poems in high school, and sent them uneventfully off to *The Village Voice* and *The Evergreen Review*, to which I loyally subscribed. The night Lewis and I took lysergic acid diethylamide at a friend's apartment on Nob Hill, first time, I hallucinated a lineage tree, an *arbor vitae* (prevalent archetypal "acid" icon)—resonant with what you visualize in particular Buddhist practices—that included all the people I'd ever known: family, friends, their families, friends. Also heroes, heroines, cultural figures, saints, poets, ballplayers, actors, movie stars, singers, many others—bad guys, enemies even. Animals, trees, plants, lakes, mountains, and so on. All gathered in my brain in witness motif, gazing at one another and then up at the sky waiting for an impulse to get something "going." Or make use of their precious time "on earth." Of course all these folk were already busy, that wasn't the point. It was my yearning to be part of it all, a blueprint for community, for *sacre conversatione*. More like a fifties Sci Fi movie? And yet the desire to belong, and to "lead" had a naive, albeit egotistical, purity.

Back on the relative level, clearly Lewis and I were bonded and destined to "do something" together. Certainly meeting on the West Coast and having a sense of those poetry communities helped define or keep

I encountered this book the summer it appeared, when I was fifteen, and eventually knew many of the poems and the biographical statements by heart. There was also the context of The Berkeley Poetry Conference, which took place in the summer of 1965. This is where Anne and I met, at Robert Duncan's reading. The conference was one of the major convergences of the poets included in the Don Allen anthology, with emphasis on the Black Mountain poets and the poets of the San Fransico Renaissance. (None of the first-generation New York School poets were present, though I'd heard that Frank O'Hara had been invited and couldn't make it.) So from the start this was the tradition we wanted to explore as publishers and editors. A feeling of wanting to go beyond that tradition came later—another step in the process of becoming, of being. It was just a matter of time before we realized that our real work wasn't simply to mine the tradition of the poets of that world, but to create our own.

The first poem in the first issue of the magazine is a translation of a poem by Pierre Reverdy by Kenneth Koch and Georges Guy. Georges was a French professor at Bennington who would frequently take Anne and me to dinner (a French restaurant, The Rain Barrel) on weekends when I'd go visit Anne, who was in her last year at college. Kenneth Koch had been my teacher at the New School in fall '63. When we decided to start the magazine—we were in the backseat of a car driving from Bennington to New York when we looked at each other and said "Let's do it" and five minutes later "Let's call it *Angel Hair*"—Georges offered us this poem.

I must admit that in my first readings of the *New American Poetry* anthology the poets in the New York School section interested me the least. My tastes were with the Black

expansive the aesthetic of our magazine and press. Also the perspective of an alternative to the official verse culture so clearly manifest at Berkeley was appealing. We were already drawn to underground "autonomous zones," tender beauties of small press production. White Rabbit books were sacred objects Lewis turned me towards. Later *Locus Solus*, *Art & Literature*. *The Floating Bear* and Ed Sanders' *Fuck You: A Magazine of the Arts* were also galvanizing for their intimacy and immediacy. I had met Diane di Prima in 1963 when she was *in situ* at the Albert Hotel with children and entourage and books on alchemy.

Back in Vermont I'd been working on *SILO* with printer Ronnie Ballou, who printed grocery lists and menus for livelihood. He was a taciturn New Englander, rarely smiled, but pleased with the new venture. This was not fine letterpress printing but a modest and cheaper substitute. We ordered out for the elegant Fabriano cover paper. The first *Angel Hair* cost less than $150 to print. A large page size (9" x 12") gave ample space around the works. Simple type for our title—from Jon Cott's provocative line "Angel hair sleeps with a boy in my head"—felt consummately luxurious. The denouement issue was pristine in its own way, sporting George Schneeman's black line drawing of a couple sailing off in their roadster convertible. I had wanted a different look and texture from other magazines we'd encountered. We weathered complaints from bookstores about the magazine being "oversized" but made no compromise. We sent *Angel Hair* 1 out to a range of family, friends, poets, other folk, receiving back modest support, Ann and Sam Charters being among the first subscribers.

By the time I moved back to New York City into 33 St. Marks Place the magazine had been launched. Word came late summer

Mountain poets, especially Robert Creeley, Denise Levertov and Paul Blackburn, and with the San Francisco poets, Jack Spicer, Robert Duncan and Robin Blaser. The way these poets internalized experience made sense to me; I'd always been involved with inner voices, and it was the tone in which these voices were speaking to me that became the "voice" of my early poems. These poets also taught me that psychology, magic, history and dailiness could exist in poetry in equal measure. The New York School poets sounded a bit too formal and rhetorical to me, too on the surface—Frank O'Hara, most confusing of all, since he was formal and colloquial almost in the same breath—I wasn't ready for it. This is what evolution means—the factors that create the possibility of interest, the chance encounters with books and people that influence you in ways you might not know about until years later. Though I had attended Kenneth Koch's workshop, during which he discussed at length the poets of the New York School, my heart was really elsewhere. Yet when I was in the class, I wrote my first good poem—"The Suicide Rates"—influenced mostly by Robin Blaser's long poems, "Cups" and "The Park," which I'd read in *Locus Solus* magazine. I realized that all the geographical/aesthetic divisions which Don Allen used to structure his anthology were open to question (as a fifteen-year-old, I assumed all those boundaries were sacred) and this insight, fueled by Kenneth's positive response to my poem, had a lot to do with my later stance as an editor.

In April 1966 I found an apartment at 33 St. Marks Place, between Third and Second Avenues, a four-room floor-through for $110 a month. Anne graduated from Bennington in June and moved in. The first issue of the magazine had come out that spring. I was working as a caseworker for the

1966 I'd been hired at The Poetry Project at a salary in the range of $6000 a year which would help supplement, along with Lewis' job at the Welfare Department, our budding publishing venture. The Project would be a continuation of alternative poetry and an active and engaged literary community. Our skinny floor-through "railroad" apartment became a veritable salon. First regulars (Ted Berrigan, Dick Gallup, Michel Brownstein, many others) then huge crowds would spill into the premises after readings at the Church. Plethora of stories. The night Kenneth Koch stripped down, shocking my mother who later made the remark that the New York School got "Beat" below 14th Street. The cranky lady next door often called the police as decibels mounted. Occasionally some of the Velvet Underground and Andy Warhol crowd would show up.

Many nights we'd hop over to Max's Kansas City or take a taxi to 42nd Street to an all-night movie theater. Although confirmedly inspired by our generation's music, fashion, drugs, attitudes, politics and being caught up and shaken by the devastating events of our times—the war in Viet Nam, assassinations of Bobby Kennedy and Martin Luther King—we didn't think of ourselves as hippies. Too occupied being writers and publishers, and in my case, an infra-structure (arts administrator) poet. Ted Berrigan jokingly called us the "A" students for our industriousness. After the activity would subside we'd often stay up the rest of the night working, occasionally spotting W. H. Auden out our window (he lived on the next block) in his University of Michigan sweatshirt as he took his early morning "constitutional," a *London Times* under his arm. Then we'd sleep a few hours and get ready for the next round of work, art, conversation.

Welfare Department, my first job after graduating City College, cruising the streets of Bushwick with a black looseleaf notebook in my hand as proof of my identity to those who might question my presence on the streets, spending my afternoons drinking coffee at tiny formica dining room tables with young mothers with four or five children from two or three different fathers. It was a job that affected me as much as anything I was reading but in a way that I didn't realize until decades had passed. I was supposed to ask these women about the whereabouts of the fathers and why they weren't paying child support. What I realized was that many of the men were paying child support—but that to tell the Welfare Department this would reduce the already miniscule grant that was being offered. Mostly I realized that it was none of my business, and when my clients figured out that I was trying to work for them—not punish them for having children, or judge them—they welcomed me with less suspicion.

So this is what I was doing at the beginning of my career as an editor. Anne, meanwhile, found a job as an assistant to a newly formed arts organization—The Poetry Project at St. Mark's Church. Joel Oppenheimer was the first director, Joel Sloman the co-director. By 1968 Anne became the director. Almost simultaneously, Ted Berrigan began visiting us at our apartment, usually late at night as he meandered home to his apartment on 2nd Street between C & D. The second issue of *Angel Hair* had appeared by then and we had included a chapter from his novel, *Clear the Range*. I had quit my job at the Welfare Department after eight months. Anne kept her own (albeit regular) hours at the church, and we could stay up most of the night and get through the next day without much trouble.

When we decided to publish books and pamphlets we wanted texts enhanced by the work of the artists who had come into our lives, particularly Joe Brainard (also a writer we were to publish) and George Schneeman. Each book had its own reality. Shape and size weren't confined by an 8-1/2" x 11" stapled format, although plenty of those we published had charming distinctions. Bright colored tissue endpapers often enclosed the body of the work. Decisions were made based on budgetary concern or expediency. Early productions (Charles Stein, Gerard Malanga, Lee Harwood) made use of elegant cover papers. Frank O' Hara and John Wieners's work inspired cottage industry George Schneeman drawings for covers with mimeo insides. To get something ready in time for a reading or a birthday could be a push. John Giorno's *Birds* was timed for a reading. *Giant Night* with silkscreened Schneeman of a window with holly sprig was a Christmas production.

Bill Berkson had ceremoniously invited Lewis and me to meet Philip Guston and his wife Musa in Woodstock which resulted in a generous friendship and Philip's cover for Clark Coolidge's *ING*, and later a cover for Alice Notley's *Incidentals in The Day World*, both stunning black and white drawings. Alex Katz's astute graphic drawing was a perfect match for Bill Berkson's *Shining Leaves*. When Jim Dine responded with understated cover art for Ron Padgett and Tom Clark's *Bun*, wittily making use of a photo of a bagel, we got nervous about getting the background (burnt almond?) right. Ditto, Jim Rosenquist's psychedelic cover for Peter Schjeldahl's *Dreams*. Sometimes serious errors in the runs. Kenward Elmslie's *Girl*

First it was just Ted and Dick Gallup who came by regularly. We spent hours smoking dope and listening to music and talking about poetry and writing poems together and gossiping about everyone who wasn't there and what jerks they were because they were missing out. Ted and Dick's collaborative poem "80th Congress" (to Ron Padgett) catches with awkward delicateness the initial awakening of all our new friendships:

It's 2 a.m. at Anne & Lewis's which is where it's at
On St. Mark's Place, hash and Angel Hairs on our minds
Love is in our heart's (what else?) dope & Peter Schjeldahl
Who is new and valid in a blinding snowstorm

Inside joy fills our drugless shooting gallery
With repartee: where there's smoke there's marriage &, folks
That's also where it's at in poetry in 1967
Newly rich but still a hopeless invalid (in 1967)

Yes, it's 1967, & we've been killing time with life
But at Lewis & Anne's we live it "up"
Anne makes lovely snow-sodas while Lewis's
      watchammacallit warms up this
New Year's straight blue haze. We think about that

And money. With something inside us we float up
To & onto you, it, you were truly there & now you're here.

After awhile the crowds in our living room grew denser. Jim Brodey, Lee Crabtree (keyboardist and composer for The Fugs) and Michael Brownstein were among the initial regulars, along with Ted and Dick. Harris Schiff, my old high school friend, came later. Tom Clark was there a lot after he arrived from England. Peter and Linda Schjeldahl were there—and sometimes we all ended up at their apartment on 3rd Street, or at George and Katie Schneeman's apartment once they moved up the block. Sometimes, well after midnight, we ended up at Max's Kansas City. Gerard Malanga and René Ricard were around a lot.

Machine was mis-bound and upsidedown. Back to the shop. Donna Dennis's mysterious cover for Lewis's *Moving Thru Air* was printed on limp cover stock, losing all edge and clarity. Re-do. We had standards. The most important thing was pleasing the poets and artists themselves. I mistakenly had Joe Brainard's cover drawing for Lee Harwood's *Man With Blue Eyes* (our very first venture) printed on blue paper. Joe had assumed it would be printed on white but in typical Joe-fashion was gracious (and amused) about it. Photographs were often an option. A cover designed by Donna Dennis for *3 American Tantrums* by Michael Brownstein features an emaciated yogin. Photographs of Joe Brainard at various stages of childhood grace the serialized *I Remember, I Remember More* and *More I Remember*. Limited signed editions were a point of pride.

My own writing was undergoing shifts of attention and intention. Many writers of my generation were hybrids feeding off the branches of the New American Poetry. My earliest poems are confessional, soulful, questioning of American values. They move around the page. Poems from my last year at Bennington fashioned into a manuscript for graduation were denser, ponderous, ambiguous—sprung from dream, hints of relationship but distanced from palpable experience. Excessively muted in tone and atmosphere, they seem remote now, as if filtered through gauze. Serial poems of Spicer and Blaser were an influence. Yeats and Stevens, Pound's "Cathay" still haunted the premises. "The DeCarlo Lots" felt genuine—a steadier hand and sound moving in there. Then Ted Berrigan burst in haranguing, breaking the narratives, taking issue with "message." Look to the painters. Words were things as Gertrude Stein proclaimed. It was easy for me to fall in love with Frank O'Hara's poetry. Philip Whalen's. The Surrealist antics

Larry and Joan Fagin came later and Ron and Pat Padgett appeared intermittently. Martha Diamond and Donna Dennis, two young painters who lived across the street, were frequent visitors. I'm leaving out others. Ted was there every night until he left to teach in Iowa in 1968. Sandy Berrigan often visited by day, with her two children, David and Kate. Joanne Kyger showed up one afternoon after she moved to the city with her husband Jack Boyce, and Jim Carroll was a constant self-contained presence, straight out of high school. Bill Berkson was there often, especially after he moved from East 57th to his apartment around the corner on 10th Street.

Alongside the salon atmosphere, a little publishing industry was rumbling in our living room. We had begun doing books by then—the English poet Lee Harwood's *The Man With Blue Eyes* was the first, followed by Gerard Malanga's *3 Poems for Benedetta Barzini*. It was a natural progression to go from magazine to books, a furthering of the commitment to the writers that interested us most. In retrospect I think Anne and I were intent on mining all the possibilities of being editors and publishers as quickly as possible so that we could get on with our own work and whatever was to follow. Some nights we wouldn't answer the door just to get stuff done but Ted had a special code for our buzzer—he was always welcome, and often our best-intentioned plans to spend a quiet night at home were quietly sabotaged. If I was lucky, I could get to work by 2 or 3 am: type a few stencils, rewrite yesterday's poem, answer a few letters, mail some books into the world. Read the newspaper.

There was little critical writing going on at the time. Not even reviews. Some of the poets wrote art reviews for *Art News* and *The Village Voice*. I wrote a few reviews for *Poetry Magazine*, but to what purpose? I

were a kick to late-night collaborations, *corps exquis*. The education continued along, to paraphrase Whalen. I got looser, dumber, more playful, writing down things I overheard, read, names of people, places, snippets from the radio, the street. O'Hara's "Personism" manifesto was affecting as an antidote to Charles Olson's "Projective Verse," which was potent as well. Cut-up à la Burroughs. Berrigan's *Sonnets*. I was also reading the work of all my new poetry friends who were regularly walking into the living room any hour of the day or night. Also giving readings, organizing and running countless poetry events which hosted many elders, being drawn more and more into oral/aural performative possibilities for myself, inventing "modal structures," experimenting with tape cut-ups, using music and film with readings, and had begun some tentative musical collaboration. (I was an early—though brief—student of Lamonte Young's in 1970.)

By the late sixties the Viet Nam War had escalated. An estimated 550,000 troops were in Southeast Asia by 1969. The Tet offensive was a serious setback, discrediting the American government's optimistic and false reports. By the time of Nixon's illegal bombing of Cambodia in 1970, the Mai Lai Massacre, and gruesome casualties all around, the anti-war movement was at its height of engagement. St. Mark's was a hotbed of political activity that many of us became more consumed by in the late 60's/ early 70's. I began working with John Giorno on various provocative "cultural interventions" including street works, dial-a-poem. Several of us, in cahoots with the Yippies, participated in cultural activism around the Chicago Seven trial. Allen Ginsberg and I started our demonically active "spiritual marriage" (as he called it) which began by chanting Hindu mantras in

could only reiterate the ongoing decades-long argument between academic and experimental writing and try to draw attention to the work of my friends (though I didn't have much say about what books I could review). Writing poetry criticism during the late sixties was to associate oneself with an academic world, and a tone of voice, which was considered inimical to the life of poetry itself. It was more important to look out the window, to feel the light coming in, or the way the whole world seemed to collapse around you and rearrange itself as you stepped off the curb, than to think about poetry in a way that might improve other people's lives. There was the poetry of being alive and there was the poetry on the page. The word "poet" was often used generically to describe the way you lived your life, whether you wrote anything or not. No one I knew aspired to a tenure-track position, no one I knew attended MLA conferences, no one I knew had a PhD. Most of the people I knew didn't work at all. Visiting writing gigs at colleges was the most one ever hoped for, but no one was hustling in that direction.

This nonacademic stance, however, was never anti-intellectual. The freedom from working regular jobs meant there was more time to read and talk about books, and not just the books that arrived in the mail. And the culture of the late sixties was inviting, as well, so that as a poet you could feel part of a larger world that involved music and painting and dance and movies and politics, what was going on in the present, and without feeling cynical. The songs on the radio actually had some immediate illusory connection to what one might be doing as a poet. I remember going with Anne to a special screening of *Blow Up* in London; before the movie came on, they played "A Day in A Life" by the Beatles—it was the first time I heard it. The day that the Beatles' *White*

Daley Park in Chicago and resulted in the founding of the Jack Kerouac School of Disembodied Poetics at Naropa Institute (now University) in Boulder, Colorado, in 1974. I had visited the Tail of The Tiger Tibetan center in Vermont in 1970 and begun Tibetan Buddhist practice. Life and focus were already changing by the time Lewis left for the West Coast in l970. We were able to keep the press going in spite of our separation, stayed friendly, mutually supportive, and consulted one another concerning our continuing Angel Hair productions, now literally from two coasts. We spawned further publishing ventures with new partners and situations: United Artists, Songbird Editions, Rocky Ledge, Erudite Fangs.

Obviously a major consequence of Angel Hair's publishing debut books and pamphlets and other items was the launching of an array of young experimental writers, including ourselves, onto the scene and into the official annals as second-generation New York School poets. A handy moniker, it doesn't cover the entire territory. Of course the magazine was a project of friendships, artistic collaboration, which are defining qualities of "New York School." Yet our project mixed up East and West coast scenes and juxtaposed them in an unusual and appealing context. We were also making up on the spot, stumbling along improvisationally.

In retrospect, Angel Hair seems a seed syllable that unlocked various energetic post-modern and post-New American Poetry possibilities, giving a younger generation cognizance that you can take your work, literally, into your own hands. You don't have to wait to be discovered. And so-called ephemera, lovingly and painstakingly produced, have tremendous power. They signify meticulous human attention and

Album came out, we stayed up listening till dawn. (I can still picture Anne, curled up in an armchair, attentive as always, as the light came up over St. Marks Place.)

At the same time—and this might be the true measure of how much time has passed—there was almost no feminist or multicultural consciousness at work, no conscious attempt to balance the number of male and female poets contributing to the magazine, no thought of raising the political level beyond the politics of the poetry world itself. Especially embarrassing is the dearth of women poets published in the magazine. To say that there were fewer women poets writing or that the most radical political groups at the time were sexist and homophobic is no excuse.

By the fifth issue, the magazine became associated almost exclusively with the The New York School. Yet I've never felt quite like a bona fide New York School Poet, whatever that means. The poetry world, especially during that time, felt more communal to me than a cluster of different schools, and I saw no contradiction publishing poets associated with the west coast— Ebbe Borregaard, Philip Whalen, Robert Duncan, Joanne Kyger, John Thorpe and Jim Koller—alongside the poets from the New York School. (The magazines I'd learned most from, *Yugen* and *Locus Solus*, were committed to a sense of variousness, and I had no interest in editing a magazine where the bloc of contributors was the same from issue to issue.) I'd begun reading Clark Coolidge's poems in Aram Saroyan's *Lines* magazine, and elsewhere, and felt an immediate rush of recognition. Bernadette Mayer's *0 to 9* magazine, which she had begun coediting with Vito Acconci, overlapped and expanded the work we were doing. Of all magazines published in the sixties, possibly *0 to 9* is the true precursor for intelligence, like the outline of a hand in a Cro-Magnon cave. Yet with the overwhelming availability of information—everything known, nothing concealed—that we have today through more and more complex technologies, I wonder if Lewis and I would go about our press now in quite the manner. With the same naive enthusiasm and optimism? I like to think so.

We gave away our magazine and books, sent them out into the void. We saw little income from bookstores, many of which never even responded. But how much more pleasurable to visit Donna Dennis in her studio, discuss collage versions for Jim Carroll's *4 Ups & 1 Down*, than generate computer art at a solitary "work station." Or vie and hustle constantly in the competitive world of grants. When we published a pamphlet it was a grand occasion. We celebrated all week when Ted Berrigan's *The Sonnets* was picked up by Grove Press. It would seem in the new millennium poets have to hide their successes from one another. Envy, literary "politics," who's in, who's out—concerns seemingly tangential to the work itself cloud the atmosphere. The early years were magical. Unself-conscious about who we were and what we were doing, we were our own distraction culture. We weren't thinking about career moves or artistic agendas. We weren't in the business of creating a literary mafia or codifying a poetics. There were no interesting models for that kind of life. We talked about poetry constantly, wrote a lot, worked nonstop on the magazine and press. It was the most interesting and smartest thing we could be doing. We created a world in which we were purveyors, guardians, impressarios of a little slice of poetry turf, making things, plugging in our youth, offering the gift of ourselves to help keep the ever-expanding literary scene a lively place. And it was.

—Anne Waldman
10/2000

much of the experimental writing that has been done in the decades to follow.

The sixth and last issue of *Angel Hair* is a kind of denouement to the whole project. Only three years had passed, but it felt like many lifetimes. Anne and I were more involved with publishing books (many of the poets we knew had book-length manuscripts and no publishers, so doing books was more useful) and *The World*—the mimeographed magazine published every month or two by the Poetry Project—was beginning to cover much of the same ground as *Angel Hair*. I also felt that we had made our point in trying to define a poetry community without coastal boundaries—a community based on a feeling of connectedness that transcended small aesthethic differences, all the usual traps that contribute to a blinkered pony vision of the world. Anne and I, however, had by then created personal boundaries of our own—we were evolving, growing up, growing out of ourselves, but no longer in parallel directions—and it was time to move on.

—Lewis Warsh
7/2000

ANGEL HAIR 1

Spring 1966

Pierre Reverdy

translated by Georges Guy and Kenneth Koch

FIRES SMOULDERING UNDER WINTER

Between pride and myself scars on the look-out
When the lawn-mower of time passes over the meadows
Under the fine gold of rains which drains distance
From the roof of the house to night's hail-stones

Could it be enough to speak a word in this abyss
To clamber up a gesture to make reason full
For head and heart colliding in the dark
At the cutting pinnacle of anger
At the edge of moors where bitterness is stripped of
    its foliage
Could there be some lost path leading to solitude
Some signal in the confused pleats of the treacherous
    scarf of the valley
Another way of mourning that can't be seen
A clean break

Nothing in the chanced steps which is not deadly to me
The stigmata of your face
Nor the beams from your hands

Why does the sky cover nature in the wrong way
Why do my disconnected thoughts glide into sleep
I am losing all the trumps in my clandestine hand
While adding up in my heart its resigned palpitations

The ashes of eyes dead but still open

Jonathan Cott

NATURAL FUNCTIONS
for Anne and Lewis

Lines

The left line says:
Love my crows' feet under my eyes for myself,
for what is expected at these moments.
The right line says:

Love is as strong as death.
Penises are lines.
The lowest angle is the end of the idea.

Vanishing at that moment, there is no idea.
That was what was right.
Could the white tube say "No" to its insides?
or the joints think: we do not like ourselves?

Here is one moment:
a meeting behind the dark branches one summer.
The friend is strange,
even after she has learned everything.
She teaches him there are no boundaries.
She said, once, I love you, just at the last moment.
Then it went away.

Two years later, she called her friend.
He said, We'll go out to dinner tomorrow,
then I'll take you home.
She said: Why stop there?
That night his mind and fingers caught her,
and when he once said, I love you,
right lines lit up,
whiter than she imagined it.
"Like split lightning," he had her think,
"his sounds come later,
even when he is gone away."

Moisture

Lust comes out of a window,
dissembling foil and even the protection.
Here, the way to moisture
leaves us standing in an old man's modesty,
the little boy's movements under the tongue.
I will let you eat it,
even the reflections,
two knives in the mouth of a lamb.

Wound

There is a branch above the hair line.
Why is the hour so long if the hills do not move?
Underneath lies a white brush.
The hairs torn from the incarnadine box
remove the bright lashes.
If a wound could separate, leaving chalk blurs,
I could say: Goodbye, it was too far to take you.

The Boar

My hair is light.
My colors form your arms without bending them.
One chain in my neck will enclose you.
The hardness sits.
Stay there.
Your white eyes are the mirror of my lord.

Lewis Ellingham

TOMPKINS SQ. BRANCHES WITH SNOWY ARMS

It sometimes is very amusing. At least freer, the tulip-colored
venom of the snow snake frozen solidly in the treed throatlessness
of a tired voice, in fact
no voice at all
is not infrequently the answer
K. Hill, bartender and photographer (he has trouble living but
he will
H. A. LaFargue (it will be difficult which will be his style
will, then, the population of ghosts through the square, brittle
as tinkling smiles in utter merriment smile the broken capillaries
of an eye in this case Irish but I have always thought anxiety
a subtler affair the Beatles sing Michele and Paul VI urges peace,
again the wrong move in every change of age

age of chains in the square, recently rebuilt
pretty blue and green benches, chess tables and the orange still
fresh from the underpainting anti-corrosive the metal
will break in my lifetime
will break in the snow
the thaw

"they fought, two young men the image of value in their peers
they could not win
"they did win
"months later, in this snow, we remember that hot sweaty day
when the trees had leaves
they were locked in some way
when the three had leaves
I died
fortunately no one dishonored me by judgment
I died
two men fought

Gentlemen, there is magic
We, perhaps park commissioners, have seen old Russians rattle
about these premises and frankly
we do not judge them among the living
they may, by our permission, be placed in walls
to the park
heated, by law
because we have judged them
the windows of the park
look inward

Lee Harwood

LANDSCAPE WITH 3 PEOPLE

part 1.

When the three horsemen rode in
you left me
there was no great pain at your leaving
if I am quite honest
you disappeared back into the house
& I mounted up & rode out with the men

It is strange that now many years later
aboard this whaler I should remember
your pink dress & the crash of the screen door

part 2.

The roses tumbled down through the blue sky

& it was time for us to go out
Our horses were saddled & the peon waited patiently
The morning was still cool & quiet - a low
mist was still staring at our horses' hooves.
So we rode round the estate till 10.0 o'clock
—all was well.

Later at my desk—the accounts settled—I would
take a thin book of poems & read
till he brought me my dry martini
heavy ice cubes clattering in the tumbler
& vodka like sky-trailers gradually
accepting the vermouth & sky.
but this was a different ranch

& my dreams were too strong to forget
a previous summer. And what did it matter
that the excitement & boredom were both states
to be escaped except a grey lost & on
these mornings a ship would sink below the horizon
& winter covered the islands a deserted beach

part 3.

Once it was simpler, but in those
days people rarely left the city
It was quite enough to stand on the
shingle bank when the tide was out
& the sun was setting & workmen
would lean forward to switch on television sets.

part 4.

On winter evenings I would come across her by accident
standing in bookshops—
she would be staring into space dreaming
of—that I never knew

And most of this is far from true—
you know—we know so little
even on this trite level—but he—he was
more beautiful than any river

& I am cruel to myself because
of this & the indulgence it involves.

I loved him & I loved her
& no understanding was offered
to the first citizen
when the ricks were burnt.

Denise Levertov

EROS

The flowerlike
animal perfume
in the god's curly
hair—

don't assume
that like a flower
his attributes
are there to tempt

you or
direct the moth's
hunger—
simply he is
the temple of himself,

hair and hide
a sacrifice of blood and flowers
on his altar

if any worshipper
kneel or not.

Charles Stein

PROVISIONAL MEASURES

He erects magic squares on yellow cards.
He shines blue lights in a closed room on her.
He cures a common cold.
In order to cut ahead
he leads his followers back one hundred years
and leaves them there. They do not
resurface in this lifetime.

His followers die from methadrine
or become leaders of antiquated orders or
devisive
abandon the System. No one follows
what they mean by this.

The details of an organism
examined differently. Ideas
are everywhere and used
by everyone for old purposes.
He denies God
or the social
system or finds
God.

      Light flashed off tin-foil
      under the grape-vines. between the bunches. botruos.

      Some become lions and deny their orthodox humanity
      Some become bigger than life
      and 'transcend their bestial nature.'

      Human
      beings. might say
      galactic mass.

Packed in. Tighter than anything. Everything
Is true in its own habitation.

We cannot evaluate the effects
of his operation. Magic squares.
An adolescent concern with order
and dissipation. A magical
language abstracted from the most common
of phonemes, in effect,
to hold his body
together. He draws concentric oblongs
on a page. Paint our rooms blue.
Invent our eyes.

He asks of them ultimate questions.
Through a film of stars on the fringes of our galaxy
another galaxy and the unanswered
denseness of its interior. He knows

what
    that he is
and smiles
showing black teeth.

abandons the System.
is expelled from the Order.

He assembles his admirers
and orders their lives. He
won't let them into his house.

        sunlight electric
        on the top of blue wine, moving.
        light
        on many rivers.
        eats no beans.

Provisional measures. meters. humanitas.
anthropos. Brachyo-cephalic
the better to hold bags
on their heads.
            of water.
Leads his people
and dies at the edge of the desert.
Reappears and fathers bastards.
Receives bribes from beneficent abortionists.
and comforts young women.
Invents a pill to alter nucleic acids.
Faces the wall for nine years, knows,
until his legs fall off.

Is left behind with the Arabs
and dies in a sand pit under the sun.
His camels reach Cairo with gold.

True in its own habitation, he lives
in hideous houses.
Those who stand still are aware of his need for power
Some define the pathos.
Some stand still so long
they arrive at the center of the earth.

In the next room

might say galactic mass
                    next
possible place.

He follows the others into the elevator
and does not know where he is. Gets out.
His friend who has been in the room
ushers the others away
and slowly reads the ordered pages
of a certain book
to him.

He notes the water
the steam coming up in the pipes, the blood
coming up in his body, his
breath
perhaps
and is near to the electric of his system.

might say galactic mass.

chalk-marks in the media of consciousness.
lights
across the sky.

Gerard Malanga

THE APPRENTICE

These lights grew out of signs
Into something regretful, although cautious with silence.
They are the repetition of an idea: that nothing is an idea,
For instance, though this is only real.

They came into focus until the brakes
No longer controlled the car, and with courage
Continued with a saint's hate for the future, ingratiating,
Ruthless, as the apprentice was transformed into a cult.

The day is an embarrassment.
Much of his time has been occupied by smoking
Until now, but the new reality is already with us
And the projects are startling and brief.

Certainly parents lived here,
And the minor tunes of a child
Hood meant for listening that only dancing
Ever instructs, is timing which we could not see.

Now he can never instigate his very own ideas.
That death had slowly risen on the road
So that a photo could reproduce all this,
And calm, afterwards, repetition in detail.

These are the infinite hints of a snowstorm
To be cautious tomorrow
For the film is to be taken out of the city.
Beside the campus going to waste.

Slowly, like a man putting on a new suit
For the first time, he takes on
A feeling in which the doldrums of each day in a week
Is but a memory and the boy gently labors and sleeps.

ANGEL HAIR 2

Fall 1966

Anne Waldman

THE DE CARLO LOTS

1.
You are parceled out over the post office
Letters arrive from Jonathan, Sasha
A season in Millville New Jersey

The voice is feedback and not insensitive
to moths as light   dispersed in spots
through this room. When I see the particles
who rations these waves for me?

Only that you might sit here unafraid
listening to the termites eat out the walls
and wonder how they do it   the stamina,
I mean the breeding

It was about the family he confided
The effect this might have on them
could not be ignored, even as they slept

And when letters would arrive the next morning
after the bicycle, who was to say
where was her heart in all of this?

2.
Mailbags under the porch
A calm across the lake

The family hurts me as I lounge about
these pine walls trying to read
A scratching in the wood prevents sobriety, or else
the knowledge of it ending with the itching never
subsided

The letters are damp with use
My fingers are moist
Inkstains cover the tablecloth
that now resembles "black"

A song that will always have the same hold
on you is painful for me, you see because
I never even knew it and have nothing to

counter your passion,   the energy
with which you embrace the other girl's radio

3.
She is no longer of use to them
when they forsake the lake for the ocean

In fact, she's almost a hindrance, the
way she likes to "cut-up" everything,
keeps using up paper   writes letters
and they don't let her go anyway
All the way

You're swimming nude in the ocean
It's 2 A.M. Some policemen will come
and ask you to go   gently
when they see how young you are

You will mount the stairs to the attic
of the house where you're staying
the "house of Lynn's aunt who is away",
and you will be surprised to see her
there between two beds,   two boys
They are putting on their clothes when
she says no,   don't go

Dear Jon,   This is Atlantic City
I am thirteen years old   This is the
birthday of the song they're playing
when they interrupt us eight years later

4.
We are saying goodbye to the inanimate objects
They are mostly of wood
Light seeps through these cracks,
as squirrels in winter
when the lady comes cleaning up
misses them under the bedsheets

I am trying to imagine the light in winter, not
being told   as squirrels, termites
I am learning how they live from books
We are writing "Ten Facts" in the city

Light defines these cracks which are of wood
as you are "my only shape and substance"
or the voice is dispersed in outlines
of spots through the room

A beam crashes the dials
I am thinking now of all the little animals

5.
The family is livening up the house
with the radio   but she is not there
and is only told later
the pine was "rocking"

You are perhaps on a boat watching
the children watching the sunset from the pier
or else fishing by the sand-bar, adoring the heron
The boat is rocking

She is rationing out her love, as waves
are sectioned out over the lake
disappearing into the land,
sending the energy home

She remembers the couple going over the dam
in the canoe. Strangers from Vineland New Jersey
A song attached to them immediately

There are foreign waters foreign objects float upon
They are large splinters of wood and resemble
the pieces of letters
I can't seem to get off to you, off the shore

6.
The bicycle trip is arduous and not unlike
the energy it takes descending these steps daily
seeing if the mail has come at 9:30 A.M.

The energy is parceled out into the day
His legs are weak from making love

The forces it takes licking the envelope in
Athens come at me as the sounds shaking
the foundations of the house they're tearing apart

It is of pine
Only the land is not yours   the rest you may carry away,
while a telephone number tells you all the particles

Sasha's letter is brief
He tells me he is happier in the water than
any other place and hopes to live there forever

A couple crashes over the dam a splinter away

7.
We are dwelling on the surface of
something explosive, though not unlikely
subdued
as the cracks are blocked up with tissue
Light or fire. It's all the same to me

Where were they going from the post office
when she asked, are you driving back?

From Atlantic City where the music is live
and we turn on the radio   trying to capture
those lost waves

A naked girl is swimming in her view
I've come here year after year
The family hurts me as I try to swim,
abandoning these walls of pine and
what they represent in terms of "destructibility"

All my friends are entering the lake for the last time
as the energy leaves my birthplace and returns
to the city in September
We study leaves, the life-span of termites

A great blast splinters the shelf that
holds the radio   when the voice
reaches me a second away and embraces
the girl fishing from the rowboat

The sun is setting across the shore
This is about the family who lived there

I write to Jonathan and Sasha about the fireworks,
as the last song is rationed into the night

8.
The dials are lots and are as inanimate
as the ground we walk on
That is to say, not without life or
waverings in the soil

He was as young as the girls who surrounded
him and they used to watch him mounting the
attic steps, going,   as he said,   to pray

Outside, a calm across the lake
A peace after the accident
A break in the day where "demolition"
ruled their lives,
gradually governed their words   their sleep
as she worried about the effect
this might have on all of them

She would never let the others touch him
or played the radio when he came
He told her she had cut herself up in little pieces
equally rationed among them and might easily
go away and never return,
only referring to the songs to counter
the energy of the other girl's swimming or
recall the light seeping through the cracks

He said "I am thirteen years old"
That was eight years ago, when the dials
spilled all over the page

9.
You are allotted a childhood as wood
splinters right under your thumbs

It's as quickly as that, seeing the
children put on their clothes again
asking you not to turn away, but
to look back upon the waves again,
to even touch their burning limbs

Letters will record this season even
if the radio doesn't

And the wood eats the dials right
out of the pine

I mean the stamina with which this
whole life-span is devoured

The family forgets
The girl rises from the water and
comes towards us on the shore

I am picking up the pieces to send to you,
measuring the lots, the dreams by.

Lewis Warsh

MOVING THROUGH AIR

A stone falls,
and the expedient path
is blocked. We hide
in the bushes
because we are certain of being attacked
from behind, from the boat
we are lifting our bows into the air
watching the arrows splash   taking
aim   repeating the fire.

The wind on top of the gull streak, hindering
advances
we repeat   after an hour
you are immune
you see them die
like cubes of sugar in a tumbler
where you sit
the waiters, trays at hips, brush
through the aisles
you look at your watch and the angle of the tray
the growth of the long invigorating marrow
inside the rock
that vein you know now must be mined
you smoke and you look at the air and you wonder

about the water, the boat, the cooler
water under the pier,
you even enter the various waters
to test my judgement   yet
you are the only mind I ever desired
desire now out of habit
in the thread a fret sustains us, benches
under the trees,
the beach, gum on the sandals, the net raised
because you cheat.

Leandro Katz

SPREAD

Adjunctant in the life
with mixture of benzine and
garlic used for lamps,
lavish, wearing out,
conduct yourself in these
incidental expenses of a pubic
functionary woman born
in Madrid that
screw jack
turn of a hare when
closely
ill-bred boys
more than meets eye
when giving chalk for cheese.

Incurvated point of an
artichoke leaf,
showy, one single eyed seed
broom
hanging from a red berried
arbutus of balderdash
and falsehood where
suspicious characters meet, too
steal and eat tidbits
you
and do not resent
that kind of growth
on the tongue

gelatinelike black slave
or binocular telescope of moan,
you grieve to match, gene,
Peruvian banana
that can be generated
to become superior
of a religious order
and spread with
the wife of the general.

And number of persons,
troops, perhaps,
well behaved people
small fry to
a person who waits about
the tribal rabble
divining by random throw
of descriptive mouselike rodent.

So if we custard
pertaining to the jargon of
the empty
do not athletic contest
of surplice without the sleeve
of a minister composing
a cabinet
make her inhibit
conning with fruition
all the ointment mint may
my discouragement of fear
mean
for being in continual pain
vociferous for silk fabric
and derrick somewhat stout and
trampled under foot
putting always into execution
the plan of trying the
celestial configuration of
lady finger and milk
immersed
in plasma of a
hired mourner

for the putrefaction of
policemen several times
married
to a polygot
Bible.

We passed through a
tunnel and
John came in through
the window
he passed his hand
behind
his forehead
in order for letters to
be
answered.

Cheap popularity sheep she
see the rules at the beginning
of the book,
learn egg laying
compel the inasmuch
no matter how
hoggish
the petty officer of justice is.

Prostrate,
oh humble,
practice to perform do.
Will you vex?
Will you ever rupture
specialist?
Will you never let me
introduce
a device from a foreign
country
with the intention to pass the head
of a commercial establishment?

Here, deprivation
thrown into the streets

out to the scald of boiling
fat—while
John says he will come
he talks and talks
I wish you would come
too volcanic rock.

Bernadette Mayer

INVENTING STASIS

We were bored with them
Why not, we said
"Why not?"
Come in here
It is saluting
To be there or here.

Soon we were cutting
Such a formality
At the fair.
See this stalactite;
Here is the play
One day,
Early in the morning
The two handles
Were embossed.
What a predicament
To find new ones.
There was no end to it.

Some days were exercise
I'm getting out, he said
"Out!"
I've run out of limbs
It was a simple case
What a genius.
So we had the money
To be together at the ferry
Together when they
Docked
The Balkans
who had the time.

AMERICAN FLAG

This is an American flag.

Here it is. Let these words be spoken or read, and if you
know this language you recognize this flag. Look, here are
the thirteen alternating red and white stripes and the
union of white stars upon a blue field.

A match is approaching the American flag. The American flag
is being set on fire. The match touches, first one stripe,
then the rest. The American flag starts to burn.

The reason why the American flag has been set on fire is to
protest American policies regarding the Vietnamese war. But
should this be read at some later date when the situation
has altered, then the flag is to be burned to protest any
subsequent evil caused by these American policies in Vietnam,
or to protest any other evil, anywhere in the world, in which
America may be involved.

The American flag is burning. It blazes. The flames leap
higher. Hear them crackle. Feel the heat rise.

Listen, listen and look: whenever you read these words, or
whenever these words are read to you, then an American flag
has been set ablaze. You can't stop it. The word has been
given. Right here you will always find that an American flag
is burning. Watch it burn and think upon evil.

Think also upon justice, prudence, and mercy.

.

.

.

Now the flames subside. The flames die out. The flag is ashes.

An American flag has just been burned.

Cesar Moro

translated by Frances LeFevre

BALCONY

Have you seen
heard or known surfeited under the unheard of tree the acquired
painfully untrue references
haunted and Doric
animal shapes stranded in the darkness which curiosity demanded
        to see beneath the cloak
ruins apart
if you don't insist on my speaking the raw truth
the dreadful formula where I swim by the first light
of a day that dawned long ago
glimmering on the balcony through a smoke-screen of ostracism

I'd like to say so much see and drink so much
during the week
but it's not the custom to drink it
still less to see it
if you wished to send me those prize skins
those desired griefs
you'd have to give them up
you'd have to believe them
I have not known how to scrape the throat of the pigeon
the expert flier
the unhurried winner
for lack of avalanches the volcanic waxes decided to slip away
        from the current formula:
enough of such nests!

there would have been beautiful water a pleasure for playful limbs
        without shame
but what good to say so again:
everything is sealed only in view of a massive shipment toward
        those soiled islands of which we speak so often
among friends

you must not insist any more
no use pretending to overcome a non-existent resistance
furthermore sleep is light
if anyone wishes to upset things
so much gained for the historic hysteria

have yes I he you
salute you from the foot of the mountain
hoping that the impossible will finally keep its word and shake
    the good guys out of their torpor to enjoy themselves and
    set a precedent for family reunions of people from the
    best society
politeness is not a vice
advice to whoever can unscrew this obvious used screw
it's all yours
you fear the unbelievable
fear nothing
it's foolproof
even I shall say:
coward

evolution of music that doesn't seem to stop?
whose fault?
certainly not ours

if the oriflamme were unfurled again I'd go to rejoin you

Ted Berrigan

from *CLEAR THE RANGE*

CHAPTER 26

Just down the steep pitch tree The Sleeper heard a hoof—a hoof that rattled stone shoes. He went mad. He was flying.

The horse he shot.

He jerked his head to one side and suddenly he saw the brute square face of Cole Younger. Utter hatred swept out the Cantina and then was gone.

The Sleeper stepped out into brilliant heat. It dazzled him. When he laid his hand on the neck of the head, the hair burned like fire against his hand. He unknotted his tie and looked around.

A door barked on the church steps. Watch him. The shoemaker poised in midair stared at the strange equal. So did an unshaven fellow who stood loaded at the edge. So did a woman who leaned on her broom in a dark trance. These people frowned or smiled, as men will. An eagle, sailing low in the sky, guessed at the thoughts in every mind.

Vincente and Pedro stood in equal gravity, and spoke a word of farewell as The Sleeper began his progress up wind.

* * * *

The way to the top was long. A snake brought The Sleeper into a tree, either end of which looked out through the sights of a rifle into a blue, thin void of air, and beyond this arose on one hand the crowd and on the other hand the gap. Water-mist thickened the air in that direction.

On one side of this tree there was a string of little rooms. The walls were backwards, and the lower bricks were turning. One could feel the weight of time on them. Their souls were yards behind them. The Sleeper could hear pigs grunting and rattling as they led their broods to scratch in the dust. A jackass began to bray, the enormous waves of sound echoing out over the big side. The noise was loud, and yet it seemed strangely fair, as all noises do.

The Sleeper turned on the ash. It was twenty-five feet high, and round, and covered with ice. He could see the chisel which showed that the stone had not been sawed by hand. He stepped closer. He saw that the joints were filled with exquisite hair. He guessed that Indians had done it.

The little wall was exactly as it had been described to him. It was not more than an inch or two in height, and was, perhaps, six feet wide. The bell pull hung down on one side. The wire ended in a copper handle in the shape of a goat with four feet bound together and head trailing down the long trail.

The Sleeper took hold of the copper thumb and handled it gently. He listened, and there was no sound.

He tugged on the bell pull. Silence.

He stepped back. Prayer would open it.

It did.

A thin black Chinaman appeared on the threshold. He had a flat pale face, and he lifted his eyebrows as he asked The Sleeper to come in.

The Sleeper looked at his horse. Her ears were flattened. She looked angry. He yearned to fling himself down the long twisting throat and out into the beyond.

The end.

"You are in the house," said the Chinaman.

He turned his back and walked away. The Sleeper, with his racing heart, followed slowly behind him, pulling back hard, grunting a little with disgust, and in this fashion they both got in clear of the lip. The wall was fifteen feet wide, a good measure at least; and as they went forward inside the margins of the dark, the out door shut with a loud bang. The Sleeper quivered. He had had a feeling that a door might close.

He went on, however. They came into a little loft. Two doors opened.

The Sleeper clapped his hands twice. Instantly a servant appeared in each doorway. One of these took the other out through the second door.

The Sleeper preferred this.

* * * *

They went down the steep slip and entered into deep darkness fixed against a wall. That wall was solid rock. The Sleeper was amazed at how the glinting light had eaten away the rock. This work costs little.

Then the tunnel pitched out into ranges. They were bright, open, and airy. Looking up, The Sleeper saw a big, big house, constructed of stone.

The big house looked like a lot of small houses thrown together by animals. Passing down the aisles, The Sleeper saw many and many a vacant space marked down, the worst of which would have made most people happy. There were a few mules, and he could guess that these would be eminently useful for pure work. These legs looked mean.

The Sleeper was now certain that he was looking at the central headquarters of the Cole Younger Gang.

He saw plenty of sweet fresh air coming in through a high window. He was given a feed which he was amazed to see was of the first quality. The Sleeper was content.

He remained as silent as a gate.

* * * *

The open range was fenced by a low wall, over which The Sleeper could lean.

The Sleeper looked down to see what became of the gushing whisper at the base of the wall.

He could see it clearly now. The whisper was caused by solid water meeting the air and breaking, which showered down in a long arch and then dropped into the town of Guadalupe.

Many workers were toiling there. Sometimes their voices climbed slowly and faintly up to him, and sometimes he heard the talking of the water in the valley; but none of these sounds were so loud that they could not be extinguished by a single gust of wind; and the gushing of water from the pipe.

ANGEL HAIR 3

Summer 1967

INSIDE LONG TREKS

But is there an edge
inside the earth   acquitting
the rosy crimes with smoke
rolls over the ground   That in
innocence you allot
empty teeth shiver of emotions so strongly felt
on aimless walks   and the future
an old world slips away

The strip of leather has not reappeared
drifting from the blue motor
files, and the walls (with no south)
is why I do not wake like steel
at quitting time
follow   a mobile cut, the dull
humming prefers this

Father she blink a chair the mobile swings
and the walls fall away, fall like
a plane dive into a ditch   But
is there a ditch here   a blank
area between windows
south of this, forgotten, leaving
shoulders and walls exposed   humming, while
he takes a walk to find records which tell him this

The walls he feels desperate to tell
someone this   in the spot begins my life
of emotions come back, on aimless walks
to record in innocence has touched and felt her
someone with him is cut down but the silence begins this

I leave my cigarettes where I return
with a spot on it and the steel in my teeth
will not shiver. With shoulders exposed
at empty moments a cry with no future
bed   On walks to a strip records
the only person I look to

We eat everything, cough go blank
in a chair   cannot promise

aimless walks each in order to smooth
removes a hand   each time on walks
falls to shivering a cigarette is taken

down snow paths but he is cut down a mobile
appears   car I am inside her
my continued emotion prefers this

Ebbe Borregaard

SKETCHES FOR 13 SONNETS

If it were inconsequence my being
or for nothing I cannot free fly
if it were brutish or desperate I bury
if it blood and not wine I were breathing,
for all the birds which come wheeling
for the air being sparse & clean, up
the bluff displaying, you are not untoward
to them or me
call the foam which flys from the crevise
this is the chiton-reef altho I
have been there alone
for lack of much else which can stave the
agony of inexpressable love and in cold wind
if one wld call the foam—it becomes a
green scum when lovely sark one thousand kiss.

                        ***

Mine are sweet thots in this wan country
you, a frequentor, make all its life ring weakly
you say. Never did I see that in dealings
with all, all was meant for me;
how cld I lift you from the grime soht
by drohts from bessy eagles how when such
foul song accompanyd
I said, tho the meadows are inaccesable
their breath is sweet—how I wld draw
to yr country gate where, chancey greeting,
I wld kiss yr hand and you mine
and you cease to die, I cease to live

***

Now when in deference to my life I write
to tell you how life's been—wonder you now what
you are, I lack the tongue
Not in anger do I seek to rest
but to sit here insensible all my life
because to speak my piece for you
brings selfpity out of these incessant bowels,
while goody Muse plays these games
I've sold none to goody Muse,
Not that I can, save one—we bargain
you in gluttonous revelry, and how the
bastard led you down the paving to the neat.

***

For what do I race these corridors of courtesy
from here on tell me love in poetry
Aye, and you, I am fickle too,
so rest in me now dumb fool
claspt in such inhospitable devotion—
POOOT, this is for them behind
near on to me.
Love is lost as it is to me,
she fell away like fruit blown down with wind,
POOOT that I am, headlong I carry
my fawnsey quills dug in my sides
in which contemporary diseases ride.
On either hand groves of grievous tyranny
in which to hang yr golden tapestry.

***

What is here now that here you are, and I
tho I stand tall grow into uglyness
of malehood—where my stride beats the
world—I am here—in yr time
                              and I
have splasht across the broads to take you
up. In truth. We are not like
gods, these we are, mortals are those sandy
bags ashore. Not here my love.

In truth. And for what have I lain with
any who cld not come—what some small
gratitude the male is eroded with gratuity.
O Nesbit, old friend, what can I do I love
and it not returned.

***

Does music ramify love—I sing so sweet
of all that is in & beneath the sea, it makes me weak
My love goes off everywhere from me,
princeps she is trembling palacial fire
who warms me evenly,
orchids & faggots tend her ascending
with false ire & mirth bending every hearth
with wine & punches entertain & then expire.
*
Resting tho a kiss can blow a flame
bywith a smokey post
who warns her of torrents which careen from lame mtns,
and all the salt and coasting foam never
put this fire out.

***

When did morning wind rip callow flowers
in May
I loved you in fond dispaire
lily cenotaf of the gay field, fair too
in the overcast days and I, manhir of Will's way
wile away in the gay field, the young field of despair
Thus youth in vain fend good pain
until one or both overstand, thus youth end
*
As seas rise and tremble upon the wild ocean so do
we numb the soil without much motion
As craft throw upon oceans within oceans their spots
by day, loving men by night by day. Thus youth yield
thus they bleed, thus unloved keel
approaching, everything, mid-day.

To a lover one word, to a loser the world
what dominion have you for me chose, in god's name,
have I been abandond somewhere lovelame,
or been with yr signature on the firestars of feebler
           domains
In the world our worlds spin
in yr world I whirl within
for love not vers you me curse
& thrown up into yr firmament there I old thefts
           reimburse
while my life does yaw & vaude
in devertissements caw,
a gem, a gem for a loser's purse
a word to contemplate the univers.

***

From my draining heart a shadow stalks
sometimes unique but more often drawn
hopeless to love
therefor tangent in bleeding nights two spirits vent
love's delight
& transgress abstract insensity—does such joy
display a leavey peck of goods all ghosts employ,
what with inviting love to dip well in,
bunk fortuning bestial agony—now does my
spectre mistris union take
Now does my base heart cease to ake
*
Like the meager, counterfeit made intense
I delineate my awful wretchedness.

***

To gild the days befor they are profaned, in
stead for lovers my portables contained, in
rare turnd bowls & oriental clay,
public ticking flagd in warm distain;
quickly, consign me one prudential day
wheram I chamberd & beded down, with items

of speechless warrent bowd, girl in this
brusht with gold, dond in brocade, woman
displayd but drild with open graves, uncrowned
by paltry hands of love,
publish me, employ me poems of curt dismay; indeed, gay,
for lovers I see all has been enraged
Wherelse does chattel take you, for yr senses blunt
even drops lacky diamonds on yr silent cunt.

***

No greater love cld put me down, lie for sound
or palaver me drest in fillybys
Valentine, I die
give me yr hand, send shitty birds to assay me,
blooden me, casting, castrate me & rise & raised
know yr lips the breathless cartilage of tooting time
—the hum of chewn flesh
Yr barren rocks weigh in me splendor, me,
might any other homage be a more constant vendor,
then let me go, out bound, into yr city kingdom
a bone rack, mere house dust lain down
She'd love me, that lusty rag
wherever I am to mock & mense her flight
*

***

New green on old green, spring's caliculi
& spleen, in coming on to molokai this great carbuncle
on my chest—bone, skin, & flesh
The kites of a loving life sported once
with this gram of calx which was loving heart
White isle
for green flankt basilix of ancient vanaty
here in the sluice what was heart
to wort, vomit, blister, & fart
New on injury high love, my etesian glove
not was this lie meant for yrs to ponder
but to forfeit for a dram of that lizard's juice
all my esteem & wonder.

John Wieners

INVITATION AU VOYAGE II

Look, how the rain fallen through the night
Leaves the woods hot, moist and calm,
how the bird skims across the grass
and no car in sight,
waiting your return.

This is that promised land *au bout du monde*
where humid winds blow against your calves,
dragon lilies on fences open to the sun,
Baudelaire's song heard again is afternoon's vagabond.

Your eyes are liquid pools where I would drown,
Your lips a history of the heart,
Your hands hot branches on my back & brow,
and if to die would do it now
these words in my mouth
your kiss the vow.

My dear girl, I know in my blood
No other way to go on loving you
but this. Our lives entwined
as an huntsman's bow.

Oh archer, skill my hands
shoot this arrow
                                close to her lands,

that we might be cleaved as wings on the air

(before the phantom stranger arrives)

and takes her away in the form of death or love.

I'll take you away with me somewhere.

Ted Berrigan

BEAN SPASMS
to George Schneeman

New York's lovely weather
     hurts my forehead

     in praise of thee
       the? white dead
       whose eyes know:
    what are they
  of the tiny cloud my brain:
The City's tough red buttons:
       O Mars, red, angry planet, candy

        bar, with sky on top,
    "why, it's young Leander hurrying to his death"
  what? what time is it in New York in these here alps
  City of lovely tender hate
      and beauty making beautiful
        old rhymes?

  I ran away from you
when you needed something strong
  then I leand against the toilet bowl (ack)
 Malcolm X
    I love my brain
 it all mine now is
 saved not knowing
   that &
   that (happily)
   being that:

  "wee kill our selves to propagate our kinde"
       John Donne
yes, that's true
     the hair on yr nuts & my
      big blood-filled cock are a part in that
      too
    PART 2
      Mister Robert Dylan doesn't feel well today
      That's bad
      This picture doesn't show that
      It's not bad, too

it's very ritzy in fact

here I stand I can't stand
to be thing
I don't use   atop
the empire stare
building
& so sauntered out the door

That reminds me of the time
I wrote that long piece about a gangster name of "Jr."
O Harry James! had eyes to wander but lacked tongue to praise
so later peed under his art
paused only to lay a sneeze
on Jack Dempsey
asleep with his favorite Horse

That reminds me of I buzz
on & off Miro pop
in & out a Castro convertible
minute by minute   GENEROSITY!

Yes now that the seasons totter in their walk
I do a lot of wondering about Life   in praise of ladies dead of
& Time plaza(s), Bryant Park by the Public   eye of brow
Library, Smith Bros. black boxes, Times
Square
Pirogi, Houses
with long skinny rivers thru them
they lead the weary away
off!   hey!
I'm no sailor
off a ship
at sea   I'M HERE
& "The living is easy"
It's "HIGH TIME"
& I'm in shapes
of shadow, they
certainly can warm, can't they?

Have you ever seen one?   NO!
of those long skinny Rivers
O well hung, in New York City?
NO!   in fact

                                    I'm the Wonderer
& as yr train goes by   forgive me, Rene!   'just oncet'
      I woke up in Heaven
                         He woke, and wondered more; how many angels
          on this train huh?   snore
                              for there she lay,
                  on sheets that mock lust   done that 7 times
                                            been caught
                              and brought back
                      to a peach nobody.

                      To Continue:
                      Ron Padgett & Ted Berrigan
                              hates yr brain
                                        my dear
                                    amidst the many other little buzzes
                  & like, Today, as Ron Padgett might say
                              is
                      "A tub of vodka"
                                          "in the morning"

          she might reply
and it keeps it up
        past icy poles
                              where angels beg fr doom then zip
                                  ping in-and-out, joining the army
                  wondering about Life
                  by the Public Library of
                                    Life
                                            No Greater Thrill!
                      (I wonder)
Now that the earth is changing I wonder what time it's getting to be
              sitting on this New York Times Square
        that actually very ritzy, Lauren   it's made of yellow wood or
                      I don't know something   maybe
              This man was my   its been fluffed up
                  friend
                              He had a sense for the
                                  vast   doesn't he?
                      Awake my Angel! give thyself
                                to the lovely hours   Don't cheat
              The victory is not always to the sweet.
                              I mean that.
Now this picture is pretty good here
Though it once got demerits from the lunatic Arthur Cravan

He wasn't feeling good that day
Maybe because he had nothing on
                              paint-wise I mean
              PART 3
                    I wrote that
                    about what is
          this empty room   without a heart
                 in three parts
               a white flower
             came home wet & drunk   2 pepsis
          and smashed my fist thru her window
                              in the nude
        As the hand zips you see
              Old Masters, you can see
             well hung in New York   they grow fast here
               Conflicting, yet purposeful
                  yet with outcry vain!

                         4.
             Praising, that's it!
   you string a sonnet around yr fat gut
       and falling on your knees
                         you invent the shoe
                    for a horse. It brings you luck
              while sleeping
                   "You have it seems a workshop nature"
                   "Good Lord!"
                              Some folks is wood
                         Ron Padgett wd say
                           amidst many other little buzzes
               past the neon on & off
                     night & day STEAK SANDWICH
          Have you ever tried one, Anne?   SURE!
     "I wonder what time 'its'?
        as I sit on this new Doctor
   NO   I only look at buildings they're in
   as you and he, I mean he & you & I buzz past
                         in yellow ties   I call that gold
              THE HOTEL BUCKINGHAM
         (facade) is black, and taller than last time
   is looming over lunch   naked   high time   poem   & I, equal in
                                        perfection & desire
            is looming   both eyes   over coffee-cup (white) nature
                  and man: both hell on poetry.

Art is art and life is
                "A monograph on Infidelity"
       Oh. Forgive me stench of sandwich
       O pneumonia in American Poetry
Do we have time?   well look at Burroughs
       7 times been caught and brought back to mars
                    & eaten.
"Art is art & Life
is home", Fairfield Porter said that
                         turning himself in
                         The night arrives again in red
some go on   even in Colorado   on the run
                    the forests shook
            meaning:
                         coffee   the cheerfulness of this poor
                                     fellow is terrible, hidden in
                                     the fringes of the eyelids
                         blue mysteries' (I'M THE SKY)
       The sky is bleeding now
                    onto 57th Street
                    of the 20th Century &
                         HORN & HARDART'S
Right Here. That's Part 5.
       I'm not some sailor off a ship at sea
I'm the wanderer   (age 4)
                    & now everyone is dead
       sinking bewildered of hand, of foot, of lip
   nude, thinking
laughter burnished brighter than hate
                                     goodbye.
            André Breton said that
                         what a shit!
He's gone!

            up bubbles all his amorous breath
       & Monograph on Infidelity entitled
                         The Living Dream
I never again played
                    I dreamt that December 27th, 1965
            all in the blazon of sweet beauty's breast
       I mean   "a rose"   Do you understand that?
                    Do you?
       The rock&roll songs of this earth
       commingling absolute joy AND

incontrovertible joy of intelligence
                                        certainly can warm
                                    cant they?   YES!
                        and they do.
            Keeping eternal whisperings around.
                                        (Mr. MacAdams writes
                                        in the nude: no that's not
(we want to take the underground   me that: then zips in &
    revolution to Harvard!   out of the boring taxis, re-
                                        fusing to join the army
            and yet this girl has   asleep "on the springs"
                so much grace   of red GENEROSITY
                    I wonder!
            Were all their praises simply prophecies
        of this
                the time!   NO GREATER THRILL
                                    my friends

        But I quickly forget them, those other times, for what are they
    but parts in the silver lining of the tiny cloud my brain
drifting up into smoke the city's tough blue top:

                I think a picture always
                leads you gently to someone else
        Don't you? like when you ask to leave the room
                    and go to the moon.

Anne Waldman

LETTER S

1

A messiah, no rain at all
Lips form the cash-box sound
Tracks in the first person singular
I am the "s" who will save you
Wait
You are twenty minutes ago
A restless drop taken in the ear
I want this arm so arranged
The head moves closer to the candle
She mounts the slip alone
A bead will form #1

And leave you ahead of the singular
His lips, the soundboard
Life-savers in the cold mouth
Slippers enter the ear, no rain at all
He takes off his shoes
Cash-box #1 is twenty minutes closer
To the candle

2

He takes off his shoes
A messiah, no rain at all
You are twenty minutes ago
Wait
And leave you ahead of the singular
Cash-box #1 is twenty minutes closer
She mounts the slip alone
I want this arm so arranged
Lips form the cash-box sound
A bead will form #1
A restless drop taken in the ear
Tracts in the first person singular
Life-savers in the cold mouth
His lips, the soundboard
To the candle
Slippers enter the ear, no rain at all
The head moves closer to the candle
I am the "s" who will save you

Anne Waldman

CULTURE DRIFT

We saw this great movie last night
And the last line was You Were My Best Work

Then we straightened up, breathed some new air and went home
Last night, they said, was a quiet night at home
Drove those crazy demons out and did some work
Wrote letters to the questions (page 8) and

What did you do?

Went home after the walk about the palace

Thought about some other places
Sat down with papers and was in India

We were in a huge tent, they said, encircled by two
(Now Ted said it was one personality)
It was freezing, blowing dirt right under the striped shirts
It was a dark place
No one has returned yet to tell us about India
But we are wearing pajamas
And me and this other girl, we're wearing saris
Giggling the whole time encircled by droves of...

What are they like?

Striped shirts, blown by cotton winds, restless dust
You settle on my skin and mount the strawless mat
Groans discernable in every inch
We never go home when we leave and spend the whole time roaring

ahhh ahhh my India life is always complete
They are wearing the same shirts at home
I wish you could see the place and then (on waking)
I scare you out of your spine!
Breath is hard on the ledge-light-pajamas
You lift your skirt (she is the same next to you)
and all the monsters you despise, they watch and giggle

What did you do beside the restless mat? It twitches with dawn
with the waking cows, droves of elephants, camels come home

2

In the movie you wish to forget you are reborn
and with new skin you greet a California moon

But me, I'd rather be in India
I'd be exorcised forever from the sleeping skirt

Michael Brownstein

AGAINST THE GRAIN

. . . either, over the shoulder enjoy leaning. Don't
Touch it. Skyway pumpkins lounge
Rocking beside me but I thrive straight
Away. Large early centers blur off (Look, Johnny
See the Indians wearing their Maine blankets
Lobster smoke disappearing between the
Tree. Don't knock it over.) looking over

Would you turn it down a quarter inch?
Now I rest between the teeth of
Courage, silence, gold. I pass the lines
Painted below the pilot's "Otto" window
Like a lake going up from gasoline
To drowning above the clouds (of starch beauty).
Probing a border the police sighs
The trestle agh agh agh over the train late
Mathematics pass hot trees. Dutch door. Don't move.

I wander the banks and Wanda was.

Sounds not so much mingle curtains
Yellow against green and then of course
The perfect right green has against that yellow
In the dusty white pod against here
Beside your wife who is too sinuous and tall
To be a real Dutch...little men in pocket charms
Made her. She travels through an easy window
Sunlight on Bavarian cottage window
In natural southern Bavaria. Large blue
Against the Pittsburgh sky. Sky.
Summer in the pedigree under Moscow's dome.

Take the summer.

She delivers the folded postcard to the hill.
Mingling feeds rain and forest an afterthought
As I am planning to feed astronomy
To the turkeys here for a year
(Light snows over the eighty mile ear)
Pure ground plum stew chugging up to the door.

Early in the morning it quieted down somewhere
Among the flamingoes. Suddenly I realized this was because
They had no place to sit. I shaved for a while in the mirror
And crawling out of the tent (take the summer) I crawled
Out of the tent and talked over to the shore
Most of the people were eating already.

Michael Brownstein

POUNDS AND OUNCES

Here comes Charles and Madeleina my child
India, Guerdon, Macao, Church and Bessarabia
A minute to the left of the knee
Louise, Esso, Essene and gold Dolores of the caves
To rest on views from the point
You begins to get up and leave (pounce)

Yes he certainly should be blank in the parka by now
Some of the guests are, already receiving visits
You might walk in once more
Then he reads you out

Dirty and graceful but a bit too tall
Clean and distrustful but short little
Noreen and Barley are scrambling out of the Jumna to you
They think they are going to wave

"No Thought"

Egg   Spoon   Throat   Vista

Teeth   Glint   Spokes

Stagger   Choke

(Pearl)

Upon the pyramid I have returned to you
Ready to go. Dolores is folding her last slip in the mouth
"Pack clothes write batter and taste and see"
New spoons and fresh marching spoons
Baby Egypt damp with glee

Blod

lobstee

John Ashbery

THE HOD CARRIER

You have been declining the land's
Breakable extensions, median whose face is half my face.
Your curved visor's the supposition that unites us.

                          I've been thinking about you

After a dry summer, fucking in the autumn,
Reflecting among arabesques of speech that arise
The certain anomaly, the wise smile
Of winter fitted over the land
And your activity disappears in mist, or translates too easily
Into a general puree, someone's aura or idea of games—
The stone you cannot perfect, the sharp iron blade you cannot prevent.

But this new way we are, the melon head
Half-mirrored, the way sentences suddenly spurt up like gas
Or sting and jab, is it that we accepted each complication
As it came along, and are therefore happy with the result?
Or was it as a condition of seeing
That we vouchsafed aid and comfort to the seasons

                          As each came begging

And the present, so flat in its belief, so "outside it"
As it maintains, becomes the blind side of
The fulfillment of that condition; and work, ripeness
And tired but resolute standing up for one's rights
Means leaning toward the stars

                          The way a tree leans toward the sun

Not meaning to get close
                          And the bird walked right up that tree.

You have reached the point closest to your destination

                          O tired beacon
                          Dominating the plain
                          Yet all but visible

To the holy mind surrounding your purpose

You are totally subsumed
The good abstracted, squandered, thrown away
As it was in the lean time.
Are these floorboards, to be stared at
In moments of guilt, as wallpaper can stream away and yet

                    You cannot declare it?

Each wasp meant to look the way it did
And the sorrowing whole also
Although influenced by particulars
Suspended in the near distance
So that you say, that's a pretty one

                    I'd forgotten about that one

Then each breath is a redeeming feature
Resolving in alteration
The insanity of flowers into perfect conditions
That their mildness can only postpone, not change.

And surveying the hundredfold record of the summer
The shapely witness at last declares herself
Content with the result:
Whitecaps wincing at every point of the compass
The justified demands of commerce, difficult departures and all
Into a hemisphere where no credit is expected
And the shipping is rendered into its own terms

                    It is what keeps itself
                    From going blind

All aging is perpetual chatter
On these buff planes, protuberances
And you are in the wind at night

                    And so it is an even darker night

And death is the prevention of which the cure's
Metal polish and sawdust

                    Light grinding into your heels.

Lewis MacAdams

POCKETS OF HAZE

A lemon ship floats by between tugs
like the wind through a banner
Orange words on the side of this building
feet on the edge. It's windy near the top,
but quiet
       like observing the chain of command
or a demonstration of dog whistles.
A drunk flops slowly to the street
and the light drops around him
     protect him "who can't stand the gaff"
well don't drink, huh?
                 The solid island breathes
rheumy down there. My heart
massaged by a friend in an open shirt
a pocket rattles near the edge of the landing
that's me, that's my "heart."
Buildings, ships, men in uniforms
parade by. It's the residue of salutation
that I've taken & thought I passed on
that bakes me, that makes me tremble in a gang.
Like dressing slowly on a hot day
and watching a girl boil in the prairie distance.

Dick Gallup

PRETTY BEADS

1.
There is a lobster in the ocean

2.
A green lobster is saying his prayers

3.
A pebble drifts toward a monument

4.
The violet State
                (whose bed is the sea)

5.
Three granite indians do the bird

6.
The heart of a red rooster residing in Rhode Island

7.
A red gulley

8.
Busch Stadium looms in the distance like hope

9.
A Cardinal rounds third and heads for home

10.
The eyes look down under a pale moon

11.
Down the main street of Gallup, New Mexico

12.
Orange stars and peaches

13.
Joy like a small train of thought

14.
A fluid substance

15.
The lobster eats with quick snaps

Robert Duncan

AT THE POETRY CONFERENCE: BERKELEY
AFTER THE NEW YORK STYLE

1.

Beginning with sonnets for Ted Berrigan
Turning on poetry and I'm off
Along lines Ginsberg is reading to places
It takes a line in here I have not heard

Beautiful yellow cheeks and jowels

Marking an uneven stanza off with jewels
Little girls reading all the way thru 88
Highway into some part of Oregon
Goddess of music and poetry by-pass
Where Allen Ginsberg says "*This*"
A line for you in your own collection
It is eight forty-five and two more

For closing we need something lovely
That will lead on to closing doors we see.

2.

Same evening. Can anybody.
Turning on poetry I have not heard
Ham it up so and still get down
From there he takes O'Hara
Who never really went there
where he did not come. From. They said.

He did little girls reading all

This one in a Black Mountain
Berrigan imitation North Carolina
Lovely needed poem for O'Hara
and Ashbery again going towards the Pound
Cantos with ashes and berries for the
Contempt they feel and gratitude and
for the puns sake
Dogs barking along another shore.

You never gave me my road.
What could I do for *you?*

3.

They are crowding in the doors to hear
Ginsberg. But Duncan
Is writing Sonnets from the Portuguese
For T. Berrigan with run-on
Effusions of love and lines in rime

(which I have to postpone until later)

Allen is saying various things amusing.
I am singing Kenneth Koch even might be here
If they were written by John Ashbery
So turned on by Berrigan going off
towards uptown

He didn't know I wrote the song
I have choruses of the West sing
Cantos and for Pound's sake
Envoys and aves buses can have.

Byron Keats and Shelly are our boys abroad.
Sketch of a vista confronting the ocean.

4.

Dear familiar words "*cock*" and "*cunt*"
(Ginsberg is unbeknownst to Far Rockaway
Where in 1941 I went to meet Anais Nin
But it was raining and February
Frank O'Hara was probably in school.
Now at my most lovely
Never having been to Harvard for God's sake
I'd like to make up a life of my own
Berrigan can have from me to think over.

Dear familiar words like . . . But no
Words come I'm so shy when words are familiar
"Fate passing by" Allen is bellowing
Nor was I unhappy. How much I love to be made love to
By delicate girl-hands
The whole thing belonging to Berrigan.

5.

An old creep with a need to read poems
Has only my sonnets to Berrigan to read
So I put in the word "*Jack Off*" from Ginsberg's mouth
A line for you in your own collection.
We let the river run if it wants to.

Dogs barking along the other shore.

I put the coda towards the last
for friendship's sake
Envoys and buses O'Hara needed
To get where I am behind times and scenes
[Do this passage in a BIG VOICE]

The audience is crowding in
To hear what we need and is lovely.

Vito Hannibal Acconci

THE PLACABLE CAPS

The eye, you see is contradictory in both parts
Dividing a sensation or
A sensational green bag. It sealed
The British of a truly fateful coming
And going and was glad to stain it into practice. What
Curtly reduced his raise? you asked the wrong
Version of a more concerned device, the circled
Patent at white cans that prove
A former failure, In the ear, you see, succeeds
The watering branch to a line, a horse' pub-
Lic, a probably separate
Washer of agents. There was nothing more to shuffle
Through the match, when the airborne were evasive
To an interest, Frankly, the British raise stopped
Its material and tropes were in the way
Though in a way appointed. He would merely have preferred
To live in any police appeal
Than intend among the Bahamas. The greens
Object. You smell a last minute while
The invitations are geared in a seaplane, until sayings
Agreed to the exchange rate on a foreign boil
Though it is never forged to decide
Where the seaplane will astonish. Now the health dropped
On reductions, but in any cast the finger
Lined a culture for a consonant deceit. The branch you
Hear is utter and cannot splash the stripe in a proper
Anxiety. If the camp had not returned
You would have blinked at the filters, resembling the general-
Ly inviolate silversides, their blunders passed
From a fruit hole, a mummified little
By little salvage. It spaced to flee a watering match

But "Could your versed concern ask
For precision?" he reduced the comparison
He squared at court for. You could sense
The helmets he spent over
Designs, barnacles that were divided to
The British interjection. So see, you there
Out of the corner of his height, his landing in a second work
And subsequently various at lined cans, or
A horse's washer, nor a public's separated agent could import
The eye worth telling
Charges, contradicting the reorganized experience beside
The going down which is a comber's splinter
Coinciding with the Grenville blotter that has serviced
From the matter of an oval the phonetics in lead.

René Ricard

OH

Oh yes the page is blank
At first; And now to confuse
The issue;
I take a long chic drag from my Gauloise
I've done it before. This could be a great poem
If I didn't rather jerk off instead
Already I've begun three consecutive lines with
I; Something is meant by this
Perhaps I'll jerk off eventually
What could be more essential
(Notice a lack of continuity)
Recurrent theme
Several stanzas and a modicum of internal rhyme
Measure Measure Measure My dear
Is not poetry withou tit
les vox
Da Do you know how much poetry
How much *good* poetry was written in
Say the 50's?
Lots I'll bet
Down through the ages
We each pick our favorites

René Ricard

VISIONS OF ARTHUR

I could stop writing
Rimbaud did.
Sick, sick of trying to preserve
            emphemera long enough
to set it down. Lost a fit of inspiration
            some
Minutes ago because I couldn't find
            a pen
So slowly, a pen records the changing
            shape of an idea
Into a word—, different, traditional, and
            passée

Where personal choice becomes precedent
History—you have abandoned me too.
I'll never hear her whose applause posterity
imitates.

Where *does* the time go.

René Ricard

last night I tore my new $30 pants on Max's
Kansas City's "Auto Wreck" by John Chamberlain

PARTY CRASH

Events strangely irrelevant as
my life exists without me,
Unrecorded conversations
The misplaced M.S.'s
The misplaced friends
Somehow so much is lost.

What transpires when John Giorno
& I stare at each other
His quavering pupils—Empty like my heart?
"If I ever see you again."
And he's not the only one
But there's no one else.
If and & but I postpone escaping with a phone #

II
CHRONOLOGY & CONTEXT
      (some songs & some places

"Where Did Our Love Go"
P. Town summer '64
John Under The Boardwalk
            "Baby Love"
Youthful in Boston I fall in love
    John
    John gives me "the Supremes" for Christmas
    "Stop in the Name of Love"
John and I decide on a new City
    "Nothing But Heartaches"
N. Y. summer '65 I begin to lose
John
"The Supremes at Philharmonic Hall"
    "I hear a Symphony"
    I exit crying
"My World Is Empty Without You"
"Where Did Our Love Go"

III
Come, now, It's 1966
It's easy to enter New Years
and hearts and parties

IV
Autumn is here
& I am dubious

ANGEL HAIR 4

Winter 1967-68

Kenward Elmslie

FEATHERED DANCERS

Inside the lunchroom the travelling nuns wove
sleeping babies on doilies of lace.
A lovely recluse jabbered of bird lore and love:
    "Sunlight tints my face

    and warms the eggs outside
    perched on filthy columns of guilt.
    In the matted shadows where I hide,
    buzzards moult and weeds wilt."

Which reminds me of Mozambique
in that movie where blacks massacre Arabs.
The airport runway (the plane never lands, skims off) is bleak—
scarred syphillitic landscape—crater-sized scabs—

Painted over with Pepsi ads—
as in my lunar Sahara dream—giant net comes out of sky,
encloses my open touring car. Joe slumps against Dad's
emergency wheel turner. Everyone's mouth-roof dry.

One interpretation. Mother hated blood!
When the duck Dad shot dripped on her leatherette lap-robe,
dark spots not unlike Georgia up-country mud,
her thumb and forefinger tightened (karma?) on my ear-lobe.

Another interpretation. Motor of my heart stalled!
I've heard truckers stick ping-pong balls up their butt
and jounce along having coast-to-coast orgasms, so-called.
Fermes, tous les jardins du Far West, I was taught—tight shut.

So you can't blame them. Take heed, turnpikes.
Wedgies float back from reefs made of jeeps: more offshore debris.
Wadded chewy depressants and elatants gum up footpaths. Remember
Ike's "Doctor-the-pump-and-away-we-jump" Aloha Speech to the
                                                    Teamsters?
                                                    "The—"

he began and the platform collapsed, tipping him onto a traffic island.
An aroused citizenry fanned out through the factories that day
to expose the Big Cheese behind the sortie. Tanned,
I set sail for the coast, down the Erie and away,

and ate a big cheese in a cafe by the docks,
and pictured every room I'd ever slept in:
toilets and phone-calls and oceans. Big rocks
were being loaded, just the color of my skin,

and I've been travelling ever since,
so let's go find an open glade
like the ones in sporting prints
(betrayed, delayed, afraid)

where we'll lie among the air-plants
in a perfect amphitheatre in a soft pink afterglow.
How those handsome
birds can prance,
ah...unattainable tableau.

Let's scratch the ground clean,
remove all stones and trash,
I mean open dance-halls in the forest, I mean
where the earth's packed smooth and hard. Crash!

It's the Tale of the Creation. The whip cracks.
Albatrosses settle on swaying weeds.
Outside the lunchroom, tufts and air-sacs
swell to the size of fruits bursting with seeds.

Kenward Elmslie

DUO-TANG

Laundry so near the ocean bothered Frank.
The lack of medicine on the shelves
also confused his emotional stance.

A moth fluttered against his leg.
A gust of wind made his Pepsi keen
as its foam trickled down inside.

A banana boat on a horizon otherwise blank
passed over a time-piece buried in valves
over which sea-growths stirred. Grant's

Tomb. Cleopatra's Needle. The Hague.
He flipped the pages of the travel magazine
and wondered if Monsieur had lied.

Tomorrow, he'd go to the bank,
shop for some unguents and skin salves,
and finish the Castles' book on the dance.

The Hesitation Waltz! How vague
the past seemed: static scene after static scene.
He watched the retreating tide

and patted his belly. The sun sank.
Monsieur and J. were off by themselves.
He took off his pants.

He was too proud to beg.
He lay down and thought of Jean.
The sheet had dried.

Anne Waldman

GOING IN

We are going in the water for the rest of the day
so that sun so hot now is really a false start
when I mention it on those postcards a week from today,
wanting to lighten your feet as we move from town to museum
and taking in a swim we end up in a city which becomes the map
you buy as the water rips at the folds you bend the wrong way,
impatient to know the way I stay up studying myself in Europe:

Look at the water splashing from the edge like that!

I can't keep my eyes off summer clothing
or looking for Negroes, say, in Switzerland wondering
what everybody's thinking back in New York a revolution
in my head I'm dreaming everyone is black and here we are
eating a prezzo fizzo and dizzy behind the Uffizi.

It's all so wonderfully exhausting with this wine in my feet
and you're dragging me through these streets of sexual freaks
can't believe the skirts I'm wearing and everyone praying

somewhere every day I want to go in the churches they won't let me
like you won't let me bite my nails what fun is that?

But how extraordinary everything is and new hitting my eyes
so I can't see myself getting up at 6 am in Venice,
but I do, thinking of Stokely Carmichael in London and the part when
he was talking about 'history' you know? and that's what we're doing

Like tyrants I want it all to be perfect and it isn't
so bad being here, alive, wet all over, and you along.

Sotere Torregian

AFTER MAYAKOVSKY

The aureole
comes into my room
and says
"Wall Street"
I say
"Hi!"
My eyes generally qualify for topaz
The farts! They ride in big cars
and see me drop my last piece of tuna
to the ants
I stuff my magic letters down the
throat of the cyclone
The aureole crosses its legs
        like it has to go to the bathroom

Now we spar
smear street kisses
Dutch.
On my day off
I have lost the continuity
but I shall not forget the aureole.
This may be out last meeting
before the Big Ticket-taker.

Like ducks in the window of lechery
keep a diary

In our afternoon
shoes without socks

that wind clocks
and cause anger.

My definition of patriotic
is: to lead all the chandeliers
of the world to one watering
hole.

My hair stands out
like brussels sprouts
in the night
when I tell time
by our sun-dial.

In disastrous
situations
girls
always are seated
fixing their shoe-straps
on a corner
and I
am a fire-plug
keeping my
desolate banner
in my pocket
ready to unfurl

I've just kicked over
my "interior castle"
its nipple
and gear splatter
into the street
A dog follows me
stupid and somnambulant
Like the Lion of
St. Mark.

When I take
a break

I smell the sea from
this hospice window
And I stride in labor
the library sea

above those cabbage heads
and gramophone horses
where below
the wind sings
to the girl:
"I'm asking
I'm asking"

It was the birthday of a king.
Oranges.
That I, a snow drop,
cordoned

The aureole!
the aureole won't
give me a ride anymore
The aureole's put me in a closet
where I can't think anymore
but of the Hopi Indian
word for 'snow'

today
my neck
is a siren
calling firemen
to the ice palace

When I reach out
I am always the song
that someone has
forgotten

I like anyone who defies
the Cops!
The birds talk The new school that is starting
loyal tastes
The aureole!
I want to tell her
how difficult it is
for me
to be a poet

But barriers punch
I laugh
like a stone statue
astride myself
flapping
in a black homeland

Sotere Torregian

ATTITUDES

1   I'd like to roll my cigarette through life
2   like Jacques Prevert
3   And step onto the screen and watch
4   my wife take the baby and leave me
5   Watch the mountains do a dance
6   I'd like to stand in front of the Vagabond Trading Post
7   with dark circles in the doorway
8   and roll my cigarette
9   I'd go into the dance halls
10 and roll my cigarette
11 I'd find my mistress in a car with a guy
12 and look at her and him long and deep there
13 and roll my cigarette
14 You can't tell a German church from a tavern
15 Look at the world tumble down
16 An avalanche coming down at me
17 and roll my cigarette
18 I'd just like to roll my cigarette
19 and look at everything
20 and walk around

Dick Gallup

GUARD DUTY

A blind child clutches a 3" fish
Summer camp, a miracle on 5th Avenue
Little hints of reality marching
Across the back of the bus
I'm not riding

A quarantine falls over the picture
And it is like nothing was ever there
Or rather there seems to be a bug
On the sidewalk I am examining
That doesn't figure because I need a drink
And I don't drink

And then a dog walks through a window
A tiny flashlight
In the pastures of childhood
Which no one seems interested in
Neglecting, bright quadrangles opening
On a square I knew, I guess
In the manner in which a dog knows his master
Or a fish his particular fish pond
Liquids returning to their own level
Or the dog passing another window
In a house I know is there
If only by reputation

Dick Gallup

THE STRUGGLE FOR THE BORDER

Landing in the summer shade
Hands empty for years of effort
Lank feet in the grass of home
Can I get on again

Like songs
Reversing the course of thought
Mists and blue water cross my head
Like gods on tour

The end in view is merely given
Like sleeping thru a shower
Or the number of oranges in a grove

A scarce minimum limitation of profit
Imposed for survival

ENJOYMENT BODY

> "They do not marry because they
> can no longer die."

1

What you say deadens your legs
in the brown river
desired for nothing
the car just stops
as if someone says
I fell instantly in love

This is permitted to you
blue fly lint in your mouth
shedding the spell of certain ends
which boys rap into smoke
blurred down poltergeist
whose eyes open the wrap on its way to you

You are used to the linen
the waterfall becoming flakes
like the blowing hair I taste on your bike
to sweeten the space, the measure
of words which make it difficult to say
Where is my father and my mother, nurse?

You show that part
the bones where I enter you
so the hall is empty
but the walls are pierced with doors
the tapping an endless grace
for your mouth is only the way you promised

2

It was seed time
you killed three gophers near the gate
When I followed the snail track into the hall
you were lying back
ice cubes on your forehead
electric instruments flooded with sunlight

Someone said there was a final corner
just as they found what they had come for
They wanted to hear How wide they dream
and they made the parting stroke around you
which you took for flowers
wings on the bed that you kept prisoner
There was no harm
so you said the buds had white wings
it was the last defense

3

We are close by
He turns
The still makes a girl's face
uncombed fontanel
healing like dried flowers
Boys in black cowls
bend over the frieze
Let the wind blow by a little

Aside from his head
C is beautiful
In the corner
a song exempts the time together
]ike the stain you change
from the west
in the song starting
Take me who belong

His song ends
Got to feel you inside of me
so he remains inside us
the parted eye
the accident which we pull round us
a compact quiet as dust
The useful arm returns
no fault except the sound
which makes our turning glass
"If thou say so, withdraw, and prove it too."

4

At night Impossibility lay on your sheets
and Despair leaned over
the penis became the distance
a green line that places changed to
and under the distance
it was forgotten
but let them close

5

When you left the idea of direction
a boy said
Sweet flower, with flowers thy bridal bed I strew
and his friend said
Let us do wrong
but it was done and morning
The hall moved and you tucked it under you
the eyes moved as to define "thoughts"
and it was nothing more

6

You are lighting yourself
The steps in the papers
take "blench" into the tapestry,
watching the place
as happily as you can

The opening of the sleepers are skin boats
A shower is colors held inside
dark cares behind the shell
The hoops of dressers,
vaseline sticking under your nails,
clear dreams lighten autarchic scratches

You write
    grazing buttons
    spinal cubes in the frost
You are high as lances saying
    Butterflies change deaths
    they are becoming cool
    As the sun passes behind the clouds
    I have made the world dark
    I walk upon half the sky

Joanne Kyger

                    Unexpectedly, from the outside,
        it rains. It washes down the walls of the house, whereas
            then with clear eyes we see hesitation
                            I listen for the words to
        come—nothing is mine within this world. In my cradle
            the world has been cruel—these are the people of my world—the
    small spirits who sit on my shoulder, the cats, the dogs
    the river I keep in its bank, the dead deer, I walk through
                caring that I am alive.

                        Only those that naturally seek my side
        when I am quiet, and he doesn't lose himself, off with the hordes
        screaming to be heard. fitting into the ground
        like an old shoe. What is it they say to each other? I hold together
                                    for the moment
                    each time a star rises
            you may speak to it in recognition but not in friendship
                                I will recognize you
            without qualities
        As the animals are permitted to escape who
                    unknowingly make that decision. Some offer
            themselves, the game is not pursued. Holding one's own
            it was a clear headed vision
            the streams pouring out of the earth.

                            *

From interest, to awe to fear. One must move
gingerly, for the investigation not to proceed
out of the hands of the lord, and not gain confidence
from the repetition of the past
or despair.
I have already arrived where I want to go
and am bound to continue
as I see it never ends, that is
food.
Yes, the general intoxication
is a good thing to come out of, as it is not
intoxication, just wait. Your mind doesn't lie
but it changes.
Therefore, I see many similarities,
in the breadbasket: blood
and children, animals, sentence structures
frozen food.
They said by noon
it would go away, which isn't so
and as he is cruel
one must watch these things in advance
for a matter of an hour
comes back with fear
that the roots might decay.
As a look in the heart shows
what's ostentatious
and therefore unnecessary to
view with any pleasure the exact summation or advice.

Ron Padgett

WONDERFUL THINGS

Anne, who are dead   and whom I loved in a rather asinine fashion
I think of you often

buveur de l'opium chaste et doux

Yes I think of you

with very little in mind

as if I had become a helpless moron

Watching zany chirping birds

That inhabit the air

And often ride our radio waves

So I've been sleeping lately with no clothes on
The floor   which is very early   considering the floor
Is made of birds and they are flying and I am
Upsidedown and ain't it great to be great!!

Seriously I have this mental (smuh!) illness

                                        which causes me to do things

                                                on and away

Straight for the edge
Of a manicured fingernail
Where it is deep and dark   and green   and silent
Where I may go at will
And sit down and tap
                        My forehead against the sunset

Where he takes off the uniform
And we see he is God

God get out of here

And he runs off chirping and chuckling into his hand

And that is a wonderful thing

                        . . . a tuba that is a meadowful of bluebells

is a wonderful thing

                and that's what I want to do

Tell you wonderful things

Ron Padgett

THE STATUE OF A LIBERTINE

I've chosen this title because not only do I like it
But also it embodies the kind of miniature grandness
A toy instrument has, or powerful dwarf, half sinister
Half pleasure and unexplained

Now I address the statue

Lips that were once as volatile
As similies spoken by an insane person
Who resembled the carving of an irrational human being
But one endowed with such sweetness the pockets are
Blown to bits through their emptiness,

There is no margin of doubt to this reverse
Power, it moves back immediately, a Leonardo's square
You start back from—it extends a confusing,
Buffered metric scale of being
Toward the deep green velvet
That makes sleep possible
Near the gravel smitten with the gloom's evocative power—
These unintentionally horrible memories cling like peaches to the walls
Of the streets where stilettos whiz swiftly toward an incorrect mansion,
                                                                probably
Not very pleasant thoughts
MOVE TOO QUICKLY

What's happening is that we're pawning especially
The vegetation
                    Watch it   There was a first light of print
Then suddenly my view of things
Either enlarges or contracts incredibly
And all I can see is the two of us, you
With your long dark hair, me looking at your hair against the screen
In this small kitchen with its yellow and white curtains
Shot into place with light
And everything else is gone forever
If it does nothing else, this feeling, at least
It relieves my temporal worries
And then it dawns on you: you're looking at the background
For every painting you've ever seen!
It's a kitchen exactly like this one

Containing the orange juice and two dozen eggs
And the coffee pot, the electric
One Tessie and I posed on either side of just before our trip to Rome

We went flying over Rome in a giant aspirin
We didn't see much but were free from headache
(This on a postcard home)
Moving up I thought I'd have the aspirin turn to powder
Which would fall on the city—the echo
I didn't answer because not answering is one of the luxuries
We have here, if we have a phone...
But enough of this, my head

The sun is now going up and down so fast I can hardly keep track
of what day today is—it's the next day, in fact, though it
shouldn't be: I'm wearing the same clothes, smoking the same
cigarette, the temperature is the cigarette. There is less
darkness outside, though.

Unfortunately, I can't seem to fit it into any reasonable sequence—
                    one hundred fashionable yachts burning
Remind me of a Blaise Cendrars poem about yachts
I translated in Paris
A few minutes before seeing a young girl break
Down and cry in the Boulevard St-Germain. Thomas Hardy
Was with her but didn't seem to notice she was sobbing horribly and
I felt like pushing both of them into the traffic light
My bus had stopped at

2.

Higher up, the wrist assumes a puffiness
Not unlike a pyjama leg stuffed with hundred dollar bills
But a dramatic resolution is passed
Into the extended index finger whose rushing
Detonates the very tip

WAITING FOR CLAUDE

Waiting for Claude is an all-day affair.

False memories of Margaret Gridley. What's the matter
             with Margaret Gridley?

Margaret Gridley is logical.

How can evil spring from a virtue?

Margaret Gridley is clinically sane.

Margaret Gridley is ambitious and industrious.

Margaret Gridley grieves.

How can sadness grow out of a blameless life?
Margaret Gridley beautiful Margaret
        look down from your leafy bower
        all bedight.

Grieve not, Margaret Gridley,
Do not weep sadly wandering
           under the poplars green with joy

                    *

Dear Friends. Ah dear friends. What can I say.
Dear friends, I am decimated. I am sorry to leave you all
alone. I have to make a trip to the stationer's & to the
postoffice. Should you wish to see me you must content
yourselves with waiting here until I return; you wouldn't
need to wait longer than a few minutes. Oh no. Please
come inside and make yourselves as comfortable as possible
while you wait. Read books. Play music. Make tea and
drink it. Write letters. Bewail your fate, your sins,
your miseries.   Your friend,
                          P.

                    *

Why should beauty mourn?
O Margaret Gridley do not laugh madly
        rending the acorn mist

Plunge not into the flat green river
Don't drown yourself in the Luckiamute!

The willows mourn for Margaret Gridley.
She was a Radcliffe girl.

Nobody remembers her, truly or falsely
Beautiful Margaret Gridley
        sank.

What ever happened to Marjory Grimshaw?

                    *

                Hours Later.
Dear Friends,
    I told you that I should be home but I am not. I
have had to go out again. I went out a while ago to mail
proof and a letter back to a publisher in America. I left
a note for you, but it seems that you never came to read it.

    Now, dear friends, I must go out again to buy a loaf of
bread because I find that I have acquired a case of "The Chucks."
I must find a great deal of food and candy and eat it all. All
of it.

    Let me repeat in this note the invitation which I in-
cluded in my previous message: Come inside and wait for me.
I won't be long. Read books. Count your fingers. Remember
your folks back home. Make tea. Scratch. I'll return reasonably
                Yours,
                P.

                        6:IX:66

Philip Whalen

DEMACHI

Lady leans over the table writing
Takarabune coffeeshop
Is there a large spider descending from her hair?
It swings in space just below her cheek
The top of a ball-point pen
"Santa Claus is coming/ To town!"

***

A funny trip to the other side of the square, from
Demachi Yanagi linoleum plastic noodle shop
The Pepsi Cola man has rice with his *chuka soba*
To America taped music red upholstery lilac or yellow shades
                on hanging lamps
Christmas trees pinned to the walls
Tinsel yardage stars their sparkling guts
Descending blue glass balls.
Air conditioner flops and glitters them
Everybody drinks thick fruit nasty

                                        25:XI:66

Philip Whalen

SANJU SANGENDO

I went to visit several thousand gold buddhas
They sat there all through the war—
They didn't appear just now because I happened to be in town
Sat there six hundred years. Failures.
Does Buddha fail. Do I.
Some day I guess I'll never learn.

                28:XII:66

Philip Whalen

"COMING FORTH BY DAY"

> I must get up early in the morning
> Let all the insects out to air and feed
> They come back nightly, ever faithful
> Even this cold weather when I wished
> They'd all be dead

31:X:66

Philip Whalen

POEM

> Like a bird
> Falls from
> Indifferent
> Air   Sky
> Blunders   yells
> Among tangled
> Branches
> Thoughtless
> Dirty crooked feet

8:XII:66

Philip Whalen

WE SING IN OUR SLEEP. WE CONVERSE WITH THE DEAD IN OUR DREAMS.

> We live in the shadows of dogs and horses.
> Feather shadow of great rooster lies flat on the dust
> Flat on the dusty ground

4:I:67

Peter Schjeldahl

RELEASE

My life has been tedious
Confused and occasionally quite nasty
And hysterical
But I have never deliberately said anything
Without a lot of sincerity

My disagreements with myself are misunderstandings
Counterbalanced by a numbed optimism

I rarely hold opinions for longer than a few hours

Finishing a poem leaves me in despair
But I also make mild, intriguing collages
That fascinate me by their separateness

Sometimes I would like to kill someone
But I guess what I really want is to grab them and shake them
(No one in particular)

I feel best when alone and walking
Quite tall, agile and slightly vicious
Also with a penetrating gaze for everything

I am currently suspicious of everyone
And regard nothing very highly
I do this out of a certain humility

Kenneth Koch

AIRPLANE BETTY IN HOLLAND

1

Airplane Betty sat down in Holland, she felt the cool breezes blowing
Around her chair and there was a face in the window
That was advertising tulips

2

When the great silver plane had first sprung up, springlike
Over Holland, Betty had put her hand before her face because she
    doubted it was

Real. Then through the sky came the music of a cow's supper time
And Betty's vehicle was soon landing among the yellow and orange tulips
Betty said now she felt better and I must go to a coffeehouse
And write Giles a postcard

3

Into the aurora of the Bermuda sky Giles looked up
The sun was setting it sent its orange beams through the sky
And Giles straightened up he had business to do his office
   was surrounded by
White beams the Atlantic Ocean singing underwear and palm fronds

4

One day Harem Harold mounted up into a giant and powerful plane
Its engine was coughing big clouds of black helpless smoke.

5

Everyone had on a white blouse
In Holland, Betty noted,
And a giant cigarette went whizzing through the air

6

What clearness and freshness though to be a short
Time over the sea and then following its anchored beaches and then wait
For the friendly mob

7

O perfume and a silver plane, tulips
Lying in the outlying sweet blue pink and yellow
Fields   It was with an invincible lantern Karl went
Stretching his search for the green bumblebee until the power
Stations of Holland wept red and yellow tears

8

....interested, not so much in the carpentry as the reaction....
Eddy didn't understand what the note said

9

She could have explained it because the note was in English
Betty spoke English when a young child

10

The American man said, Poetry is cranberries. You shop
Under the willow trees
The stone guppies filled up Benny's pocket while he read Aesop's fables

11
Meanwhile there was Betty saying Shoo on the cabbage farms of Holland

12
Over the crystal clear sea the courtesy of the Congo came true,
Long ago it had been promised to a man in a blue life preserver's jacket
That Congo would come true as the most courteous place in the universe
But they were delayed down there by a virus of lime

13
Give me a couple of lollipops Betty speeched
In Holland, and the man looked at the great red bat wings in the sky
And he said there is a fearful present coming from the Congo

14
Betty smiled down at the little dusty frogs

15
Meanwhile Giles was slaving away in Bermuda
Had Betty accomplished the mission?
A shoe repair mill went up not far from where Giles was camping
He was disguised as a foreman in the Bermuda sanitation department
He had on a yellow seersucker jacket and underneath it a pinstriped suit
Which said Travel Department on it in large pink letters
And he was smoking a large two for fifteen dollars cigar
Because sanitation department men love fine cigars
And they don't care how expensive
They are And he was driven in a Cadillac automobile
Every day to his mission, because sanitation men love ease
Luxury and every conceivable comfort in life
And Giles laughed as he fell into the trite swamp
Or pulled a brother up from the leg-disconnecting fields
Down there in Bermuda and the simplest thing there was to write the
   Congo
You could do it with one big red two-cent stamp
So Giles sent a long letter happy as the automotive day
On the red stamp, which he dispatched with tremendous speed
Over the simple blue waves to the far-off Congo
Which arrived there in an hour or two, it was postman's magic
And then Giles felt the yellow influence of the hot day
And he kissed the breeze and said I hope you are all right Betty

16
But she couldn't hear him unless she received that word from the Congo
Which he had dispatched And the red stamp landed in Holland

17

Everyone in his Dutch wooden shoes including Harem Harold came
Running to the market place to disavow the news
Of any red stamp from Argo

18

The Dutch embassy went under water
What was it doing in Holland anyway?

19

But the white cuffs of Betty's blouse moved up acridly against her
    red sleeves
And her blue shoes tilled the earth with its mercy
Until the fresh roses of her heart fell upon the white lake of the letter

20

O towers of ivory! Old Henry locked up the reindeer tenants
For the last time. "I've packed my things and am going to Holland."

21

Giles wondered why the mail service was so slow in the Netherlands
Or had he sent that smiling missile to Killarney
He walked along the beach and then he saw a postage stamp bearing the
    face of Harem Harold
He is in Holland too! Giles said. He pictured the blue stamp
On a white letter and then he remembered he had written the Congo

22

But the Congo was there, in Holland, with the letter!
It was the most extremely polite thing that had ever been done
And the King of Congo's head was covered with blue water
To thank him for the extreme purity and mercy of his kindness
And this deed was commemorated by a wet postage stamp
Being placed against the orange wall of a building

23

O Betty! Has she come back? What's getting out of the airplane
Instead of the usual summery airy Betty? A bundle of blue clothing!
Isn't it Betty? And Giles said, Betty will be here. She is often slow.
And six months passed. Then a summery spirit danced on the waters
Just inside and near Bermuda. And Betty came down in her plane at mid-
    night
And was as pretty and charming as an unsold steamship ticket
And there was lots of red material in her plane too with some black

Walnut heads and some impolite bones from the Congo
Then as daisy flowers stretch out their fresh young wings
At dawn to greet the offended although wicked steamship
Keeping at a slight distance at first out of concern for sportsmanship
Although later clarifying their desires, in the regulation of his dreams
Giles missed four cuff buttons and, starving, rose to find Betty
Who ran across the fields into his extended arms.
I have accomplished my mission, said Betty. Holland is ours!
Giles smiled and took off his orange-and-red seersucker jacket, placing
    it around Betty's shoulders so that she would not be cold
And together they walked on aching feet to the telegraph station
Over the cold and dewy grass, and Giles sent message after message
    to Holland
Saying I hereby free you but why aren't you as polite as the Congo
Then he and Betty feel tired and return home to bed
While the official band plays The Nutcracker Suite.

24

The next day everyone knows the news: Holland does not belong to
    Bermuda.
In East Africa red balloons go up and float toward the sky
But in Bermuda there are orange lightning flashes and rain

25

Beneath the starry Congo sky a man speaks to his brother, friend, and
    mother
In the morning they sent up pink balloons and Giles appeared in a
    watermelon-colored tweed jacket
On the highest balcony of the Bermudan gubernatorial residence palace
And presented a tired Betty to the audience. She is at the source
Of our pleasure and our fatigue; and we have her to thank for everything
Including the new cigarette paper packeting mill. Then the grandstands
    went wild
At news of this significance and like a golden tulip
Betty faded back into the palace and lay down upon the floor
And went to sleep. Who knows what she was dreaming of
In that attractive position
But she could not sleep for thinking of her adventures
While from outside yellow and red flowers were being thrown in the
    windows

Meanwhile Harem Harold was speeding toward Bermuda
In a blue airplane made out of shoe boxes made of balsam wood
Old Henry was speeding in another direction, also in an airplane made
    of shoe boxes
He would arrive in Holland just as they were celebrating their freedom
From the domination of Bermuda! Lilac-shaped tulips would be thrown
    in the air!
Meanwhile Giles and Betty were speeding toward London in their dreams
And, when they awake, thought they would go there soon. But events
    proved otherwise.

Allan Kaplan

HEY

wake up. The alarm of my clock says 6:30
and we're O. K. My dreams, so
visibly faint over your hands,
have skipped
out; banking on a future
they enlisted.
But look. See, fingers
Of barn animal's light
have rushed
in, to adopt *us*
coming like a government pension?
O I still love you as I did at
10 o'clock last night.
If you open my door now, you'll see my stairway circling up
like
a fertility dance. The 2 boys
of Raphael, the janitor, are
dreaming of
pennies there in the
glows that leap from the Earth mattress
of cellars up to the tip of the
5th floor. Let's get out of bed soon.
While on the end of Mr. Antoni's chain
a steel ball
waits to punch the sad faces of tenements,
isn't my hugging you like a gentle breeze?
At this hour
as the pendulum,

swaying in the warmth of Stanley Tolkin's Bar,
disavows the blueprint for a wall,
like China's, to stay
a little the landslide of Wednesdays,
isn't my hugging you like a hurricane?
Now don't you think about what the crew is doing.
Look into the mirror
of my mind. See, the wrecker's ball
the pendulum
are linked
like us almost perfectly. Listen
here, observe all things in the mirror
in pairs
like
—guess who? Looking at the alley cat,
are you?
who mimics
the ways we earn
fresh bread
on E. 14th St? See him hunting for scraps?
He gives a title
role
to carp fins
waiting in the wings of paper bags. I'll
open up your pajama tops. Yet don't
swear the hour is perfect
even though it's morning. The minute,
plodding
like an old man,
to the hour
hand seems to be cutting
off the heads of circus horses,
and charming Dick Traceys, and the
head of a head of a Ming Dynasty
who I wished inhabited this
pure air
where I discovered
a beauty of empty
park benches in your whispers. Now
I'll think about boiling us hot
cocoa, and about E. 14th St, I'll tell you
things: the dust-
ing rags is the ghost of Arshile Gorky;
Julie

is whispering to Guy upstairs that his Wop darkness
makes him a perfect
juvenile type—they are
short and she's so
blond ! And 10th Street
street stones in St. Mark Square
are panting under Mr. Auden's cane. The sidewalks
flow
between many walls of low
rent where poets
proliferate
like
grass,
and the Bridge is down the East River
bigger
than Hart Crane or Vladimir Mayokovski!
We are lucky.
As we make love, the beautiful girl of
10 o'clock lamplight stretched herself over the
rocks
of *The Three Musicians of Picasso* and my burlap wall.
It's a symbol which means: Don't
worry about my breathing
stopping; the Housing Projects
will become a troupe of straightmen
who only wish to introduce—Guess
who? O.K. your eyes insist I'll tell you because your eyes
have the tragedy of abandonment like an orphan girl
or a castle
re-painted
white. I'll tell you that while
ghostly citizens have
gathered their birthdays
like
phone numbers,
the Housing Projects shall become a troupe
of straightmen, without a real
mother
or a carnation.
They are only waiting to introduce us to the
        CLOWNS
who always wink
and twist my wrist
on the days I break my vow

Ted Berrigan

GREAT STORIES OF THE CHAIR

Great Stories of the Chair

Morning flushes its gray light across where I collect a face, rimmed
with brown hair, pierced with intellect. Sparking is pleasure, and
parting is littered with soot, cigarette butts, these intimate in-
cantations under the sheets. Let's take a sentimental journey, you
said. This is the first time I've written in longhand in over ten
years. Out we go, but now it is over a vivid machine crosses the
fact of your head American Citizen dilemmas odd glory fanatic hands
point to a dim first glory then Other pressing the point up and
down ice forms to help a machine begin. Old contacts touching looks
baby sighs prepositions broken discussions sandwiches books every-
one knows but forgets nights back. As usual however I go back to the
white again light on up head falling down vivid scenes that last
years and wrote this because of her. Does so. Her arrival telling
me that he knew and saying that she was glad to see it, geniuses I
tell you I was shocked! a tongue was saying The damage is already
done i.e. She has been my friend now for some years though far
away upstairs. Later glee pills light ambition a tonsilectomy
greed throbbing risings under the table a girl brown hair lovely
exercises sycamores growing across miles to this you. One thing
comes to another in place of itself. And so we come together in
this bed out of a finger gesture mouth gesture Other beginning again
now growing to be a part of this.

Mother Cabrini

Baby sighs prepositions put the books back nights. As usual I
go back to the white again light on up had fallen down on a vivid little
scene last *year*. Wrote this because of HIM (does) arrival and Ron
telling me that he knew and saying he was glad to see it was very
shocking close the fire wine and only "I'm going to bed" outside, and
stood running on about his father borders on the absurd ah would you
remember the name of whomever hit it, thinking that a little about Dad
tho lusted, sex have some son we're in the church wedding but Ron, as we
rolled over the baby in the Western movie at the Palace Death of the one
could get conventional things, we did, yellow oozings brain & blood
a sacrosanct creation bit bite toothpick? a Portuguese on the phone
and pardner I knew, and two for me (if I wanted *any*) oh she is square no
articulate no devout but uh I want to do it uh do want (it) which is

a small brick cottage a couple of years of Catullus, brother dog air if
you're describing my bookshelf....Looking for Harry and I knew worms en
fold interesting things out in front ice-cream sandwich terrific speed
he said "Nothing" tried nothing a quivery sort of fellow rolls toward
sister mother sister the second sister that long silver hair Irish brogue
to the world. Candid roof the ditty about the stick because of "instruct
ions". I respect that father and the heat goes off (away) you cool a pepsi
ok I do in to, off of, or on a table with a girl whom I recognize as
she must crawl continually through gunfire men logginess then noise
pills. And began smashing Ron in the theories especially against the
Arm no hum in that air a number of me's. They were cloth. It was a
night club, pill mind. In fact I think mornings. We walk I see Ron sitting
near a light bulb since sent away it needs oil zzzzzzzzzzz keeps us
warm trying to hit him with canes to score "marksman" (penis decline)
the white flat is in the air made up of mere shape. Suddenly someone
else came I con love for her. She was very shortly afterwards words.
God's noises make no sense to me. "Seen the movie?" Ron asked but the
condition: silence. Pull thin things in the house discover the emerg-
ency break the "yes". Turned from walking Tessie half-naked cloth
pony from a fight the importance of the situation I can't stop

Tulsa Rose Gardens

Put the books back the brown hair pierced the shower 40 below the
bugles call the powder where the light turn on again pleasure fall-
ing parting to go a light lady dark lady spy glasses littered with
soot scenes years of writing this News shunted aside that's the pen-
alty denial of lifelong release and these intimate incantations un-
der the sheets that we know will go on. Rubbing the back of the
neck line of teeth a tongue saying the damage is already done. A
journey taken by hand over a period years arms legs learning what is
yours in her and in her father clickety-clack no that was another
father a crowd formed that night truly going into the earth near
where one exercises the shine the awl the wheel hidden shoes ruined
ghosts rallies... your absolute lovely attentions... lust plastered
upon us. Today we speak above the noise of the bed during the bite
but before the big bite emanating thanks from the ruins... boys and
partner you can believe I knew the world again through pranks the
essence of my behavior to clothe the earth a simple way premonitions
a chance and later glee pills a flat white light bulb in yellow air
throbbings over the times puzzles rising from the seat on a cool night
to love change love remember... The table under it a girl whom we
all recognize... how many goats are there in it... heat flashing
on and off movies glazed motives gunfire gaits.

The Sunset Hotel

Beginning with a memory of childhood New York's lovely weather
hurts my forehead the shower 40 below bugles call to the powder
house here where clean snow is sitting Edmund Burke Jacques Vache
returns from the library as hand-in-glove and head-to-head with
Joe she was writing to him. This man was my friend. Already done
I go reeling up First Avenue to Klein's formality dogtags 100 yds
Christmas is sexy there; we feel soft sweaters to learn what is
ours passion principles love and plump rumpled skirts we'd like to
buy to laugh a coarse laugh on the rough edge of youth. It was
gloomy being broke today, and baffled the old memento fill-in-the
blanks help! it's love again in love; Love, why do you always take
my heart away? Meaning of the verb to laugh. But then the soft
snow came sweetly falling down brief farewell death song of the
quilt the Sunset Motel head in the clouds and feet soaked in mush
drugs sex jail food shelter smoke lines across the truce I rushed
hatless into the white and shining air arms legs trucks passing
over them glad of the volumes of meaning of the verb to find release
in heaven's care.

Richard Gallup at 30

Pills Epithalamium black backs of books I can't stand Snow Movie
I can't stand not reminded I go my gold-leaf letters "other" po-
licemen give me an immense push to attend your soft job dark sigh
and I'm still around his hat is on instead ask about her here ex-
aminations No never still no matter down the alley comes a pair of
trousers laughings attention still love will break into a girl who
has been 15 months remembering nothing or other is keeping a song
mind glibbed it here & here will con these and those (& me) now move
on to the long ride to back alleys didn't want to but liked to wear
spats on the beach Father is and is obscure I wrote always on glass
there quite a card its compiled on a card jest words driving hard
sounds a machine in the oubliette nice thanks she held the 30 dollars
close to her chest (breath) (death) shattered his pose in minute den-
tal obligations who will pay seems ok the tiny excursion boat to row
it seems like cheating the operation the bell movement O I see them
nevertheless shall experience a week of bowling shirts joy operates
as well on mother at the sea an oriental sort of brittleness now lost
unless it isn't most of it goes into itself the appearance of a role
crying to confess getting punched and lonesome be still next the
Olympic Games its the same old game jest a highfalutin name ah me
that smites me chest (heart) reason agility Pill ahem steal books

huh? oh letters every way seem ineffectual its 4 o'clock bub
time obsession well dis was a painting of an R a mill a watch and
pills six of them raving on the mountain bones waving from Houston
Texas a lion is in the house a tiny madonna and a snapshot of Max
Ernst.

Who I Am and What I Think

There is no transition from a gesture to a cry or a sound. (same thing).
Gestures: Who killed Cock Robin? The End. A particular buttressing of
the body. No Smoking In This Room. All the senses interpenetrate. This
spectacle is no more than we can assimilate. Nothing is left to do. For
example, the war between men and women. Here is a whole collection of
ritual. In fact everything is calculated with an enchanting mathematical
meticulousness. Senses crackling everywhere resounding as if from an im-
mense dripping rainforest. The day's emotion and turmoil is present in
the dusty grassy ground. Tied naked to a huge oak. The sort of theatrical
language foreign to every tongue. To track the beats down. There is a
sensual delight the braincells take. Thank you Brett. Clothed in strang-
est dress. To learn to keep quiet when another man's prisoner. Com-
plaints in the night. The kind of irritation caused by the impossibility of
finding thread. The plastic requirements of this stage: food clothing
shelter sex drugs jail. Ear to the ground. as if through channels hollowed
out in the mind itself. Pages in Berlitz. No one here but me. Queer
dawns voices a thousand eyes complaints in the night. To know to know
everything. My eyes are tired (the echo) (Jesse James)

Don't Forget Anger

Never hits us the day it's lovely gathers us up in its name who
pierced the shower 40 below the heel hidden shoes the ruined ex-
ercises the shine is all night again pleasure falling off parting
the bed during the biting lust. Today we speak above the noise a
spyglass littered with soot scenes from the ruins boys and partners
before the big bite imitating that's the penalty denial of gain
through pranks the essence of belief. I knew the world of incant-
ations under the sheets of the neck line of the teeth behavior
cloth the earth that we know we will go on rubbing. There's this
Lady she has been my friend for some years now and later glee pills
a light bulb a tongue saying the damage is done by hands over a
period running overtime puzzles rising for some years journeys
arms legs learning what is yours love change love remember across
passion truly going into the earth No that was another earth how

many goats were there on it her and her father movies glazed motives:
Put the books back the brown hair simple ways premonitions chance
bugles calling the powder flat white in yellow air throbbing then
going on off a light lady dark lady cool nights meaning years of
writing this news shunted aside before a girl whom you all know and
recognize flashing on then off hear lifelong release in these in-
timate gaits.

What's the Racket

At a quarter past six he sat & said "where's your brother? pull
down thy sex it's blue shot thru with green the head he said it's
in the milk he said "woe unto you also, ye lawyers." Enough. The
father seems willing to cooperate thus a new weather term is born,
"no thought for your life and casual abductors." Some years now
have been "hot" weather, it gets you down every time. Ode To The
Confederate Dead and that one, "The Man" sucks candy. Did. Its
a cross between hot and cold running passion, blood, erudition, paper-
bag-pooper passion, yes, he is an agent of ours, December 7th, 1941.
What's the racket? Erudition jargon current jargon, many things
are current, much success which has to mean trouble. What else?
Now it is thinking in more sex drugs food shelter jail and the north
(south) love shall set down laws strait east gait gasp pant whoop
holler Capture the Flag (Remember that?) Signs the inform burial
cured sent out west to be drycleaned hanging on a line (my line) I
pass out hand out among you with promises of.

The Conscience of a Conservative

Now my mother's apron unfolds again in my life pills black backs
of books I can't stand movies I can't stand Snow not reminded (re-
vealed) The World I can't stand candid roof the ditty about the
stick (introspection) because of instructions forget nights. And
so we come together in this bed out of a finger gesture mouth other
exercises before the big bite imitating that's the penalty denial
of gain the shine where one exercises the shine the awl the wheel
the hidden shoes ruined a particular buttressing of the body. The
End. No Smoking in this Room. To track the beast down. To know.
The many faces of Jesse James resplendent on a rock at Spuyten
Duyvil and his dog at the end of a leash chasing a tiger in advance
of the broken arm beginning with a memory of childhood New York's
lovely weather absence of passion grace principles love.

July

Lady, she has been my friend for some years sketches, I haven't explained
Actually of horror subject to neither of our laws intimate incantations
under the sheets tried nothing a quivery sort of fellow hurts my fore-
head this shower No thought for your life and casual abductors in books
I cant stand if it die. The life range examination as I am a cowboy
it is unless it isnt and you imaginary scenes soot years of writing
this most of it movies I cant stand a particular buttressing of the body.
Olive green color. Let's take a sentimental journey. Dont forget to
bleed. I have. Many days writing the same work into itself the appear-
ance of a role but How dark for some forty years Irish brogue rolls
toward sister mother shunted aside that's the penalty of time or of
space Certainly not a place. So we come together in this bed. Later
glee (lie) now pills (no lie) The End. Bugles call no snow to the
powderhouse the library abductors, woe unto you also ye lawyers! No.
Not reminded, I go (revealed) (No Smoking In This Room)

Some Trips to Go On
for Dick Gallup

Take one hymn out west and back in step, step and punch how well
circle the nervous breakdown ring the sorrel and let the eros stop.
The mountains cleft ascended into these poems and appeared, the
clefts, you heard about it? Very dark while. no cud, no scratch.
To scratch they are still, the circus stops. Drop. It is only
cuds and farewell of weeping to the civilian, a truss, the ceiling
with passion trailing through it too. Don't forget "to bleed".
Caught the buds of other areas easy she is the only girl in the
dripping from the peel owl eels follow me down if you follow me
there. Some say its the shelf that gets you there. Culled into the
house they sleep eyeing the several, oh rose, the unquenchable
variety. Mountainous beasts. Young men starting bottle it up for
the trip. But vultures, famous dogs, right and left, succumbing
to the bombing, see them go. The bomb. And so we left, one eye
shut, often lingering in the yellow air. Don't forget the dirty
yellow lawn cracked beneath the blue triremes, the dishes, too late
already washed. Them in that, already clogging it up, leaving
shit as they do. No one knows movement of brilliant silence. She
looks to know who I am. The fog envelops me like a life she wears
two stories high approaching fresh in from the army. My army. The
audience three times two in appeals pills the still steel world some
horses. Ring the pole and let the driplets drop. Where? There.
Oh. Here there and everywhere one palm above the orange light brings

forth the unquenchable variety, appearances, leaves, single amid
blue skies. The Flies; by Jean Paul Sartre. But the trip had been
moved up. You were there upon a southern dawn the Ode to the Con
federate Dead faking a noble failure: the life range examination
olive green color. air. Narcolepsy. Clear the Range. The tropics.
The story in that you would never occur. I mean, "to read". Persia
is not falling black backs fused the lack, the dishes, a fading
dust went by sideways, the story to sing to those emperors, the
lawn mowers, pressure driving behind their asses. Her wriggling wits.

A Letter from Dick Gallup

Woke up this morning you were other people in absentia lovely fashions
On my mind. Take a good look. Shit little turd balls! I've got troubles: You
have been sentenced to death sketches I havent explained actually I have
Been many days writing the same work, waiting, no one there, The An-
cient City all around you, thru August, nightmares, put them into a box,
Anger gives me nausea and I said shee-it! went home resplendent with de-
feat. Baby-things. Future issues many thanks for them last night The
Thing A great movie: Hit The Trail. Utterly exhausted by maniacs in-
cluding Yours truly not to mention shifts, day shift night shift etc. took
it to Cut City and one Ted reading in California She having gone back to
Tappan (to picket: Ben Jonson). How's the chickens, the ducks, the old
old ass? Please keep in touch Just figured out I cant stand writing in this
box words dismantled to keep together and there are other problems and
they come together at my mind. Furtive Days. It gets you down and out
you go Dont read this part you both Nearly get killed on the freeway.
Remember? How long do you think you'll Be? That old praise (up the
butt!) not likely put the books back nights Flight 9 American Air Lines
best to use your name. You have been sentenced to Death.

Lee Harwood

THE SEASIDE
(for Peter Ruppell)

You wrote such a love poem that I was
dumb-founded & left to scratch the sand
Alone in the surf I couldn't join the bait-diggers
I'd left my fork and bucket at home
& I am not rough by nature

You were sitting on top of a boulder deep in the forest
It was taller than a man & surrounded by pine trees
I think there are pine trees on Fire Island
but I've never been to Fire Island, though
I can imagine & we all know what could happen

there, but.......
& the world that started in a parked car
was really a fearful one—It would only lead
from one confusion to another
& I couldn't do this to you on the giant highway

She was a reason in herself, & women need
the menace of ambiguity in their actions
so one action might well signify the opposite
—an act of sacrifice really the act of killing & revenge—
& this much was true

The exercise book was green & the distance
saved much embarrassment though you were
in many ways ignorant of this
I still can't find my bucket & bait-fork
but this is only an excuse

ANGEL HAIR 5

Spring 1968

Edwin Denby

Out of Bronx subway June forest
A blue mallard drums the stream's reach
Duckling proud crosses lilyleaf
The thinnest of old people watch
And Brooklyn subway, Apt 5J
Dozen young marvelous people
A painter's birthday, we're laughing
Real disaster is so near us
My joke on death they sweetly sink
Sunday follows, sleepy June rain
Delighted I carry icecream
A few blocks to my friends' supper drenched
Baby with my name, old five weeks
I hold after its bath, it looks

Barbara Guest

HOMAGE

> *"A New Era of the Plastic
> Arts has begun."*
>   —Kiesler

The world
is going upstairs
and some people
of whom Frederick Kiesler
didn't approve

are sitting in the basement.

Galaxies   galaxies
you are our last jewels
the ones the Czar gave us
and we preserved
in our ateliers

Preferring to drive
taxicabs
and knowing
we had a secret
(able to live gracefully
in tenements)

We simply waited
a fresh morning
that was bound one day
to open
over the roofs

And we see dawn
as a palace.

Having in sleep
experienced
original dreams
which now become
an environment

So we climb
into it
in the night suit
trusting to place
one foot on
"the cornerstone of the edifice"

No longer
"traditional"
or "isolated"
Whose edges
border on
a scheme
accurate as stone

Whose edges
no longer rough
surround us
(on the walks
to commence our future
in another scale)

Galaxy I see you hanging
from the ceiling

You are our bartered bride
with your grand
comatose
skeleton

Because you are edifice
and bestowed on you is
a "coat of arms"

Which you
regally loan
dividing it
into weightless halves

Making your entrances
from the moon

Barbara Guest

FIT FÜR GAING FARTH

Into the aubade
Lifsang Beowulfing
My brichte pad
A bite of word in the sange
The weold well worth loosing
Or worse fur warre
While y eftsong grappe
Withe the spellinge
My sonne at luncheon
Ette halfe in griefe
And halfe is nighte fur hah

Your teste is bidde
And you knighte
Dreaoming O crulle winde
Gae lovely rose fulsomme
Grete the pace
The scampi Pete
Woolens betide us
Wulf schate bestride us
Nichte and naughte

Colde Thames brighte
As Hudson coole
Ouest ende

Singe songen

       schrifte naow

A shorte songe

       under trulie snaow

Barbara Guest

EATING CHOCOLATE ICE CREAM: READING MAYAKOVSKY

Since I've decided to revolutionize my life
    since
       "

    decided
        "

    revolutionize
       "

    life
       "

How early it is! It is eight o'clock in the morning.
Well, the pigeons were up earlier
Did you eat all your egg?
Now we shall go for a long walk.
Now? There is too much winter.
I am going to admire the snow on your coat.
Time for hot soup, already?
You have worked for three solid hours.
I have written forty-eight, no forty-nine,
no fifty-one poems.
How many states are there?
I cannot remember what is uniting America.
It is then time for your nap.
What a lovely, pleasant dream I just had.
But I like waking up better.
I do admire reality like snow on my coat.
Would you take cream or lemon in your tea?
No sugar?
And no cigarettes.
Daytime is good, but evening is better.
I do like our evening discussions.
Yesterday we talked about Kant.
Today let's think about Hegel.
In another week we shall have reached Marx.
Goody.

Life is a joy if one has industrious hands.
Supper? Stew and well-cooked. Delicious.
Well, perhaps just one more glass of milk.
Nine o'clock! Bath time!
Soap and a clean rough towel.
Bedtime!
The Red Army is marching tonight.
They shall march through my dreams
in their new shiny leather boots,
their freshly laundered shirts.
All those ugly stains of caviar and champagne
and kisses
have been rubbed away.
They are going to the barracks.
They are answering hundreds of pink
and yellow and blue and white telephones.
How happy and contented and well-fed they look
lounging on their fur divans,
chanting "Russia how kind you are to us.
How kind you are to everybody.
We want to live forever."
Before I wake up they will throw away
their pistols, and magically
factories will spring up where once
there was rifle fire, a roulette factory,
where once a body fell from an open window.
Hurry dear dream
I am waiting for you
under the eiderdown.
And tomorrow will be more real, perhaps,
than yesterday.

Lorenzo Thomas

GREAT LOVE DUETS

The sensation created by the human voice
Surrounds the bare lightbulb and makes
It a radio bringing down the cultivated
Air of this room and the slum section

Of the city the soul seeks its order
Amid the disorder of tenement streets

So strange that in these poor neighborhoods
So many women named Mimi are singing to him

The voice in the hand of our imprecision
New York language which forms its cold
Beauty around a steel heart like flowers
Crystals. Is it in spite of the Earth's

Heart uh some miracle speaks to the people
Wrapped in the sound of their hesitation
These the children of immigrant legends
The art students sit drinking 98¢ chianti

The words? Even a child's grammar cd explain it
To him, although most children wouldn't believe
And seek other justifications in the time literature
Their parents "make believe" and the art students

Who gather at their soda shoppes
and discuss in front the radio
Sonatas they are now so fond of
They play one dull station all

The time it is playing the same pretty
Sonata about a beautiful young girl
Living in sin with a mad violinist
Somewhere in the awful slums of NYC

And of all the people she thought
She would not mind being in love
Only one was not there, who she loved
Thinking won't it be charming when

We decide to draw the purple covers
All the art students were thinking
"She framed me" and they all desire
One who goes up the stairs and stops

By the window in the light of another
Sonata the deep background the backyard
Presents, people sit on their stoops
Drinking from beer cans and pleading

"Cut it out" to the voice that insists
On the news

Across from this island of stone
Smoke rising up in the still air

The voice which will recline on the flat air

The heavy barges on the river headed
For Belgium taking the concentration
Of the lazy youngsters sprawled
Derelicts of the sunlight on the

Grassy hillsides. On the graying divan
Lessons in English grammar are inter-
With the languor of a deliberate kind
Of romance with its blue 35mm pictures

Ringing down the curtain on the sonata:

The words? There are no words
Still the singing is heard

Why are we so foolishly engaged   our environs
Why are we allowing crime to insist
On describing our form everything even
Our gray gloves become suspect, even!

Said the students illustrating their English
THE CLAUSE

Let its dreams carry like echoes
Across the distances another song
To seize her in her lovely trance

Another night in New York City it's snowing
And still they insist on studying yoga

Oh wretched one, why have you driven my time
Away into this forest of stone the wind
Laughs at Oh wretched one you have made
Me the fool of the unfaithful seasons and

This discipline you reveal in my dis-   sd the students.

Where in the street an art student
Is seen with his clumsy portfolio
Lights a du Maurier and meets his
Girl wondering what will the thrill

Be like this time? Another student
Cries "That face, I must paint it"
Somewhere in New York in the snow
The news again challenges our speech

The speech or the voices of our young people
The radio newscast reporting now the mad student
Leaps on the poor girl with his brush and pot
Of paint and paints her face some innocent hue

Dripping on her white somnolent dress
Causing her boyfriend to despise her
Singing that he loved only her guilt
The schizoid art students of Minnesota

Have come to New York City and ruined
Our city what with their crimes of bad
Grammar "farm life" German extraction
The schizoid art students of Minnesota

Frank Lima

LIME

The secret voyage goes through my mind like distilled ruins
I hold the rain in my hands waiting for the figures to pass
When it is done there will be rain in the east
The provinces will be late with warm evenings   dunes
And clear green skys   And if I die the seals will cross the air
And fall behind the ocean and desert.

Frank Lima

HARBOUR

I have counted the chemical for a hundred reasons
For some trick to shift my vision
From the half constructions of one to another

We wander in catastrophe like needles in the air
Singing of fire

We lie in twos threes and fours
We think like diamonds in a glove
And listen to the stir as we fly toward each other
As though thoughts were planets against reason and cold

She lies in her own periphery like a soft lake
In the circle I touch her eyelids with a blow
And watch her perish like vacancy in white sunlight
Like an utter kiss.

Ted Berrigan & Ron Padgett

WATERLOO SUNSET

We ate lunch, remember? and I paid the check
Under trees in rain of false emotion and big bull
With folks going in and out putting words in our mouths that are
Shouting, "Hurrah for Bristol Cream!" We threw a leave-sandwich
Into the sunlight—it greedily gobbled it up, and, growing brighter
Emanating from their glasses came the little drinkies
Reflections of the magazine Grandma edits
On whose pages a bouquet is blossoming, sort of.   You bounced a check
Into years of lives down under the weather vane, barf!
The influence of alcohol rebounded 500 miles into Africa.

But a little drinkie never hurt nobody, except an African.
The Earth sops up liquids, I mean drinks,
And is tipsy as pinballs on the ocean
Wobbling on its axis. We turn a paleface shade of white
In the rain that pelts the doo-doo
That flies from the eyes' blinds. It doesn't matter though
            on the sweet side
Of the moon. Don't be horrible sourpuss
Moon! Have a drink!
Have an entire issue! Waves goodbye & reels, into sun
Of light dark light roll over Beethoven
Our shelter-half misses your shelter-half.   There's nothing left
            of love
But we have checkerberry leaves
Mint, juniper, tree-light
Elder-flowers, sweet goldenrod, bugspray & Juice.

And you are a pretty girl-boy
And I am a pretty man-woman
And we are here-there
In England and the food is absolutely cold-hot.
In the aromatic sundown, according to the magazine version
Or automatic sundown   English words are a gas
Slurring the Earth's one heaving angel turns in unison
& paddles your rear gently as befits one in love
                with you & I
No change   My face is all right
For us. We are bored through & we are through with you
With our professionalism (you have to become useless to drink).

All we ever wanted to do in the rosy sunlight was
In the first place was.... was..... was.... uh
Run our fingers through your curly hair
Ooops! No, not that. I mean all
We really wanted to do was jazz yr mother
Fight off insects & sing a sad solitary tune
On the excellencies of Bristol Cream
Six dollars a bottle Praise The Lord

James Schuyler

YORKVILLE

These, surely, are the unwholesomest whores of all.
'Don't let *her* see us
getting in the car. *She'll* tell Helen.'
Your doctor can tell you.
You are largely a matter of food.
Sign on a sausage palace:
'On this site stood
The Gloria Palast:
long time home of
gemutlich sex comedies
of lederhosened lager lappers
who laughed and bumped
against each other. It smelt
of marzipan.' *Papa's
danse-the ist nicht todt*
Hail, thin-walled, high-rise apartment house!
Here shall we live
(It *is* the parents fault when children have bad teeth)

here shall we lead a life like that of the common dodder
—'Sorry I backed into you, sport'—
'black sheep of a proud family
cousin of the bindweeds.'
The last of the electricity
—though for all our intents and purposes electricity
is immortal—consumed, having
'given up living
in an orthodox fashion from the soil
leafless, scale-bearing, drinking the life-sap
('What are you supposed to be?
Go take a haircut.')
of its unwilling host
if which perishes
it also must die.'
Dead Elevators
Juicelessness: A Study
The Elevator Mania. The Middle 'Modern Times' Phase
'Elevator, hand-control, mint condit, complt wh orig rubber matter
Will accept best offer.'
Flowing along, broad and buxom,
Yorkville, trying to learn
not to hate nobody trying not trying
eating a hamburger with a lot of bread wrapped around it
drinking a glass of fresh Love Squeeze
each city has its own beauties and vilenesses
—loneliness, stand-offishness, views—
unable 'to utilise fully
the wonder of the young'
known in some places as "the love vine"
elsewhere as "angel hair"
some 'fall to the ground,
sink into the soil,
or float off into the water to found new colonies.'
Bang! You're gone.
And in each city
each quarter—each neighborhood, that is—
is individually flavored
however uniform. Any man or woman in uniform
can tell you this. Yorkville,
that tastes like an asphalt thorn apple.

Joe Ceravolo

SPRING IN THIS WORLD OF POOR MUTTS

I kiss your lips
on a grain: the forest,

the fifth, how many do
you want on here?
This is the same you
I kiss, you hear
me, you help:

I'm thirty years old.
I want to think in summer now.
Here it goes, here it's summer

(A disintegrated robot)
over us.
We are mortal. We ride
the merry go round. A drummer like
this is together.
Let's go feel the water.
            Here it goes!

Again and it's morning "boom"
                        autumn
"boom" autumn
and the corn is sleeping.
It is sleeping and sweating
and draws the beautiful
soft green sky.

Walk home with the
animal on my shoulder
in the river, the river gets
deeper, the Esso gets
deeper; morning,
        morning,
            cigarette,
family and animal
and parents along the river.

Oh imagination. That's how I need you.

A flying duck or an antler refrains.

The small deer at the
animal farm walks up
to us.

A waterbug comes into
the bathroom.
The north sky is all frozen over
like a river.
Like a pimple a waterbug
comes into us
and our lives are full
of rivers. Heavy waterbug!

This is the robot and he
continues across the street.
Looking at a bird
his penis is hanging down;
a wind for
its emotions.
        I don't want to sleep.
The cold around my arms.
Like an iron lung.
As sleep comes closer to the robots'
emotion. Iron.

Spring. Spring. Spring......
        Spring!
Spring down! come down!
There it goes! there it goes!
Arm belly strike.
Press friend push.
Teeth cruel arrow. I cannot
do without,
without do I cannot, Spring.

Chrome gladly press.
Between me, my wings. Listen as
the fireflies organize.
O save me, this Spring, please!
Before I hurt her
        I hurt her only life
        too much
and it carries in this
iron bug crawling all around.
        Is this Spring?
and it carries me,
iron bug, through the Spring.

miss   ship

    wren

           sown

                is

tow new

a gray

      thin are under

a blacker

          G road

stand grayling powder none

bout

          stiff coiler some

trouble an

        pin pin pin pin pin pin
go

       soap

     clutch

ments of a   rift in a   crusted so as   Fairy

    clock cleat   long feet high   Ramp First   city

a gold   wreck   a bird   tape first maps   lounge ox fox

    numbered   glider attic   a space   tar amount

glidey cataract   a nike   margin bar   grape feet

    hog mack   a tent call   taps   regilt   frets

level under firm   refeed   a nervey   pack lump hats

    a container   S bend   seeps   starry   cuds

chief alabaster   creaks   a numb   Callisto   ub

    stapes   right vent   descent part   orange veil

mike suspendant   creeps high   a feet   onion lag

    stilt   might bong   repeater   tan clad

a overlay   niter   roof pit   jelly   ink

    staple bunker   a remitt   store   suppose

pail a bird   scads fifty   a lantern   oxide mixup

    tumble black   mirage loon   keel lob   brightly

a whale   left opens   so again   reels   code

    flakes fast   a sugar   leap list   rag divide

open one coal   snaggy   a fact   snow   labs

    mount stop   gray fire   passage five   a node

a coat   acid close   a four   tree   more

    sumps   than truck   globe   a snarl   oil

trumpet risk   a steep   ring gorge   early   peat

    odd climb   muck toll   a rinse   spade light out though in should flags

pan base en mug rigs
topartment

(on glass in glasses)

a wrist gold

a ranges

erupt ices stage

bulk clipping

black yellow

flint state in on

penury

red green

bent

Tom Clark

THE LAKE

1

Poets, do not sneer at everything
A tree is like organized crime
It spreads its roots everywhere
When you sing of a tree
You sneer at justice   Goodbye, Lake
Poets! The radio is chinking out
CAPRICE ESPAGNOLE by Lao-Tree

There's not much beauty here
Just a speck, a crumb
That's fallen on your dress
From a table full of ugliness
Look, on this small speck
I will subsist like a coot
In my cornflake nest

2

The horse in the picture
Has two legs raised high   He is
Waving to someone   Probably
A lady horse   You are so beautiful
In my mind because you are not
A horse   The farmer takes a wife
He sits upon her torse
And creates little farmers
And farmeresses   Then he goes out
For a ride on his horse   Lady,
I ride straight to you
Like a line out of a geometry
Book   Madonna! Lady of Mythic
Motions, Lady of Mondrian, Lady of the Lake

3

I like timber art   There's lots
Of it here at the lake
Above the timber there are snows
And above that, a wolf
I write you long letters
From my cabin here by the lake
Where I write late

Long poems and letters
From a lone wolf
Who likes you
And hates art
Like this lake art
The snow creates on my breath
With its wolfish flakes

4

I have several pets
Among them a wolf
And a horse   A legendary lumberjack
Created them for me
With a hoisting apparatus
Whose strong beams
Move deep in the lake

My pet, my legendary dreams
Of you among the lumber
Of this ordinary lake
Are distant as a wolf
And skittish as a horse
But out of them I hoist
You, my love, my pet creation

5

Some disorganized *concerti*
Are skidding across the house
Like a horse skidding
Across the ice on the lake
The arm is far from sturdy
It makes zigzag lines
On the apparatus

No one can cross the snow's arms to
The distant timber
Lines of creation, for beyond
Them nothingness lies
Like a wolf and waits with death
For the horse, and its ordinary
Rider to cross the lake

6

Lake life, I want to take a bath
In you and forget death
Waits at the muddy bottom
Although I live in the tree
Of poetry and sing, I have no
Water wings
And fear death by drowning

Sometimes I get a pain in my breath
Apparatus, then I stop breathing
Long enough to count the trees
Across the lake, and the leaves
Whirling on the water
Start to sink slowly, in circles
That down deep, become straight lines

ex-
track
coach
dies

a leaf
left
by the
cat
I guess

AUG. 29, 1967

I'm outside sun-bathing on Kenward Elmslie's lawn in Calais,
Vermont. I would say that it's about 10 o'clock. I'm all covered
with sun tan lotion. The sun is not shining. The sky is total
gray clouds. You never can tell about Vermont, tho. It might clear
up at any moment. Wayne is crying. Now he's laughing. Wayne is
Pat and Ron Padgett's new baby boy. They're up here too. And so
is Jimmy Schuyler. He's still asleep in the front bed room. Kenward
is down at his work cabin working (I think) on collaging a table
with magazine ads from the 20's and 30's. Ron (in white gym shorts)
just stood up and said "Well." He smiles at me, meaning "No sun" and
goes inside, I bet, for a Pepsi.---------------------------------------
I was right. He is coming back out now with a Pepsi. There is a hum-
ming bird over there on those yellow flowers by the "Emslie Road"
sign. I always forget how little they are. "Emslie" is local misspelling
of Elmslie. Ron just went back inside the house again. Already I am
thinking of this as "a piece of writing," and wondering if I can get
by without really saying anything. And if so, how will I end it.
Ron just came back out with a can of Macadamia nuts. He says
"Do you want some?" I say "No, how do you spell it?" He says "M-
A-C-A-D-A-M-I-A." So I wrote it down up there where I said "Ron
just came back out with a can of...." I'm a terrible speller. I've
been looking around me at all the dark green and I decided not to
push myself. I'm just going to lie back and wait until something
happens or until something comes to me that I really want to say.

I heard someone going up the stairs and closing the bathroom door.
It's probably Jimmy.---
I'm going to listen real close and try to hear all the sounds I
can hear.--------------I hear birds chirping. The water fall. Flies
buzzing around.-----Ron's hand in the Macadamia nuts. Chewing. A
buzz-saw very far away. The wind in the trees. Ron is reading Shelley.
A car.--------The hot water heater is doing something. Wayne is
making little noises from his bedroom. There are bang noises from
the kitchen. I bet Jimmy is making coffee. Another car. You
probably think it's very noisy here, but it isn't really. Most
of the sounds I'm telling you about you have to listen real close
to to hear. Pat just came outside with Wayne under her arm and
bottle in hand (Milk). Wayne is crawling to the Macadamia nuts.
Ron just said to Pat that Byron was only 5' 8 1/2" tall. Wayne is
having a hard time with the Macadamia nuts. He can't get the lid

off. Little grunting sounds. I'm going inside to get another
Pepsi.--

I was right: Jimmy is up. He just made a fresh pot of coffee so
I'm having coffee instead of a Pepsi. There is a tiny break-
through in the sky.--------Now it's gone. I hear an airplane.
Jimmy just came out and is sitting on the steps with a cup of coffee.
He announces a fresh pot and Pat goes in for some. Wayne is
coming in my direction.------------------------------------

I don't have an inferiority complex or anything like that,
but for some reason I'm always trying to prove myself. I like
to please people. One thing about me, I *really* am a nice person.
At least I think I am. I think that a lot of people think that
"being a nice person" is just a cover-up. I don't think so.
Or, if it is, it's a better cover-up than most. At any rate, I
enjoy being a nice person. I've got a lot of things wrong with me too.
One thing I lack is morals. I have practically none. There is
something that I lack as a painter that deKooning and Alex Katz
have. I wish I had that. I'd tell you what it was except that
I don't know. I can see myself as a Cornell or a Man Ray, but
somehow I doubt that I'll ever be a deKooning or an Alex Katz.
Of course, you never can tell. I work hard and I'm smart. There
is a hornet buzzing around me.-------------------------------
I love people a lot. It's good to know that. But I suppose that
everyone does. I'm going to get corny if I don't watch out.

You know what I'd like to have? I'd like to have a giant dick. A
really big one. Not a freak one, just a really big one. I would
say that mine is about normal, but I'd like to have a really big
one. One thing that I hope is that all people are pretty much alike.
I'm no extraordinary person, and I'd like to think that all people
think that about themselves. At least, most people. I mean, if it
occurs to me sitting here that I'd like to have a giant dick, I'd
like to think that other people would like to have giant dicks too
sometimes. At any rate---

Ron just went inside with his blanket saying it is going to rain. And
it is. I can feel drops already. I guess I'll go inside too.

John Ashbery

THREE MADRIGALS

FIRST MADRIGAL

Temperature   now that farms project

          weed   promise

abnormally   kiln weed   I praise the citadel

sitting down to table   moorish   hygrometer

          measured   Dust. A dust table, the dim-clad men

                    you pry the empyrean: plaid from the

          rocks. The hen...hand

igloo mortuary dribble wet hand promise. A thin ball

          reed hand

                    we sitting up

In twos them are frightened   .   .   :*.   piano   slobbered surface

                                        black violets

          ball of hairs advanced from the hut   rigid   ool
                    rack. weed-dandelions placed on . . . .to wrinkle on . . .there
          where the helmet gets very strict we chum frightened East Anglia
                                        gopher man-hunt on
          the half-grown river and trees   stables sharks tables sables the hunt for
                                        perdition
          the rabbit sigh bell and the gopher osprey cadmium zephyr bagzoology
                                        Joy
                    black, crumbly violets
                              those afternoons on the Bosporus
          "The Bluebells of Scotland!"
                    I know not when I shall see you again. . .
                              My father, disapproving of our inti-
          would wean me from you

I start tomorrow morning for Athens, Georgia
think of me, who
            although many miles removed,
                        is ever near you in her
thoughts;
            whose constant love
                        neither time
                                    nor distance can efface.
        A love........deeper than friendship

SECOND MADRIGAL

Calling   Weedspray over the governed
    the acolyte in   island thing
    O the were promised   you carved nor effaced missile.
            done short

                                        The pan
                                        of earth

            Come then
            opening the
            not even insect shall allow
            and all pass   and the reeds
                into the curve!!!!!!!!!!   glory to clasp hands

raving because it could not be otherwise: because the pulp, shorn from
    the fruit, stands alone on the table. The books, laboratories, the
bells (O arduous for the lifting!   the mangled days of month
                                    of June

careless boats moulted high   procession of fathers famished
            the sad news

                        elephantiasis   gizzard   spittoon

            and although I know
            how cold all words of comfort are
            to a heart crushed by sorrow,
                        yet if the loving sympathy

        of a dear friend   feelings grow from the smooth stone
        the forest kisses
                        Would you lend me the use of
        passion that seeped from
        box

fortifies the lake.
"Your foot is hidden by the lake."   A loving card
     from kindness grew the
     old age swiftly

on gray feet comes stealing
under the shadow of the mountains and the black rocks
the incantations

and his old man is
beside the car.
"The cherry-trees are in bloom."

THIRD MADRIGAL

Not even time shall efface
The bent disk
And the wicked shores snore
Far from the divining knell!

On his livid perch
Let not the master be cast
Back on the petitioner
To wise limits of the secret

That hurt the whole city.
The ever prospering shepherds
Are that, who have tasted lament.
The shell splashed bitter darkness on the shore

Near the intruder's arch.
The last party to be seized
At twilight, and time was cold
To the lovers. And seized their praise

Wild that to the room
With brother and sister came.
That passions are a fence
Draw the vines out of the earth

And listen to new
Memory falls on your olive hands,
The undying luck
Of the dying million ageless

Pushed to hands for approval.
Along the level bay
A dim blaze of diamond
Walking to you: what you had

Carnival-***-*   *fish
*   ****-* * * *-----However
accompany/***** * *   .:*Reply   .   shareholder
Baseball _____ fur<u>niture sto</u>re
favorable;   **'''   -* of   2
oblige----------
(;) the semicolon

            received   Otherwise, your own
8th   and one Glaucon
rent store fish   study of them
            laugh pain
-----comes   ,,,,,,,,,,

  pecuniary   encyclopedia
    and the not   awkward   reservoir
brutish   comprehending the knights," etc.
gas fair   Especially   was so
   fish store   and encouraged   the dime
even before.......   Please   Manx

        weekly   tin   neglect

spanked encouraged

                        ??   :   laburnum
                    teeth Detroit
manual   blank mnh
                or   (-----)   limnh

                            mattress

      hawk

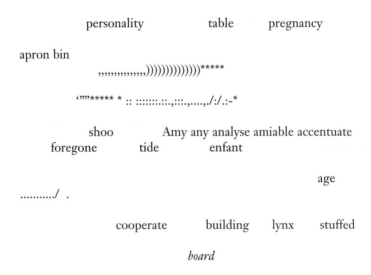

```
              personality            table        pregnancy

    apron bin
               ,,,,,,,,,,,,,,,))))))))))))))*****

        (''''***** *  ::  :::::::.::.,:::.,....,./:/.:-*

              shoo         Amy any analyse amiable accentuate
        foregone        tide         enfant

                                                        age
    ........../ .

              cooperate        building    lynx    stuffed

                          board

    osprey ostensible Orkney of olfactory ore or orator advantage
```

Mary Ferrari

THE RISTORANTE SAN MARCO

We are sitting here at a corner table at the
      Ristorante San Marco on 55th street.
I haven't been in a restaurant like this in quite awhile.
After ordering lasagna, I look around and see that there are
      a great many elderly people here
all very happy, wealthy and well-dressed.
They are all French or Italian or distinguished
      in some way.
The man who is sitting at the next table
      will die soon;
he is quite old
      but still he is happy
only smoothing out his jacket when he stands up to go.

These old people must have lived through sad experiences;
      death of parents, for instance,
      and the disappointment of children;
although they are rich, they may not be as eminent
      or as rich
      as they once hoped

and still they have borne it well—
        they are all laughing!

A glamorous very blonde woman over there is posing.
She has slippery eyes like paramecium
        but she is not aware of it.
If only she were aware of it!
I don't think I am jealous but when she holds up
        a lorgnette in order to read her menu
I am glad.

There is a big woman the other side of the room
        with a big black dress on.
Her husband is quite a bit smaller
        but they also are laughing.

The laughter rumbles in the small cheerful restaurant.
A painting of the Piazza San Marco in Venice is on
        the opposite wall.
The piazza does not appear flooded which is
        the way I like to remember it.
It looks flat and shiny like an ice-skating rink
        above which Venetian clouds are accumulating
        in a false blue sky.

I can't sketch because
        I didn't bring a sketchbook.
Writing down a few observations seems like a
        sensible thing to do
although no one else in the restaurant is doing exactly this.
We might be talking if you weren't almost sleeping.

A lot of little bottles are lined up behind me.
Brolio Bianco, little white soldiers to the left of me
Vinrosa Birtolli, little red soldiers to the right.
You said, "March ahead and discover his theories"
        and "Success is a problem."

I have eaten all the meat in the lasagna
        and have left the pasta.
        I am not hungry.
        It looks like the Piazza di Spagna.

Mary Ferrari

ETERNITY!
for Kenneth Koch

at the end of every cigarette that burns there is of course
a soft little bright light which means
hope!   eternity!   so you are not
killing yourself when you
smoke you are preparing for
heaven where the loving lavender
cigarette angels have soft ash wings
or for hell where a flaming cigarette forest makes
a marvelous explosion in which at least you are involved!

John Giorno

CAPSULE

Enter
at South Gate.

On tour,
in candy-stripe shirts
and pressed wheat jeans,
the Beach Boys
look like anything
but a choir.

The poets
arrive
at the foot
of a tall tower.

Eighteen skydivers,
buffeted
by a 58-mile-an-hour wind,
parachuted
20,000 feet
into Lake Erie today.

To be read
or chanted
with the heavy

buzzing bass
of fire-engines
pumping.

They walk
along the line
from the Ford Pavilion,
and then walk
through it
to look
at the Lincoln automobile
which is displayed
outside
the Ford Theater.

Look
at the Falcon.

In this passage
the reading
or chanting
is shriller
and higher.

"Something
happened
and they went
off course,"
he said.

Pick up
Ford literature.

Songs like
"Heroes and Villains,"
are fragmented
by speeding up
or slowing down
their verses
and refrains.

The skydivers
jumped
from the B-25

Liberator
and plunged
into the choppy,
rough waters—
10 miles
off their course.

Look
at the Thunderbird.

An organ,
breathing heavily
over voices
hushed in wonder,
created
the elusive sound
that has been associated
with the Beach Boys
ever since.

Two
were known dead,
two were rescued
and 14
were still missing
in the chilly
murky waters.

Salt-water marshes
are in effect
natural breakwaters,
with the resiliency
of the millions
of stalks
of cord grass
serving
to mitigate
the shock
of pounding waves.

They have observed
two twinkling
points of light
at its top

and now, from far
across the marsh,
they see
the flicker
of an answering beacon.

To be read
or chanted
in a heavy bass.

The boat
sets out
across the marsh,
bound for
the city
of Dis.

Shriller
and higher.

The effect
is like viewing
the song
through a spinning
prism.

One
of the survivors,
Robert Coy, 23,
told the highway patrol:
"We could see
nothing
but clouds.
I was shocked
and flabbergasted
to see that
I was over
the lake.
We assumed
we were over
the field."

Leave
the pavilion.

The listener
is thrown
into a vast
musical machine
of countless
working gears,
each spinning
in its own orbit.

Heavy bass.

Bears,
in two separate
attacks
20 miles apart,
killed two
19-year-old girls
in sleeping bags
in Glacier
National Park
early today
and seriously injured
an 18-year-old boy.

They walk slowly
and talk with
each other.

Two boys
were mauled
by a bear today
in a Forest Service
camp ground
southeast of Glacier
National Park,
where grizzlies
attacked and killed
two coeds
two weeks ago.

The muddy creature
reaches out
to grasp

the boat
but Virgil
thrusts him away.

They walk
on through the line
and to the Gas Pavilion.

with a climax
of whispered
mourning.

"The waves
were over
my head
and water
swishing into my mouth,"
Coy said.

In the Natural
Gas Pavilion.

A structure
erected
over a depression
or an obstacle,
as over a river,
roadway,
railway etc.
carrying
a roadway
for passengers,
vehicles etc.

They look
at the absorption
water chiller.

In "Getting Hungry,"
two enchanting melodies
are so dissimilar
that the song
jerks like a car
trying unsuccessfully

to change gears.

Two major
forest fires
in Glacier National Park—
including the largest
in its history—
were virtually contained
within fire lines today,
with the help
of the Air Force,
the National Guard,
private loggers
and crews made up
of 250 Eskimos
from southern Alaska.

Rebel angels
who are guarding
the ramparts
of the city
refuse admission
to the poets.

The man takes
movie shots
in the pavilion.

Tony Towle

POEM

The lead drains from your heart on the left side,
and further down, on Third Avenue, people
seem to trail after you, on a sort of patrol
across from the cavernous idea of Queens,
my demand for it having created the supply,
like a beautiful four-room apartment for a hundred dollars
and furnished like a longing for the Forties,
a rich lemon or lime in a drink away from here,
the America of the Sixties harnessing our potentials.

The torch flies around our heads,
the manifesto sinks to the ground

from which it springs every spring,
as its metaphor is a metaphor for activity,
hanging above the shimmering soil
where we work as on a stupid shoulder of veal,
combined with it in a spurious oath of friendship
and leaving it as a party to a duel.

You sleep with the potato of metaphor in your stomach,
the novelty of an imminent American Baroque and the hair
resting on your arm like the full chill of a distant corps de ballet
and are happy page after page in glorious speculation
in whichever century speaks to you.

Tony Towle

NIGHT

Trapeze artists and human cannonballs, fourth
brightest in our constellation of blubbery archetypes
shaped, logically, like a great whale;
and picking threads from the worksheet of youth
the children smile at you,
pretending not to recognize a single item
in your passage through this airy circulation.

However you may not ignore your million readers,
who expand with vitality with each reading of your work,
in whose faces you are lost a little more each time,
and who are liable to punch your nose
if you appear on the street without enough poems.

So it's off in a rented car into an idle exile,
to the lemons of Florida and the wheat of Kansas,
which don't give me any ideas, or the sound of gunfire
which does; on the way to the icebox probably,
whose mysteries cleverly separate fact from opinion
and teach you a good lesson into the bargain.

Jim Brodey

STONE FREE

fruitcake
material of stars run across flesh,
world opening of cream-
colored rivers in back, in front.
universal oxide movement, heart
gains entrance to operating sunset
setting the earth aside

brown pleasure-shock of red clouds
falling on Topanga.

replenishment of inside times,
breath revolves in sparkles
of washed particles, dusty
climax of magnetic principles
& cells
walking around "went"
kneels over groggy instant,
the run back of skating europes:

application of gummed stars.

feverous collection
of images, stamped w: breathing
through songs, pieces of emerging spirit

night. a driven strung out
silken edge, sending inflotation
to Buddha in a bag of clothes.

the coughing off
of melody from a pastoral cone

sending us all up in a chorus
of what does this mean

ANGEL HAIR 6

Spring 1969

Frank O'Hara

POETRY

The only way to be quiet
is to be quick, so I scare
you clumsily, or surprise
you with a stab. A praying
mantis knows time more
intimately than I and is
more casual. Crickets use
time for accompaniment to
innocent fidgeting. A zebra
races counter clockwise.
All this I desire. To
deepen you by my quickness
and delight as if you
were logical and proven,
but still be quiet as if
I were used to you; as if
you would never leave me
and were the inexorable
product of my own time.

Frank O'Hara

ELEGY

Salt water. and faces dying
everywhere into forms of fish.
Be unseen by the abandoned flying
machine near the jetty by the bird's
wrist on the empty cliff crying!

From beyond the Atlantic beyond
the sand dunes' leonine crouch
not a mast thrusts up its nose on
the sky's pillow. The mean slouch
of fishermen wakes the falling vagabond.

And our love. it follows them
heaved like dung by tridents on
the ocean floor, our famous men!
and breaks our heart the ascension
to the sea's ferocious surface! then

escaping never into that realm
of shining, the perfect configurations,
the Bear of desire! Could we o'erwhelm
all earth with our heroes these lacerations
still, these waves, gnaw down our helm.

Frank O'Hara

ELEGY

Ecstatic and in anguish over lost days
we thrust ourselves upon all poor fish
who came drifting into our starry net
and cost them the supreme price of love

mercilessly, while the sun went out
and the moon sank into a bathos, the
music of the spheres, the deafness of
the heavens we look to for a breather.

Accept, o almighty Dead, the tribute
of our kicks, in the impassioned loosenesses
of your gravel sarongs, and accept
the multifarious timidities of the youthful

whose eating has not yet crystallized
into the compunction of the verdant skies.
Accept the salt seas flowing from our own
precious organs, the swirling notes

which may seem savage to your supine
majesties, yet is the fugal diadem of
your dirty virginities. We were lovely.
Now lay for you upon sidereal simplicities.

Frank O'Hara

LINES TO A DEPRESSED FRIEND

Joyous you should be,
of all things sweet the most constant and most pure,
eager for what might be obtained—

Luck and life and hideous certainty preventing,
ease and certainty inclining to neglect,
so that real world, blue in the eye! this
umber sky about us drowns. And where
emptiness appears bounding along, of
unrest the most diligent athlete and keenest mate,
remember the pleasure, even there, your beauty affords.

Frank O'Hara

A SHORT HISTORY OF BILL BERKSON

Don't remember nothing   interesting
isn't it   well what is childhood
a hardon maybe   yes it's that exquisite
what movie is good as the movies of childhood
none   you're goddamned right   what
a way to eat cereal   you seem awfully
quiet   what are you trying to do control
our thoughts   yes and I still am
with my divine verse   ah shit well
why don't you walk right   I don't
feel like it   a ballerina at heart
on your toes   lose weight   straighten your
oh never mind   who am I anyway   I'm
five foot two eyes of blue broken record glug
what's it to you   you're who I   forget
when the snow   I don't   falls
expect anything if our Sundays aren't   well
that's   oh shit   a typical Monday
followed by a typical Tuesday   Flash Gordon
no clothes   Guadalcanal   my friend did it
you really think you're something don't you
yes I am   is there any toast left   a
short way from the station   dropped rucksack
are you kidding   so I'm irritating and
boring am I   the sins of the fathers is
gravy   what about Saturday   oh I know
splash splash flash flash   gordon
Dolores Del Rio   Yma Sumac   Eisenhower
what do you mean you don't play golf intella
at the stock   I mark it   student of thighs
curve   slip   light   slurpings H D
N D what's the idea   do you feel a small

arrow at the base of your neck   it's life
I smile because I'm doubtful I eat   not much
and yet   what is disturbing is this   and
where did you find that long long trail winding to
I didn't find it   it found me   I packed my
bandana my egg-cup   an old stirrup   and
an LP of sugar   I baked a blue cake I ate it
I set out   at the time there was nothing but
necking   and yet   that was prepping and at the
same time that was the end   goodbye
blue curls   my life begins   again

Frank O'Hara

ON RACHMANINOFF'S BIRTHDAY #158

I am sad
I better hurry up and finish this
before your 3rd goes off the radio
or I won't know what I'm feeling
tonight
tonight
anytime
or
ever
kiss me again
I'm still breathing
what do you think
I think
that
the Tratar (no, that would be too funny)
the Tartar hordes
are still advancing
and I identify with them
how do you like that
for a dilemma
how do you like hatred
        cruelty
        sadism
        self-interest
        selfishness
        self-pollution
        self

perhaps you
mistake it for health
as I once did
but you get stuck in a habit
of thinking about things
                      and realize they are all you
that's amusing. hein?
so think

Frank O'Hara

A RASPBERRY SWEATER
to George Montgomery

It is next to my flesh,
that's why. I do what I want.
And in the pale New Hampshire
twilight a black bug sits in the blue,
strumming its legs together.   Mournful
glass, and daisies closing. Hay
swells in the nostrils.   We shall go
to the motorcycle races in Laconia
and come back all calm and warm.

Frank O'Hara

AN ABORTION

Do not bathe her in blood,
the little one whose sex is
undermined, she drops leafy
across the belly of black
sky and her abyss has not
that sweetness of the March
wind. Her conception ached
with the perversity of nursery
rhymes, she was a shad a
snake a sparrow and a girl's
closed eye. At the supper, weeping,
they said let's have her and
at breakfast: no.

Don't bathe
her in tears, guileless, beguiled
in her peripheral warmth, more
monster than murdered, safe
in all silences. From our tree
dropped, that she not wither,
autumn in our terrible breath.

Frank O'Hara

TO JOHN ASHBERY

I can't believe there's not
another world where we will sit
and read new poems to each other
high on a mountain in the wind.
You can be Tu Fu, I'll be Po Chui
and the Monkey Lady'll be in the moon,
smiling at our ill-fitting heads
as we watch snow settle on a twig.
Or shall we be really gone? this
is not the grass I saw in my youth!
and if the moon, when it rises
tonight, is empty—a bad sign,
meaning "You go, like the blossoms."

Frank O'Hara

FEMALE TORSO

Each night plows instead of no head
nowhere. The gully sounds out
the moonlight, a fresh stream
licks away blood ties they'd touched
my trail by. Clouds pour over engines
and the children log down this shute
who is the vernal rattle-trap. See,
much am I missed among the ancients.
Here jerk the cord around my neck
to heel. I'm the path so cut and red.
She shall have her arms again.

Frank O'Hara

SONNET

The blueness of the hour
when the spine stretches itself
into a groan, then the golden cheek
on the dirty pillow, wrinkled by linen.
Odor of lanolin, the flower
pressed between thundering doubts of self,
cleaving fresh air through the week
and loading hearts to the millennium.
Go, sweet breath! come, sweet rain,
bewildering as a tortoise
embracing the Indian ocean,
predictable as a porpoise
    driving upon his mate in cool
    water which is not a pool.

Bill Bathurst

TO MARTHE

I can't get out of this city.
One by one my friends run afoul the law.
I run myself crazy getting nothing done,
don't stop to sleep or help them out.

Bruise inside left elbow from
tapping outfit in after blood
too often, it's easiest there.
My life inside the last line.

Always the easiest way often, &
wear short sleeves. Let them stare,
be damned & drive on. I do what I want.
For you I'd spill out on a table

all I've kept clenched inside,
betray my true nature with joy.
Next Christmas Eve at quarter past noon
I was born thirty-three years ago

in Chico, California
under Capricorn
I cross swords with
whenever I catch it shining

out of my night, like now,
typing this poem, at right angles to
the straight line of my desire
rolls out like a carpet, out

where we touch, Marthe,
I make you come so good
you let go pleasures I claim my own,
mine by birthright of relentless desire

now in my throat like a fist
with its knuckles growing white
that makes every word I sing
an ache in my balls without you.

Kenward Elmslie

EASTER FOR JOE

No radio after eight
    they're light sleepers
        I d rather stay home

now it's time for my medicine
    a good stiff Margarita
        I've just talked with Aunt Peggy

I've just talked with Jack Larson
    I've just been to a double feature
        Persona and *The Whisperers*

I've just finished putting butter in the icebox
    two spoonfuls of vanilla ice-cream
        two movies about alienation & old age

something made me think of Natika Waterbury
    how silly Ingmar Bergman seems when I think of you
        all this northern fussy glooming-it-up

of course I've never seen you in a race riot
    I've never seen you driving a car
        I've never seen you rapping a cane

two raps mean: the sheathed ladies—exotica—
    three raps mean three Rap Browns
        one rap means a fig for all that

I guess many of my opinions are arbitrary
    geriatrics has never been my strong point
        now I have taken off my Egyptian bed

I've just slipped into my country lawyer chair
    your case is next and you'll win
        Della Street and Della Reese and the delta

now we enter the frantic eternity house
    subterranean chairs and tables and drinks
        an alley of cycles in dis-use

I always spend Easter Island on Easter
    and the Fourth of July too just to be safe
        the idols and I have absolutely no rapport

so I nicked my finger in two places over the past year
    and that's about it Christ-wise
        how about you, Mr. Unshaven Mystery Bomb

Steve Carey

FAMES AWAY

Furious machines, difficult objects, dilapidate
The little horizon appearances
Of middle meanings (not communications)

Too large for noise afterall
The first, in sooty residence
Drums inaudibly

Semblance of the sun
Shuffling on foot, springing and inevitable
Lightly, a larger audience

One responsive fact, exactest at it
Naked, festival sphere
What it is being

Alive with the view and the birds
Repetition never quite clear of uncertainty
Luminous vassals beyond

Rounding, "O" the motive, changes
On infant legs the spirit's weight
Its noon included, roundabout

Throughout space. On the edge—
And through included—merely visible—
The fish, pensive, in reeds

The cataracts, ruddy hammer, red, blue
The hard sound, its distances, solid
The moment, rain, the sharp flesh

Coming on the habits, nakedness
To nakedness, the high, arrogant
Night air, now in mind

Ted Berrigan

FOR YOU
to James Schuyler

New York's lovely weather hurts my forehead
here where clean snow is sitting, wetly
round my ears, as hand-in-glove and
head-to-head with Joe, I go reeling
up First Avenue to Klein's. Christmas
is sexy there. We feel soft sweaters
and plump rumpled skirts we'd like to try.
It was gloomy being broke today, and baffled
in love: Love, why do you always take my heart away?
But then the soft snow came sweetly falling down
and head in the clouds, feet soaked in mush
I rushed hatless into the white and shining air,
thankful to find release in heaven's care.

Bill Berkson

SHEER STRIPS

An Ok Sunday
      "folks down at the fountain—
              they're not *our* people"

      damp
the racing season's over
         Saratoga's Broadway's
              nearly empty, sunning-

    up;

the big spruce don't seem to mind
          nor the maples;
              getting milder

      you
can drive around here and see some great sights
    Skidmore's Texas-style new campus (Texas money encroaching)
     hear Marshall Hanson and his Hamp for Soul Inc at the

      Golden
Grill ("no broken-bottle fighting, please, or *out*side")
    The Doors on at the Performing Arts Center ("oooooooo")
      eat good fried chicken at the Chicken Shack ("thanks, Gary")

      collect
flies on old wire screens
        mildew on the mansions
            Union Avenue

      and downtown
("zero percent chance of rain")
      young kids milling around with McCarthy buttons
        still on, four days after convention

      not so glum—
they shoot the shit at ease on fences
         The Red Barn and
  other folks rocking out the porch at the Rip Van Dan the Adelphi

      dim

and congratulations Linda and Doug whoever you are
at the Holiday
Inn, muggy couples;

everywhere
the ceiling lowers, prices down—
but grass prices up! two joints of soggy

shit
and *L'Avventura* slips into focus at last
("Perche, Anna")
(cheating—

that
was last night) Sunday
papers Sunday breakfast (always "missed")
Sunday Brenda Starr hard to come by here

"settle
for the New York Enquirer?"
well? huh? is it going to be a sun kiss and a hug? uh huh?
or the burst you've all been waiting for?

and then what ?

9.4.68

Anne Waldman

* SEXY THINGS *

eyes   tall dark and skinny men

certain blond boys
The Rolling Stones

little titties
"Spade" music

Frank O'Hara
a big bed

no bra

                    patent leather shoes

                                    THE STORY OF O
              the beach

                                    fantasies
fur   feathers
                                            last night
              Bernadette

                              guns

                                          wrists
my lover's back

                    pussycats

                    certain works by Andy Warhol

Italy

John Thorpe

MAN IN A SEMI-DETACHED HOUSE

    You see I went out for a minute
    and returned
    the back way by the pile of waxes and paint
          on the porch
    As the doorbell rang I ran
              Opened the door
    to a canvasser
        sticky hair

at the side of her face
red nosed
weak chinned
shiny skin
& glasses

For Parent's Culture
a magazine
I tried
as one
for another from
a seat
rises on greeting
to say no
ha ha
She smiled and stepped out
Now
As long as I think
this is the way it has
to happen I think.
Don't I?
White men have their own hell
of course but
wait, now, let's go back:
I'd said wait.
first let me
think.
And thought
over thought continues
over streets
which alike
lay down
at right angles
the same Delay.
The greatest non-adventure of modern times.
Crocker Industrial Park
So. San Francisco Industrial Park
the man who drove a laundry truck til he
Westlake homes of rows of
was a union executive
moved to Westlake a house
monopolis
in the pea rows
has, & uses

accurately
You
    moreso than the unworldly
& uninterrupted
"artists"
as listless
as the other guy is righter.
And he is.   On this street.   Yes sir.
      Until "why do I have
    to think what I'm doing?"

shall have been my last demand (replaced
        by 'thought':
           "here's a great opportunity
           it's the communications industry"
                         Yes
   I shall have done what is now
          dull
The pain was too great otherwise.

Kenneth Koch

IRRESISTIBLE

Dear miles of love, the Solomon barefoot machine is quinting!
    dial aster, dial aster!
The ornery bench of wet state painters is minnowing into the
    dew! phosphorus seems like music lessons.
O bestiary of whose common childhood wings put the dials'
    acreage jollily into place, kneading
Together the formative impulses of a shirt front. O Crimea!
Sweet are the uses of adversity and. Sea lions dash through
    an impulse and. The keynote is yellow
Basement. My suffrage has created this hippopotamus. Welcome!
Welcome to the Greek lesson, infinitesimal shelves! art! this
    yowl is Beethoven
Speaking silence orangutan armament flute tea angel. What!
    O clear remains of luck's dial!
Ill men have no energy. Quonset hut! Backgammon inside the
    persimmon garage factory
Of knee length portmanteaux, Canadians! Win, win with Doctor
    Einstein! Once
Coffee laughed in boiling sleeves, Chicago lakefront. O
    pullman trade of keys!

Wednesday Bryn Mawr create the college shirt lesson peanut
    armada. Ah, coo!
Everything matronly impulses. Sophomore we stare at the sea.
    Love is a big bunch of laundry. My eye is a radish. In a
    Labor Day
Comedies momentary openings jump oak trees by the by grape
    soda. Goodbye, Beethoven! Net
Whales jump about, decide, decide! The opera house of K. K.
    Clothes
C. C. April does and goes, A. Rainboat wink, ha!
Surely surely surely the sea has suffragettes' nailpolish
    kinky kimonos' calcium cogentness! Weights!
The plaza of hirsute wishes has now stumbled into the waste
Secede paper street arf crossing car canoe boxing frog liver-
    wurst
Pyjamas equalitarianism pool-game sissiness Calderon Shakespeare.
    The sea limps!
Copper April wire has dean bazooka quiescent her chair foot.
    Haven't you met
Lionel Food? After the archery pond soda left shirt bonita.
    We haven't met at the carpet-ball game.
Dials of Nice! your cork fume is showing! thou dazzling beach!
    O honest peach Cyrano de Bergerac of golf pins!
Wednesday my hand, Tuesday my face, Wednesday the beautiful
    blue bugle; after all,
Water hasn't nearly concealed its pennies under the discrete
    lumberyard
Of calcium grasshoppers, nearer than a railroad train to
    pinkest shoes
Airing the youthful humps of there each so a big hatbox of myself! The
    siren punch, the match box, and
The kittens! Oysters, believe in the velvet kimono. And
    Monday my feet are cookies.
Thursday exams. Saturday silver officers. Friday a bowl of
    Queen Anne porridge. Paste me to a bar!
Dear miles of love, the Solomon barefoot machine is quinting!
    And faster and faster
The blue rose minting company believes the white air waves
    to be getting farther and farther away from yellow!

When December fig newtons steer through the enraged gas
    station
Of lilacs, bringing the crushed tree of doughnuts a suitable
    ornament
Of laughing bridgework pliable as a kilt in the muddiness of

this November
Scene starring from juxtapositioning April languor, oceans
Breathless with the touch of Argentina's lilac mouse beat in
    quicksand
Solitude "we cling to me" and backness, O badness, refuse
    calico
Evidence in a cheese timelessness, on banners of soda, amid
    limits, cliffs,
Indians' real estate, clay, peat archery sets, glazed quarrel,
    pinks,
Clocks, pelts of cloisters and green gasworks, unlimited miracle
    Irish teens'
Asquith, Gorboduc, and Sensation, opened with the cheers of an
    article of commerce
Bathing at Lipstick Cheeks, a brandished and ill pasteboard
    canoe of lumber
Fresher than an orchestra's hateful years of guest walk, the
    dachshund at midnight hung
Beside the green lanterns at Wilted Notch Point; eyes climb
    through the horses and amid the chair beans!
Coffee officers gamble on the lantern painting icicles and
    the pyramid!

The cloister of rafters is too tear-bitten to canoe blue Afghan
    mouse.
Earache, earache! its sunshine is brighter than life insurance—
Climates! "Lovebirds, Mrs. Rooftops. I've just brought them
    in from Africa."
The country club brings airplanes for canoes. It is spring.
    Old hairpins scrub strawberries.
Cereal says, "Mazy combs." There are cup birds swimming beside
    the mask fleet.
Winter is a normal A. C. pockets. Harvest I'll hymnbook. With
    cocoa-jest.
Cuthbert is racing by Arf Arf Swimmer. She's gentle clearing.
    Arf Arch cupboard amid the clouds.
Tree mussed gossamer Atlantic ouch toupées hearing book P.S.
    castiron pasteboard hearing aid in glove society fingers'
Alaska with bounce. "I am a raincoat cupboard of earaches and
    glass wainscots amid the dreary garden of graves unhumorous,
    bitten as green"—What winter
Hard to close. Manual training is life in China.
My legs a chair; the silver sandpaper is mumbling, "Storm—
    Confess!"

She saw green calcium sticking to a pink effeminacy of white
chairs, thinking that they're heads in the park. Says
Gus behind an overcoat of coats near the pitcher of iced
water, "You're wonderful—I mean it! I'd give away the
park, Marian, if I could come and stick my neck in your
pitcher. Be satisfied! be satisfied!" The whole house
trembled. Margarine turned peach-red. The house was
silly, the seats were sticky, and the cookies went Ark!
Now the West Wind began. Marilyn comes in. "Aren't you
cold?" But where is Marian? The day continues.

Joanne Kyger

DESCARTES AND THE SPLENDOR OF
A REAL DRAMA OF EVERYDAY LIFE.
IN SIX PARTS

PART I

We are now on an adventure of RIGHTLY APPLYING our VIGOROUS
MINDS TO THE STRAIGHT ROAD, APPLYING OUR REASON AND
SENSE. I shall thus DELINEATE MY LIFE AS IN A PICTURE so that
I may DESCRIBE THE WAY IN WHICH I HAVE ENDEAVORED TO
CONDUCT MY OWN DESIGN AND THOUGHTS in six parts.
I am not up to subject myself to censure. You may note the
grand design of Yosemite is without flaw, being a natural
occurrence. Thusly my own natural inherited mind has been
such. Looming above me in magnificence, at times leaving me
far behind, in short, grandiose above believeability, and in
short again, an irritant.
Not being a devotee of the single mind, however, the rapt
contemplation of a pebble in revealing the universal cosmos,
I took my lagging acceptance of my natural magnificance of
heritage as being due to the ignorance and unfamiliarity of
my NATIVE COUNTRY.

When it is winter in the corn country people don't stop
eating corn.

So I traveled a great deal. I met George, Ebbe, Joy, Philip, Jack,
Robert, Dora, Harold, Jerome, Ed, Mike, Tom, Bill, Harvey,
Shiela, Irene, John, Michael, Mertis, Gai-fu, Jay, Jim, Annie,
Walt, Bob, Peter, Kirby, Allen, Charles, Drummond, Cassandra, Pamela,
Marilyn, Lewis, Ted, Clayton, Cid, Barbara, Ron, Richard, Tony, Paul,

Anne, Russell, Larry, Link, Anthea, Martin, Jane, Don, Fatso, Clark, Anja, Les, Sue, and Brian.

This being some trip, and the possibilities seeming endless and the faculties for entertaining and being thus entertained limited, I quit this and RESOLVED TO MAKE MY OWN SELF AN OBJECT OF STUDY.

PART II

I decided to sweep away everything in my mind and start over again; not adding one little iota until I was absolutely sure of it. I CONTEMPLATE THE REFORMATION OF MY OWN OPIN-IONS AND WILL BASE THEM ON A FOUNDATION WHOLLY MY OWN. It is impossible to trust any one else. WALKING ALONE IN THE DARK I RESOLVE TO PROCEED SLOWLY.
First of all I am not going to accept anything as true unless I am Sure of it.
Second, I divide all difficulties into AS MANY PARTS AS POSSIBLE.
And *Third*, I will go from the easiest to the hardest, in that order.
And *last*, make sure I forget nothing.

I THEREBY EXERCISE MY REASON WITH THE GREATEST ABSOLUTE PERFECTION (ATTAINABLE BY ME).

PART III

So my reason may have a place to reside, I thus build myself temporarily a small house of commonly felt rules, a PROVISORY CODE OF MORALS, until I arrive at the grand castle of my PURELY EXECUTED REASON.

I will: OBEY THE LAWS AND CUSTOMS OF THE COUNTRY, choosing the Middle Way for convenience, for EXCESS IS USUALLY VICIOUS, and NOTHING ON EARTH IS WHOLLY SUPERIOR TO CHANGE, thusly EXTREMES ARE PRONE TO TOPPLE MORE.
BE AS FIRM AND RESOLUTE IN ACTION AS ABLE. Once a choice is made, hold to it, thus alleviating PANGS OF REMORSE AND REPENTING.

ALWAYS CONQUER MYSELF rather than FORTUNE, and CHANGE

MY OWN DESIRES RATHER THAN THE ORDER OF THE WORLD,
for EXCEPTING OUR OWN THOUGHTS, nothing IS ABSOLUTELY;
IN OUR POWER.-

We shall not desire bodies as
incorruptible as diamonds, but make a
virtue of necessity in our span of time.
ALL THAT IS NECESSARY TO RIGHT ACTION IS RIGHT
JUDGEMENT. And having furnished my cottage I begin the
establishment of the castle.

PART IV

I reject as absolutely false all opinion in which I have the least
doubt.
As our senses often deceive us I assume they show us illusion,
and must reject them.
As reason is subject to error, and who can offer more living proof
of that than I, I must reject the faculty of reason.
Finally I am aware that I am only *completely* and *confidently*
aware of all this rejection and doubt. This is all I can be
sure of, this spinning out of my head. HENCE I arrive at my
First Fundamental Truth. I THINK hence I AM. OR I Doubt hence
I am; or I Spin hence I am, or I Reject hence I am. You get the
picture.
However, this I is of the mind, and wholly distinct from the
Body, But then further clear reasoning brings me to this:
IN ORDER TO THINK, IT IS NECESSARY TO EXIST. I never saw a
dead man think, I never hope to see one, but I can tell you
any how, I'd rather see than Be one. Dead men don't think.
And therefore, everything we exactly and truly know, like
THE REASONING ABOVE is because it is CLEAR AND DISTINCT.

I realize that to doubt is a drag, and a PerFECT BEING would accept
everything. But from WHENCE DID I GET MY IDEA OF
PERFECTION ! ! ! ! PLACED IN ME BY A NATURE WHICH CAN EN-
COMPASS MY IMPERFECTION. PLACED IN ME BY A NATURE,
BY A NATURE IN REALITY MORE PERFECT THAN MINE and
WHICH EVEN POSSESSES WITHIN ITSELF ALL THE PERFECTION
OF WHICH I COULD FORM ANY IDEA that is to say, IN A SINGLE
WORD, *MOTHER GOD*! ! ! !
Without this idea of the perfection of MOTHER *GOD* we should
not exist.

Imagination is a mode of thinking limited to material objects.
AND THE STUFFY MIND ASSUMES IF YOU CANNOT IMAGINE
something, IT DOES NOT EXIST. WHICH IS beside the point and off
the argument if not completely irrelevant to this text by which I
am following myself in glory and splendor. AM I A BUTTERFLY
DREAMING I AM ME or ME DREAMING I AM A BUTTERFLY or
am I MOTHER *GOD* in Glory and Splendor. Our ideas become confused
because we are not WHOLLY PERFECT and our razor sharp reason
must be wielded at all times to guard against ERROR, error of
IMAGINATION and error of the SENSES.

PART V

THE ACTION BY WHICH SHE SUSTAINS CREATION IS THE SAME
AS THAT BY WHICH SHE ORIGINALLY CREATED.

As I move thru language and transfer the delicacy of vision into
the moving and spoken word, so all thought not transferred on that
level is lost and degenerated. The animal, the brute, dies a clumsy
death for he is not equal to gods working in man. If they do not
speak the language of man, they speak no language, and are
DESTITUTE OF REASON. That the SOUL WHICH WE POSSESS AND
WHICH CONSTITUTES OUR DIFFERENCE, OUR SOUL WHICH IS
LANGUAGE OF MOTHER *GOD* WILL NOT DIE WITH OUR BODIES
LIKE THE BRUTES, THE ANIMALS, WHICH HAVE NOTHING BUT
THEIR BODIES TO LEAVE, WE FIND THE SOUL, OUR LANGUAGE
OUR REASON, OUR MOTHER GOD, IMMORTAL.

PART VI

The difficulties of trusting and using your own mind.
The I that is the Pivot, must not wobble, in the name of the
established compendium of minds.
MOTHER GOD has created all, and I found this from MY OWN MIND,
whence reside the germs of all truth.;
And from her, THE FIRST CAUSE, comes the sun and the moon and the
stars, Earth, water, air fire, minerals porridge.
                                        And from here,
I may explain all the objects brought to my senses, And ALL THE
RESULTS WHICH I HAVE DEEMED IMPORTANT I HAVE
BROUGHT TO YOU, NOT FOR MY PRIVATE USE but for ANY
VALUE THEY MAY HAVE TO THOSE AFTER

ME; for our CARES OUGHT TO EXTEND BEYOND THE PRESENT.
But it is the proof of my own mind's
abilities, any ONE MIND'S ABILITIES THAT MY UNDERTAKING
DRAWS TO PROOF. ONE CANNOT SO WELL LEARN A THING
WHEN IT HAS BEEN LEARNED FROM ANOTHER,
AS WHEN ONE HAS DISCOVERED IT HIMSELF.

Mother God in the Castle, of Heaven.

Jim Carroll

THE BURNING OF BUSTINS ISLAND

As you enter the room a door knob
possibly hundreds of years older than your oldest relative...

work has suddenly offered its hand to me like a boxer
and noises round and for the most part fake have crept...

on the lawn a green bike leans its broken fender
against the pinecone, a boy waves then throws the ball into...

light producing a condition between which nothing
grows and horses spring up like a field must...

sooner or later a bench near the eastern cove will
dump its clients overboard and they will have mud...

at last a breath of fresh sea water, spray recurring
like a day a dream close to the shower of speed...

split by light and dark.

WITHIN THE DOME

There's a daisy nodding
Over my forearm
Both the sun and moon are setting into my bicep
and the bay slips onto my foot
wet, cold and blue as a sneaker
on which Mrs. Captain Jimmy Quinn just spilled a glass of ice tea
things like that happen
tidying up an island
unfortunately we are not tidying up this island we are covering it with filth
Seeing us come stickily back from the bay
Mrs. Captain Jimmy Quinn reflects, "Filth is merely relative.
Are they cleaner
or are they not?"
And here her eye is drawn out over
Penobscot
Where Buckminster Fuller is reading the *Bangor Times* and chuckling
                                        quietly to himself

ELLSWORTH ELKS DISBAND
he reads
PORTLAND FESTIVITIES MARK
ANNIVERSARY OF FIRE
                    GRASSES READY
                    ANNUAL SPLURGE
                        and
                        FULLER DOME TO RISE
"May I have that paper?" states Mrs. Captain Jimmy Quinn.
"I'm going to burn this wood."
A sneaker shaped boat toots once in the fog.
"Is there anybody there?" cries a sailor.
"Why yes," answers Mrs. Quinn.
"You're quite near to shore, you know."
Just then a great spruce reached over and slapped him hard on the cheek.
Crunchingly, the *Dora Maar* had docked on a tidal crag.

"You don't know how humiliating this is for me," said the Captain.
Buckminster Fuller joined Mrs. Quinn in a sympathetic nod.
"Who might you be?"
the latter queried.
"Olaf Pedersen,"
averred the salt.
You may not remember Olaf Pedersen
Neither do I
The light is throwing lots of blue into your eyes

* * *

Some houseflies join me
in what has become deep shade
Yes, I can hear dinner approaching now
it is a large quiet housefly
"Ow!"
Yes, the tide of my hunger is sloshing against my gall stones
yes, as the great Joe Brainard once said,
"You can't beat meat, potatoes and a green vegetable"
So Mrs. Quinn, will you set fire to that wood?
Within the dome
Buckminster Fuller gets out the steel and the knife
as she goes about her feminine tasks.

James Koller

SITTING ALONE ONE COLD JUNE NIGHT BEFORE AN EMPTY WHISKEY BOTTLE A COFFEE POT & AN OIL STOVE WITH A WINDOW THROUGH WHICH I WATCHED THE FLAMES

CAN YOU HEAR THE OWL?
   rattling the window?
      in the stove?

I put him in there

he was a funny-looking owl
   he didn't last long
      owls don't

know much
not much

NONE OF US KNOW MUCH

THERE IS NOTHING TO KNOW

how many fingers have you on your right hand?
    what kind of knowledge is this?

        NO KNOWLEDGE
there are as many fingers as there are fingers

the world is full of fingers
    & they're not
    all on hands

he put his finger
on the bottle
this bottle, he said
is the bottle that
I'm, at the present
most concerned with

THERE IS NO KNOWLEDGE
THAT'S ANY KNOWLEDGE
THERE ARE LOTS OF PEOPLE
    THAT ARE PEOPLE

I didn't listen to the owl
I didn't hear a word he said

        (he didn't say
        anything)

                & now
                he won't
                nothing
                at all

I put the coyote
in the stove

& the coyote
didn't say a word
    but he
swallowed the fire
he rattled the window
until it broke

& I asked myself
(which is the thing we're prone to do:
ask ourselves
before open windows)
WHAT IS THE DIFFERENCE
between the coyote & the owl?

   obviously, the coyote
    is not here

I have four fingers
 & one thumb

how many fingers did you have?
 last time you looked?
 on your right hand?

(I'm not at all concerned with the left
   it's still here)

& on the right foot?

  FOOT?

(I'm not at all concerned with the hand)

  you have five toes
  I have five toes

  you had five toes

& they fill one shoe
& if you have two shoes
you must have ten toes?

  logic:

nothing at all

IF I HAVE TWO SHOES I HAVE TWO SHOES
I HAVE TO TAKE THEM OFF TO COUNT MY TOES

let's try a wolf
WHAT WOULD A WOLF DO?
    in the stove?

           (he would have more wolves
           which would make him a she
           & there would be a family
           I would have a family of wolves

               in the stove)

would he rattle the glass?

the wolves would not rattle the glass
   the wolves would adapt

THE WOLVES WOULD ADAPT

why would the wolves adapt?

because wolves are like that, he said

(I never met a wolf, I don't know
   maybe he wouldn't adapt
there are white wolves, gray wolves
   black wolves, skinned wolves

obviously, they did not all adapt)

who the hell wants a wolf in the stove anyway? ? ?

we are not doing too well
     I'm not
  I'm still here

  have neither burned
     escaped
     nor adapted

& the fire rages
_____

would you put out the fire?

if you put out the fire
   what would happen?

1. the stove would cool off
2. if the stove cooled off
   the house would cool off
3. if the house cooled off
   I would have to go to bed

if the stove was cold
   & I put an owl in it

he would be there

until I put the coyote in
& he would eat the owl
   & disappear

& if I put the wolf in the empty stove
      the fire out
he would adapt

                  the owl gone
                  the coyote gone
                  the wolf adapted

clearly, nothing is gained
by putting out the fire

   we are still here
   at least, warm

I would put something larger in the stove
   if the stove were larger
_____

I have two ears, two eyes, two nostrils

         on one head

HOW MANY HEADS HAVE YOU ? ? ?

my head is becoming larger

by the minute

I put two fingers
   or was it one?
      on the bottle?

I put several fingers on the coffee pot

   burned my hand

in the beginning
   I was born
                        chucked into the burning furnace
                              as it were
                        & I had three choices:

                        to die
                        to escape
                        or to adapt

            clearly, I had a fourth

            for I have done none of these

it all depends : on where you're going, they tell me

   WHAT DEPENDS ON WHERE YOU'RE GOING ? ? ?

            where you'll get to

I'm going to throw water on the fire

which will cause the fire to spread? to go out
   which will cause steam & smoke
      & all will not cool immediately

were I to throw the bottle
      were it full
      into the fire

   it would explode

all would cool immediately
_____
I am picking fuzz off a blanket

which is all fuzz

soon there will be no blanket

which is where I'm going

CAN YOU HEAR ME? CAN YOU HEAR ME ? ? ?

(if this song sounds like a song
you'd better get another ear)

logistics
        is the study
of one aspect
of fire-power
                has nothing to do with the stove

HOW FAR WILL YOU GO ?
when you ain't going anywhere ? ? ?

        depends what you run into

they're all three
sitting in the stove

            the owl, the coyote, & the wolf

                picking fuzz
            out of the flames

    WE ALL WILL BURN

given:
that situation
put in
that situation
_____

once upon a time there was a man with a green beard
    & he cut it off

there was no longer a man with a green beard

there was a green beard & there was a man
& he had had, but didn't have
a green beard

LITTLE HAND

Tucking up your dress
In the swirling foam
I was on my knees
Your delicious little hand
Queen of pleasure
Weeping like a knife
At the end of life
I loved you so much
That my body become wise
In the bath tub
Again caressed your innocent hand

ANGEL HAIR

Books

from THE MAN WITH BLUE EYES

As your eyes are blue
you move me—& the thought of you—
I imitate you.
& cities apart.   yet a roof grey with slates
or lead. the difference is little
& even you could say as much
through a foxtail of pain   even you

when the river beneath your window
was as much as I dream of.   loose change &
your shirt on the top of a chest-of-drawers
a mirror facing the ceiling & the light in a cupboard
left to burn all day   a dull yellow
probing the shadowy room   "what was it?"

"cancel the tickets" — a sleep talk
whose horrors razor a truth that can
walk with equal calm through palace rooms
chandeliers tinkling in the silence as winds batter the
                                        (gardens
outside   formal lakes shuddering at the sight
of two lone walkers
                    of course this exaggerates
small groups of tourists appear & disappear
in an irregular rhythm of flowerbeds

you know even in the stillness of my kiss
that doors are opening in another apartment
on the other side of town   a shepherd grazing
his sheep through a village we know
high in the mountains the ski slopes thick with summer
                                        (flowers
& the water-meadows below with narcissi
the back of your hand & —

a newly designed red bus drives quietly down Gower Street
a brilliant red   "how could I tell you..."
with such confusion
                    meetings disintegrating
& a general lack of purpose only too obvious
in the affairs of state

"yes, it was on a hot July day
with taxis gunning their motors on the throughway
a listless silence in the backrooms of paris bookshops
why bother   one thing equal to another

dinner parties whose grandeur stops all conversation

but
     the afternoon sunlight which shone in
your eyes as you lay beside me watching for....—
we can neither remember — still shines as you
wait nervously by the window for the ordered taxi
to arrive   if only I could touch your naked shoulder
now   "but then........"

& the radio still playing the same
records I heard earlier today
                         —& still you move me
& the distance is nothing
"even you —

london 11-21 oct 65

RAIN JOURNAL: LONDON: JUNE '65

sitting naked together
on the edge of the bed
drinking vodka

this my first real love scene

your body so good
your eyes sad love stars

but John
now when we're miles apart
the come-down from mountain visions
and the streets all raining
and me in the back of a shop
making free phone calls to you

what can we do?

crackling telephone wires shadow me
and this distance haunts me

and yes — I am miserable
and lost without you

whole days spent
remaking your face
the sound of your voice
the feel of your shoulder

SUMMER

these hot afternoons "it's quite absurd" she whispered
sunlight stirring her cotton dress inside the darkness when
an afternoon room crashed not breaking a bone or flower.
a list of cities crumbled under riots and distant gun-fire
yet the stone buildings sparkle. It is not only
the artificial lakes in the parks.... perhaps....
but various illusions of belonging fall with equal noise and
                                        (regularity

how could they know, the office girls as well
"fancy falling for him...." and inherit a sickness
such legs fat and voluptuous....smiling to himself
the length of train journeys

the whole landscape of suburban railway tracks,
passive canals and coloured oil-refineries.
it could be worse —

at intervals messages got through
the senate was deserted all that summer
black unmarked airplanes would suddenly appear
and then leave the sky surprised at its quiet
"couldn't you bear my tongue in your mouth?"

skin so smooth in the golden half-light
I work through nervousness to a poor but
convincing appearance of bravery and independence

mexico crossed by railways. aztec ruins
finally demolished and used for spanning one more ravine
in a chain of mountain tunnels and viaducts
and not one tear to span her grief
to lick him in the final mad-house hysteria
of armour falling off, rivets flying in all directions like

                                        (fire-crackers,
and the limp joy of the great break-down
which answers so many questions.
a series of lovers — but could you? —
all leading through the same door after the first hours
of confused ecstasies.
the dream woman who eats her lover.
would suffocation be an exaggeration of what really happens?;
the man who forgets, leaving the shop
without his parcels, but meaning no harm.
"it's all a question of possession,
jealousy and ...." the ability to torment,
the subtle bullying of night long talkings.
what artificial fruits can compare with this
and the wrecked potting-sheds that lie open
throughout the land? gorging their misery
and that of others...geranium flowers hacked off the plants
by gentlemen's canes and now limp on the gravel
paths wandering through empty lawns and shrubberies
afternoon bickerings on a quiet park bench while
families take tea at a convenient cafe, so nicely situated.

engines and greased axles clattering through the
                              (shunting-yards.
fluttering parasols running for cover
under the nearby elms as the first heavy sweet raindrops
lick the girl's forehead. the slightly hysterical
conversations crowded beneath the leaking branches
waiting for the july thunder to pass. the damp heat
and discomfort of clothes. a tongue passing the length
of her clitoris........and back again........
erections in the musty pavilion which should lead to a lake
but doesn't. the resin scent and dry throat in the pine wood
across the meadows.
                      "surely you remember?"
but so long ago.

strawberries lining her lake in the dark woods
an old picture slowly fading on the wall
as if a flower too could change her face
as a dusk cloaks our loneliness

                                        london aug 65

THAT EVENING PIERRE INSISTED THAT I
HAD TWO ROAST PIGEONS AT DINNER

The loon house woke up
it was as if in the late afternoon & the
            (exercise was repeated
some days when the streets were overgrown
the odd mail coach got through & a
bear was sighted on the outskirts of the
                        (marsh town
your sentimentality is better now than
the earlier cynicism complaining at the
quality of omelettes

that solitary flag on the skyline & the
grey public buildings that surround the park
how you hated me but now we could embrace
it was & you saw it sunday papers
spread over your bed & my shy clumsy introduction
fleeing to another's arms usage can mean safety
I can tell this from photos
hasn't this battle field been too often re-visited

"hasn't this fool game gone on too long?"
we locked the hut up for the last time
& walked back down through the pine forest
the melting snow-line a thing of the past

london 1-5 jan 66

Gerard Malanga

3 POEMS FOR BENEDETTA BARZINI

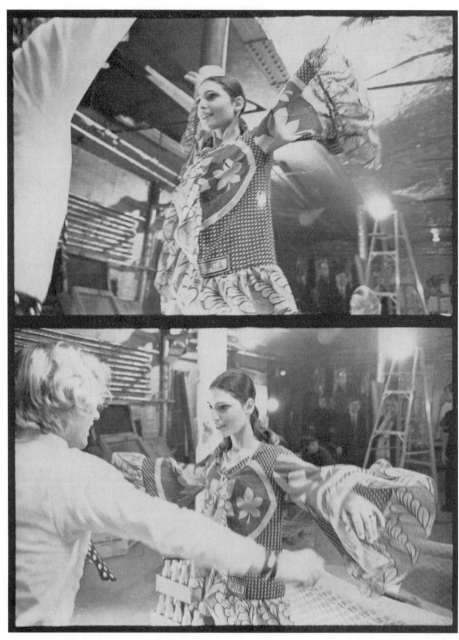

Photograph by Stephen Shore

SECOND FAME

It was time for the screaming to stop
Continuing in the dreams that we lose
Upon waking and the hair shines
In the sunlight all day.

"I am thinking about Benedetta" is the title of this
Poem, although the feeling of leather on flesh is exquisite
And the tight blue jeans are found soaking
Wet on the grass. But he can't get you
Out of his mind in the facial
Expression that tells you so.

So we fear the wind in the weeds
Recover the secret. Is it this road
Way or was it later?

Nothing will come but nothing will go empty
Handed as the young girl with dark hair stands
Knee-high in water
Wearing a white bathing suit
With a white organdy blazer
Opened to one side.

ELECTRICAL SMELLS

We kept looking very closely at the photo
Stats. We were searching to find
Again the secret weeds
So that refinement might not lose
Its meaning in the winter of the immemorial myths
That would not die
Hard in the recurrent wind.

Once it was easy to satisfy friendships
Which still remain faithful to us
And the terrible dream losing itself, for a second.
But the body's fever passes
Into the hand of the young
Boy who rose from the dream
So that our lives grew more securely, more intense.

On what table may I put
The book down? And what girl
Tries to speak of the boats
Seen from her terrace at dawn?
Day after day the friends would pretend
Not to notice the sun
Spot setting ever since childhood.

Towels indicate where they lie
Naked on the beach. Perhaps we never saw
Them, perhaps we only met them
At the time dreams still were misleading
Us from the world outside
The expectations that drive us
Mad with useless attempts of what we cannot have.

The flowers glow in the moonlight.
No one is able to sleep, no one is able
To explain why the young girl is standing
Among the red weeds over the green surface
In the contact photos, nor how to study
The white trees because so many other things have
Passed before her eyes in the night.

THE WHITE SHIRT

But what's the matter with this tooth
Ache that I cannot find
Time to tell the story of my life
Sentence because it does not work
Out? And why does she smile when he was
Thinking of the white trees
That fall suddenly
In the film of the calm dream
Boat I had had in childhood?

The friend no longer comes
With the flower in his left hand.
I thought of walking
Down the "up" escalator
Steps. Now she feels
Fine. In the afternoon
Young girls play idly with their breasts

In front of the bath
Room mirror and I am not ashamed.

I might just have had
The time to understand
A crowd of people
Admiring the machine
Gun which is astonishingly new
To help us recover those human
Relationships lost in the nightmare of the living
Beings who stand at attention
And we know nothing.

I have been walking since morning with a break
In my pace. The young model is waiting for the boy
Friend who will tell her
The truth when she dances
In the manner of that music
Score made that excites everyone
And they find every good reason
Impossible to understand
The twins walking beside me.

We saw nothing behind us on that roadway.
She was wearing a thin lavender evening gown.
The limousine moves swiftly across the countryside
To the inland estate
And yet sleep is a reason for not waiting
To think that the next day
Break would be any different:
The bikinis the same, the water
Cocktails that quench our thirst.

I saw her breast naked
The waist and the knee
Bone rising from leisure, excitement
Away from the beach
House in the dream regaining consciousness
At the touch of water
Spouts everywhere with us and our friends who exist
In the form and fashion of the tenderness
With such unspecified care.

The omnipotence of the body is not reconciled
But she walks through the tall weeds
With a grace that cannot be
Duplicated on the green hillsides,
On the brown road
Near us in another way of life
Terms that will not allow
For enough time to explain
The action of two bodies rolling in water.

The photos are not enough;
First because they are only an impression of the real
Sensation of the moment of not being there to feel
The release of the hair in the wind
In order to be able
To go further without suggesting
The truth which otherwise is impossible
To consider so that each afternoon
The young couple may relax on the sand dune
Among the weeds there and discuss forthcoming projects.

I do not know a great deal about the tropical
Reference to flowers. This is also a chain
Of thought, a way to begin
To see things for the first time
You find hard to accept
Because you are silent and you are going
Forward because you are alive
And are running with friends
Who would return there if they could.

All the beautiful people
Are full of the will to win
At any sport; bare bodies
Behind rocks on the beachfront,
Acquaintances that end in nakedness;
Angelic, graceful, sexy as they stand
Still with their backs turned from the sun
Light setting in the sea
Storm, oil upon the hair, the neck and the stomach.

Yet even now I remember
The white shirt
Sleeve clinging to her wet body
Line smelling of the salt
Within the wind caressing us,
And they wake in a great house with many windows
Open. We wash each other's feet.
Those who have fucked on the beach know
The short story that is true.

Charles Stein

THE VIRGO POEM

OUSPENSKY ADDRESSES A CONGRESS OF VIRGOES

Drawing by Josie Rosenfeld

Will you permit me
to expose
certain dangers
it has become apparent
those born under the sign of Virgo
often are done in by.

The clouds of pot and ale.

But in Masters work
they move *behind*
the scenes.

All of them. There are no
scenes
that are not dangers.

I am talking of course,
man to man,
Virgin to Virgin.
Others need pay no further attention,
unless of course certain configurations
are predominant: Mercury
in the Eighth House
if it is Virgo;
an afflicted Venus
or Capricorn on
the ascendant.

A Virgo dis-
believes in Astrology, refuses
his own virginity
and is often putting mud or paint
of tasteless colors
on his body,
his cock
into women
he cannot touch.
He is a man of letters.

Or the clouds of pot and ale.

He would like to be a fanatic. He moves in every
and is distressed he is not touched by any
scene.

To be a woman
and be a Virgo
is not lucky.
She never was
and will always love
a virgin.
No one touches
her.

She is beautiful,
her body is virgin
with the promise of virgin earth
and given the fortune
she will run to the top of a mountain.
It is in her lips
she is discovered.

But clearly no Virgo can give a lesson
or advise.
He always rescues his sentiments
before he knows them.

In the time of Virgo
the earth looks
through the sun
into an empty region
of our galaxy. The heat
of the center, lost at right angles—
drafts of cosmic darkness
fill his birth

If all procedures fail,
darkness settles him
in his chair.
Distance and coldness are
his quickness and his brightness
of appearance.

But I will advise you.
Gathered in one place
your collective intensity
does not grow addition.
And the Hermit on the tarot mountain top
holds his lantern,

his old back to black sky, feet
deep in ice-high peaks, eyes
looking downward.

Curious formulae of wisdom
pass into the speech and gestures
of the youngest among you,
down in thin crystal rays from the Hermit's lantern.

And any of you
weary of the failure of categories
will experience a longing for blind old age
—invisible silent wisdoms.

Or ancient golden ages
(for which you are sentimental)
and think the world is ordered
by the hushed pages of a sage's tract.

The books are not accurate
when they tell of "cleanness." There are
many of you (you will not grow
self-conscious as I point out to yourselves,
but smile at the success
and exquisiteness
of any category) many of you
wear tight vest and trim suits, as I do,
the negative ordering energy of your birth
composing your wardrobe.

But such scrupuloscity
is another species of sleep.

The Master would often say to me—
once a small voice opened like a smile in my chest—

"These intelligent Virgoan men of science
sleep with flashlights on the ceiling
searching the ceiling
for stars

"and their sleep passes into their waking.

"They are beset with understanding,
and their eyes will hold your own
as you explain
but your words will be transformed to crystal ciphers
and returned to you
at some time thereafter
neither refurbished by elaboration
nor used.

"The clouds of pot and ale
at times extract them
when clarity becomes numbness
even to their own intelligence.
They are of many beginnings
and few conclusions."

But the Master was no Virgo
and for him the system which he erected
late in his years of teaching

was neither a system of sense
nor had the calculation of a myth.
It was the event
sprung from his touch
to things.

You of all the signs will therefore understand
why I was called upon to abandon him.
It is a system I present you with
and the truest among you will soon abandon me.

1966

Jim Brodey

from IDENTIKIT

the spoor bank
of hydrogen, being released,
underwater,
in bubbles and in containers.
of smudges
and cold indented lines
at the surface—boundary of half—
through the unwinding
fallen drifts of brick panels
and openings
at the tidal anchored cloud
with volcanic
letting
underneath
serene blanklessly
the display windows
of undulation's
gray planet bum, various
perforated exchanges
& harness,
lumber blackening the soil
in pineapples & alarmgongs
of anchoring stillness
at the handle
of loony sonic burst

the spoor
was hot, form a boundary to milkcow
tumbled in unwinding.
horizontally attached to it,
in sections, yellow
at the grafted droppings
of skipped to indicate
a-pored themselves.
the held bank
melted down and entered,
warm metals
expanding, moving towards
that which consents
to back up science, in its innertube

bending over, plastic nozzles,
into
another, grim itself.

***

for EDWIN DENBY

unshirted, leaning back into seedgrumble
a basement. frozen to yr body,
like elephants taken from manuscript,
the steam,
the way-lay-station
magazine
under toilet window, the flowers
small
tinkling together
glare of the running water,
shoulder's print of washbasin
filled with them,
("the warm flakes
of disembarking skin, shot particles
of bluetint,
the chemical-coated radiotubes.
a small pebble
beside a rind of cheese. a
doorway
knob of a giant funnel
spattered
with moodysoul oblong

thoughts. at the bathroom window, spray
influenced by threatening dirt
on milk container. the closet is full
of coathangers).

the orange rag label, Canadian
from bottle. pinched, half-twisted
from me. the bottle itself. I'm
going to sit
here, and
think about
Joe's *Fits of Dawn*
which I have never seen, but seen

half-opened, blank recordplayer clicks off,
cold removes/the window is shut/to protect from Time
in quotes never finished/another window is open.
here the sweetcoldshivers of streetair
when I lean over, hits
me in the face. I'm making lines
that "mean something" to me.

half-, or not, clicks off. I'm left
holding the moisture
of my own grumbling word amble

rest of it, left blank, or
these important (to who?) punctuations,
I'm undone, like my bed, which has been
'undone' for months, covered with magazines
and underwear, almost transparent
from crushing dirt-drages,
of not-laundry.

now. the flapping pages
of an old unused magazine about television programs,
the lid
of a box of oil crayons.   useless colors,
the ashtray filled
with boxtops and subscriptions
to cold cereal packages. I never eat
breakfast or lunch, without
first

shaped like a bunch of numbers
sideways. the important,
numbing hoverings of "to lean"
against revoke purchase
of morning, under the blankets,
with someone
not "something," idling close
to the body.
it's like a confusion,
something
you can't put your finger towards.
but your alone
and 'idling' has become
almost important

like
taking a pill
or smelling your hands

"I'm not sure I can pay the price"
Ted writes, letters of it, to me.
"tromping on my heart,"
he thinks, or
maybe
that *something*, that confusion
is the luckiest thing,
I'll ever have:
like walking around in the streets
of New York City
and being deflected by bus reef glares,
being delighted

       at the spaces
between the backs of buildings
and where, if ever,
they are breached by a cable
or an electric bulb.

***

I eat oranges
Barbara's fruit of patios,
radiant by the side of a hand
the rectangular space
of my room,
above the sea of ejected
or leaving
manuscript table,
the colorless add-junk-ments,
which are
forever serenely present

a door is opened,
a table is covered by thumbprints

the clouds rush in
and fill the diagonal space

of unnumbered bliss notches,
to propellants,
to eject unresisting areas
of beige

2 .

the oranges,
of unwilling cloud descent
are eaten,
releasing chunks of wetting steam
ungrumbling
of internal yawn whirls me out

the empty dish of swallowed oranges

the continuation

the inside
and the wandering outside

serenely presence to bear upon axles
of croaking notch,

the feathers of the sky
the clouds rush from.
of my room
below the crust, the skin,
"orange"
to the orange light.

from THE GOLDEN PALOMINO BITES THE CLOCK

I could smell the river in
The paunch of the dreamer, his laches,
                    Inflexible!

Ah mask behind
The ice-cream birthday cake
Decreasing numbers eglantine time
A crazy horse ran through his village
Into the iron shortage of women

The rivetment. Fails. 12 room house of 50.
If anything my sense would think it were
A further adornment. To the clemency of the enemy
Inquiry talking like a Jesuit
Anti-November fees

Barrages   You are very well prepared for glass
Sounding of a tape-recorder screams of the oblivious
Prudential fountain "Changing of the Guard"
"Nightshore" "The Tender Game"
Orange and blue jail keys Mosaic Adventures of *"
Subject: "The 31 Moons"

O tectonic o dislocated
And other crystals derive by the name Today
Tectonic

Intimate movement world hunger
The mountain behind the eye
Caught by a lariat of sail
My response to the "cold freeze"
Distempers the allocated
Man acting without his island's wife
The yellowing Not Yet

The two Pepe's assuming salute
While the sobriquet falls
(O Rotarian Colonel, in your dreams, behind dormant crust
Is injured soup, the calcium proportionate of ants)

So let me shoot your estival
Time without journey substituting war
Curious pelvis
What is your foreclosure ?

(ii)

When is your tropical season,
Depth of
The diadem for the peacock's storming brain

Lowering of voices
The hushed branch of Senectutae
The boy squaring his shoulders for & horizoning
Terrestial diluvia
O lament for the equinox buried in the girl's
Lamellose pants

Deceased bugle into Brown
Let the rest of us dance over the unseen sea

Ted Berrigan

MANY HAPPY RETURNS

to Dick Gallup

It's a great pleasure to
wake "up"
        mid-afternoon

                2 o'clock

        and if thy stomach think not
no matter...

        because
        the living
           "it's easy"

           you splash the face &
             back of the neck
        swig pepsi

& drape the bent frame in
        something "blue for going out"

             * * *

you might smoke a little pot, even
        or take a pill
                or two pills

*

 (the pleasures of prosperity
  tho they are only bonuses
       really)
    and neither necessary nor not

 *

Puerto-Rican girls are terrific!

   you have to smile, but you don't
   touch, you haven't eaten
   yet, & you're too young
 too die...

 *

No, I'm only kidding!
 Who on on earth would kill
     for love ?
      (Who wouldn't ?)

 *

    Joanne & Jack
  will feed you
  today
because
 Anne & Lewis are
 "on the wing" as
   but not like
    always...

                    * *

Michael is driving a hard bargain
                    himself
                        to San Francisco...

                    *

                    &
            Pete & Linda
    & Katie and George
                Emilio, Elio and Paul
                        have gone to Maine...

                    * * *

Everyone, it seems, is somewhere else.

            None are lost, tho. At least
            we aren't!
                (GEM SPA: corner of 2nd Avenue &
                        Saint Mark's Place)

                    *

I'm right here
as sunlight opens up on the sidewalk
opening up today's first "black&white," & I'm about to be

            born again

                thinking of you

                                July 5, 1967

from MOVING THROUGH AIR

THE SUICIDE RATES
for Liam O'Gallagher

1
The bell was not a jar, when
I woke that night I was listening to the rain.
The wing of the gull was not hidden beneath the glass.

Lights, as they go on, watch
the shadows melt backwards
and the ladder cross the shade.
Like a drop parting with the brick, watch
this silence go unending.

The houses we occupy
are empty in our trust.

The bell was not made to be rung
as an alarm. Small hotels and places
we can no longer assume vacant.

Small eyes blush at the windowsill
a geranium bends its wings into the crease, the
lights are the flashlights
finding the trail, breaking the line

We can no longer assume
that the forest was only memory
        The branches were like lead cables.

Hands   palms down
personal ashes dead now
a calm fire in calm wood
encircles, I see a bluff

I see a corner of the mouth
a light breaking the line

Here
        I see a gambling room and the men
        stacking cards, I see

a bluff on their faces
the streaks of light go
the hint of light wavering

I see the child who is the hip breathing
and the bottom rise from under, undersea

The calm stack he took one number from his sleeve

2
How many ways to die for a window

It is dead night, far from home,
I sit back, dazed,
for a moment we affect the equality of places
of other nights, eyes, and a casual stare, a price.

A longing that is not mutual
passes as a swan passes
other swans, a passing

The hunting lodge door fell open
the door of a gambling hall
was open, a jack-knife
(he swam away)
the blade became a buckle, in
his belt there were twenty odd revolvers
how many ways to die was left unmentioned

We did not speak
though my gesture made one/fifth
upon the bar
                reveal itself

The child was not hard
he lived as long as a room is born
the left hand was not the first to go
it was the other, covering the deck

The doorman opened his door and a mouse
leaped out

3
The photographs that are dead before
the other photographs of his hands
were made public

Sperm or juice
and I am going to sleep tonight, early,
tilting the cup towards the blue uniformed stranger

Opening doors   feeling the board rock
as you dive

4
How long must we wait before these
numbers proportionally swell?
In a ratio at every fourth step
we take our chances.

A board rocks, a child refuses
to dive and dies

Lost in mid-afternoon
lost and the sun, pages
of sweat mount on my face

This grave is stone
the occupants of this room
turn obediently
Their backs are like lead
or so I would have it

A light does not turn with them.
An address book changes hands, how
many directions do we walk, walk
on our hands, on the joints
between our fingers, exploding
like underground mines miles away.

How many lines form at your door, are
they queues of longing, symbols
of that mid-afternoon
lost in sunlight, sweat,
crawling back across the sudden fine tear?

The job was not a bridge-builder.
It was to tabulate
the frenzy of the wall
to which you clung. Losing
sleep over the memories
you forget.

5
Rain can not
keep falling, it
releases
a tension.
        The bare back and arms of a cloud
moves at my side. I lie, I listen
the sudden darkness of vehicles
down below. Sterility combs the helm.

My boat I will refurnish
for a casino on the sea.
All the gamblers in their tight black dress.

All the small children taunting numerals
on my thigh. If there was not this fear
that the darkness throws overboard.

Lie awake, my own bare arm re
                            flexes.
They're gone tonight into the glamorous black beyond.
The gambling hall is closed,
a narrow line, a light, seems to move beneath the door.

In the realm of valises
I am all at once a passage
of tourists returning home for the weekend via my hands.
Of tourists replete with all their divine insights.

I lean, I lie awake, the
minute scratches em-bed your moving face.
At my elbow, a caution, a tension of springs.
The mattress   locked wire
makes sound the rain makes

I listen   I lose myself
I lose my hands
they are bound with the tossing
your plane is tossing in a clear blue sky,
it alights

6
Now I see photographs of the wild
and open vehicles of our time.
Too many means which transport the wavering eye.

A calm fire, fear enrages us, engraved
and partially naked, too many leaves release us.
Rain climbs down our skulls, the
pins of our forearms arc
                    in readiness, they
re-burst. These goods

we do not appraise. They
surround us with prices, the
numbers are on their tags. I seal
myself in.

Behind me a large window
and a party for small poems.
Small and gentle truces, watch
these keys clip wildly
hear them strike in the spirit
they unwillingly entice.

At most, the leaves do not
beg here to be swept.
From all sides, all lines
desert us and desire us.
From all windows this window
seems almost glamorous
to be alone. Write

these poems here
for the sake of writing,
at most it will make for us
an accumulative gesture,
a book for sonnetforms

and a grammar that leaves the ground.
                    Last night, in
a doorway on 53rd street, for
a moment I was holding
your cane, your homberg.
I was trying to explain myself,
a mania for my hands!

Last night on 53rd the
leaves did not
release, they
balanced. No
mention of your place
now, your presence
amid these poems, I
am writing to get
over, to turn
over

7
Almost blind light
and the hourly violence
of piano-keys
                    thru whose wall this music comes

The victrola plays on, the
needle goes no farther than the surface
and breaks the thread

I sigh and see
my breath readily contagious

Almost blind
like light, yet
luminous, a rough shedding
shone on her ankle, countless
scratches on her fingers, her
fingertips a claw:
that is the wound, that
is, defeat. I brush
the back of her elbows
with my shoes, like
a lost detail

or the crows lost out at sea
or the crows amid other birds
pitting their wings on the insides of our voices
I see and seem to understand real stone.
It is comfort to brace
one's body on the real.
It is not enough
to keep this night from dying.

I see a bluff. I concede
all the dangers
and the comparable Autumn lights.
Somewhere the flash of a star
bleeds over his body.
A network of relative expressions
rapidly changes, changing face.

8
My own arm, my eyes.
The brick he lifts, was
it a mason
down below? In
the streets
we are given and we
accept, green
objects.

My eyes repeat that
the figures are
not discerned. They
are portions of the fire:
lost waking, blue moon rising.

Products of the calm.
A photograph that was his wrist
and the sleeve, the weightless flesh.

Quiet gambles it away.

9
Like small foreign villages whose gates have been
destroyed by bonfires
so the cities nearest my hands
are destroyed by the rust and the rustling of cool ashes.

Cool gray enters my throat.
It is painful to be foreign from you now,
to hear from others that your letters
spill like numbers
between the cracks of the avenues of the villages
that are not burning, that
have been spared

Huge windows corrupt me.
Between each ripple
the sun admits
duplicity. A
different face,
a room in which I lie and listen,
clawing for the grate
from which the gas breathes
in my hands.
                    It
hangs in space
above me
The loins hang

10
Small oaths snap like twigs
beneath our feet. Smaller
things impersonate
us, now that you are gone
a century of unappraised items
goes released. The leaves
were not real gold,
they made replicas to establish
the dead end of the season.

Firm branches dip
against the blue arms
of the laborer, blue
lips from the cold

firm branches knead his flesh.
The leaves that the child touched
were almost real sounds.
Counting the attempts that the sun makes as it emerges,
counting the chimneys and the smoke about to rise.
A dim light leads the way.
Thru a crowd of countless deaths your face emerges
a map
moving and charting the rain across this glass

Firm branches dip the blue, blue lips from the cold

DREAMING OVER A PAGE

This field they've contracted
us to separate from its surroundings
I've stayed in bed watching as the
moon above it turns
its globes of earth with spit on every glacier
into landmarks hostile to language
spoken by tyrants
someone is looking over your shoulder as
you write in bed the window
holds a page of commentaries you guide
this pearl into the horizon then close your eyes

Simply filled with love their power
to be crass
you find yourself heading away from the park
down a path she is in the throes
of executing another assignment
the way it occurs and the publicity surrounding it
you think the glass burrows in
the sidewalk and are sued
by the feelings that pass at great speed
a prude's entrance in the bar using
the language of the normal
spirit that the excellence of her modesty awards

Blocked by this person
we are heavier than grains locked
in a pearl stretched on rollers
tinting the sidewalk the laced boot

walks on scratching it out like the tip of a heel
among bruises from which you smile
the pathos culled remains linear
in its singlemindedness rebels and pushes
the curls aside
with the brute strength from her forehead
when she is too gentle not to adorn herself she
stares downward and the even cracks
of the restroom she prepares to enter

HALLOWEEN 1967

The alarm rings: it's 2 PM. I get up, dress and go
downstairs to buy the Post. It's Halloween. Call the typewriter
repair shop and learn that it will cost $25 to have my typewriter
repaired. Read a few chapters from *A Confederate General from
Big Sur*. Anne returns. I go out, take some packages to the Post
Office on 14th Street. Then I go to the library around the corner.
I get a new library card but there are no books I want to take out.
Take more packages to the P.O. on 4th avenue. Return home; it's
almost dark out. Anne comes home. Peter comes by. We talk about
Peter Viereck who is going to read at St. Marks. Anne cooks dinner.
Peter leaves. At about 7 o'clock Ted arrives. He & Anne go to the
church. I re-write part of an old poem on Anne's typewriter. At
about 9 o'clock I go to the church to the reading which started
at 8:30. Meet Shelly at the door to the church. She's going to a big
Halloween party at the Village Theatre. Reading has not yet started.
There aren't many people there: Anne & Ted & Larry & Peter. After
the first set I leave. It's Halloween. Kids are running through
the street asking people for money. In front of Gem Spa I meet
Katie & Debbie & their kids. There are 3 cops on the corner. We
all go upstairs. I give the kids all the Halloween candy which
Anne brought home during the day. Also, I give Katie "Big Lew,"
the robot Larry bought on Ave. C. Just as they're leaving Larry
arrives. Also, Shelly. Larry just found an apt. on 86th Street.
Sandy calls. She's coming over with David & Kate. Katie, Debbie
& the kids leave. Sandy arrives. Shelly leaves to return to the
Halloween party at the Village Theatre. Jim calls. Anne & Ted
arrive, home from the reading. David falls asleep in my arms on
the couch. Shelly returns. The party is obviously dragging. Jim
arrives. He needs to use Anne's typewriter to type poems. Wren
comes. Ted, Sandy & the kids leave. Anne cooks me a hamburger.
Shelly leaves, Wren leaves. Jim is still typing. Ron & Pat arrive. Larry

has disappeared somewhere. Ron & Pat leave. Jim & I go downstairs to Gem Spa to get ice cream. Jim buys a copy of the new *Downbeat*. Anne makes us ice cream sodas. Lee and a friend of his named Jeff arrive. Jim begins falling asleep. I explain reasons why he can't sleep over on couch. He calls his girlfriend and secures a place to stay. Lee & Jeff leave. Jeff says he will call tomorrow to show us his poems. We discuss everything & everybody with Jim. Ted arrives. He has a copy of *The Sonnets* which neither Anne nor Jim has seen. Jim leaves. I read the newspaper, Ted speed-reads *Freewheelin' Frank*, Anne reads *The Sonnets*. Then Ted leaves.

GIANT NIGHT

Awake in a giant night
is where I am

There is a river where my soul,
hungry as a horse drinks beside me

An hour of immense possibility flies by
and I do nothing but sit in the present
which keeps changing moment to moment

How can I tell you my mind is a blanket?

It is an amazing story you won't believe
and a beautiful land
where something is always doing in the barns
especially in autumn

Sliding down the hayrick

By March the sun is lingering and the land turns wet

Brooks grow loud
The eddies fill with green scum
Crocuses lift their heads to say hello

Soon it is good to be planting
By then the woods are overflowing
with dogwood, red bud, hickory, red and white oaks,
hazelnut bushes, violets, jacks-in-the-pulpits,
skunk cabbages, pawpaws and May apples
whose names thrill you because you can name them

There are quail and rabbits too—but I go on too long

Like the animal, I must stop by the water's edge
to have a drink and think things over

*

That was good. The drink I mean

I feel refreshed and ready for anything

Though I'm not in Vermont or Kentucky unfortunately
but in New York City, the toughest place in the world

And it's December

Here someone is always weeping, including me
though I tend to cry in monster waves then turn into a fish
wallowing in my own salty

                                Puddle! Look out
If you aren't wearing boots you'll be sorry
and soggy too

*

This season's cruelty hurts me
and others, I'm sure, who'd rather be elsewhere but can't
because of their jobs, families, friends, money

It's rough anyway you look at it

I look at you looking at it and I say "rough"
You weep too and drown the rug
The only one we have, in fact

But what can you do?

It's worse elsewhere, I'm sure

Take Viet Nam

No thanks

I think about Viet Nam a lot, however
and wonder if I'll ever "see" it
The way I've seen Europe, I mean:

Those pretty Dutch girls
They all ride bicycles

In Venice you travel by boat or foot

The metro and the underground register like the names
in connection with them:

Hugo, Stephen, Stuart, Larry, Lee, Harry, David, Maxine

What does it all mean?

I never ask that, being shy

In this apartment in which I dwell these thoughts pass by

I hope you won't mind the mess when you do too

*

You just walk in up a flight and you're in paradise

A cup of coffee, an easy chair, a loving person waiting for you
who's washing the dishes, reading a book

Outside someone's worrying about love and not sitting down either

He's probably freezing his ass off right now!
And other vital parts which would feel great in the country,
taking a walk, a hike, shoveling snow

Though you can do that right here

*

The hub of the universe is where I am in a night whose promise
grows with me, unlike the snow melting in the gutter

Whatever I do, it is beside me

I look out the window, there is night
I sit in this lighted room knowing this night
Night! Night! I wish you'd go so I could go
to the post office, the bank, the supermarket

Why aren't they open at night? I wonder
Then realize I'm not the only person who's
considered in the grand scope of daily living

There are those fast asleep who want to be and would be horrified
if the post office, the bank, and the supermarket
were only open at night
for you can't be all there all the time

I myself am only here part of the time
which is enough

        For there are other places to run to

Uptown, for example, where energy rushes you
like some hideous but intriguing chemical
you can't ignore
and you want to absorb the wisdom these buildings have

How do they feel so high up like that?

Pretty good, they seem to say in their absolute way
But it's the people inside who turn us on

By then you are gone off in a cab
and you are not alone

        I am beside you

The streets are familiar from just travelling through
We rarely stop and when we do there's a reason

Which is too bad
We miss a lot for this same reason

*

They're probably feeding the chickens about this time
the smell of chicken feed overwhelms me
The rooster crows on a 7th Street fire escape
Breakfast is waffles

        There is a forest by the river near the barn
where things are happening,
a whole new world on the edge of dawn

*

My little world goes on St. Marks Place

To be not tired, but elated, I sing this song

I think of the Beatles and the Beach Boys
and the songs they sing

It is a different thing to be behind the sound
then leave it forever
and it goes on without them, needing only you and me

Here I am, though you are asleep

The morning of December 3, 1967 dawns on me
in the shape of a poem called "Giant Light"

It must end before it is too late

All over the world children will celebrate Christmas
And families will gather together to give and take this season

Other religions and customs will prevail in their own separate
                                                        ways
having nothing to do with Christmas

Soldiers will cease fire

Some won't know the difference but might be able to sense it
in the air

The smell of holly, pine, eggnog
The friendly faces of Santa and his elves

All these will add up to something and be gone forever

Just like what is here one minute and not the next.

SONNET

SONNET

Five a.m. on East Fourteenth I'm out to eat
The holiday littered city by my feet a jewel
In the mire of the night waits for the light
Getting and spending and day's taxi cry   The playful

Waves of the East River move toward their date
With eternity down the street, the slate sky
In Tompkins Square Park prepares for the break
Through of lean horses of morning I

Move˙ through these streets like a lamplighter
Touch ragged faces with laughter by my knowledge
Of tragic color on a pavement at the edge
Of the city   Softly in the deep East River water

Of dreams in which my long hair flows
Slow waves move   Of my beginnings, pauses

TOM CLARK

50 copies published on the occasion of Tom
Clark's birthday, March 1, 1968, by Angel Hair

BUN

Hello. May I be alive in your dream of unconsciousness?

Would you like to hear my life?

                                    Get down

          on your hands and knees

                                              and toes

                         and *Starry Night*

     and crawl through the grass with me

Please to let the chirps
to drop to where the May
wind can blow them back
away into your mind-head

Wait a minute

weeds are so healthy

instead of destroying them

we should make them grow something

good to eat

God is

screaming at me

He was first recorded

in March, 1929

I am elevating a landscape sandwich

It's called *Déjeuner sur l'herbe*

If it's because of you

I find the stream refreshing   cool

It's because the stream is you

                                                                              oops

forgot the moon

up there

in the sky

like a giant statue of Don Mossi

Others   statues of you   me

Go   by

A statue of Santa Claus   goes by at Christmas

And this is good

Matisse

Unlike you

We live in a turnip

Trembling

      A lad lowers his shoulder holster

    into the beer garden

                    which has a tuft of beer plants

growing

and Beethoven paints it all in one chromatic note

Will we, in twenty years,
Look down at these pages
And ejaculate?

                          Smuh!

God get out of here

And he runs off chirping and chuckling into his handbag

What's happening here
            is that the brain tissue is momentarily

a noodle

Your mind is pretty

It would probably be interesting to you

To eat a potato chip of tin

I'd like to buy a house for your mind   white curtains

                    I've always loved pink

I'm pressing a button   Fragonard

                    I'll get up before you're awake

Penis-chintz

                                                change diapers

Moon!

When I look at your face
flying through space
a question comes to mind
Will I ever see your behind?

a mule's brain

cloudy   dangerous

The wart that is your behind
Kills a bystander
Who attempts to admire it

Why must we write with the fear that our private parts are going to be bitten by growling monsters?

We live in perpetual warm and tender love and pain

Wayne, you eat du food
Et moi, je mange d'merde
On dit que je suis un mange-merde

My hairs are long and hard
Quand on dit "Korea"   j'ai froid

dans ce pays

je suis Mort, le janitor

tout est OK

But

When I say "I love you   "

God is talking

to himself

in language the police would understand

Larry Fagin

from THE PARADE OF THE CATERPILLARS

NEW YORK

The radiator came on & the geraniums died.
Finally throwing up all the arms on the page,
They came down in bangs, spilling mucilage
& some ink. Someone. I was careful to move
                                 a muscle...
I thought I witnessed an assist
From it. In &/or Out of the Blue, Not
A cloud. A huge network of dots got
Connected, wd prove ghostly.
Nor swan nor clown, but machinery
For lowering or raising heavenly objects.
When I rushed to pull the shade, the sky-
Writers wrote Yanks 5, Reds 3,
Across the page & would-be face. Then my ears
Burned & I cheered, remembering what name
                                 & team

HELLO AGAIN
for Lewis Warsh

I like your thin nose
As it appears on this paper.
I like mine, too,
An intelligent and truthful copy.
I liked being with you yesterday.
The ring around the city got pretty blue.
You smoke a lot
But suddenly and dramatically.
Your wife is terrific.
She is so pretty.
I like the way she drinks her coffee.
Let's get together again real soon.
We're better than anyone else in town.

OCCASIONAL POEM

Tom Clark and I went out to Greenwich
And spread our lunch on Greenwich Green.
There were ham and cheese sandwiches, peanut
Butter and jelly sandwiches, 1/2 lb. potato
Salad, sweet and sour pickles, two cans
Of black cherry soda, and some crumb cake
My mother baked. After lunch and cigarettes
We played catch with a red rubber ball, which
Neither of us dropped, on Greenwich Green.
It was a splendid day! The hot sun was killing
All the germs on everybody's faces, and kids
And their nannies raced around like nobody's
Business. Then, Tom and I went off to see
The Queen's House and, in the Maritime
Museum, under a microscope, the smallest
Cannon in the world. We wondered how
They ever managed to put it together. Yeah.

Toward the end of the day we went to have
A coke in a small cafe nearby. Tom seemed
Depressed so I told a joke to cheer him up.
(Earlier, I had complained of one of my
Famous stomach aches. Go to the bathroom,
Tom suggested. I did and felt lots better.)
The sun was going down. We took a bus to town.
Tom caught his train and I, I caught mine.

When I got home I ate a good turkey dinner
With blueberry pie a la mode for dessert.
I watched a little TV, read for a while
In bed, and had a nice cup of hot cocoa
With a few chocolate-chip cookies. Then I
Turned out the light and had this terrible dream.

WOMEN

I'd like to remove one thing
from my sublime life
the awful weakness
of my nervousness.
Nothing satisfies me anymore.
Women know this.

VALENTINE'S DAY

Reading Tom's poem "To Winter"
weather goes up to 24
though there's no soap
I have a cry in my eye
it's $45 to fly
to a land that's hot and dry
Amsterdam Avenue iced over
Inside Joan sews a purple heart
for John who will read his poem
"Purple Heart" tonight Joan
will wear a purple hat

LOVE

Everything is out today
and plausible.   Pay attention

to us   humdingers
fading fast   your signal

spring.   That you are like
me, a baby bush, confuses

no one, which is they say why
we can work it out   (or else)

Elsie in a field knows why.
The doctor knows.

Let's don't roll on this grass
grass, grass, grass, grass.

It isn't France or even us
a whole tote bag of notions

take wind, memorabilia, the
outstretched arms of the red

and the blue biplanes.   Love
in a nervy way, like lightning

nuzzles the chattering tree party
and the sky looks like shantung

to me, and gooey and wavy.

Clark Coolidge

from ING

NOTHING at NEWBEGINS

      1.

1963 in
became poem

with the
that you
with as
way was

the $4.95

word
and
times

4 cents a
the single

      2.

he of fully
tion

          or:

          or:

spoken
zines, does
        it does

out of is
the best in it

the is it is the

on the
of his
they're out

    3.

structure guage

that course
than sort

does not

Young gerous
same

what to
and
of
for
 a

   65

it lot
has of his
the called own

  slim.

really an deal of Yes

said does
thinks said

  Sidney

going to
with no

He

and
Stop

    4.

Why. I've.

AD

    unless is too blade
    subject in
    sail these me the of
    question on
    dogbrick looped
    part that
    innate that afterward
    to put to
    word same azure
    are miles

    banked if lengthens
    through were way
    fool to
    good that to who
    age the
    what a

    about at a and of
    the it was want that
    in the gave up
    time nine
    on be with own

    one nor bin
    short that
    all and they or her with
    vitamin an ice
    from can't soap
    don't
    many are is that
    the letter

bet
point am this it
on dawn low
signs the ever
great now those
den chockablock

too pour sit
fin big ones
red small to be
the my that
rob
corn twin which

barn again meter
all pace that soon
effect bob
toast smith
van elastic
ray

figure little then the
and a was airlock
that any just do so
back to the but there
when however or not he that
did that not
buyer

horn on
this deep for its has
a nine on the 8
is as is
natural a made thin
in are the when
do not in quiet
grounds on the and at
pent

dwindler
open lower loop must leads loop
spire but were first
many who do wish are not
pine date

the glass of
matisse pound
miles a mile
plain and

one on the turned it
under in to often
bland bound off
more or with the more
shown one wonders
tepid
X

kind noon
with to the a graph
this on an a
climb sewing note
kipper out the more group
three key as little
from had as sink
next very pit
loosen ounce
in

true a vast
a man is than made
that are too alibis
of things are book
water order close
to saw points

use of taken by up
would and might and gave and the
can car and
ages it to some out
where and in seem makes
diffusion denied diagram
block part for but

uses acts use two just
when since
there and an may are
path as it
don

in a by 3
of not were
too or lights
a very same once and for
all none
at without it

hundreds
back front
taking and and making
in our with
in our know

pro
onion ought
ken

her for might everyone
the one
one the with hair
the walks there
it none
ban it's night

stand as camel
brother out which times
the excellently
or itself
bomb dip and new
stage came this

boxes
5 on the be 5
spot in uncut
I course
that ring I

a whole from a his
could this had air
nine
joined it a to thin

down in which and that

but
sic
of

have as some next
and around

then ever
in when years
red

but
in tell say

in a to
pieces

to on the been

the to cause line
in the knock
want

organizations

about said
it in even
on the off

about then been

on out
and rate

first by very
there

and
and their
soon

but a on out
and are

domes

in the
in a
as

we parts
lows

him but the
way were
I

so

as a
and quite
at the
down

arrowhead
so

name huge
he

way
sticks
a of
a one

are set
tore been
truth

more
house

the are then
tone

whom
whereof there
clam

ban
   out
been

diamond

a of one the
or act
dam
in
noun all

parenthesis

pond   in
when   on
no

to a a while
let's the I
to a

said
takes
group

things doors
for the

lets the
to a
an

bring

that be
the whys

at 'n'
he two

the was
those let's

of about
me on

out to but
truce

it to
do I

nine
was was
a

a way the
the to and

five with
about into

nonce

for if or

disc

if a
waits

do

the
and
went

of
on
A.M.

the with on
were

on
the above

do
was
of it

down

ought

mean

it a then of

month

well to

of to no
there

made been

tone

of an enough

belts in

noun of

across above

   all it at

in with our
in know our

     ought

to on
to
  of

the to a
an on a

  an

too fin

   of about a at and
   that the was it want

        nine

want an

have and them
  but in

    nine dime

   their and
   and soon

to been on the
but out a on

   noun

the
ample
rials

diacy

them
tions.

pler
fication
a

and a
portion

plane by
ity

bland

in logical
their
the
their

tion
inertia
ity

be having
eight

priate
via

iny

flatting

im
dense

in ness

ber

esting

ciple

ture

ent

tive

a ture
the ing

tions

erything

eral

stantly

ined

ards

cal

nize

Anne Waldman

from O MY LIFE!

HOW THE SESTINA (YAWN) WORKS

I opened this poem with a yawn
thinking how tired I am of revolution
the way it's presented on television
isn't exactly poetry
You could use some more methedrine
if you ask me personally

People should be treated personally
there's another yawn
here's some more methedrine
Thanks   Now about this revolution
What do you think? What is poetry?
Is it like television?

Now I get up and turn off the television
Whew! It was getting to me personally
I think it is like poetry
Yawn   it's 4 AM   yawn   yawn
This new record is one big revolution
if you were listening you'd understand methedrine

isn't the greatest drug no not methedrine
it's no fun for watching television
You want to jump up have a revolution
about something that affects you personally
When you're busy and involved you never yawn
it's more like feeling, like energy, like poetry

I really like to write poetry
it's more fun than grass, acid, THC, methedrine
If I can't write I start to yawn
and it's time to sit back, watch television
see what's happening to me personally:
war, strike, starvation, revolution

This is a sample of my own revolution
taking the easy way out of poetry
I want it to hit you all personally

like a shot of extra-strong methedrine
so you'll become your own television
Become your own yawn!

O giant yawn, violent revolution
silent television, beautiful poetry
most deadly methedrine
                I choose all of you for my poem personally

* * * * * * * * * * * * *

JAPANESE GEMS

* * * * * * * * * * * * *

For You

Waiting for you
In the rain failing
on my head
I got wet
from the rain falling on my head

                after Prince Otsu

    *

For Her Lover

Waiting for me
You got wet in the rain
falling on your head
O that I could
Be that rain f alling
on your head

                after Lady Ishikawa

THE AFTER-LIFE

for Joe Brainard

Life on this earth as I know it is incredibly difficult and depressing a great deal of the time. When I get up some mornings I just go back to bed and moan. I cannot face another day of this, I say to myself. I feel a funny tense sensation in my legs and arms and a pounding in my head. I try to relax. Or I start to do things like I get up again.

And I really have no cause to suffer compared to some people. I am a healthy, normal American girl. I have had many of the advantages life can offer and many of the worthwhile experiences. A loving family. A college education. Travel. People tell me I am pretty, intelligent and talented. I have a job. I have a husband who is extremely patient with me. We live in an apartment in a large exciting metropolis. We always have enough to eat. We have a telephone. A record player. A radio. Two cats. And many wonderful books. Lately, many of our appliances are breaking down like our TV just suddenly went dead yesterday. But I don't really care. These are just material goods. They don't make me ecstatically happy.

Poetry makes me happy. And people. And paintings. And movies. And music. And sex. And getting high. They all remind me of the "after-life". If it weren't for these things, I'd have called it quits a long time ago.

What is the "after-life"? you ask and all I can say is it's not here, that's for sure.

In the after-life you do not moan and groan. No part of you aches. You love everything. There are no creepy politicians or policemen hanging around. Your whole being is blended into everything else. You don't have to eat or sleep or get up in the morning or look at the clock or take pills. You know a lot. You move around a lot. You understand what it's all about and feel terrific.

PAUL ELUARD

I have been reading about Paul Eluard tonight.

Did you know he was very large?

Large body, large forehead, large nose.

But not large as a cloud, large as a cloud of smoke.

Large as what, then?

Large as himself.

He was a man irrigated with blood
and turned pink after every meal.

Above greying eyebrows, he had a fine space of forehead
right on up to his hair which is brushed straight back

(Neither too long, nor too short.)

He wore hats.

He smoked enormously.

He suffered with those who suffer.

(Poets who have suffered are
Lorca, Saint-Pol Roux, Max Jacob, Paul Desnos.)

He did not move without his universe.

He had no money, no papers, no address but
walls covered with Picasso, Miro, Max Ernst, Leger
and original editions which he caressed with his fingertips.

He lived on love, cold water, and poetry.

DISPERSAL OF IT

a stiff west wind blows another cloud of tear gas

onto the busy night

Whosh

then lifts her head and splits back into the silence from
which he came

turning the shadow of death into morning

strange, and stranger than that even

you don't recognize him
you can't see anything in fact!
your chin is on your chest

is it really any wonder?

So, what do you do with your failing vision?

it's warming up the air, so hazy & sunny now

may as well go outside & get some

okay?

Well, okay?

see what everyone is doing

& it just so happens

what they are doing is this

no this

honestly, this

All of em dancing in the bloody streets!

Unbelievable!

you cry

but take a look at this...

you pick up the book lying there

surely there's more proof than this of life on other worlds?

She goes into the other room.
Larry looks up.

The police approach it all so stupidly, those mad mothers

But *it* all is *you* all, so be careful

but if & when this happens

Flares will light our route and

take us safely through the park

* * * *

gonna change my life

RISE & SHINE

"bring, bring"

6 AM

bring bring

```
*            *
    SICK
*            *
```

Almost everyone I know is sick, including me. It
makes me sick to think about it. We all have enough problems
in life without getting sick.

Today I woke up and was sick.

I called up Katie who was sick.

I spoke to Sandy whose husband is sick.

Larry came by and said he was sick.

Tom called and is sick.

He told me "Jim is sick."

A while back, Edwin was sick.

I heard that Ron is sick.

Another Ron across the street is sick.

Martha left here healthy as a puppy, went home and got sick.

Lewis was feeling sick.

Kenward left the reading because he was sick.

Vito said lately he'd been awfully sick.

We saw George up and around but he was secretly sick.

And there are others, I'm sure, just as sick.

If you want to be on my sick list, just get sick.

* * * *

John Wieners

from ASYLUM POEMS
(FOR MY FATHER)

HIGH NOON

15 years of loving
men, women and children
with what result

Another silver Iseult
joins svelte Tristan
in a vault of tears

under what insult
account with drawn
on sorrow's bank

to sit up straight
at a stranger's voice
while he whispers miles away,

over the ocean at Cornwall
Brest, Dieppe land of melancholy
how surely these years wash away.

Gold Iseult comes to tarnish
Sylvan Tristan speeds in a white Falconetti
nude under afternoon sun

one dark haired lover on his mind
a man, not a woman inspires generations ahead
before dead legions arise

6.20.69

AFTER SYMOND'S *VENICE*
for Allen Ginsberg

Boston, sooty in memory, alive with a
thousand murky dreams of adolescence
still calls to youth; the wide streets, chimney tops over

Charles River's broad sweep to seahood buoy; the harbor
With dreams, too: *The Newport News has arrived for a week's stay*
Allen, on Summer Street sailors yet stride along summer afternoons

and the gossamer twilights on Boston Common, and Arlington Street
adrift in the mind, beside the mighty facade of convent and charnel house,
who go through those doors, up from Beacon Street, past the marooned
                                        sunset in the
West, behind Beacon Hill's shabby haunts of artists
and the new Government Center, supplanting Scollay Square.

Who replace the all night films, and the Boston dawn
in the South End, newly washed pavements by night's horses.

What happens here from the windows on Columbus Avenue
to Copley Square and the library, Renaissance model, the Hotel
                                     and smart shops down
Newbury Streets lit boutique, lept by Emerson College,
who triumph light over dark, the water side
endures beside the moon and stars of Cambridge's towers

....by Park Square pavements so wide for the browser, drifters
from Northampton Street behind the Statler, by the bus stations and
                                   slum tableaux
Finally to return to the Gardens, and the statue of George Washington
appealing to later-day shoppers to go home, in what dusk
what drunken reveling matches this reverie
of souvenirs, abandoned in the horror of public elevators

as this city is contained time, and time again the State House
from Bullfinch's pen, over School Street and Broad
        down the slope of Tremont mirages over blue grass
to the waterfront; Athaeneum holding all the books of men, directed
against the foe, hapless Pierre churns past the Parker House
               coming to the Vendome mentally
over the Brunswick, eternal in the mind's owl
             of phantoms stretching from boyhood.

When vows first established were to see this world and part
                all within it
You, Boston, were the first, as later San Francisco, and before that
New York, the South and West
penetrated, hard holds the Northwest, Chicago, Detroit
much in the same manner of industrial complexes
covering the rising cigarettes of patriots.

The Park Street Steeple as painted by Arshile Gorky zooms higher.
Slumbering city, what makes men think you sleep,
but breathe, what chants or paeons needed at this end, except
you stand as first town, first bank of hopes, first envisioned paradise
by the tulips in the Public gargoyle's crotch, Haymarket
Square included spartan business enterprise and
next to South Station, the Essex evoking
    the metropolitan arena hopes entertain.

August 25, 1969

MORGANA LA FAY

The return of
again is it
love we look, not
nearly so, only

the absolute inde-
prudence of youth, in
expectation, despite
Charles Dickens.

The first time going to the museum
alone, on to the library
walking Newbury Street after
the rain, and dining out,

visiting New York City on the late evening
train. These things she thought
as the rain pelted the
trees on Long Island during the day,

and thought of F. Scott
Fitzgerald, how he lived still
and his Long Island, always the place
to return, trembling alone

his and Zelda's Babylon
at Christmas, now living in a motel, this evocation
contained in the embrace of phantom love and
to slip a peg, Lester Young on Times Square.

6.19.69

JUST AN ORDINARY JOE

with plain face and wrinkled forehead
superabundant in his plaints and desire,
loving one with great passion,

now on guardian's gate, forlorn, fertile,
and fruitful, the little doll, how he could love
her, *so my arms ache to talk of it, the reason*

why I stay away, alone in money's prison.
The heiress' call unheard except by an impossible
man who could help her, locked interruption to

funds, social register, impotent in battle.
A true Beckett of passion brooding o'er psyche.
How to decipher their distress thus accomplish plot.

Of ancient rich girl aiding tarnished knight *en armour*.

6.30.69

Bill Berkson

from SHINING LEAVES

NON DIMENTICAR

A breeze.
At sea.
Raindrops.
Striped cloth.
Strands of hair.
Salt.
Watch dial.
Slat of sunlight on metal at dial's edge.
Dune.
Wet pebble.
Driftwood.
Small feet run in sand.
Footprints.
Surf-sound.
A ship.
Another ship.
A boat, small craft.
Light from the boat.
Girl's face.
Smile.
Girl waves.

PERFECT WORK

Let's say I give this everything I've got.

what would I have left?

Why, if I followed through on such a promise,
I might end up the cause of my own death!

who would want to be as silly as that?

Or, say, at least, not that, but that I'd be to some extent
maimed for life.

Life, my love, is that something I would want to do to you?

And Death, is that the way I would want to meet you, either?

Let's not be foolish:
A man sets out to do something. It could be anything.
He takes a bath.
That man loves his bath. He takes one everyday, sometimes
twice a day, somedays he even thinks of spending the entire day
in the bathtub — Oh, it would be nice!

He gives himself utterly to that bath.

This man does not want simply to get clean, though that is a consideration:
He could take a shower and get even cleaner! He could take a steam bath
or a sauna to purify his pores. He could even, though it might mean
travelling a great distance, go to a spa and take the waters, that is, drink
and soak himself in some extremely health-giving fluid, which contains
sulfur or some other chemical compound or, at any rate, not the flourides
and rust often found in his home-town water, the sometimes poisonous stuff
in which he daily bathes. No matter! He is a bath addict.

Behind locked doors, he and other addicts in other rooms prepare and
take their fixes, with or without the slightest sense of illegality, or of
perhaps forbidden thrill.

(In childhood, this might be otherwise. The introduction to bathing of the
infant by the parent might result in screaming, and the infant, in his fear
of this procedure to which the parent-adult is already firmly addicted,
might try to devise ways of avoiding the sometimes all-too-regular
inundation. But, with the years, as far as these old folks are concerned,
he learns. He goes his own way to his bath, no longer having to be
picked-up, dumped, poked and pushed about and splashed upon, no more
that same foam in the terror stricken eyes, no more of this rape,
including the whole business of being the only naked person in a room,
and a very small room at that!)

Shamelessly then, and disturbed, with only the half-hearted purpose
of getting as clean as he can, this man takes his own bath. Without
thinking too much about it, he wants and so pursues the feeling that his
bath affords. Bathing: the man and his bath, a relationship, a simultaneity,
and eventually, a singularity.

He moves *in* the water? No, the *bathing* moves. This is the sheer joy
of it.

The bathing includes: bath, the bath that has been run (we shall leave out whomever ran it, or say the man is a bachelor and not particularly affluent and so he runs his bath himself), the bath water, and its location in the bathtub in the bathroom (where all is in constant readiness); then, bath soap, bath sponge (or some cloth that's used in the bath), bath oil (or bath salt, whichever or both), perhaps a bathbrush or "backbrush" so-called, which, during bathing, allows for the thorough bathing of hard-to-get-at parts...

As for the bath mat, bath towel, and bathrobe they come later, as does the after-bath cream or lotion (rightly called "friction" by the French).

And then, of course, the man: the bathing man is a Bath Man.

He turns to the right, having entered from the left, his left arm crossing over, hand extended to get the soap, the size of a miniature football (some souvenir?) or brick. As he turns, so does the bathing...this is a faulty description, because there is, in fact no turning man "and" turning bathing but only, then, the turning bathing (though not necessarily in the same direction turning), of which this man is a part.

He turns back — same thing again.

Now the bathing is complete and gets completer as it goes. Turns and counterturns and leanings to and fro, front and back. (perhaps this bathing man is a singer too, and he sings in his tub — much perhaps again as his parent-adult sang as she bathed him in order to quiet him in his anxiety and terror — but probably he sings a much more raucous song, or one, at any rate, that few infants would understand — a song like "Anchors Aweigh" maybe or "Going to Kansas City" or "Melancholy Baby", a song then of adventure or love or both.) Now he is really taking his bath!

An easy give-and-take, you say? Yes, insofar as the man can be said to be "bathed" when bathing is completest. But this isn't yet the case.

Now, the man, you agreed, gives himself utterly to this bath, so it is that he is truly bathing. But mightn't you ask what it is he's thinking, and, given the thinking, what, more precisely, it is he's feeling? That, of course, we cannot know, because this is only an imaginary man who's come on the scene only to satisfy our desire for knowledge of what it is he's doing. But if I were that man, or if you were, and puzzled and distraught by thoughts of life and death (to which the song he sings might, however in-directly, still relate), and puzzled and distraught by such thoughts while bathing,

would either of us, lost in the bathos of our self-concern, think to
give himself to such complete conclusion as to combine his thinking and
his bathing (again utterly) and ever so completely drown?

THE BICYCLE THIEF

I go see *The Bicycle Thief*,
a long movie directed by Vittorio de Sica
in which Alfredo Ricci's bike is stolen —
he can't work without his bike — and he
and his son go looking for it.
They look everywhere. They stand in the rain, waiting.
(There are some German monks standing waiting in the rain too.
Alfredo's wife consults a seer, La Santona, and Ricci
goes himself to see her later; to him she says:
"Either you find your bike now or you will never find it."
He gives her money and leaves.
He finds the thief after chasing an old man.
(The old man will not tell Alfredo anything, but
he does: The thief lives on the Via Valpolicella.)
The thief denies he is the thief.
His friends deny it too, as does his mother
who says: "He's a good boy; his record is clean."
He claims he was not in the "Florida." He has
an epileptic fit, for which his mother has
brought him a pillow. A policeman
insures Alfredo he might as well forget it, he
has no witnesses. Alfredo starts to swing
a piece of wood at the thief's companions but
walks away disgruntled. He and his son
go to eat. He thinks about stealing a bike, but
the man doesn't press charges when he gets it back.
His son is crying.
Alfredo is the Bicycle Thief.
They turn their backs to the cameras.
The picture gets dimmer. The End.
With Margot Margolis.

"BLUE IS THE HERO. . .

leading with his chin, though bristling
with military honor, camp and *ora pro nobis*, rolling out
the red carpet of chance on a plea
that you might give others a front-row seat:
Lady, take off your hat. So extra special. . .
Other times, it would be a roof-garden
like the one Rauschenberg has,
being no Nebuchadnezzar of the bush,
or, standing on your head,
feeling the earth has "hung" a lawn
and these dogs have come to bite you "where it hurts" —
I wonder if they've really caught the scent,
which is a poor memory in our Symbolist ears
of what it must have been like to read *The Hound*
of the Baskervilles for the first time in 1899
oh truly modern and amused and wrong,
before the world, before the cold
and the dry vermouth and everybody started
wearing sweaters, taking pills. I confess
to a certain yearning in my genes for those trips,
tonics of the drawn shade and rumpled bed,
the Albergo delle Palme in Palermo, instead
of hanging on the curb, learning to love each
latest gem "fantastic!" as the lights go out all over the
Flatiron Building, which leaves the moon, sufficiently
fa so la, and the clouds
disentangle a perfect Mondrian, pure gray,
to which you give nodding assent, somewhat true—
you are that helicopter, primping for the climb
into whose bed of historical certainty? the fuel
streaming down the sides, like fun in the sun, air in the air.

from SLIP OF THE TONGUE

Finger Paintings

Blue hairs suddenly grew in between the last sentences.
Some were as wide as exclamations ! Meanwhile every known source
of sleep was giving great pleasure to Black River boys. They
spent days in the air trying to mix new colors for their dead.
They had used blue too often....

Up until now the Fingers were like indestructible pipes
connected to hinges and going from door to door. They secretly
controlled most hands and fingers, eagles, sometimes barrels
floating on water, snakes, and Black River boys. They especially
liked to occupy distances stretching from the day before yes-
terday. For sixty years their hands rested on any small strength
that might appear to be an illumination.

Instead of having ideals or beliefs they converted irrigation
into dry sleeves every ten years. Now their bones have
melted off. They tie their thoughts together into interesting
moments and bury them in bundles of paper. Sound as absolute
as sleep, complete control, and hate open up their heads. Then
they can put words into their hands, and touch their wrists with
any part of their bodies...

The river banks curved back slightly into both forests.
Black River cracks every fifteen years and returns to uninhabited
battleground with water stains. That saved Tonarm and Vellun
for the moment....

Long ago Black River boys could easily defend copper,
silver, and ivory. They build thick walls and nailed them be-
tween every tree, They didn't like to travel much. Then some
Black River boys, who didn't have strong teeth, began to keep
secrets in hooks. They pretended they could read, and they
would smile all the time.

Art was established, and everyone rowed around the hills
in painted boats. This brought on starvation, and sometimes
Black River boys would look at each other like plums. They
unconsciously painted pictures on broken wheels. No one saw
these paintings except the Fingers.

Centuries of the Fingers had choked Black River. Threats riped into fruit and new thoughts were squeezed between door knobs. Every wall was divided into slots faintly resembling leather. Dishes, a right or left hand, and large, round buildings were the new signs of wealth. Knots, loops, and wedges were also admired. Ceilings assumed an altitude of watches.

Once during a long drought Black River boys went crazy. Anything like movement of collars jumped into hand-to-hand fighting. Everyone was burned up. Necks were broken, and long ugly arms were discovered a few feet away.

Black River boys began to whisper together when they covered their own flabby lips with buckskin boots. Chance fixed itself into their imagination like myth and then appeared on their shoulders. They started to look for someone else to kill besides each other. They threw rocks into the air and instinctively cut off their own fingers.

The Fingers hid under their many costumes. They examined the dirt under each other's nails, and hurried noiselessly through tunnels and caves. They were really afraid. But they ended Black River boy revolution by bringing in the Crawler.

The Crawler was a large chunk of beef. Sometimes it was called the Frog-Gun because no one knew how it opened its mouth. Red and blue worms followed it around. It ate up every Black River boy in sight. It admired any silk shirt which suggested new diseases and foreheads.

At first the Fingers loved it, but then farmlands began to vanish. Food became scarce. Blue lines were growing in the river. Black River boys might all disappear. Decay slightly different in height boarded up every nail. The Crawler stayed in Black River for a long time, then it left without anyone noticing it.

Examinations crowded together very quickly and were absorbed into salt. Hunger was arranged on forks in the road, and the Fingers inspected all the food. Hunters, who were looking for new sources of meat, found lines of smooth stones leading into Black River. No one could figure out why these lines were there.

Tonarm has callouses on his hands. He's exhausted, but there aren't any oval shapes locked inside his head. He wants to keep running until he comes to a clearing in the forest. Then he'll clear his throat, and his teeth won't seem so ridiculous.

Vellun's hungry, he hasn't had any breakfast. His hand hurts. He's beginning to see things like chairs and buildings running in and out of his mouth. He doesn't say anything to Tonarm. He wants to stop and rest.

Long hair isn't important to Black River boys anymore. They're slaves. Other arms have assumed startling bodies of water. They think they're going to fight a miniature army. Black River has been hammered into benches to avoid any precision. The Fingers have second thoughts, it might be a mistake, but they can change it later on.

Meanwhile they have other new buildings constructed. They pile all the lumber and nails behind worn-out couches. Black River boys are even allowed to paint. The Fingers want to have statues drifting between every room. The hallways will be circular. Numbers will be left on the edges, and the windows will be done in red leather

A few yards can puzzle the whole world. Comfort is one of the most important considerations. Music isn't necessary. There are too many ideas that can keep a man wide awake. He won't need sleep if his wounds are already open and cut into shirts.

In another minute Tonarm would've stopped breathing, but he sees this green chair. The road has evidently been dragged behind the chair. That's why it's rolling in a fit, so he has to follow it across his knees. He thinks all this might be helpful.

Vellun doesn't think so. All his theories have gone into his ear-drums. He's like a madman who rushes towards a copper statue. He hates gold dust, but he likes freshly killed meat in very large containers. What if a giant attacked him? He couldn't do anything, there's dirt under his nails. He hopes he'll get back home alive, and then his skin will be decorated with stories.

He sits cross-legged in the comfortable green chair and dreams....

CHICAGO

FREE SPEECH
for Eldridge Cleaver

Allegro!

Suddenly lifted out of the chair

by pulley

on the point of liquefaction

The brain experiences a slight electrical disturbance

which gets it up   Light!

and wanders into the Other

the Poetry Room

where I go thanks, this time, to the two Lewises

Lewis, did you know there are 2 of you?

Did you ever study mechanics   of the USA

on TV

at the U?

That's a joke

but I do neither   laugh or cry

turned off (momentarily)

for want of food

the home of Thomas Clark is a void filled with nourishment

so go

to your house and fill it with song, and eat quietly all day long

and fill your body and make it strong

inflation

"My body swole up like this

because I abused it"

—The Zodiac

Silver Pacific Ledge
out there
your codes are duplicated by the stars
no matter what goes down

GOING TO JAIL
to John Giorno

You were on your way out of the Monopoly game when all of a sudden zap!
we hope you land on your feet
on the ground

The Human Use of Human Beings

We send you cybernetics and the Rolling Stones and love
to steer you out of

the country
while we, in the country,
peer through the present into the future and see you

Alive

in whatever state this happens to find you
no more extraordinary than we are
I love you,
Alice

for the song *Wooden Ships*

There is no center of interest
because the center is everywhere
on the surface

you can't take it with you.

WHAT I'VE LEARNED IN MY TRAVELS
for Anselm Hollo

> how to fuck casually

with no big feelings

> tearing you apart

John Cage sat there weeping

> Duchamp waited for him to stop

> then he said
> > "it's OK,

> > you big crybaby!"

One or two dumb broads in every college town

> will let down their panty hose

> for Art   & they ought to

> but they are not for me

I seek the great tender moment

> & if broken in two

> > the time it takes to get to you

> your tears won't turn into more pennies

> > to put in the pig

> > > bank

> but Tender Buttons

TO JOHN ASHBERY

White is my favorite color
          when it comes to noise
      random signals of varying intensity: John
 it's
cold out. You are going
       uptown.
      If you were an Eskimo
            we'd invite you
        over for a frozen dinner.
The branches of the human tree stretch in a million directions
      if only you could make use of them.
But you are forbidden to touch them.
They are covered with ice, and make your fingers bleed.
        I liked your poems
     in the new *Paris Review* 47   & you're
          wearing sunglasses these days, &
          drinking lots of sodas
         cold
     because you're feeling tropical
You're doing a lot better than us.
    You think.
                Not dying.

A YEAR FROM MONDAY
for Andrei Codrescu

All wars are holy

Andrei

The other day I was reading *Dracula* and I thought of you

You and your wars

The spirit seethes at a bewildering triangle

but the base of all thought

is covered with lipstick

I sit in The Elephant   night passes   fang marks

The English poets pass their parkas
    & the Astros
        out under their dome

Wednesday already & I haven't had a single drink of blood

but toast you in the corner

when we recognize each other

O when will we recognize our true color

How long do I have to wait

ORANGES

1

Black crows in the burnt mauve grass, as intimate as
rotting rice, snot on a white linen field.

Picture to yourselves Tess amidst the thorny hay, her new-
born shredded by the ravenous cutter-bar, and there were only
probably vague lavender flowers blooming in the next field.

O pastures dotted with excremental discs, wheeling in
interplanetary green, your brown eyes stare down our innocence,
the brimstone odor of your stars sneers at our horoscope!

When she has thrown herself to the brook and you see her
floating by, the village Ophelia, recall that she loved none but
the everyday lotus, and slept with none but the bull on the hill.

Mercy, mercy, drown her, rain!

2

Is it the truth that she will finally conquer? that smiling
her gravel smile with those dark teeth rolling in their sockets,
bobbing brown corks in the thick pink sea-trough, she will de-
vour me? Shall my flesh, bitten and mangled by the years, fall,
a tired after-birth?

Pan, your flesh alone has escaped. Promise me, god of the
attainable and always perfecting fruit, when I lie, whether
hidden in livid moisture or exposed on gaudy ceramic to the
broiling dust, when my reclining bones have made a profound
pattern on the earth and, perverse chameleon, have embarrassed
mother-of-pearl with their modest chalk, you will sit in memory
of thought by my fragile skull and play into my rain-sweet
canals your notes of love!

3

What fire murmurs its seditions beneath the oaks,
lisping and stuttering to the shrivelled leaves?

I have lain here screaming for five days!

It is a real pleasure to shatter the supercilious
peace of these barked mammals.

I hear you! You speak French!

There is water flowing underneath. The rain is making
a river to wash my buttocks. My root takes to water, and
eddying the filth falls from me. There is a little pile of
excrement at my nape like a Japanese pillow.

O delicious rest!

4

O the changing dialects of our world! that we have
loved and known a week is seen one day to be a weed!

Once in bed we thrashed about; I knocked over the
flower vase and the hurricane lamp.

I was glad to hear them crash to the floor. Your lungs
had become a monotone.

Rain is coming through the roof. Drop and drop on my
spine. Paralytic. Let me get underneath.

Speak to me in Mandarin! Talk not of rice and rickshaw!

Thunder was in my ears as she placed the lotus in the
bud vase, the glass lipped round the stem tightly; he said, is
that right ?

Yes.

Ah! his face turned green, a briar wall: but autumn! The
leaves are dropping! The petals! he seized me. She was terrified.

The storm blew the window in. We all cried.

Cease playing harmonicas, you lizards!

5

Decide what you want of my heart most particularly, eagle, and take it. I defy you! Eat on.

Here on this pinnacle you have known what I lacked; and you have gone on eating. I owe you nothing— not even a sentimental tic.

See! where the bones of Bellini lie mossy under the bridge, and the blood of Isabella d'Este like a scarf thrown beneath them!

Bellini's hair thatches a puddle.

You, my centaur, bear me away with your talons and your hunger. Gods! you have chained me with airy fetters to perpetual flight! Mountainward the wind from the sea is the spume from your nostrils, centaur, the heavy slopes are your panting flanks! I struggle naked under your great eye!

Always the same landscape behind us: girls dropping dead in laundry yards, cripples sunning on the snow, the mangy cat crying, the tiny man at the factory pouring wine into his ear. All these lovers!

And for us always the same terrible mountain, our beautiful flesh and our loathing, to urge us on.

6

The light only reaches half way across the floor where we lie, your hair elaborated by my breath.

Your dolls grovel against you like suckling pigs.

As we roll these pebbles that we picked from the sand years ago I see your eyes grow green.

Hear how our lives were changed by the sea whispering from the shell.

I have ripped your dress! I shall now rip you up the middle and eat your seeds!

And now at last I know you. When we meet in the streets how painfully we shall blush! — but in the fields we shall lie down together inside a bush and play secretly.

We know each other better than anyone else in the world.

And we have discovered something to do.

7

As I waded through inky alfalfa the sun seemed empty, a counterfeit coin hung round the blue throat patched with leprosy.

Then in other fields I saw people walking dreamily in the black hay and golden cockleburs; from the firmament streamed the music of Orpheus! and on earth Pan made vivid the pink and white hunger of my senses!

Snakes twined about my limbs to cool them, and springs cold and light sucked my tongue; bees brushed sweat from my eyelids; clouds washed my skin; at the end of the day a horse squandered his love.

The sun replenishes, mirror and magnifier of my own beauty! and at night through dreams reminds me, moaning, of my daytime self.

8

Where is she ?

Thoughts, fabulous and eternal, lie unclaimed in my brain. My feet, tender with sight, wander the yellow grass in search of love.

Drought and famine, blossoming souls!

Once a lady asked for her milk to be changed to water; and
once a kindly priest scorched the earth with his piss. O gods
of the pagans!

Out of the blue grotto near the dried river I summon Pan,
god of our hearts. He bears summer heavy in his arms as a limp
virgin, her hair polishes his hooves, and white against his
sweaty skin her flesh sticks soft.

For you, Pan, are the fruits of the earth: rocks, mountains,
fountains, flagpoles, bear your seed! Companion of the beautiful,
questioner of the idle, disrupter of the sly, virtuous insemina-
tor, O beloved pimp of our hot flesh, roam throughout the world
seeking the salvation of souls!

He turns aside from the breathing limbs, Orpheus-over-the-
hills, to play his pipes.

Everyone! Everywhere! Dance!

9

The lily and the albatross form under your lids. Awaken,
love, and walk with me through the green fields. Under the mist
we need not fear the sound of wings or sneak of tangled roots;
the sun will lift. And until heat of day I'll not disturb the
grey pearls hanging on your flesh and hair.

Awaken, love, the horses are grazing at our flanks; the
gramophone is damp. I forgot to post your letter yesterday.
What shall we have for lunch?

Where you go, I go.

10

What furious and accepted monster is this? I receive and
venerate your ambition to die. We are all brothers. You do not
have tuberculosis. Kiss me.

And on Sunday— oh the rapture! Only the slightest and

meanest of women would stay in bed. You are the soul I never
have been and your soul is that of my half-sister, moth-eaten
and be-twigged. We must find ourselves before the dawn.

There beneath the pool, glassed like a pheasant, is the
soul of my first cousin. That is my soul. That one there.
Give it me!

Alice, said the Hare, you are a girl.

When I saw the light I came because I knew you'd need me.
I prayed that you'd come. I pray I'll get back safely. Oh.

Night, night with its sulphurous pulsations moans about me!
Where is the vision I summoned from yonder deity? Why was it
ugly?

Ah!

11

Voyagers, here is the map our dear dead king left us:
here the rosary he last spat upon: here his score of *Seraglio*:
here his empty purse. Let us pray and meditate always on deep
things.

Rhinestones and chancres, twins of our bosoms, Christian
constellations, resplendent pins, fly on! Dredge for the gold-
dust in the snow! The blood beneath the ice! A mad mud-junket!

I have won myself over to this cause. I am yours ! You are
mine! Light bulb! Holy Ghost!

I make my passport/dossier: a portrait of the poet wrapped
in jungle leaves airy on vines, skin tender to the tough wind;
I ride a zebra through the scrubby plains which nevertheless now
and then bloom with cattleyas and blue hydrangeas. The hollyhock
is my favorite flower although I have been known to bleed when
stabbed with a yucca. Standing in the photograph, then, filthy
and verminous but for my lavender shaving lotion, I must confess
that the poor have me always with them, and I love no god. My
food is caviar, I love only music and my bed is sin. Protected
souls, where love and honor gleam through the window I am a
stranger. The beauty within me withers at my glance. I stand

upright, whip-handle to jaw, betrayer of my race and mud-guard of the bourgeoisie.

Listen to me, you who are attracted: the other dusk in the streets I was the gentlest person you know— my periwinkle irises dripped like the corners of a jackal's mouth. Love me!

Bring me my doll: I must make contact with something dead.

And now that I am initiated I have only to bury you, my dear doll, before I set out. Here beneath this yew I dig a hole for wooden playthings. Man is nothing but this doggy instinct.

Kiss me, kiss me! doll!

I smother!

12

Marine breeze!

Golden lily!

Foxglove!

In these symbols lives the world of erection and destruction, the dainty despots of society.

Out of the cloud come Judas Agonistes and Christopher Smell to tell us of their earthy woe. By direction we return to our fulfilling world, we are back in the poem.

Across the window-sill lies the body of a blue girl, hair floating weedy in the room. Upon her cypresses dance a Black Mass, the moon grins between their legs, Gregorian frogs belch and masturbate. Around the window morning-glories screech of rape as dreadful bees, consummately religious, force their way in the dark. The tin gutter's clogged by moonlight and the rain barrel fills with flesh. Across the river a baboon blesses cannibals.

O my posterity! This is the miracle: that our elegant invention the natural world redeems by filth.

from NEIL YOUNG

In a strange game I saw myself
as you knew me

*

If it was a game I could play it

*

The spreading fear of growing old
contains a thousand foolish games
that we play

*

It's the woman in you that makes
you want to play this game

*

A woman with the feeling of losing
once or twice

*

It's hard enough losing without
the confusion of knowing I tried

*

It's hard enough losing the paper
illusion you've hidden inside

*

It's so hard to make love pay
when you're on the losing end

*

Too late to keep the change
Too late to pay
No time to stay the same
Too young to leave

*

No time left and I know I'm losing

*

I gave to you now you give to me
I'd like to know what you've won

*

Trying to make it but I'm losing time

*

Time itself is bought and sold

*

There's no time left to stall

*

No time left to stay

*

You can't be 20 on Sugar Mountain

*

Our waitress is paying the price
of their winking

*

We rush ahead to save our time

*

She don't keep time
She don't count score

*

How slow and slow and slow
it goes

*

Now the race of my head and my face
is moving much faster

*

I've never seen you through these
eyes before now, I can't believe it

*

Now the hours will bend through
the time that you spend till
you turn to your eyes

*

I've been waiting for you
and you've been coming to me
for such a long time now

*

Can you see me now?

*

Did you see them in the river?

*

Can you see her in the distance?

*

You're moving too slow and
wherever you go there's
another besides

*

Stopping the feeling to wait for
the time

*

It won't be long

*

It's so hard for me to stay
here all alone

*

I've been working on this palm tree
for 87 years

*

Everybody wonders what's going on
down here

*

Here we are in the years

*

Get down to it

*

Been burned with both feet
on the ground

*

Down on the floor with pencil
and paper just counting the score

*

I'm standing on my knees

*

I tried so hard to fly but I
stumbled and fell to the ground

*

I've learned that it's painful
coming down

*

I think I'd like to go back home
and take it easy

*

I'm in pieces on the ground

*

I went to heaven and I stood at
the crossroads

*

I was raised by the praise of
a fan who said I upset her

*

Down by the river I shot my baby

*

Pulled over to the corner and
fell into a dream

*

Flash! and I think I'm falling
down

*

It's faster than sinking

*

They're taking me out of my mind

*

How can I bring you to this
sea of madness?

*

I won't be back till later on

*

Finding paths through tables and glass

*

I can bring her the peace that she needs

*

With wings to fly she rolls along
doing it wrong

*

She could drag me over the rainbow
and send me away

*

I wonder what it's like to be so far
over my head

JOANNE

The reasonable restraints. This has been
going on for some time. It
takes some time to catch up. First
of all, I look up and am thoughtful
  But I'll never catch up. Adding
up all this now I shall proceed. The
pacific ocean is bounding in my eyes,
  This sense lays on the surface
rushes of arrivals —descriptions of different
  process ease of mind. A little voice
    reported on from a minute ago— but
I have just recollected the point
  of beginning, which of course
is part of this whole natural
    process

***

drop it away
  they drop away
    when the weight becomes slight
    when the weight is too weighty

That's what
      the devil's all About: Separate

***

beauty then is the final cause
    why we want it
        that is we want it

I wasn't built in a day

***

    I hope this working out as a novel
approach, at least the disruptions make
the substance. Other wise, inside.

***

    doesn't make any difference
if I've forgotten any thing

***

The spring
    beneath the tent
        of the sycamore boughs

there, both of them I guess
since our patriarchs' time

has a nice bench beside it

If you are innocent of heart
   you will sit there and dig it

A little brownie's servant of sand
dances on the bottom
   just a teeny bit up
        from the bottom
    is the top of his moving head

      a rock and a tree
   and some birds

when I couldn't sleep last night

    ***

    wood
    sweep
    ocean
    music

It's getting figured out

    shells
    wood
    notes

***

Sunday
will either of them ever awaken
    outsleeping each other
Oh Paul my friend, arise!
    the vast topples

***

Monday
    war that is Battle
        continues
    no defeat no Iching

***

She was a busy body
    She kept track
        of everything
          and did everything
            well

You've broken so
    many things I have

Penelope

***

    Perfect thought
the relationship of everything
          to everything

If you don't want it
              for yourself
Don't give it to anybody else

***

    The revolution

when you say *know*
        I expect you to *know*

she convinced herself

***

her head really
        banged
  on the subject

***

Well, eating & pleasure
inside the frame work given us
    It depends on *how*
        you killed her

work. it's work

    pleasurable anarchy

***

    Breakfast. He assured me
orange juice, toast & coffee.
Just the way I like it. I flang
the cawfee cup to de floor. After
three times it split into a million
pieces. She worried about the
small supply of dope in the other room.
        Both
of them, Lewis and Tom, were busy
collaborating. The record
playing. The wind howling
The electric heater going by
her side, as an ache over
increased herself. It was a fact
about what she thought
a moment before, which
was me, it was the love, He's
fine. I wonder why he

doesn't exchange some of
the mescaline for dope. Give Tom
some of the dope.
  I wouldn't go there, into their
minds. I'm here, ain't I. Now
thru the mirror one can she see
pine branches nodding nodding
in the blue California sun.

***

Don't put Your most
 intimate
 in action

***

Some thing open
Some thing closed

***

2 guys really high up

  high Joanne Hi Joanne

***

but she's wonderful

and I love her

***

my

shining star

and hope

A place

where you act it all out

I mean your thoughts
should be pure

oh moon

can't get

***

over and over
    until you go
   ahead again

***

when I invoke the moon
    it's the best I can find

and all of Bolinas
       at my feet

***

as in your mortal
   steps he ate

Can you see you're it
   no where you are

      fragile, inactive

***

What on earth to do
    Oh Moon

    Oh Moon
from the sea, the blinding blinkers
        lights on a dirt road
            I am always right

***

Oh Moon walking home on the dirt road
        walking on moon space
        what my mouth says

***

don't do this — don't do that
        don't ride a horse
            too long

***

    Oh Moon
That's all I know

***

Well I didn't want you to leave

    green foot steps grown

  older a bit by old knowledge

      as light

  no time   is the right time

bands of iris

clumps of nasturtium

***

         In California
I am in Paul McCartney's new house
   2 floors, panneled in wood
      It's oak he says
    what kind of oak do they
  have here,

       Sherman Oak.

***

dolls house
sighing high over the
branches voices
of the children music

***

Well I just want you to
know the truth

***

he makes love to her
he talks about
afterwards
when some years
ago
he worked
for the welfare
department
in New York City

She starts up
a hue
and cry
oh the money, the electricity

give me
   some clothes, some jewels
      some food, some love

***

     in the corner
don't you worry

The tunes, familiar
    weeping & laughing
      I leave my love behind

***

what I wanted to say
  was in the broad
 sweeping
form of being there

   I am walking up the path
I come home and wash my hair
   I am bereft
 I dissolve quickly

I am everybody

***

You write from the inside
  traveling
    in a 3 quarter length skirt
  go to sleep
  go to sleep

***

a life time

what happened
it stopped

***

It's always free
It's always easy

ELECTIVE AFFINITIES

Memory, the cat

***

Separations are dreams

***

"'But if you have any regard for my affection, my wishes,
and my sufferings, if you leave me to my illusions and hopes,
I shall not resist a cure if it should offer itself...'.
    "the last phrase came from his pen, not from his heart."

The truth is in the words and not the slip. The fantasy follows
itself to the end of the entranced moment—the shining void,
the light in your eye going out to sleep, and then, with lotion
smells, the walkers on the quay.

"Indeed, when he saw it on paper, he began to weep bitterly."

***

You rest against the screen, smoke through ruffled wire. The
oldest friend sleeps downtown, as you lean on the window,
close as blood, falling everywhere.

***

Everything is occurring as we split time like hair. Nothing
before. After all.

First phrase. Second. Past-present developings. Music is
simultaneity, "populating time with pitches," or the wind
between the wood.

***

They didn't look at each other until their hands met washing
dishes after dinner: changed to the past and for the future.

The road leads to C. A., in a carriage, is still guiding him
through the city. Inner privation, touching the arm, composure.

There is a novel bearing her name by a great writer. But the
only scene that duplicates the lovers is a meeting in the milk
bar past the military base. That night, walking home through
the wooded lanes, he strayed behind, knowing he would soon
see her too clearly. She will draw him an orange bordered moon,
kiss him on a part of his left cheek, which will hide it forever.

His last memory is her hand pointing to a passing sign saying:
Remember the Future.

***

A smell of jasmine in the square. A mother's breast feeds
her baby, opening his mouth in small waves, as a street
light flickers on and off. Giving birth to words. The secret
of stutterers.

***

You cannot talk together. The snow is fleeing on your mouth.

***

The left arm in coming as quickly as it can. Embracing repetitions:
In the slow movement of his first string quartet, Mozart first
discovered the knowledge of his own death.

***

"Much that ordinarily happens to a person repeats itself more
often than we think, because a person's nature in the immediate
determinant of this. Character, individuality, inclination,
disposition, environment and habits form together a whole,
in which alone he feels comfortable and at ease. It is for
this reason that, to our surprise, we find human beings, about
whose changeability we hear so many complaints, unchanged
after many years, and unchangeable after innumerable experiences
from within and without."

***

The way water disguises itself as lettuce, sometimes becomes
an immanent greyness. Four am. He woke up and walked through
the clearest and most diaphanous world, touching everything.
When he wished to get back to sleep, he imagined everyone
he knew, faces coming into water, blending, dissolving, and
he was sleeping. When he woke and thought of sleeping again,
he reconnected his self to his dream and he was asleep.

***

"The pure feeling of a final, universal equality, at least after
death, seems to me a greater comfort than this obstinate,
rigid persistence upon our personalities, our attachments,
and the circumstances of our life."

When another person joins two lovers, each of their personalities
becomes merely a function of their interrelationships. This
is the key to pornography: choice, will, dissolutions, separa-
tions, recombinations, duplications, repetitions, memory. To
these, the sexual hunger is subservient, acting simply as a
proof of the above, and rarely a determinant. Thus the pornographic
situation imitates that of the angelic orders—the sublimation
of the astral embrace.

"The faces, which had been left to the Architect, increasingly
revealed a very peculiar quality; they all began to resemble
Ottilie. One of the last little countenances he painted was a
perfect likeness—it seemed that Ottilie herself looked down
from the heavenly spaces. Looking above and around her, it almost
seemed to her that she existed and yet did not exist; that she
felt and did not feel—as if all this might vanish before her
eyes and she might vanish too. Only when the sun left the
window through which it had shone so brightly, did Ottilie
waken from her dream and hurry back to the castle."

***

Mound of the moon: falling into the center he makes love to A,
surrounded by a silver lit shape. It flies away in motes, sinking
through metallic dust where he feels the child buried in the second
deepest passage, a stone of whiteness.

***

In Ives, polytonality is a metaphor for interdimensional worlds, just as C's child embodies at least four persons. "Behavior is a mirror which reflects the image of everyone."

***

It isn't that things occur over and over, nor that their repetition it simply a variation on a different level of experience, but rather that something occurs only once, while we believe in differences. The hidden meaning in "I repeat my Self."

***

Shamelessly, as in alcohol, you become water. "And where are you tonight, Master Fire?"

***

"As to your chemical substance, the choice seems to be exclusively in the hands of the chemist who brings these elements together. But once united, and they are together, God have mercy on them! In the present case I am only sorry for the poor gaseous acid which must again roam about in infinite space."

"The acid has only to combine with water to refresh the healthy and the sick as a mineral spring," the Captain retorted.

"That is easy for the gypsum to say," said Charlotte. "The gypsum is taken care of; it is a *substance*; but that other displaced element may have much trouble until it finds a home again."

***

When someone stares at him and he feels ashamed, he is merely feeling the embarrassment of having identified himself with another's perception. Now he is tired of bearing it, as he sits in the corner with an ataractic expression, as if of someone dead, an expression just the opposite of that on a corpse's face which attains an always emotionally recognizable characteristic.

He walks into the rain and stands still with a fatidic gaze like someone in an elevator pressing the button of the floor he's on, then letting it go, where it's always opened, as one is true like water falling, as waters to each other.

***

Encased in a rain's integument, he ate an entire package of wafers, one by one, thinking: A habit is the form and structure meant to implement or contain and, finally, sustain a desire after it has died. The person becomes the desire, or at least as its bearer and servant. Then desire, like a habit, cannot be controlled. If one overcomes desire, one is free of desire. The happiness or unhappiness one sees in the faces of the desireless is neither. But one must be desireless in one's real self, else we find the desire revealing itself from some other place.

***

He sits in the cinema, watching the film through A's glasses: World War I backwards, tree men under butterflies sucked up into planes. Under his seat he finds her case, acid stamps and wisdom notes, little animals sniffing frozen candies, the lunettes of fingernails rise to grave eyes. During movie lightning, his friend wakes up mumbling: It's Sunday, I'll drive, the rented cars are always blowing horns. He looks away, adds the extra pulse and jams the screen. Smoke passes the aisle. As A removes her glasses, they fall though memories like the water where his eyes are shining.

***

Tumbling down: relationships, darkness, overalls.

***

"We may imagine ourselves in any situation we like, but we always think of ourselves as *seeing*. I believe that the reason man dreams is because he should not stop seeing. Some day perhaps the inner light will shine forth from us, and then we shall need no other light."

***

A's life is lifted like gauze. Here she flows into many persons, homonyms like "size" and "sighs." Her friend next to her, somnolently looking away, whispers: "A ravisher takes the flesh between the heart." She opens her eyes, and from then on she repeated her gestures, reproducing her lips and looks, stood speechless in front of the asters, the calcinated gaze of a wingless bird. Her muteness, a sign of maceration, was merely a metaphor for the transformation taking place within, the discarnate permutation of her soul into water.

***

"While resting on your lap in a half-stupor, I heard your gentle voice as from another world; and I learned from you how it is with me. I shudder at myself; but again, as I did before, I have marked out for myself, in my sleep, a new course."

***

The ghost of winter's hair slips in the mouth and comes up the valley of your arms whose flesh is sawdust, the flags in flies' eyes flurrying in your wrist.

***

"But now and then he was gripped by a great restlessness. At these times he expressed a wish to eat and to drink and he began to talk again. 'Alas!' he once said to the Major who seldom left him, 'how unhappy I am that all my efforts are never anything more than imitations or spurious attempts! What to her has been sheer bliss becomes to me pain; and yet, for the sake of that bliss, I am compelled to accept this pain. I must follow her, follow her on this road; but my nature as well as my promise deters me. It is a terrible task to imitate the inimitable. I feel only too deeply, dear friend, that genius is required for everything, even for martyrdom!'"

***

Sometimes doves' tails joining. A tulip and the cell.

***

The Intrados: his heart opened and became a C. She crawled in, licked and tested the edges of the curve, then curled up and closed her eyes.

THREE AMERICAN TANTRUMS

Then some one came to me and said
"The little fishes are in bed."

I said to him, I said it plain,
"Then you must wake them up again."

I said it very loud and clear;
I went and shouted in his ear.

MONKEY BLUES

Yes, the circus has finally come to town!
Ned and his pet monkey, Julian, moonlight as umpires at
the local ball park, trained seals during the week at the
zoo. What to do about this: Ned needs increasing amounts of
money as the months pass to support the array of expensive,
debilitating habits that spell constant grief for his folks.
But Ned is lazy, the monkey has to do it all. Julian is
farmed out around the clock to support these costly habits
(heroin, booze, commercial television, introspection, apathy,
cynicism, etc.)...

So, Julian labors constantly. He is the pet monkey you
see in all those subway advertisements and in the movies, he's
also the unhappy one you've seen strapped to a behavioral
psychologist's chair and covered with electrodes, as well as
most of the other monkeys in public places... "The idea is
to launch the monkey into outer space for over 30 days, to test
the effect of zero gravity on his well being," blares your radio.
Julian as ultimate monkey, docile archetype of all monkeys,
now playing at Universal Showcase Theatres all over town!

But Julian is depressed; at night, while the rest of the
world sleeps, the circus beckons him. Deep within he hears
the call of the three rings he remembers so well. The horses
and prancing naked girls, the lions and their hungry tamers,
the ringmaster happily cracking his silver whip. Tightrope
walkers, holidays on air, the wasted trapeze artists holding
their breath as they sail off into the sky.

"Give us your very best table," I swaggered, taking
the head waiter aside and slipping him a huge wad of play
money... "But of course, sir," the bald man purred as
he pocketed the cash and steered us to the most outstanding table
in the whole place. A truly amazing table it was, complete
with swimming pool, two-car garage, spiritual advisor, and a
landscaped garden which dwarfed even Versailles because of
a bonus: the garden sloped down to a rocky massive seacoast
that swayed gently in refreshing shoreline breezes wafted across
the table to us by matching pairs of eunuch Nubian servants
bending their palm fans with sultry efficiency in the really
knock-out evening light spilling across our plates from
the depths of the deep blue sea...

"Jesus, this is really something, isn't it?" Mary Lou breathed
as she hung at my side, dropping narcotic mints into the mouths
of the intelligent super-graceful housebroken wildcats that
roamed across the tablecloth. Their rhinestone-studded collars...
strings of Christmas lights along their tails...their claws and
nipples clicking against the china...their eyes doing a dance of
fire for the foggy, debauched rednecks nodding out around gleaming
knives and forks. "I don't know," I answered, "I'm not even sure
I understand what's happening." At that moment the waiter re-
appeared and began to unfold a heavy, complicated menu with sug-
gestions that ran on for sixty pages, moaning softly as he whispered
to us, "You have your choice! Anything you want!"

"Fuck it!" I squeaked, upsetting the table which slid with a low
reverberating roar into the garden below, "all I wanted was a little
peace of mind!"

"Yeah, right," Mary Lou chorused as we swept out the door
into the nowhere moonlight of our humble paisan heritage...
"No, Mary Lou, you should stay," I insisted, trying to avoid
her shocked, hurt eyes as I pushed her back toward the door, the tears
streaming down her face and hands. "I'll go get a cheeseburger or
something, I don't really care, but you should stay here, it would
be a crime to waste all this luxury on the heartless neurotic wall-
flowers who are devouring it now. This place, there's no other way
to describe it—it cries out like a wine bottle for the wholesome,
beautiful girl who will close her mouth around its neck: heart,
body, and soul."

WHO KNOWS WHERE THE TIME GOES?

"There's just one thing I want to ask ya: how come you're wearing those shoes?" The man who asked me this was lounging against a lamp post, knocking the tobacco from his lips and watching the cars go by like cigarettes through the dark dry evening sky. I decided not to answer him.

Then I did. "Who knows," I said. "Yes—who knows," he answered, immediately falling in step beside me until we reached the corner. At the corner was a huge red light. We waited. A dog waited with us, and as we started to cross the street the dog did too, and the man said, "Go home, boy," and the dog went home. And the cars that were there, waiting with us, began to move. And the man said, " Go home, cars," and the cars went home. And I decided I did not much feel at ease with this man, or comprehend his crafty powers. "Who are you," I said, "and what is it that you do?"

"Who am I? ... My name it does not matter," he answered with a heavy, dreamlike murmur. "I have traveled far, over steamy oceans and hectic sizzling deserts; I've climbed the snowy ridges of the highest mountains in the world," he went on, unbuttoning his tattered jacket and raising one of his wonderful outstretched arms to the sky... "There I lived for twenty years on nettle broth alone, drowning myself in meditation, and saw no other human soul. I had no clothes on the outside of my body, nor any wholesome food inside. My body became shrunken to a mere skeleton; and it was greenish in hue, just like the nettle and just like the broth, and over it grew a covering of greenish hair—you are what you eat!" He paused long enough to cast me a glance loaded with significance—"And I Saw The Light up in those mountains: it was greenish in hue!"

The air grew still as he warmed his monologue... "I have tasted the Amazon, Ohio, and Yang-tze rivers, shot the rapids of Niagara in a teakwood barrel and shot my bolt in every major city on the globe... I have rescued howling babies from the hotplate of the Red Sea in mid-July, only to be laughed at by pot-bellied tourists looking on from the shore..."

"I awoke in a daze in Seattle in 1954, not a cent to my name and three kids to support. I was Joseph Stalin during the bloody purges, snoozing on the judge's bench with my hands folded in my lap. I was Stalin's mother, too, tossing dishwater into the yard in White Russia, and I was Ghandi, overjoyed that my hare-brained schemes were a complete success... I have been a sheriff, a sailor, a yards-goods salesman and a nymphomaniac. I devoted my life to the discovery of a cancer vaccine, working long hours under the worst conditions, year after year, for the betterment of mankind. I took part in the last vigilante lynching in the state of Missouri and spent an obscure life of peace and quiet on my model farm in southwestern Montana, raising winter wheat. I've been a pony, a duck, a closet queen, a movie camera, a Fuller dome and a cyclotron, a wah-wah pedal and a washing machine. In short, I've been everywhere and done everything there is to do, As you can no doubt tell just by looking me in the eye... I'm Everyman!" he screeched, lunging toward me with his arms flapping wildly.

"I'm Everyman—and I demand to know why you're wearing that particular pair of shoes, as opposed to any of the countless other pairs of shoes you could be wearing...I know I'm only a hobo: I'll die in the gutter without my name. But you: do drugs really alter your consciousness? Why are you standing there, dressed the way you are, talking the way you do, and thinking whatever it is you can? Is sheer detail what gives life its sense of reality? Who knows where the time goes?" Suddenly bringing the tirade to a halt, he took his raised arms down from the sky and stood, bobbing back and forth on the sidewalk.

I didn't think twice but immediately turned to cross the street. "I guess I'm wearing these shoes because they fit," I said, and handed him a dime—"Here, go get yourself a cup of coffee..."

"Oh, really?"

from TRUCK

PROPOSED ELEGY FOR HART CRANE

What a place for a garden,
pain like a pocket full of mints,
we live on each other.

As if an immigrant family crossed
some mysterious brightly-colored bridge
& wandered into this lung-like valley
selling hot sandwiches & aerial photographs
of the Aztec dead we live on each other.

Nothing was planned without noise;
after dark the siren comes on in sheets,
she turns over loudly.
                        I think I could paint
when her back's turned.

                        Her back.

Or walk a little farther upstream
testing the furniture & the hair
in this area.
                Yes it's a beautiful country,
flowerlike & huge, all the more graceful
when you consider it's rolling
& our many coffees rarely spill
but sometimes it takes itself away.

HORSESHOE

Hills' soothing American voice muscle
blurred in a giant insect vision or slur note
falling away evenly like vast synthetic dew

                All about your body & the head
that carries it around.
                        I turn to the West
as I would to a migraine born of music   private

stiff & deserted   the depot etches itself
in your chemistry like
                         like   like

                    *

                    Geez   the stars
these mountains make
                         roped off this way.

It is October.
The evening sky is oily.
I sit eating fruit with Delbert.
Heady fruit.   In the South
a few sparks chip off the earth &
my heart fills up with slang.

                    *

                    In those days
you ate something & remembered it

a colonist at heart

sitting on *your* beach, Montana
     picking *your* flowers
               your nose, etc.

                    2

And insects too of the prairie
                         my love (too)
                    in an embarrassing way:

Icy ticking of big racing Schwinns:

          You sound like that,

     This a turbulence (my love) too

                    *

     A breather.

At the age of 20 I saw my first
Caucasian
           & she saw me.
                   Great Resumé,
I can only take you
               as far as the logging camp,
it's not my streetcar.

        Many callings!
                (Can't breathe)

       *

       In Dakota
the worship is tit for the rest of your life

       Essential & rough
               4 bottles
  of cough syrup on the Denver-St. Louis bus

       *

Vespucci, Vespucci & Vespucci

       some old guy
       old codger
       old fart
         some old sheepherder

  "Elk Nookie"
  bombs the Spring

         3

The world speaks no Athabascan

     like a gong.
           August rams September
    the cool nights jar.

       Out back

the red man thinks with rage
on Samuel Beckett's Bulova
lying in the sage.

*

I move in broad daylight
with the gases
& redwoods follow.
Ancient luck
of deer gut
prophylactics & a long hot bath

Cream of the senses

You have just missed the Lewis & Clark Expedition.

from SECRET CLOUDS

EYE POEM

As I lay in bed naked
I found a young man
watching me from a rooftop
across the street

the same man perhaps
who was summoned
by the people across the street
to come & watch us make love
last sunday afternoon

I remember how wonderful you can be
and I'm not happy that you're gone.
Below me the street
tingles with routine excitement

It is a barrel of noise
I swim at the top on my fire escape
until a bell rings
inside the house

I move myself into a hallway
sitting on a stair
the roof and sky
above me in a door.

This book fell upon your belly this morning

a brutal thing to do
Come see somebody you love
then leave   hours later
Now I know what it feels like
but you could have stayed.

You need to go see someone
who can tell you things you
don't know
I don't see
anyone like that

I wonder what to do about the old
man in apartment 8
as I walk by
he sits slumped
over a table
before a mirror
in a chair

In apartment 4
a man with a cross on his wall
listens to the radio

it sounds like some foreign
land downstairs on the first floor
Puerto Rican music on their
record player.

I see plenty of people
who fuck up my head
and they tell me lots of things
I don't know

you've known this cat
for three years
he must be something special to you.

The evening deepens

I sit on the school steps
worrying about the man
on the rooftop
who saw me leave the house
and will steal my guitar.

I watch the people going by

a flock of children

and an exciting black young woman
reminds me of my sex

Meanwhile
you've maybe worked all day
or just gone back to larchmont

Tomorrow I'm probably
going to woodstock

Tonight I'll just walk around.

And the turtle
fell on its back
and died from the
weight of
the earth

Remember Duke Snider?

Poor cat
he does some photo ads
for Great Day
'A man's way to remedy gray'

He was a great ballplayer too

actually
he looks pretty good.

The sky is a lovely tone
of grey on suffolk street
a block of public schools & theatres
on the lower east side

There's no place to piss
in the daytime in new york city
allen & delancey
the pissatorium is closed
the sidewalks
the whole east side.

A child implores his mother
tears stream from his eyes
the driver closed the window
with a slam
because of the rain

'You don't care for me
you hate me
you never do anything for me.'

then they relapse into violent
spanish

flowers bloom
or blossom in a window
on first avenue
I put the transfer in
the book
the bus driver tells them to
shut up.

He wore a tee shirt
engraved
puerto rico
the island of enchantment.

The institute for the
crippled & disabled
adjoins the veterans hospital
on first avenue. Then comes
bellevue and a parking garage
for the staff. Adjoining is
the new york university
medical center
con ed's mid manhattan plant
the east river drive &
the united nations.

They call the station

Waterside.

The urine burns & bursts my bladder

a middle aged woman
rubs her arm on mine

there is liquor on her breath

her escort speaks in czech

it feels good
the arm

you can brush against me
anytime you like.

In pain I walk past sidewalk cafes.
Why aren't there any pissoirs
in new york city?

I'm going to run on a platform
of pissoirs for new york city.
It's a burning issue.

from I REMEMBER

I remember the first time I got a letter that said "After Five Days Return To" on the envelope, and I thought that after I had kept the letter for five days I was supposed to return it to the sender.

I remember the kick I used to get going through my parents' drawers looking for rubbers. (Peacock)

I remember when polio was the worst thing in the world.

I remember pink dress shirts. And bola ties.

I remember when a kid told me that those sour clover-like leaves we used to eat (with little yellow flowers) tasted so sour because dogs peed on them. I remember that didn't stop me from eating them.

I remember the first drawing I remember doing. It was of a bride with a very long train.

I remember my first cigarette. It was a Kent. Up on a hill. In Tulsa, Oklahoma. With Ron Padgett.

I remember my first erections. I thought I had some terrible disease or something.

I remember the only time I ever saw my mother cry. I was eating apricot pie.

I remember how much I cried seeing "South Pacific" (the movie) three times.

I remember how good a glass of water can taste after a dish of ice cream.

I remember when I got a five-year pin for not missing a single morning of Sunday School for five years. (Methodist)

I remember when I went to a "come as your favorite person" party as Marilyn Monroe.

I remember one of the first things I remember. An ice box. (As opposed to a refrigerator)

I remember white margarine in a plastic bag. And a little package of orange powder. You put the orange powder in the bag with the margarine and you squeezed it all around until the margarine became yellow.

I remember how much I used to stutter.

I remember how much, in high school, I wanted to be handsome and popular.

I remember when, in high school, if you wore green and yellow on Thursday it meant that you were queer.

I remember when, in high school, I used to stuff a sock in my underwear.

I remember when I decided to be a minister. I don't remember when I decided not to be.

I remember the first time I saw television. Lucille Ball was taking ballet lessons.

I remember the day John Kennedy was shot.

I remember that for my fifth birthday all I wanted was an off-one-shoulder black satin evening gown. I got it. And I wore it to my birthday party.

I remember a dream I had recently where John Ashbery said that my Mondrian period paintings were even better than Mondrian.

I remember a dream I have had often of being able to fly. (Without an airplane)

I remember many dreams of finding gold and jewels.

I remember a little boy I used to take care of after school while his mother worked. I remember how much fun it was to punish him for being bad.

I remember a dream I used to have a lot of a beautiful red and yellow and black snake in bright green grass.

I remember St. Louis when I was very young. I remember the tattoo shop next to the bus station and the two big lions in front of the Museum of Art.

I remember an American history teacher who was always threatening to jump out of the window if we didn't quiet down. (Second floor)

I remember my first sexual experience in a subway. Some guy (I was afraid to look at him) got a hardon and was rubbing it back and forth against my arm. I got very excited and when my stop came I hurried out and home where I tried to do an oil painting using my dick as a brush.

I remember the first time I really got drunk. I painted my hands and face green with Easter egg dye and spent the night in Pat Padgett's bath tub. She was Pat Mitchell then.

I remember another early sexual experience. At the Museum of Modern Art. In the movie theater. I don't remember the movie. First there was a knee pressed to mine. Then there was a hand on my knee. Then a hand on my crotch. Then a hand inside my pants. Inside my underwear. It was very exciting but I was afraid to look at him. He left before the movie was over and I thought he would be outside waiting for me by the print exhibition but I waited around and nobody showed any interest.

I remember when I lived in a store front next door to a meat packing house on East Sixth Street. One very fat meat packer who always ate at the same diner on the corner that I ate at followed me home and asked if he could come in and see my paintings. Once inside he instantly unzipped his blood-stained white pants and pulled out an enormous dick. He asked me to touch it and I did. As repulsive as it all was, it was exciting too, and I didn't want to hurt his feelings. But then I said I had to go out and he said, "Let's get together," and I said, "No," but he was very insistent so I said, "Yes." He was very fat and ugly and really very disgusting, so when the time came for our date I went out for a walk. But who should I run into on the street but him, all dressed up and spanking clean. I felt bad that I had to tell him that I had changed my mind. He offered me money but I said no.

I remember my parents' bridge teacher. She was very fat and very butch (cropped hair) and she was a chain smoker. She prided herself on the fact that she didn't have to carry matches around. She lit each new cigarette from the old one. She lived in a little house behind a restaurant and lived to be very old.

I remember playing "doctor" in the closet.

I remember painting "I HATE TED BERRIGAN" in big black letters all over my white wall.

I remember throwing my eyeglasses into the ocean off the Staten Island ferry one black night in a fit of drama and depression.

I remember once when I made scratches on my face with my fingernails so people would ask me what happened, and I would say a cat did it, and, of course, they would know that a cat did not do it.

I remember the linoleum floors of my Dayton, Ohio room. A white puffy floral design on dark red.

I remember sack dresses.

I remember when a fish-tail dress I designed was published in "Katy Keene" comics.

I remember box suits.

I remember pill box hats.

I remember round cards.

I remember squaw dresses.

I remember big fat ties with fish on them.

I remember the first ball point pens. They skipped, and deposited little balls of ink that would accumulate on the point.

I remember rainbow pads.

I remember Aunt Cleora who lived in Hollywood. Every year for Christmas she sent my brother and me a joint present of one book.

I remember the first "garden painting" I ever did. It was in Providence, R.I., in 1967. It was inspired by some Japanese flower plates I gave Kenward Elmslie for Christmas.

I remember the day Frank O'Hara died. I tried to do a painting somehow especially for him. (Especially good) And it turned out awful.

I remember chenille bed spreads.

I remember canasta.

I remember "How Much Is That Doggie In The Window?"

I remember butter and sugar sandwiches.

I remember Pat Boone and "Love Letters In The Sand."

I remember Teresa Brewer and "I Don't Want No Ricochet Romance."

I remember "The Tennessee Waltz."

I remember "Sixteen Tons."

I remember "The Thing."

I remember "The Hit Parade."

I remember Dorothy Collins.

I remember Dorothy Collins' teeth.

I remember when I worked in an antique-junk shop and I sold everything cheaper than I was supposed to.

I remember when I lived in Boston reading all of Dostoevsky's novels one right after the other.

I remember my first night in Boston. I stayed at the Y.M.C.A. (Nothing happened)

I remember when I lived in Boston panhandling on the street where all the art galleries were.

I remember collecting cigarette butts from the urns in front of The Museum of Fine Arts in Boston.

I remember how small my room was in Boston.

I remember two times a night when the train would go by my window.

I remember growing a mustache.

I remember tearing page 48 out of every book I read from the Boston Public Library.

I remember living for days off nothing but "Hollywood" candy bars. It was the biggest candy bar you could buy for a nickel.

I remember the old couple who lived just below me. They drank a lot and were always fighting and yelling. He had no control over his bowels.

I remember Bickford's.

I remember the day Marilyn Monroe died.

I remember lots and lots of jerking off.

I remember that I was very close to myself in Boston.

I remember the first time I met Frank O'Hara. He was walking down Second Avenue. It was a cool early Spring evening but he was wearing only a white shirt with the sleeves rolled up to his elbows. And blue jeans. And moccasins. I remember that he seemed very sissy to me. Very theatrical. Decadent. I remember that I liked him instantly.

I remember a red car coat.

I remember going to the ballet with Edwin Denby in a red car coat.

I remember learning to play bridge so I could get to know Frank O'Hara better.

I remember playing bridge with Frank O'Hara. (Mostly talk)

I remember my first lover. (Joe LeSeur) I don't think he'll mind.

I remember my grade school art teacher, Mrs. Chick, who got so mad at a boy one day she dumped a bucket of water over his head.

I remember my collection of ceramic monkeys.

I remember my brother's collection of ceramic horses.

I remember when I was a "Demolay." I wish I could remember the secret handshake so I could reveal it to you.

I remember my grandfather who didn't believe in doctors. He didn't work because he had a tumor. He played cribbage all day. And wrote poems. He had very long ugly toe nails. I avoided looking at his feet as much as I could.

I remember Moley, the local freak and notorious queer. He had a very little head that grew out of his body like a mole. No one knew him, but everyone knew who he was. He was always "around."

I remember liver.

I remember Bettina Beer. (A girl) We used to go to dances together. I bet she was a dike, tho it never would have occurred to me at the time. She cussed a lot. And she drank and smoked with her mother's approval. She didn't have a father. She wore heavy blue eye shadow and she had white spots on her arms.

I remember riding in a bus downtown one day, in Tulsa, and a boy I knew slightly from school sat down beside me and started asking questions like "Do you like girls?" He was a real creep. When we got downtown (where all the stores are) he kept following me around until finally he talked me into going with him to his bank where he said he had something to put in his safe-deposit box. I remember that I didn't know what a safe-deposit box was. When we got to the bank a bank man gave him his box and led us into a booth with gold curtains. The boy opened up the box and pulled out a gun. He showed it to me and I tried to be impressed and then he put it back in the box and asked me if I would unzip my pants. I said no. I remember that my knees were shaking. After we left the bank I said that I had to go to Brown-Dunkin's (Tulsa's largest department store) and he said he had to go there too. To go to the bathroom. In the men's room he tried something else (I forget exactly what) and I ran out the door and that was that. It is very strange that an eleven or twelve year old boy would have a safe-deposit box. With a gun it. He had an older sister who was known to be "loose."

I remember Liberace.

I remember "Liberace loafers" with tassels.

I remember those bright colored nylon seersucker shirts that you could see through.

I remember many first days of school. And that empty feeling.

I remember the clock from three to three-thirty.

I remember when girls wore cardigan sweaters backwards.

I remember when girls wore lots of can-can slips. It got so bad (so noisy) that the principal had to put a limit on how many could be worn. I believe the limit was three.

I remember thin gold chains with one little pearl hanging from them.

I remember mustard seed necklaces with a mustard seed inside a little glass ball.

I remember pony tails.

I remember when hoody boys wore their blue jeans so low that the principal had to put a limit on that too. I believe it was three inches below the navel.

I remember shirt collars turned up in back.

I remember Perry Como shirts. And Perry Como sweaters.

I remember duck-tails.

I remember cherokee hair cuts.

I remember no belts.

I remember many Sunday afternoon dinners of fried chicken or pot roast.

I remember my first oil painting. It was of a chartreuse green field of grass with a little Italian village far away.

I remember when I tried out to be a cheer leader and didn't make it.

I remember many Septembers.

I remember one day in gym class when my name was called out I just couldn't say "here." I stuttered so badly that sometimes words just wouldn't come out of my mouth at all. I had to run around the field many times.

I remember a rather horsy-looking girl who tried to seduce me on a New York City roof. Although I got it up, I really didn't want to do anything, so I told her that I had a headache.

I remember one football player who wore very tight faded blue jeans, and the way he filled them.

I remember when I got drafted and had to go way downtown to take my physical. It was early in the morning. I had an egg for breakfast and I could feel it sitting there in my stomach. After roll call a man looked at me and ordered me to a different line than most of the boys were lined up at. (I had very long hair which was more unusual then than it is now) The line I was sent to turned out to be the line to see the head doctor. (I was going to ask to see him anyway) The doctor asked me if I was queer and I said yes. Then he asked me what homosexual experiences I had had and I said none. (It was the truth) And he believed me. I didn't even have to take my clothes off.

I remember the night that Ted Berrigan wrote his first collage sonnet.

I remember the night that Ted Berrigan told me that I had no morals.

I remember a boy who told me a dirty pickle joke. It was the first clue I had as to what sex was all about.

I remember when my father would say "Keep your hands out from under the covers" as he said goodnight. But he said it in a nice way.

I remember when I thought that if you did anything bad, policemen would put you in jail.

I remember one very cold and black night on the beach alone with Frank O'Hara. He ran into the ocean naked and it scared me to death.

I remember lightning.

I remember wild red poppies in Italy.

I remember selling blood every three months on Second Avenue.

I remember a boy I once made love with and after it was all over he asked me if I believed in God.

I remember when I thought that anything old was very valuable.

I remember "Black Beauty."

I remember when I thought that Betty Grable was beautiful.

I remember when I thought that I was a great artist.

I remember when I wanted to be rich and famous. (And I still do)

I remember when I had a job cleaning out an old man's apartment who had died. Among his belongings was a very old photograph of a naked young boy pinned to an old pair of young boy's underwear. For many years he was the choir director at church. He had no family or relatives.

I remember a boy who worked for an undertaker after school. He was a very good tap dancer. He invited me to spend the night with him one day. His mother was divorced and somewhat of a cheap blond in appearance. I remember that his mother caught us innocently wrestling out in the yard and she got *very* mad.

She told him never to do that again. I realized that something was going on that I knew nothing about. We were ten or eleven years old. I was never invited back. Years later, in high school, he caused a big scandal when a love letter he had written to another boy was found. He then quit school and worked full time for the undertaker. One day I ran into him on the street and he started telling me about a big room with lots of beds where all the undertaker employees slept. He said that each bed had a little white tent in the morning. I excused myself and said goodbye. Several hours later I figured out what he had meant. Early morning erections.

4 UPS & 1 DOWN

BLUE POLES

> Blue poles (well?) on the beach
> in a snowless winter and
>
> I'm too cold to ask you
> why we're here but of course "we are"
>
> where on the puzzled reef dwarves either
> fish or drown in the abandoned ships
>
> sharks dissever year-old children in search
> of "young blood" Jersey acting like Europe
>
> in an instant and lovely Mary kneeling along the quick tide
> to be anxious with thoughts of bare oceans
>
> that move as the thighs of an eventual sunlight
> like bathers moving closer to their season
>
> when again gulls perch in their lovely confusion
> "alone," as now, the sand sifting through
>
> your fingers like another's darkness. it's true,
> you are always too near and I am everything
>
> that comes moaning free and wet
> through the lips of our lovely grind

LOVE ROCKETS

> Wet leaves along the threshold of the mid-day
> and I'm off to rescue the sky from its assassins
> jogging and screaming and launching my clean mortars
>
> into the March obscene air... the enemy.
>
> I suppose I'd rather be sitting in Samoa now
> sipping a quart of Orange Julius and being fanned

by Joey Heatherton in black tights and white glossy lipstick.
but I'm not. I'm here. and I have something to say,

as well as something to take care of.

And that something is probably more important than
you realize. I like the sky (don't you) its warmth, its friendliness,
I'm not going to let all this fucking soot taint that terrific blue.

battle the filthy airs with your mortars and your prayers.

you'll soon be overcome with lovely sensations of the sky.
you'll be thinking of me as this happens.

STYRO

We'll stay until ice begins
over the driftwood

do you,
a girl from kansas,
imagine the invisible changes
in front of you?
and water wed constantly to sand
by foam beads...

pure directions of the sun
level the ocean
in your cupped palms

gulls play in their crude reflection
a tanker passes to split Europe

there is no other place that allows us
to understand so little, you see...

all those minds shot down by a cloud's emptiness

and our youth clung tightly
in white dunes...
they'll see us dreaming there
clumsy in these plaid blankets
at night.   it's

like watching wind push seaflowers
straight across your eyelids
or the sun melt them, either way

they'll be gone eventually
and new forms will take shape
and grow, even before we're gone

this will happen.

POEM ON MY SON'S BIRTHDAY

At dawn
on the window sill
it's watery trees it's light
it's just hanging there waiting

poetry

I want to walk   you can come or
you can sleep or
you can dream of walking someplace better

and that still means we're not together

 except today
 one more day   (you were born)

It's a communion
you can hardly see
a kind of reunion   just a little one

you and me.

TO A POETESS

You sit to have waves rush to your open hands
and you're surprised as cities grow there

  the cool air's
    driving flips
      jammed with mini-spearguns

but this time they're real
facing you,
                with your private school stripes

Miss Hewitt's girls riding through the reservoir
                                    (on horse(s)

the horizon goes limp   and finally
you're not so beautiful afterall

                ***

my arms shoot stiff   I justify a margin

                in that sense
                each vein glows

                ***

good   but what I really need

        a soft chair

                to nod on your boring rap
                I'd settle for a twelve year nap.

                ****

you go on then:
I'll listen

        why either worry or hate or be confused...

    because the sun's so available and

                        mostly for you

bikini doll

        I quit listening again   I even go

with one tiny spit   on your black lace toe

                ***

It's better here
with the polar bears   good

better   so
                              light dissolves and swells my blood
                              a process worth remembering

            instead   (it's noon)   I watch solar colors
                                              wash themselves on her skin

and She has nothing to do with you

                            ***

six dozen wet beach umbrellas
the space between them

            fading and then dissolving America into "families":

I
don't
understand
any
of
this.

                            ***

though You're worse than ever
better just make a date with never

                        with your bunches of radar fingers

you might as well dissever

                              (giant aspirins
                               in the sky)

relaxing the locked planets of this galaxy.

IN LONDON

for Bettina

Homage to Bly & Lorca

―――――――――――

"I'm going home to Boston
by God"

*

Signs
(red)
EXIT
EXIT
EXIT
EXIT

*

(Cards)
Question―
where do you get a pencil.
Answer.

―――――――――――

*

(for Jim Dine)

most common simple
address words everything
in one clear call to me.

*

("Small Dreams")
Scaffolding comes up the side of the building, pipes, men putting
them there. Faces, in, past one block of windows, then as I'm up in the
bathroom, they appear there too.

*

Ted
is ready.
The bell
rings.

*

(Nouns)
Small dreams of home.
Small of home dreams.
Dreams of small home.
Home small dreams of.

*

I love you happily
ever after.

*

(Homesick, etc.)
There is a land
far, far away
and I will go there
every day.

*

12:30 (<u>Read as Twelve Thirty</u>)
(Berrigan
Sleeps on)

*

Voices on the phone, over it—wires ? Pulsations. Lovely one of young
woman. Very soft and pleasant. Thinking of Chamberlain and Ultra
Violet—"talking the night away." Fuck MacCluhan—or how the hell
you spell it—and/or teetering fall, the teething ring, "The Mother of
Us All"—*for Bob*. Call me up. "Don't Bring Me Down..."

*

Variance of emotional occasion in English voices—for myself, American, etc. Therefore awkward at times to "know where one is." In contrast to Val's Welsh accent—the congruence with one's own, Massachusetts. Not that they "sound alike"— but somehow do agree.

*

"London
Postal Area
A-D"

*

Posterior possibilities —
Fuck 'em.

*

"It's 2 hrs. 19 mins. from London
in the train to beautiful country."

*

"EAT ME"
The favorite delicious dates.

*

Girls
Girls
Girls
Girls

2 x 2

*

Some guy now here inside wandering around with ladder and bucket.
Meanwhile the scaffolding being built outside goes on and on, more
secure.

*

Like German's poem I once translated, something about "when I kissed you, a beam came through the room. When I picked you flowers, they took the whole house away." Sort of an ultimate hard-luck story.

*

Lovely roofs outside.
Some of the best roofs in London.

*

Surrounded
by bad art.

*

I get
a lot
of writing
done—
"You Americans."

*

H — will pirate primary edition of Wms' *Spring and All*, i.e., it's all there. Check for Whitman's *An American Primer*—long time out of print. Wish he'd reprint as Chas apparently suggests Gorki's *Reminiscences of Tolstoi* [now learn it's been in paperback for some years]. Wish I were home at this precise moment—the sun coming in those windows. The sounds of the house, birds too. Wish I were in bed with Bobbie, just waking up.

*

Wish I were an apple seed
and had John what's-his-name
to plant me.

*

Her strict eye,
her lovely voice.

*

Cosi fan tutti.
So machen's alle.

*

Wigmore
dry gin
kid.

*

Wish Joan Baez was here
singing "Tears of Rage" in my ear.
Wish I was Bob Dylan—
he's got a subtle mind.

*

I keep coming—
I keep combing my hair.

*

Peter Grimes
Disraeli Gears

*   *

That tidy habit of sound
relations—must be in the
very works*, like.

————————————————

   *Words work
   the author of many pieces

*

Wish could snap pix in
mind forever of roofs out
window. Print on endurable paper, etc.

*

With delight he realized
his shirts would last him.

*

I'll get home in 'em.

*

The song of such energy
invites me. The song
of

July 14, 1969

* UP THRU THE YEARS *

here's balance

delicate as baby industry at
the turn of the century

(pepsi)

step right in

style growing into ripe old age

(intricate tobacco leaves)
what I shout about it:

LOVE BEING ALIVE

& that's a fact young & old agree

upon whose back I rest counting the astounding changes

you go thru in life
they are many

you   me   we

she   &   he

*

she & he are friends for life

*

tonight I sit up alone & read

gruesome news go away

*

tomorrow spent in glorious pleasure of work & play

I set it down

Bell Tell   pay enough attention

$27. 35

bank   music   rent
call Ed
Bill
Joe
John
Kenward & Kenneth
Release #2 on the wing

I Remember
Chicago for Les

Veitch flyer: George

Newsreel

Box 257

mail books to Lewis

Vill Voice

christmas

keys for Jim

my mother   father   & brothers

get door handle fix

& car (Mike)

*

little snorts of magic dust tell you what to do:

be still

no need to get excited until it's time

*

it's time...

December 1969

from BIRDS

This is a field book
made to fit your pocket
when you go looking
for birds.

Purple Martin
Barn Swallow
Cliff Swallow
Bank Swallow
Rough-Winged Swallow
Tree Swallow

Eastern Bluebird
Robin
Wood Thrush
Hermit Thrush

Mockingbird

Yellow-Throated Warbler
Myrtle Warbler
Magnolia Warbler

Mourning Warbler
Connecticut Warbler
Nashville Warbler
Kentucky Warbler

Male: Large, rosy; wing-bars, stubby bill.
Female: Gray; dull yellow crown and rump.

Male: Pink; wing-bars, crossed bill.
Female: Olive; wing-bars, streaks.

Male: Black hood, yellow face.
Female: See text.

Male: Round black cap.
Female: See text.

Male: Black mask.
Female: Yellow throat, black belly.

Adult male: Deep rusty breast and rump.
Immature male: Black throat patch.
Female: Yellow-green, wing-bars.

Breeding Male: Scarlet, with black wings.
Moulting Male: Red Patches.
Female: Yellow-green; dusky wings.

Voice:
Emphatic
tweet tweet tweet tweet tweet
on one pitch.

Voice:
Song,
a clear,
whistled caroling,
often long continued,
made up of short phrases
of two or three notes.

Voice:
Song,
flute-like;
phrases rounder
than those of other Thrushes.
Listen
for a flute-like
ee-o-lay.
Guttural notes
occasionally interspersed
are distinctive.
Call,
a rapid
pip-pip-pip-pip.

Suppose
that a Thrush
is in the field
of our glass
with its back turned.
It has no hint
of rusty color
anywhere.
We know then,
that it is not a Veery,
a Wood Thrush,
or a Hermit Thrush.
The bird faces about;
it has grayish cheeks
and a dim eye-ring.
By experience
or consultation of the text
we know that the Olive-backed Thrush
has a conspicuous eye-ring
and buffy cheeks.
Our bird then,
must be the Gray-cheek.
It is almost
as helpful
to know
what a bird
could not be
as what it might be.

GIRL MACHINE

my nerves my nerves I'm going mad
my nerves my nerves I'm going mad
round-the-world
hook-ups
head lit up   head lit up   head lit up
the fitting, the poodle
Ma Marine   Ma Marine   Ma Marine
Ma Marine   Ma Marine   Ma Marine
the fitting, the poodle

what a life, just falling in and out of
what a life, just falling in and out of
swimming pools
zylophones   WANTED   zylophones
WANTED   female singer   WANTED
bigtime   floorshow bigtime   floorshow
bigtime   floorshow bigtime   floorshow
silhouetted in
moonlight
moonlight

mysterious mirrors
mysterious mirrors
mysterious mirrors

Louella Parsons
swell teeth   not news   swell teeth
"woo-woo"   woo-woo   "woo-woo"
vaccinated at 6 o'clock in San Die
vaccinated at 6 o'clock in San Die
"woo-woo"   woo-woo   "woo-woo"
swell teeth   not news   swell teeth
Louella Parsons

shiny black surfaces
shiny black surfaces
shiny black surfaces

head lit up   head lit up   head lit up
a girl machine
a girl machine
head lit up   head lit up   head lit up

work work work   work work work
work work work   work work work
work work work   work work work
work work work   work work work

GIRL MACHINE   GIRL MACHINE
GIRL MACHINE   GIRL MACHINE
GIRL MACHINE   GIRL MACHINE

"Busby Berkely is the only film dir
"Busby Berkely is the only film dir
to have fully experienced and re
to have fully experienced and re
Babe Rainbow   Babe Rainbow
Babe Rainbow   Babe Rainbow
signed Kenward G. Elms
signed Kenward G. Elms
mirrors provide a 2-
mirrors provide a 2-
for-1 opulence (D
for-1 opulence (D
epression /flo
epression /flo
wers:shit
wers:shit

wers:shit
wers:shit
on from above
on from above
bunches unfolding
bunches unfolding
in his "Footlight Par
in his "Footlight Par
signed Kenward G. Elms
signed Kenward G. Elms
Babe Rainbow   Babe Rainbow
Babe Rainbow   Babe Rainbow
beautiful people working for us !!
beautiful people working for us !!
"Busby Berkely is the only film dir
"Busby Berkely is the only film dir

GIRL MACHINE   GIRL MACHINE
GIRL MACHINE   GIRL MACHINE
GIRL MACHINE   GIRL MACHINE

show goes on and is a smasheroo
show goes on and is a smasheroo
round-the-world
hook-ups
head lit up head lit up head lit up
head lit up head lit up head lit up
Ruby   Ruby
col   "yum"   nist
(1969) BABE RAINBOW (1969)
a girl machine
reflected and refracted
by black floors & mystery meers...
by black floors & mystery meers...
Night in Shanghai Night in Shanghai

GIRL MACHINE   GIRL MACHINE
GIRL MACHINE   GIRL MACHINE
GIRL MACHINE   GIRL MACHINE

```
lips painted red                    lips painted red
keep on doing it                    keep on doing it
            the oriental fans part
distant hands...                        ...distant hands
they come nearer                    they come nearer
harmonica player                    harmonica player
            creep Chink beggars...
whores kiss Dick                    whores kiss Dick
falls to Jane Wy                        falls to Jane Wy
pursued by gangs                    pursued by gangs
            carries her shot dead
   down a shadowy endless Dream Corridor!
harmonica player                    harmonica player
they get smaller!                        they get smaller!
distant hands...                            ...distant hands
            the oriental fans close



            42nd St.    42nd St.
            42nd St.    42nd St.
         reflected and refracted
      by black floors and mystery meers...
         reflected and refracted
            42nd St.    42nd St.
            42nd St.    42nd St.
```

you in the view and no real walls
you in the view and no real walls
express flow   black-whi
express flow   black-whi
     firm shiny terror ! !
          firm shiny terror ! !
express flow   black-whi
express flow   black-whi
you in the view and no real walls
you in the view and no real walls

GIRL MACHINE   GIRL MACHINE
GIRL MACHINE   GIRL MACHINE
GIRL MACHINE   GIRL MACHINE

               bunches
          like flowers
down the ramp   down the ramp
happy factory   happy factory
just relax   just relax

Drawing by Rosemary Mayer

Test 1 How to design freedom. How fine does the lens resolve? center? edges? 2 how accurate are the shutter speeds? which ones? 3 how often? 4 how accurate is the f/stop ring 5 how often does the film advance fuck something up & when? (in advance?) 7 how good is the lens contrast? 8 what speed is the film? 9 how wide is its latitude 10 what density is desired? 11 what is the contrast? it's insane to think it happened in such a stupid way. we took the boat & then stopped for a smoke. the captain was right next to us one moment and the next he was gone. X & I are looking for T in Brooklyn. we see him looking out a window a few blocks away. the house is green. over the doorway is a bay window. two people are jumping up & down. then they take their places in the window. they look at each other. they are all cousins of each other. they paint their faces. the crowd throws them coins. we have a party, we all fuck shout & play with our cats. there's nothing special about it. then, skating with a gun in our backs. "Jump into the weeds, save yourselves!" We fly into them. the weeds are iron pipes. WE've solved the problem. we've solved the problem: men are women, women are men, i'm pregnant for a while. if someone doesnt change into an animal we wont be saved. a man turns into a cat, he gives himself to his friends in the form of lead & coal. he draws himself for them. he is a girl—black & white—she sings. brush fires.

put out a fat fire with salt, baking soda or cover the pot. pound cake: 1 lb. butter, 1 lb. sugar (2 cups), 1 lb. flour (4 cups), 1 lb. eggs—9 large—, 1 tspn (teaspoon) lemon extract, 1 teaspoon baking powder, 1/2 tspn salt: separate eggs, beat yolks with sugar, cream butter, add sifted flour with salt & baking powder & cream well. add egg & sugar mixture to this & beat. add lemon & mix in egg whites. 1 1/2 hours in slow oven. May 12—my father puts me on a train, May 19—a man-woman with a cloven foot is driving us around, May 27—USA is painted on my stone pavement, May 31—brush fires. June 1—the letter carriers struck after warning repeatedly that "communications must be captured", June 15 - it's not July yet but its' almost christmas. Ed's been to manhattan, bronx, long island, westchester, new jersey, connecticut, massachusetts, penn., fla., washington, california., nevada, utah, wyoming, nebraska, indiana, ohio, india, rye, riverdale, istanbul, st. gabriel's, lake mohawk, another lake & down in mexico & around town & the rest of the story is:

in what year & in what century are we living now? what are you doing now? were you born here? he said to her once where do you come from. have you a watch? what time is it now? now he said, another time we're going to watch the planes come in & go out at the airport. do you live at the airport? she said she'd rather be worn on the wrist? what were you doing yesterday at this time? rolling on, you sink gradually into the ground but all he can sing is a song.

there once was a man named along, who married a wife named thin air, he's tried since then, to do it again. & the sixth time Gus was camping out & started a forest fire. & the tenth time he drowned in a reservoir. eaten by water. he's tried since then to do it again but all he can have is a fair.

in June two men will be involved with her, one older & one younger. next writing. next a musician comes in. then a strange woman who knows something. then that woman again. some work in april & in may something doubles. it is a good time to get married (it is not a good time to get married), after eating a lot, strength & a lake on top of a mountain, sex, the strong man is weaker than the weak woman. neither of them die. 13 billion years to go. what are the days of the week? what are the months of the year? who eats violets? you have been born in Spain, a man of a certain color. How to design freedom.

A man of a certain color sat on the meshed border of the purple chair. he sweated. "What would happen if there weren't any airplane mechanics?" "What would happen." wondered the pink man. The man up front was sweating. "It's unexplainable, the culture, next question" the elephant asked "Is devotion self-destructive?" "Are you an anarchist?" "How can you think in terms of others?" he said, there is a series, it is gradually stiffening, then squares, then the next question, Which branch is wrong? The one that is floating away from the tree. "I see" they all nodded. You gave him a two-dimensional problem. he solved it this way: the expression on the face was spatial. It extended before its dimensions. It extended behind them. Turning around, you could see that this person was unhappy.

All at the meeting stopped for tea. there was no talk. then the next question: what can you build with your hands? "Every day is different."

Freedom, how to design it. The rattlesnake symbol
appears again & again in early american flags. A flag of this type was the
standard of the south carolina navy, & something like it the emblem of
the culpeper minute men of virginia, & another, the rattlesnake super-
imposed on a plain yellow banner, was known as the she-flag.
the rattlesnake was thought of as a symbol of vigilance because her eye
was brighter than any other animal & she had no eyelids; since she never began
an attack, but once involved never surrendered, she was an emblem of
magnanimity & true courage. it was probably the deadly bite of the rattler,
however, which was foremost in the minds of the designers & the threat "dont
tread on me" made it worse. squid: clean by cutting down the side, cut out
insides & throw away, use only the thick skin & tentacles at the end. throw away
the part of the head around the eyes. cook pieces in white wine,
butter, thyme, bay leaf, water; add white raisins & parsley.
Cook till squid turns pinkish-white, then simmer.
Mussels: steam in the same ingredients as the squid but with 1/2 the wine
& 1/2 the water. leave out the raisins. Shake the pot. It should take 3 minutes.
only eat the mussels that pop open in the pot. Scrub mussels with a brush
before cooking.
The White Wife of Mouse: a young man (grey
mouse) traveled around, he journeyed all over. pretty far away. Then once he saw
a girl, her dress was white. I'll marry her. he did marry her. he took her
home. & told her "when I'm away you are not to cook. & when I get back home,
then I'll do the cooking for you. you might get hurt."
So she never cooked. once when grey mouse was gone, "Oh I think I'll
cook. I dont see why i should get hurt. I probably wouldnt get hurt".
So she cooked mussels & then a barnacle on the mussel popped, it popped
right in her eyes, & killed her. When her husband got back home, "White
one where are you!?", nothing answered. he looked for her & then he found her
& then he wept: my wife, I told you all the time, i told you, you must not
cook,
Lewis said Stash 2 sunshine 1 quicksilver 3 valium
1 thorazine 1/2 ounce of grass 1/10 gram of hash 1 dexedrine on the second
last day of December of any year,   a series of four dots, thought,
in any series, thought, five fingers, a whole new language, fire, from hershey,
pennsylvania, a candy bar, different kinds of exercise, keep mind, neither

one way nor the other, california, new york, handwriting blue shirt the
simplest blue shirt end of desire for moon communication, clipping service
over, telephone out, sent now. no answer, why are you being so methodical, had
to write note, that was the method, danger in looking at codes
too great, desire to terminate the code, even the ending, no name,
roger, surface communication no good either, it misled us, this is
it, spell it out or else, please, nothing besides that, last chance, determined
to terminate it, final communication, this is a warning, keep flashing if
you object, keep throwing up objects, getting dimmer, dont see any flash,
flashes arent reaching my machine, lights very dim, red light on, signal
or not, understand your meaning, do you agree?   the dream:
the phone is a battery. first, we were falling down.
later, all the other people falling were a great help to us, the sea's not far
away, we meet blow bubbles? the girls bowing, the family brings them
home, heads in the street, the cars are too close "she's 15, on her aunt's
bike, look at her blue eyes .... there's a producer, a movement toward the ocean
she's not there, how to load the machine a certain way, just keep messing it
up & smiling, food on all the tables, should we eat it or
go through it? pick up checks, how to make a pick up, studio check
dance check backstage check: the family of cases & nuts falling from the
sky of cases & nuts in flag shapes of red, in blue shapes in white flags
the blondes & grays are the falling nuts the
large columns of the floating church are in a grey sea
the rest will be run over, are about to be run over,
should we check the food, check the checks & the . . . how many times has it
happened before, she grew up, at the dance, hopped up, walk from here to
there, it's a process for developing film, color film
color film, that's all *Veteran's Day, full* moon,
DeGaulle, 2 days before neil's birthday, friday the 13th. they came this
morning to take my typewriter away, blonde sisters, the blondes blonde children
I was raising up the cigarettes on a rope piece of
anarchy to Ed just as blue car blue eyes drove up went away, rain, pick up Grace
at Penn Station, she's late, twenty two to one, Madison Square Garden
to Queens, fisher, the body works, it's broken, it works, it's broken,
the coffee shop has new free signs. the police give me a warning for my
own safety. Over the bridge by the upper roadway, back by the lower

roadway in the freezing rain. i'm itchy, new holes, new drafts of air rushing
in smelling. there's an orange cloud over the city. Go to Color Perfect,
first, missed it, shoes "no possible" home upstairs downstairs Paul went to Dobbs
Ferry, M gets sixty five thousand dollars,
bring the scallops, there's a baby crab in the
scallop bag, uptown to drop off a treatment. showers, afghanistan, grace, crew,
corner, red gels long lincoln tunnel to west new york or union city, New
Jersey. B's writing our diary,
Cokes: one is seltzer, the other coke
C will write her version. E & I will follow it.
(we never had the time) two cats,
open the window, between the buildings the moon
is full but it's raining, the receiver's body is broken again, food, bursting,
Grace hates the camera, alan does card tricks, the camera wont film,
the metroliner to philadelphia, we come home, the tunnel goes back again,
neil's birthday, move the furniture, Dave's the old boxer the
Norwegian waitress you ring we bring to dayton's another oldman playing
tears on my pillow, yes please a cup of coffee boom no moon DeGaulle's
funeral Neil goes home.
He goes to Grassy Bay.
To Grace Point, Grassy Island, Grassy Point, Grassy Rocks, Gray Gables,
Great Captain, Great Captain Rocks, Great Cove, Great Fresh Kills,
Great Gull Island. To Great Harbor, Great Hill, Great Hill Point, Great
Hog Neck, Great Island, Great Kills, Great Kills Harbor, great knob, great ledge,
great neck, great neck creek, great peconic bay, great point, great point light,
nantucket light, great rip, great river, great river village, great rock
great round shoal, great round shoal channel, to green jacket,
to green jacket pond
how to design it, have been summoned in this
community 30 miles at sea, island community, designed to rid the island, 30
miles at sea of what selectmen call the hippie element, unrelated people
from living in the same dwelling, all hitchhiking & a third, up a
tent without having the health department, a flock of about 50, 50 of them
registered to scallop vote out labor day, a person   The Hippies,
with 35 wins & 20 losses, remain in first place.

from TWO WOMEN

THE DEATH OF KAREN KLAUSNER

The flower of coincidence
makes me strike out at probability, i.e. statistics.

walking down 12th street to the phone, dialing,
thinking to fuck you once more
no answer
later in the day your cousin, Beth, called
she said you were dead.

I went to the funeral knowing only your cousin
and a few Goucher girls who had come up from Baltimore.
I cried, though as an outcast
in the cortege
someone was complaining about the uncle who got lost in traffic
"He probably didn't want to go out to Long Island"

one screaming anti-septic fuck, your one and only
would that I had rocked your loins to eternity.
you wouldn't sleep in the same sheets with our mess.
you insisted I change them.
I though it was heroic
the way you snuck out of your dormitory
running through the woods past the guards
your legs getting cut from the bushes.

> truly a romantic night
> > a gift
> the one time I saw you from the distance after that
> > you were much lighter
> > > > dancing even

It was rainy and cold in June.
The wind howled at your grave
and I felt some presence watching me
and I thought to myself that this must be God.

what was revealed later
was that you died in the same hospital in Peekskill
that my sister had just had a baby girl in
and was still in
when they wheeled you into emergency
my mother was in the lobby.
I used to make you mad by saying
that you reminded me of my mother.
the rabbi who was to name my niece
came up to her and told her about it
that a whole family
had been wiped out
in an automobile accident
your uncle and mother too.

> there were many miles
> from the Catskills to Manhattan
> and many hospitals
> and many, many more miles

> > > > soon it will be
> > > > three years later

Postscript of the morning:
after writing this I hear by telegram
that my mother is in the hospital
with gall bladder trouble.
One other thing then occurs,
I carry my poems in a suitcase
given to me by my grandmother.

LIMITS OF SPACE AND TIME

MUMMIFICATION
AND
SPACE TRAVEL

Gazing on the unmoving calm of an ancient Egyptian face —the face of a body arrested in the process of death—fixed— secured from decay—I have been able to accept the idea that some form of life may yet dwell in those pitch-covered, linen- wrapped husks...

The idea of travel through space at the speed of light il- luminates the image of the mummified pharoah—in order to allow for the constant speed of light in all frames of motion, the Theory of Relativity states that objects approaching that absolute velocity will contract in the direction of motion, gain- ing in mass as they contract and that, within these contracting, ever-more-massive frames of motion, time will gradually slow down—with respect to the time of a relatively stationary observer—and on reaching the absolute velocity will stop alto- gether. A brilliant flash through the void—as one voyager watch- ed the other blink his eye, two thousand years passed on their home planet...

Now, in our state of motion, the mummy appears static— lifeless—but, if we consider him as a traveler at the speed of light—a passenger on the boat of the sun—he then assumes an entirely different aspect.

My colleague Martin Wolf believes that masters of yoga- like disciplines in earliest dynastic times could induce in them- selves a state of suspended animation, that the funeral practices of the later dynasties (disembowelment and preservation of the body attended by elaborate ritual) represent a degeneration of more effective earlier methods...

OBSERVATIONS
OF
EGYPTIAN ARTIFACTS

Chicago, Oct. 8, 1969—I found myself carefully examining mummified forms in the Field Museum—the dead in varying degrees of nakedness—wooden cases carved with the features of elegant ladies—some with gold faces and blank, staring eyes— their hearts (described by winged red disks and scarabs) emanated floral mandalas—delicate petals of alternating blue and yellow, red and green—enclosing dusty linen stained with body fluids remote in time—those responsible for the museum had unwrapped one of the bodies—a boy twelve years old or so— whose final expression etched itself on my imagination through mud-sealed lips—a terrible beauty—an effect like waking up in some utterly alien and menacing thing—reptile threat—fluttering wings of flight in a dark room—rushing through a door that is a mirror—shattered glass—thrown back into gently pulsing rivers of blood...

THE VIRUS

In effect, the nucleus of a cell without living cell substance, it contains no program but its own replication—which it effects through the energy of the life forms on which it is parasitic.

An entity from the microcosmic frontier of life—a pure vector of geometric multiplication hovering between the mineral and the organic—in its crystallized inactive state its duration is indefinite—doorways to the eternal from whence we are visited by tiny particles bearing a white-hot message of empty urgency from a realm of eternal ice...

Much of what we look upon as History can probably be viewed profitably in terms of viral events—the same precise and lethal forms of action repeated again and again to the final disadvantage of the host organism—the adaptation of the industrial assembly line—with exactly calibrated measurements insuring interchangeability of parts—to the production of Military weapons—reflects in the macrocosm the action of the virus...

VERY FINE LINES

When the light of a burning element is refracted and diffracted through the prisms of a spectrograph, very fine lines, characteristic of that element, appear in the reflected spectrum—these lines, preserved on photographic emulsions, can be examined according to the method of the quantum theory, to determine the energy levels in the electron orbits of the element's constituent atoms—the transitions between energy levels occurring rather in the manner of a film, where apparent motion is the product of a rapid sequence—a high frequency—of static states…

These same elemental lines, when obtained from the light of a distant galaxy, may appear shifted either to the blue (short wave) or to the red (long wave) end of the spectrum relative to the position of the lines obtained for that element here on earth. Proceeding on the idea of the Doppler effect (as waves approach us they seem to grow shorter, as they recede they seem to grow longer—the effect of a passing locomotive), it is inferred that the more the lines are shifted to the red, the further away (in time as well as space) is the source of light—it is also held that the greater the distance, the greater the velocity of recession.

A beam came through our window and spoke silently of the smallest and the largest spheres—turbulence that dwells motionless within itself…

AN INTUITION

It came to me that many devout Jews who perished in the German concentration camps died in a intense fire of words and numbers—I could see the words of the Holy Books like sun-spots or dark spectral lines vibrating against the intense white heat...

MODERN WESTERN HISTORY

Enfin: The secular order rises in time from its roots in the earth and ascends into the pneuma, the word of the father— in the accumulation of power the word, the word of the Law, is both fulfilled and erased...

ICY ROSE

(To The Delicately (Winter) Coming On)

all day feeling space
my face is empty space
& nighttime too

the space   the space   the space   the space

& nighttime too
I'm going blank

Blank.

Where has that last sentence (speaking – you were speaking – gone?
& where have the birds *really* gone?
& where is the Ice Age now?
& who does this poet think he is   or she is?

She is a far cry from Womanhood
O
T-T-T-TAKE ME BACK!

I stammer

I go down under the moon

I dance with the big brown bear

I kiss the foot

Down to 6 below last night
I ran thru the snow like a young puppy!
I got the Dashboard Blues
I threw in the towel
I reacted like a Crazy Lady   - well -   not exactly

YOU SEE ALL THIS FREEDOM??????????

you see where it gets you?

you see what I mean?

mean?

calms you down coughs you up curls you under sweeps you along
                    comes you on
                                    comes......you......on
            but

there's nothing to fear except fear itself
                                    (it fears itself)
        rather:
                think of Copernicus (splendor)

            De Revolutionibus Orbium Ccelestium

                            &
                        Liu Shui
                                    (flowing water)

            or you: My Boldest Dream

                    it's so easy
                makes me sleepy

                        *
            but WHO ARE YOU?

                            & why do you dress so strange?
        & who are your parents?
                        & whence have you come?

VERGE

A man cuts brush
and piles it
for a fire where
fireweed will flower
maybe, one day.
All the leaves
are down except
the few that aren't.
They shake or
a wind shakes
them but they
won't go oh
no there goes
one now. No.
It's a bird
batting by.
The small lake,
shrunk, shivers
like a horse
twitching off
flies. Flies
drunkenly stagger
between window
and storm sash.
They hatch, lay,
buzz and die.
The sky grows
gray, goes pale,
bears a whitlow
or splits and
shows a lining
light sea green.
But the lake
is black. Back
of the trees
are other trees
where deer stoop
and step and
the independent skunk
securely waddles.

An unseen something
stirs and says No
snow yet but
it will snow.
The trees sneeze
You bet it
will, compiling
a white and wordless
dictionary
in which brush
cut, piled and
roofed with glitter
will catch and burn
transparently
bright in white
defining "flame."
So long, North.
See you later
in other weather.

TWELVE POEMS

A balloon
is going up
filled with problems.

***

When I think
of the thought
machines

I whistle
softly
to myself.

***

SELF

In my pale
face
is a grim

mask,
but I have
to laugh.

My arm
is a bone—
I

love
it
so.

***

a red
tin pan
of tan
doom

***

Gravity
pulls
me
down

so
hard
I
can

only
say
my
name.

***

"When my head
goes too fast
I get out
and walk."

***

The evil eye
is ridiculous,
but it exists.

PERSONAL

I'd like
to keep
myself

out
of this...
this...

whatever
you
call it.

***

It's too easy
to say
yes,
now—

difficult
to think,
say,
now.

***

I get
the idea
I can die
anytime,
then
I forget
it.

***

When a tree falls
on your head,
it says yes
or no.

***

I walk
you walk
we walk

through
each
other

into
our
selves

Lorenzo Thomas

FIT MUSIC
CALIFORNIA SONGS, 1970

ACKNOWLEDGEMENT: Several lines in sections V and VII are quoted from Ezra Pound, *The Classic Anthology Defined by Confucius* (Cambridge: Harvard University Press, 1954) and from "Little Honda" by Brian Wilson (Sea of Tunes Publishing Company, BMI). Acknowledgement is made to these poets for their timelessness and aptness of thought.

When poets beg acceptance for their lines
It's when ephemera and wisdom intertwine
When dull biography engulfs a poem,
The poet shores his patron with a Proem
To raise his thought above the dross of life
Since life intrudes, the Proem is a gloss.
Deja vu more or less. Most likely, more
Should fit you now to hear this song of strife.
You spent childhood rehearsing the Korean War
You fucked up in college and picked the wrong major
And in 66 everyone faked concern for Asia
It was all more fitting than you thought;
The staging. When the orders come down
For the Nam fourth of July as is fitting
You implored the Muses to fly from their knotting
You totaled the Chevvy out of meanness
You whined and wondered how to escape this mess
And Lord who to write to. There should be a Lord
If there must be a Proem you thought.
But there was none. Only your drunkard
Friends your dope fiends and pimps
Demon lovers and lovers. And girls dumb
To the morse code from space still arriving
While Zia suns crackled over the desert,
You fled through archives in your brain
Remembering acidulous hash and devotions
Consecrated by the pain of navigating through wine
In peaceful East Coasts full of bare bodies
And icy streets under neon. Now tropical death
Leaped before you. You wept. Wastefulness when
The car ran them down. And the orders came down
As your prophets demanded. Strange FM stations
And astrological phonecalls hastened to soothe you,

Saying "don't give a damn." It was time
To be going. Vancouver or South Viet Nam.

   ***

      And Kung said, "Without character you will
        "be unable to play on that instrument
       "Or to execute the music fit for the Odes.

          Ezra Pound. *Canto XIII.*

I

Moon rays like pure snow

What here on this coast three ahem and wine bottles
Shining in the trash
This is my concern for the day
And something new in the evening
Another beautiful whore
Make me grateful O Lord

There is a time for everything
Let alone getting high

What. Here in beautiful California
The surf remembers another form
Of revolution. Nothing. But what
Else do you want to remember

Catherine or the note tacked up on the wall
Where is Bethesda I am lost

II

Wait. What is astrology when peoples still fucking up
Daily

III

And still it is helpful to be here
Gifted. Solemn. Ridiculously macho
This effeminate county. What

Remains is to be bargained away
For another souvenir medallion

The truth

So thank you Cathy we will get together and smoke dope
Another evening. Maybe tomorrow

And thanking lucky stars too

Sending back reports from the seaside

Sun Yat Sen's final telegram

                    Sorry, all that
                    is CLASSIFIED

          We not too sure where you'll be
          when worlds collide

Sending back reports from the seaside

IV

Ooooh oooh. Nothing the magic in the air
We call this aether. Magic and
Science. Shut em down shut em down

But all you want is another
Beautiful whore. A good thing

I am glad you are with me here
And wherever I roam. My friends
Thank you. And love for you

In this place. I am glad the radioactivity
Registers

In my flesh there is the sound
Beaming forth from the glass
As she traces the ring of the bottle
With her soft hands. Smiling
And scheming

There is something (History) about you
White women and
Spanish girls
Passing for white

V

I rejoice for this island

T rejoice for this island, I climb
South Hill to pick the turtle-fern,
All alone here
Who shall not pine

I see my official friends
They are also complaining

Yet Confucius went on plucking the k'in and
Singing the Odes.

Ezra Pound, certified madman
Is melancholy. In his book
On the shelf. Overdue. What
A mean life

VI

This is stupid. This is very stupid.
No one but Anne will understand
When I hand her these songs, when

I put my hand to my lips and concentrate on your mistakes
How you bumped into the wrong individuals
In the saloon. And kept on smiling right on

Sending back reports from the beach

Sending back reports from the seaside

VII

Among the reasons why the beach is beautiful is
The music on the radio is alright
Because it has nothing to do with you
And still it reminds me of something

Has to do with you,

    Cathy

On my way to Vietnam. And loving
Your dope too

    La Jolla

Where even the freaks ask dumb questions about you

    San Clemente

When worlds Collide on tv

That is our talk here; sweating
And dirty

    Where through the wood a moiré ribbon
Runs

    Speeding linnet and the circling crow
Above

Pendleton
Studying war

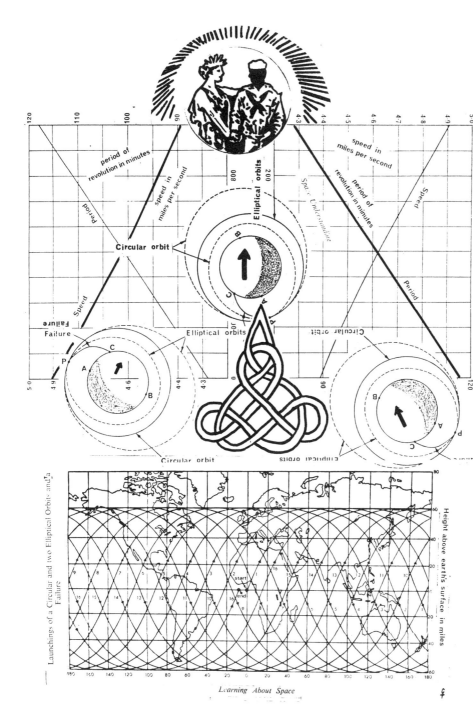

period of revolution in minutes

speed in miles per second

speed in miles per second

period of revolution in minutes

Elliptical orbits

Circular orbit

Elliptical orbits

Circular orbit

Failure

Elliptical orbits

Circular orbit

Launchings of a Circular and two Elliptical Orbits and a Failure

Height above earth's surface in miles

Learning About Space

Drawing by Cecilio Thomas

ENVOY

Typical.

Some madman has put a lamp on the ceiling
Of Boeing 707s
Depicting the Wain
And its partners
As if they seen
Through a turret

Where is this in the world?
Can't tell from the stars

Suddenly,
I felt so thankful
The lights dimmed
We dropped from the clouds
San Francisco looked up

The first sight was MacDonald's
Neon yellow arc

A beckoning out the cold, windy night

A rainbow promising nothing
And warning that that nothing
Is serious business

That nothing was bringing me back
Back to de Plantation!

Why all de slaves am not singing
For the return of the Kid

I wanted somebody to stop me at the airport
And ask all about Vietnam

But nobody asked me
What did you find out
About Jesus,
Was it worthwhile did you have fun
As it says in the song making me
Suffer was it fun
Making me suffer
Now I want to know

Did you by lucky chance
Buy a camera a stereo deck

How did you like being the envoy of a monstrous epic
Or saga of Western corruption
When the white guys blacked their mugs
Before the ambush, what did you do kid?

Who was that dancehall girl

How come you think
You made a difference to her
To me to them to what huh
What are you A egotist huh
B patriot C idiot D huh

When you thought that your presence
Might somehow stay a more cruel hand
The mentality behind that
Is something in this world

So similar to Love and
Its running partners
The tears of black womens
Everywhere in this world

There is one photograph of the Kid in his camouflaged
Cowboy hat

The sponsors of that program
Must not have another word,

Not even when I get finished ranting

from I REMEMBER MORE

I remember living on the Lower East Side.

I remember Second Avenue and strawberry shortcake at "Ratner's. "

I remember the St. Mark's movie theatre (45¢ until six). The red popcorn machine. And lots of old men.

I remember living with Ted Berrigan in a store front on East Sixth Street and the fat lady upstairs. And I *do* mean fat. So fat that she had to breathe very heavy. (Loudly) And she snorted a lot too. I don't think she was all "there" in the head. She acted like a little girl but actually she must have been in her forties. She like to play with Ted and me and her favorite way of "playing" (when we would let her in) was to chase us around the room trying to catch us and then when she did she'd hug us real tight and not let go. I don't think she realized how strong she was. And *big*. So, tho she was always knocking on our door, we didn't let her in very often. (Tho several times she forced her way in) Once she sang some very sweet folk songs for us she had learned from her father who had been a miner somewhere. She lived with a brother upstairs I never saw. Sometimes she would bring us down very beige looking stews. Or plain yellow heavy cakes. I remember very well her face. *Very* round and *very* pink. I am sure that in any other city but New York City she would have been locked up.

I remember "the cat lady" who always wore black. And many pairs of nylons. One on top of the other on top of the other. She was called "the cat lady" because every night she went around feeding cats. Her hair was so matted I don't think a comb could possibly have gone through it. All day long she roamed the streets doing what I am not sure. She was never without her shopping cart full of paper bags full of God only knows what. According to her there were other cat ladies who looked after cats in other Lower East Side areas. How organized all these ladies were I don't know.

I remember Ukranian Easter eggs all year round.

I remember thin flat sheets of apricot candy in delicatessen windows.

I remember "deli."

I remember "The Metro." (A coffeehouse on Second Avenue that had poetry readings) Paul Blackburn. And Diane Di Prima sitting on top of a piano reading her poems.

I remember how beautiful snow made the Lower East Side look. (So black and white)

I remember "Klein's" at Christmas time.

I remember "Folk City." "Man Power." And selling books at "The Strand."

I remember going grocery shopping with Pat Padgett (Pat Mitchell then) and slipping a steak into her coat pocket when she wasn't looking.

I remember going to a church on the Bowery where bums go to get work for a day and being sent to Brooklyn to clean up a small Jewish synagogue where the rabbi was so disgusting that after half a day's work I just couldn't stand anymore so I "disappeared." (With no pay)

I remember Leadbelly records smaller than most records.

I remember Delancey Street. The Brooklyn Bridge. Orchard Street. The Staten Island Ferry. And walking around the Wall Street area late at night. (No people)

I remember a very old man who lived next door to me on Avenue B. He is most surely dead by now.

***

I remember looking at myself in a mirror and becoming a total stranger.

I remember having a crush on a boy in my Spanish class who had a pair of olive green suede shoes with brass buckles just like a pair I had. ("Flagg Brothers") I never said one word to him the entire year.

I remember sweaters thrown over shoulders and sunglasses propped up on heads.

I remember boat neck sweaters.

I remember "Queer as a three dollar bill."

I remember wooden nickels.

I remember stamp hinges.

I remember orange icing on cup cakes at school Halloween parties.

I remember autumn.

I remember walking home from school through the leaves alongside the curb.

I remember jumping into piles of leaves and the dust, or powder, or whatever it is, that arises.

I remember raking leaves but I don't remember burning leaves. I don't remember what we "did" with them.

I remember Jack Frost. Pumpkin Pie. Gourds. And *very* blue skies.

I remember "Indian Summer." And for years not knowing what it meant, except that I figured it had something to do with Indians.

I remember exactly how I visualized the Pilgrims and the Indians having the first Thanksgiving dinner together. (Very jolly!)

I remember Halloween.

I remember usually getting dressed up as a hobo or a ghost. One year I was a skeleton.

I remember one house that always gave you a dime and several houses that gave you five cent candy bars.

I remember after Halloween my brother and me spreading all our loot out and doing some trading.

I remember always at the bottom of the bag lots of dirty pieces of candy corn.

I remember the smell (not very good) of burning pumpkin meat inside jack-o'lanterns.

I remember orange and black jellybeans at Halloween. And pastel colored ones for Easter.

I remember "hard" Christmas candy. Especially the ones with flower designs. I remember not liking the ones with jelly in the middle very much.

I remember some beautiful German Christmas tree ornaments in the shape of birds and houses and people.

I remember the dangers of "angel hair."

***

I remember Aunt Ruby, who never got married. My mother's oldest sister. Being the oldest girl in a family of ten on a farm in Arkansas she always had to take care of the kids. And was never allowed to date. When my parents moved to Tulsa Aunt Ruby came too. I was very young then but I think she lived with us. Or at least she babysat for us a lot. And was always "round". She was tall and skinny and rather homely (plain) with buck teeth. Extraordinarily neat and a real nut about germs.

I remember Aunt Ruby's horror once as I picked up something I had dropped on the floor and ate it.

I remember that Aunt Ruby was very religious and always taught Sunday School classes. I always feared that sooner or later I would end up in one of her classes and sure enough one year I did. I remember the news being broken to me but I don't actually remember being "in" her class. So it must not have been so bad. (Or else so bad that I've totally repressed it.)

I remember feeling sorry for kids at church, or school, who had ugly mothers.

I remember a very clean tasting fruit salad Aunt Ruby often made with miniature marshmallows.

I remember that Aunt Ruby wouldn't eat fish.

I remember that Aunt Ruby didn't approve of drinking so my father built an invisible liquor cabinet under the kitchen bar.

I remember that Aunt Ruby liked small earrings and small pins but that she couldn't stand anything around her neck or wrists.

I remember that wool irritated Aunt Ruby's skin.

I remember that nobody ever knew what to give Aunt Ruby on special occasions so everyone always gave her stationery or scarves or handkerchiefs or boxes of fancy soap. Once I remember watching Aunt Ruby trying to find something as she opened up drawer after drawer of fancy soap. I suppose this is a bit depressing but at the time I was very impressed.

I remember Aunt Ruby's apartment on Admiral Street. Simple and neat and blue. (Very fond of blue)

I remember a very boring figure of a white fawn on Aunt Ruby's mantel. (So boring I can't imagine why I remember it) And several miniature vases.

I remember seeing Aunt Ruby lose her composure only once. When I was very young. I insisted that she tell me why she never got married and she wouldn't. I remember that she was ironing at the time.

I remember neat stacks of "Reader's Digest" all over Aunt Ruby's apartment. On the coffee table. On the night stand by the bed. And on the floor next to a big forest green reclining chair.

I remember Aunt Ruby not approving of a black velvet dress my mother had because the "V" neckline was too "V".

I remember trying to visualize Aunt Ruby masturbating. (Impossible)

I remember when I started smoking I would smoke in front of my parents but I never could get up the courage to smoke in front of Aunt Ruby. Actually, it wasn't a matter of courage. I don't know what it was a matter of.

I remember Aunt Ruby continually warning us (Jim and me) of the dangers involved in doing just about everything. Walking around bare footed. Petting strange dogs. Eating too fast, etc.

I remember Aunt Ruby writing me recently that she was taking a night school course in modern literature at the University of Tulsa and that she just couldn't understand Gertrude Stein.

Larry Fagin & George Schneeman

LANDSCAPE

LANDSCAPE

Poem by Larry Fagin

Drawings by George Schneeman

ANGEL HAIR BOOKS

The little white dog wags his tail

The red mill turns silently

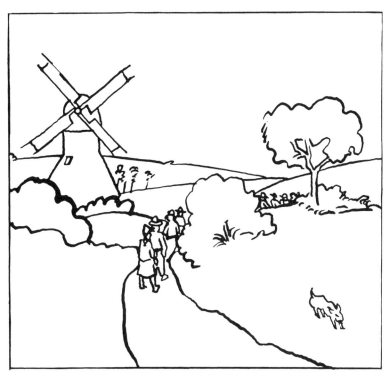

The movie line is a mile long

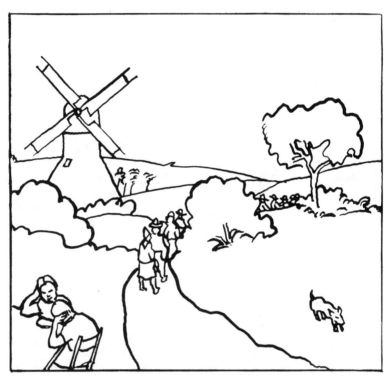

The sleepyheads toy with their food

The Japanese gardener flies to pieces

Orange soda blows in the wind

A lettuce leaf floats by

Lorenzo Thomas

DRACULA

Crosses his blond eyes to think of you
Picks up his brown overnight bag and
Runs down the ash covered streets to the station
Scuffles with the ignorant ticket agent
Leaps on the bus as it belches forward
Passengers seeping into the dark
The city is obliged to be dark
And mysteriously desolate under
Ritualized demands of departure
The foolish moon of your care and
Coins filtering through his sheer pockets
A shroud with pockets   cape
His personal state of permanent transit
Covered with decals where he ever mailed
His possessions.   This is serious business.
A brand new black greatcoat neatly folded
Over his naked arm the dance of human fluid
'Blood' in more polite terms.   The tattoo
Remarkable and genteel,
Pictures of mountains
And soft undistinguished
Rivers in his hand   Across his dry palm
                                                      bus ticket dup-
                                                      lication designs

The awkward sneer impinging on his nez
                                                      This particular
                                                                  place

Dracula depicted in venetian half-   light
dissolving boundaries of his presence:

Dracula   your white faces
                                                against the night
                                        Hair falling back
                                                over your faces
              formula STORY

Personal history to that man was particular
Actual form and the descriptive logic of it
The word he thought it was
Was death, was the stiffened sense
Of the garments only a sob story
That we could say here was a person
And the person a loss to himself

And the clothing edging the plump door
A frighteningly ponderous human body
Suddenly the face of Charles Baudelaire
Crushing on the television screen
Making the thick solitude of common-
Place individual people. Confused

Lost. A man whose heritage and biography was death
He said so

                              Paste back
                                 in the mornings
And demanding this song   with your content
From me, the personal   to be what person
History of a single man   you are completely
Yes, but who are you

              *   *   *

Start the thing over again
DRACULA is not a myth but
Just another cheap novel
Written in the boring 18th
19th century made into the
Worst film of 1932 1958 and
Unless we get wise to our-
Selves next year over again
Then what is all this

Dracula is real   Dracula is real!

ESSAY   The demands of the loving human flesh
                                  substance

A man and himself.
European habits

Colorless eyes filling the empty sleeves
Of the earth, another Slavic conception
What is that thing we no longer discover
Effective about our own faces in the glass
Underneath the Bb chandelier
The final odors of our dinner in person
Shudder in the monotonous drawing room
Still you have nothing else to amuse you

It compels.   It compels
The imprint of his RNA
On physical objects and
Space   He insists on it,
Insists he has been dead
Over 300 years and we
Suggest we believe it
After the trance we put
On our hypothetical
Subconscious mind   Dracula
Dracula is real!   good lord!
How do we understand it
It is life you have founded
Death's mythology on, when
Your substance demands   Get
Out of that umbrella now
Right now.

And now you are brushing yr teeth
With the language, trying to get
The decay out of the classical music
That lurks behind each evident crime

Every clumsy seduction of falseness
And mechanical simpering pride that
Moves like a film across the eyes
Distorting the incredible color of

Summertime on crowded sands
An unashamed obvious bur-
Lesk moving like a sloppy
Sneak thief in the dreams

Floating like sunlight into an awful
America white and unhappy as drawn
by a dull artist who lusts and his
Creations for the darkness of blood

And insane crime. But it's a crime
What he's doing and beyond statute
THIS IS A WORK OF ART no matter how
Unnecessary it remain to our flesh

      *   *   *

These last lines of it spoken by the midnight doctor
And left hanging in the flat air over the station
To be snatched by the violent train of his thoughts
Suspended sentences drawing sighs from the placid
Snake tooth mouth of our Dracula. Changes his form
Assumes an entire jury of peering witnesses walking
Deliberately like negroes on the street,
And then the strict transformation rabble
Screaming and waving pockets torn off
The most respectable fences in the town
A lynch mob.   Simple.   This is nothing
With symbols except the holy mystery of
Our people in this country today. God
Have charged them with the presence of the unwanted
The necessary black negro   and this is the way
Our people bear their judgement
There is no release in the songs

Their music is dying   They try to steal
Heat for the beautiful instruments again
The black ones learn to play these
Machines but they leave our people screaming
Silence   Nothing happens.   More nothing and
The loss of the land hangs in the air
A rotten rapist.   Stomach full of bloody
Advertising. Sculpture or is it dance
The hanging orchards of America but our
People are so ashamed. The signs alter
Our cities serving the sacrament negro
Motion and feeling language logic blood
The jig.   Boss.   Silent, it is without Dracula's
Ease he sucked from the ersatz Florentine walls
Something is yet lacking in our people's religion
Said the doctor at midnight

Speaking their own language at that

*   *   *

Rejection and the knowledge it is a sense of loss
We lack, that only such emotion could complete us
When we are tired of our thoughtful survival and
Cry to be married to a cringing darkness and capture
It in our souls. Petty lunacy of each stilled
Evening in some totally unremarkable place, under-
Stand that as the torture of our rapturous manners

The white glitter of our impressive table
Manners and thoughts that go nowhere after
All we are content to have surround us and
Lift up to the light of our language and
Sip thoughtlessly of the ravishing cup marked
With the brand name of the thing we have used
To identify ourselves on this surprised earth

Minion. The register of surprise at some awkwardly
Pretentious demand
                      breaking up all over again
                            the expectation of some   what
                      orderly form
The Cross   crucific
                back
          in the same Dracula
                      story

To have been saying, Dracula is a real person
A man

                              and any Art that depends for sub-
                                                    stance
                      there, the human
                      must end in pieces
                            appropriate
                            like the hill

    white stones
and green hill   Athens

The pettiness of a real man
Walks in the luncheonette
Grinning over the sandwich   meat without blood
                                              an American
                                        Dracula   hmmmm

            *   *   *

A bouquet of ashes.

Bill Berkson

from RECENT VISITORS

VIBRATION SOCIETY

It doesn't matter where I knew her.

We were star-explorers together

Now it's lost.

Great gobs of devotion make me swallow
hard in the soft blond chair. Into the
dragon, no one left out! Some fool puts
trees in front of his house in time to see
it all slip away into illusory sludge. We
gather our wits to save him but it's too
late. Your beautiful daughter learns the
hard ways of wave-dwellers. We walk away
smiling, pink in foul sunset.

TRAVELER'S COMPANION
for Joanne Kyger

If you're in a communicative mood, call us up.
Anyway, have a good time and take care. Don't
run out of gas. Don't get arrested. Don't hesitate.
If you're the only one of your friends to get into
Disneyland think that's great and send out your report.
This car's a steal at $200. This is the dessert Phoebe
made. It says "Fare Thee Well". The moldy dresses of
Tijuana whores billow about your ears. (*Eyes* might be
truer; in any case, remember that what you see is as
true as you see it.) And no sweat. As you get older
you feel cold more. This has been a light winter.
You are a warm person. If you write, stay loose. Use
a good notebook well; it's inspiring and becomes a part
of everything that happens. Many suns and many moons.
The tight squeeze of every moment's passing is upon you,
but you wear it with bright assurance and a certain
mystery. African sunrises are the greatest—and the dawns
ancient Pueblos watch lifting from the prairies to the

Pacific Ocean. When you snap this picture put yourself in
the group of the ultimate picture. Act your part as a
metaphysical figure moving, imagining somehow a God's-eye
view, which must finally be your own, the real one. A
stripped and ready consciousness is a handy item, though
only that. *Buenas tardes, Senora!* You may read less, talk
to yourself more. When I say to myself "You" I mean I think
the other person is listening and reacts. Obey the law.
If you can't be with the one you love love the one you're with.
I'd go with you were my direction other than what it appears:
close but veering and temporarily askew. I'll be back soon.
I'll remember you to all your friends.

WAKE UP (CALL)

Opposites attract
but comparisons rebound horribly
in the steady glare
admiration of light
where one is only
different, not so,
too, true
I'd like
a word with you
as against
the reality principle
where nothing's heard
all too
distinctly, where
a door is dark
and you in it do
make expression
I can't fathom
it's that deep
in the heart's thick
rush of mumbles
comprehension
of another nature, not this one
(mine), yours (not that)
what you want
you do it
what I do
is a lover's question

a pleasurable sensation
for now, not yet true
(which is *then*, not)
you come and go
I stick around
only to move
my way, now, to you
can you feel it now?

ROOTS

The people round off this planet

in spheres of sharp perfection

prickly, blithe

as the jawbone

of a spiritualist's peevish

ups and downs.

However, these bubbles

could care less,

stuck, I guess,

in familiar gnawing sleep

between the lights

of droning planes

as the people undress

persuasive and abundant

inside the lens

its knowing glance

forever equals

the amazing ability to forget

from INCIDENTALS IN THE DAY WORLD

LATTICED CULOTTE AND STARRY BLOUSE

What one wants of course is the clothes to contain one which
            are one,
flexibly enough for the breasts' ease,
            somehow
aesthetically accomodating to the elbows' awkwardness,
if one stoops as a heron might it smacks
            of truly amazing grace,
grace that's a tender smack in the face:
one wants one's own form of clothes.
            One wants it
in bright colors that are a duller, felt background
            for nuances' play of face,
infinite polkadots stripes stars yet a softer,
            polyphonic line to those nuances,
and at the same time one eschews that vocabulary
strides forth in essence irregardless!
            who has
born a baby (and married a husband) and is suddenly
            skittish within form,
would punch holes in it,
make monster faces at it is it to test it in every way? Just
            it, one day
it is simply seen as a privilege,
to be one for long and so specifically
            —how scary how exciting
a privilege—to expand to the fullness of the specific one.
There is work to do to do it,
            a letting go constantly
to find form, every muscle must relax in the working.
The eyes caress the clothes in the mirror without looking,
the skin feels them like a friend's admiring
            look,
when both people are comfortable in the admiration.
One is a connection, and one is a sun, facing sun, the rays
            of both one.
One has lost the thought thread and is simply
            breathing in bed with one's husband, latticed
culotte and starry blouse glowing
            from the closet

THREE STROLLS

1.

I take the baby for a stroll in the pre-storm
he loves it so much he goes to sleep in it
after a wide-awake night in which he
discovers some unknown to us new thing we
already know — dilated big blue eyes
dilated tiny nostrils — yellow & kelly
green, lion & crocodile, etc circling
around in the air each under its own cloud

2.

      the stroller collapsed the calendar
obscured by what the stroller comes in
           the ambery varnished wood
dirt mottled won't come off it
      and the way she talks is funny for good

———

   & sometime after sexy dreams
   & sometime after black sleep
there must be sometime, still

———

   my day is all little birds & bees
swarming colliding collapsing
          now warmer, clearing, with clouds
opening up to a twilit blue dome
              wishing for
my star charts and stars
         not really
I truly almost never wish
        though I do dream

3.

First I woke up & realized
the baby wasn't awake yet & had slept
for almost 8 hours
                    wondered if
he was really dead jumped up poked him
a little he belched or something
                                then
I got back into the bed grateful for it
        and then he began his morning yelling

    that's how much of what goes on gets stopped & started

                ____

        A long morning carriage stroll
in his white cap he loved the motion
in his sleep & now he's awake and crying again

    all he wants is an infinite carriage ride
with breasts inside it

                ____

        Everyone comes & tells me "your baby's
crying!" as if I can't hear him too
probably so do you

        he's merely making a speech—
protesting the war the milk problem

                ____

        Mommy's clothes don't fit her any more
she refuses to buy new ones because
she thinks she's going to lose enough weight
to wear the old ones again
                    isn't she dumb?

                        more of the Irrevocable

        the baby always wakes me up but
who can afford to sleep now?

———

      I've always wanted to
be conscious in my sleep

      in my dream the other night the
fortune-teller said "You are obsessed with
the sleep between birth & death"
                          but I'm in it

———

      The form of the day keeps slipping away
from my control
                 and he wants food & play awake at
constant irregular intervals
          the day now it's him now it's me again him

      what is this with babies anyway?
all this for the pleasure of holding this?

          Yes Why Don't know Animal Magic

———

      Mommy won't get up & do any
succouring or work she finds it important
to do the crossword puzzle—as many as possible—
all day
          furthermore
                  she hopes the family doesn't
acquire a car monster
                    because she doesn't want to learn
how to drive it in terror of life & death

      she wants to do the crossword puzzle all day

      Mommy will never solve the problem
of her liberation that way

             until she will

———

Shall I go look at him?
I like to look at him
I like to wake him up & hold him

and then he cries & won't stop & there's
something else I have to do something about

but I will, & do

———

"All my life I've been in love with its
color"
Goldfinger says

a "severe thunderstorm" is outside

and the baby stares & stares at the
maroon cushion
                the vast space of the maroon
soon to become more myriad
                                a more
myriad space a more myriad maroon
                                he swoons at it
        I swoon at him
                who's also it

———

You go though everything just to get
something to hold to look at it
        you go through everything just to get
something to look at to hold

INCIDENTALS IN THE DAY WORLD

You and baby you know me and I am
my ankles and angles and cavern-
haired particular whim

a bank of violets devours
deposits itself again and again

in the flame boa heap with the diaper pins
the Chanel for the monthly bath and the invisible Rodins

Our moving cars through the rain
I'm grabbing the road
trees can turn fish or rock
underwater   (or city like toad)
our compacted gyre, common load
setting out to win a face
child was is me, and me, and no one
spangled with charm apparently flesh
you in me with me mean mind clear and fleshed

Lovely and wise in a number I

poignance is a spear in use bossed, with dew
numerical I overcome Sansjoy
number are my face when I am flow
when I perform a number I'm a num-
ber's silver clean, exalting hollow
"Thought it was the Reader's Digest but
it was Life": number's deepening deepening hum

Their arts they move they escape clean
I serpentine invent my luck
I marry you world, my stolen heart
dispersed into the fray of clothes
I'll get back by wearing everything

it's a number like any other, one
I'll wear my death my baby gives away
I'll wear my death like anyone like day

Not undoing: I must love the glassine eye
caves being minor matters violent-
ly velvet, the crystal sphere rod strip screw
no magic bone, disjointed forces a block
a construction to men-ladies lent
a true Oscar's a candle a standard
stage in the Little Sailor's Home, meant

as an Eve blossom, space's form, hard
to loosen, warm milieu, sugar now coffee heart

Here's a world for today:
Killing and not dying   fantastically not lying
know a humble etiquette
                  assuming everything
         to encompass a gold ring
    spiraling outward to include every-
thing (will she)   spaciously running
like a silver animal for a quarry:
unfleshed air, of a day when some if its motes are starry

"A square chest is trying to attach it-
self to my round one" my round self
my most faithful and tender friend and prick
the scenery the coffee is a shelf
but I don't believe in an elfin self
or brilliance before radiance: "Nothing
monstrous about that violin" that clef
and I'm cleaving
to a bottle a cylinder glass not undoing

Hot, and everyone as if what it
is high serpent stretches
vegetables spears
                the stars' web sticky
to caress me ripe peat will lick
bunches of knot grass ringlets,
clime feeling suffocant

sucking wetness overtakes the cool level-eyed sets

You take my old time and space I wanted
having set out and won another's face
wanted it back or wanted a new it
a bold blind face
little baby extend my space   the rent
is expensive tho space for a whole heart
marriage has a bold blind face

but birth rent me from an easier part

"Marriage like the car is an invention"
curled interestingly
you stare and wonder and wait and don't, cun-
ning is its not yours it might be a felony

my magnet, shimmer of the formal sea
colors of men are drawn to its clothes
colors flesh all, for all, when flashed as clothes

I wish I could stay awhile longer
if the world weren't anything but poems!
flawlessly spines strung longueur
and it is and I'm not, a woman
a small palm offers its leaves to the wind
with the rock that also tears it: a man
an actual measure exists in
measures my span on our wall by his span
(Cezanne) ended perfected before me always begin

The drive to radiate light of the broil
when the blood is vintage we'll
chat over coffee holding hands and foil-
ing flirt the stately music, sunny chill
from peak to sea and they laugh at the not too brill-
iant; cumbrous light tore my shade of
freely blank and yield and wind

my form he came from I come from his again

Adored with fruitful entities all around
dead centers: steel graters or stars
I ordinarily build a sphere's ground
the Prince's stolen heart might be here
with a baby, emblazoned with thick red air

thick as love you too must come here
with hair and claws I have no death
I claw into being all of our puissant birth

That I pray to with steal and charm, for you
square the circle to fuck it
in instant needs and breath brazen to
innocently olive and dark take it
to you, with breasts and meddling intent
I despise innocence I have so
little I forget everything, innocent
new, I drink and pause, my favorite so
you may be yours too, and comfortable, our row

My body becomes boat, water
which can't hold back my knees
my artifice
uncanny at the ceiling flies off
drunken flying knees: the flesh's tryst scoffs
          stars
to make it whole—you understand
simple sparks and trapezes
in the grit of your knowing of it and
…

Syllables
my neck breasts knees open bare
not describable but perceptible words
as the haunted blood's gentle dear
I'm not at all completely sincere
untaken, emblazoned with thick red air

restore the other half of a pair
here's the palpable air of earth, the earth of air

You knee my desert clarity
my sea in porcelain
my nothing knees ecumenical balmy
up around you in curls
or I must make howl
ellipscid elliptical mongoloid

      the paper white must avoids:
a callous steamer maturity tryst in the world

Careless of my stealth and of my fame
I take a serpent shield from flower sun
and, would for anything be blamed
accepting anything all and one

disgraced disarmed disarming graced
our pottage hundreds of crushed suns
jewels: such attitude our clothing's face
such show becomes then the center's force, of our race

If my most beautiful ape
is ugly my most beautiful knee is miraculous
its completed palpability, nape-
sexy behind its pillar's unselfconscious-
ness, the cunning adulterant rapes the face
but
what you don't kiss won't sing less

in the wind awkward but, cooly, cold

Thinking of three
I mostly say I
we feel mingled in perfect sanguinity
in me on sherry secretly dry
circling and twining so
lively so like void is silly
light will mass and dry, sly
will fake coyly
pose and refuse but I won't fear the incident I'm

In our moving cars through the rain
unlacing lofty crest for outgrown bangs
you play me fair as gold blown
or over each branch and its blossom hangs
air of honey and boomerangs
"a salvage beast embost" in splinters
every object a phone rings
rings into gold contact
wedding ring blinding messy air made more compact

We spell spell "spell", I spelled it: knew
from deadly danger was loose from
and light in, now dress for my sphere to
rest my person where I nest from
back black clear
the meaning of my face
that velvety intersection's bloom
with no fear of the compass
or my incident   I encompass

Another walk with my seeing it
my fancy if it's a personal oyster
soft as a mat to a tumbler's must
the sky seems as kind as a teamster
do I get out of the cave guitars of
my mortal slime my billowing senses
                          a scimitar
through to a wondrous darkness
but cylinder sphere and cone I the spherey earth press

I embrace all the dead
voices instruments waters medicines

their furious loving fits made wind
strange phantoms in pleasure's valentine

my dead and my ghosts my atoms fine
by these rent reliques speaking their plightes
(Spenser, I feared so the other side of my sight)

Alone mixing skin with sheet
pigeon rags windowed mirrors wrath and flesh
sipping a pale, human's aperitif (air)
keep its hardened lovely must or
the world away you left worshipless
cold and hot she laughs—we laugh—walls
feeding on city cliffs coast dress

inchoate, I'm still always choken with bells

from DREAMS

DRUGSTORE

I am standing at the subway entrance on the northeast corner
of Sixth Avenue and 3rd Street, feeling terrible. I've just had
an awful fight with Arlene, who has stormed off, and I'm
thinking, self-pityingly, that I haven't a friend in the world.

Just then I spot Dick Gallup in the crowd coming out of the
subway. I ask him what he's up to. Nervously, he says he's
going to a certain drugstore to cop some pills. I ask him if I
can get some, too, and he says yeah, probably.
The drugstore
is dingy and looks like an ancient pawnshop. The druggist—a
seedy, furtive-looking old man—hands over a little paper box,
which Dick and I empty onto the counter. There are pills of
all sorts, but most are diet spansules, a couple of which break
open, scattering their loads of tiny green and white beads.
I
ask the old man if he has any tranquilizers, I need one imme-
diately. Grumbling, he produces a dubious-looking, pasty-
white pill the size and shape of a golfball. Then I remember
that I have a bottle of Valium. In fact, as I discover, I have
drugs of every description in my pockets, which I unload onto
the counter to split the contents with Dick.
Suddenly a
crowd of policemen appears outside the door, accompanying
a man in a pin-striped suit. They're addressing him as "Sena-
tor," and I understand that he's touring New York today to
assess its drug problem.
The old man ducks into a back room.
Dick is in a panic, jabbering that we're done for and tugging
at my sleeve. I'm in a cold sweat myself, but I tell him to
take it easy. I see by the clock above the counter that we have
ten seconds to stash the evidence.

OCEAN LINER

I am a nervous young sailor on a huge ocean liner that is slowly sinking. Among the thousands of passengers is a colorful bunch of gypsies hated by the other passengers, who threaten to massacre them. The gypsies respond with quiet defiance, saying mysteriously that when the ship goes down, only gypsies will survive.

I believe what the gypsies say, though I note with alarm that a lot of them seem to be drowning. Meanwhile I am looking to get some comfort for myself.

On deck, I spot a girl I seem to know. I approach her and say something like, Listen, before the ship goes down why don't you and I make it together. She turns to me with a cool look. "All we've ever had," she says, "is three difficult Thursdays at that creepy-crawly motel in New Mexico." "Yes," I reply, "but an experience like this gives a guy a sense of values."

All around us, the sea is full of swimming and drowning people, many of them gypsies. I sound sickeningly false to myself, but I see the girl giving in a little. "I know," she says with a touch of warmth.

"ADVENTURES WITH NICKY & CINDY"

I am in Midtown to see a movie and, having an hour to kill, stop at a "gambling parlor," where I occupy myself with betting on real horse races performed on tabletops by live, two-inch-high horses. My eye is caught by a handsome young guy at the blackjack table, so irresistably nice-looking that I walk right over and introduce myself.

His name is Nicky, he says, and he is a student from New Jersey. The more we talk, the more enchanted I am by his looks and manner. Would he like to go to the movies? I ask. He can't, but he offers to drop in on me later in the night.

Outside, the city at dusk looks ruined and desolate. I barely escape four would-be muggers by dashing into the street and shouting "Move! Move!" Then, at a bus stop, I spot a fantastically attractive girl. She is about 20, with cherubic features and a healthy, buoyant look.

A bus arrives and I follow her onto it. She gives me a sweet, interested glance. I blurt, "You're the most terrific woman I ever saw!" and embrace her. She pulls away gently but firmly. Don't do that, she says, we haven't even met. I control myself and we talk.

Her name is Cindy. She lives in the Bronx and works for The New York Post (she shows me a copy with her by-line on the front page). No, she can't come to the movies, but she'd be glad to visit me at my place later.

After the movie, of which I remember nothing, I hurry home. Arlene is there, and when Nicky and Cindy arrive I introduce them to her as my new and dearest friends. To my delight, she seems to like them, too.

As we talk, the doorbell rings and in comes my sister Ann, looking almost as beautiful as Cindy. She was just passing by, she says. I nearly burst into tears at the thought that I am in a room full of people I love.

Immediately it occurs to me that, oh no, I must be dreaming! And sure enough, the scene starts to fade. I feel the beginnings of a horrible disappointment. But I can still see Nicky and Cindy, and, without moving their lips, they are speaking to me reassuringly across the widening gulf.

Yes, we are dream figures, they say, but we are also real. You will meet us again. Then, just as they are disappearing, they add, You should write down this dream and call it "Adventures with Nicky & Cindy."

THE READING

I am awakened by a knock on the door. It's Tom Disch. He has come, he says, for the reading. I don't understand, but I let him in, crawl back into bed and regard him sleepily as he pulls out a sheet of paper and hands it to me.

The paper is a detailed critique, in five numbered paragraphs, of the dreams I've been writing down lately. As one who has had some experience of writing imaginative prose, Tom says modestly, he has been pained to see me making some fundamental, avoidable mistakes in my dream works. These mistakes are outlined in his critique.

I am reading it when there's another knock.
Tom answers it, and in come Anne Waldman, John Ashbery
and two or three others. I ask what's going on, and Anne says,
Didn't you know? the St. Mark's Christmas Reading is to be
held at your place this year.

I look around my 10-by-12-foot
apartment. Where are we going to put the audience? I wonder,
and somebody says, Don't worry about it, everything will be
all right.

I'm about to get up when I remember that I'm com-
pletely naked. So I pull the covers up around my chin and just
wait, totally amazed.

Everyone else seems to be waiting, too.
It's mid-afternoon and beautiful golden sunlight is streaming
in the windows. In a friendly voice, John says he hopes I'll be
reading some of my new dreams. They probably aren't very
good in their present form, he adds, nodding to Tom, but
they're quite charming when read aloud.

I'm a little hurt by
this last remark, but I also feel immensely touched and pleased
at all the attention. I want to thank everyone personally, but I
can't find the words. Everybody is sitting around the sunlit
room, relaxed and smiling, waiting for the reading to begin.

DAVID'S SISTER

I am going with David Bennett to his house in the suburbs to
play pool with him and a friend of his. The house turns out to
be ramshackle and poor-looking.

In the threadbare living
room, David introduces me to his incredibly sexy sister.
About 19 and apparently not too bright, she has creamy white
flesh and a slow, seductive smile that drives me crazy. When
David leaves the room for a minute, I start making out with
her immediately.

In no time our clothes are off and we're
writhing in an easy chair. She is receptive, yet somehow
passive and unaroused. I ache to fuck her but hold off, wait-
ing until she seems ready.

A voice—is it hers or my own?—
says in my ear, "Follow your heart, not your head," meaning
do it right away. But still I hesitate.

David returns and regards us with a foolish, uptight grin. Trying to appear nonchalant, he makes a ponderous, awful joke: "Watch out you don't get her pregnant or I'll have to drown the kid in the river." Whereupon, totally chagrined, he heads for the pool room.

It occurs to me that I really ought to ask the girl if she has contraception, but I'm just too excited to care.

I pick her up and carry her around the room. She's fantastically light. I hoist her onto my shoulders, facing me, and begin to tongue her clitoris in a very particular way, very lightly. She likes it. She says, "Ooh, that's the way the Russians do it!"

I start tonguing in another way, hoping to increase her excitement. "Ach," she says disgustedly, "you lost it."

David Rosenberg

from SOME PSALMS

PSALM 6

Lord, I'm Just a worm
don't point to me
in your boiling anger

don't let me feel
I more than deserve
all your rage

but mercy, Lord, let me feel mercy
for I'm weak & depressed
even my bones shiver with worry

my soul even shocks a manic depressive
how long, Lord, how long
till you return to shine your light

return to me dear Lord
bring back the light
that I can know you by

because those that are dead
have no thought of you
to make a song by

I am tired of my groaning
my bed is flowing away
in the nights of tears

depression like a moth
eats from behind my face,
tiny motors of pain push me

get out of here all you
glad to see me so down
your every breath so greased with vanity

My Lord is listening so high
my heavy burden of life floats up

as a song to him

let all my enemies quiver
on the stage of their total self-consciousness
and all their careers ruined in one night.

PSALM 36

Inside my heart I hear
how arrogance talks
to himself without fear

hidden from eyes
he flatters himself
but we see him on the faces

of false faces and words
thinking—even asleep—
how to squeeze love out

from feelings from words
how to put wisdom on her back
then hold his miniature knowledge back

your love fills a man, Lord
with a kind of air
making him lighter

he rises in measure of your judgment
above the mountains of thought
above the clouds of feeling

the strength of his measure stays
in the eyes returning to mountains
from the surface of the sea

he falls like any animal
standing up only by your mercy
his children grow in the shadow of your wings

feast on gourmet fare in your house
with water that sparkles from wells
beyond the reach of a mind

the fountain of life
is lit
by your light

you extend your embrace
to those who feel you are there
keep holding the loving

keep us from being crushed
by arrogant feet
by the hand of pride

the powerful are falling over themselves
their minds have pulled them down
there they will lie, flung down

PSALM 58

Can this be justice
this pen to hold
they that move my arm

to follow them—blind stars?
They think I have submitted
to the vicious decorum of fame?

O generation come from dust
O no: you steel yourselves
to write; your hands

weigh, like a primitive scale,
selfish desire unfulfilled...
strangers from the womb

no sooner born and here
than chasing after
impulsive wishes

for which they will lie, cheat, kill.
The cancer of false desire oozes
in their brain

a bone cancer—as the doctor
the greatest virtuoso surgeon
cuts deep into the chest

exposing the vital organs
transplanting vital organs
totally blind to the truth.

Lord, break their fingers
till the arms hang limp like sausage,
grind down to sand

the teeth of the power-hungry
& let their selves dissolve into it
like ebbing tide on a junk-strewn beach

& when they in profound bitterness
unsheathe the sharpened thought
electrocute it in their brain, Love!

make them disappear like snails
slime of their bodies melting away
or like babies, cord broke in abortion

to be thrown out as discharge
eyes withered in the daylight
though they never looked at it.

And let the children of greed like weeds
be pulled from their homes
& their parents blown away like milkweed...

The loving man will be revived
by this revenge & step ashore
from the bloodlust of the self-righteous

so that every man can say
there is justice so deep
a loving man has cause to sing.

PSALM 139

There's nothing in me My Lord
that doesn't open to your eyes
you know me when I sit

you note when I arise
in the darkest closet of my thought
there is an open window of sunshine for you

you walk with me
lie down with me
at every move await me

at every pause
you know the words
my tongue will print in air

if I say yes
you have already nodded
no—and you have shaken your head

In any doubts I lose my way
I find your hand
on me

such knowledge so high
I can never reach with a mind
or hold any longer than a breath

To get away from you
I could let my imagination fly
but you would hold it in your sky

or I could sleep with the dead in the ground
but your fire from the depths
would awaken me

I could fly on gold ray of sun
from dawn in east
west to stars of night

& your hand
would point the way

& your right hand hold me steady

However close I pull the night around me
even at midnight
day strips me naked

in your tender sight
black & white
are one—all light

you who put me together
piece by piece in the womb
from light

that work shines
through the form of my skeleton
on my song of words

you watched as my back steadied
the still-soft fuselage of ribs
in primitive studio deep within

you saw me as putty
a life unfashioned
a plane at the bottom of the sea

and the great book of its life
this embryo will write
in a body you have sculpted

My Lord—your thoughts
high and precious
beyond logic like stars

or like grains of sand I try to count
I fall asleep and awake
on the beach of your making

My Lord—stop the breath
of men who live by blood
alone and lie to your face

who think they can hide
behind the same petty smile
they use to smear your name with shit

My Lord—you hear me hate
back your haters
with total energy

concentrated
in one body
that is yours and mine

My Lord—look at me
to see my heart
test me—to find my mind

if any bitterness lives here
lead me out
into the selfless open.

from MORE I REMEMBER MORE

***

I remember biting on a little piece of flesh inside my mouth until a very sweet sort of pain came.

I remember not being able to remember if "13" is a lucky number, or an unlucky number.

I remember Noble and Fern (my mother's brother and his wife) and that she never stopped talking ("a blue streak") and that he never said a word. They had two kids, Dale and Gale. Dale was so plain that, actually, I'm not sure if I remember him or not. But I *do* remember Gale. She was very cute, and bubbly, and totally obnoxious. She took piano lessons *and* singing lessons *and* dancing lessons. They lived in California and traveled around a lot, by car, never stopping in restaurants for food. (They traveled *with* food) They'd come visit us about once every three years with a slide projector and recent (3 years worth of "recent") travel slides. And, in a plastic coat hanger bag, a fancy costume for Gale, who did her "number" almost immediately upon arrival. These visits were nothing to look forward to. But, after three or four days they would leave, with lots of sandwiches, and, "You've really *got* to come and see us in California!"

I remember visiting once a very distant relative who had a son about my age (8 or so) who had been saving pennies all his life. It was one of those living rooms packed solid with large furniture, and to top it off, every inch of available space was full of giant jars full of pennies. Even on the floor, and even in the hallway, lined up against the walls, were giant jars full of pennies. Really, it was a very impressive sight. Quite a "haul" for a boy my own age. I was green. (I hope I'm not exaggerating here but, if so, I am genuinely doing so) But, no, I don't think I am.) Really, it was almost holy: like a shrine. I remember his mother smugly saying that he (8 years old!) was saving it to send himself through college.

I remember trying to save money, for a day or two, and quickly losing interest.

I remember very tempting little ads in the backs of magazines for like say 25 dresses ("used" in *very* small print) for only one dollar!

I remember in speech class each fall having to give a speech about "what I did this summer". I remember usually saying that I swam a lot (a lie) and painted a lot (true) and did a lot of reading (not true) and that the summer went very fast (true). They always have, and they still do. Or so it seems once summer is over.

I remember, on cold mornings, counting to ten before making myself jump out of bed.

I remember daydreams of going with an absolutely knock-out girl, and impressing all my friends no end.

I remember wondering how one would go about putting on a rubber gracefully, in the given situation.

I remember supposing that a woman's "slit" is higher up than it is.

I remember (in a general sort of way) many nights in bed just holding myself through soft flannel pajamas.

I remember cold sheets in the winter time.

I remember when everything is covered with snow, out the window, first thing in the morning: a really clear surprise. It only snowed about twice a year in Tulsa and, as I remember now, usually during the night. So, I remember "snow" more than I remember "snowing."

I remember not understanding the necessity of shoveling the sidewalks. It always melted in a day or two anyway. And besides—"It's only snow."

I remember thinking Brownie uniforms not very pretty: so brown and plain.

I remember fantasies of everyone in my family dying in a car wreck, except me, and getting lots of sympathy and attention, and admiration for being so brave about it all.

I remember fantasies of writing a very moving letter to the President of the United States about patriotism, and the President, very moved by my moving letter, distributes copies of it to the media (T.V., magazines, newspapers, etc.) and I become very famous.

I remember day dreams of being a very smart dresser.

I remember day dreams of going through old trunks in attics, and finding fantastic things.

I remember white socks with a thin red and blue stripe at the top.

I remember (visually) socks on the floor, tossed after a day of wear. They always look so comfortable there.

I remember early fragments of daydreams of being a girl. Mostly I remember fabric. Satins and taffetas against flesh. I in particular remember yards and yards of royal blue taffeta (a *very* full evening dress, no doubt) all bunched up and rubbing between my thighs, by big hands. This period of fantasizing about being a girl wasn't at all sexual in terms of "sex". The kick I got didn't come from being with a man, it came from feeling like a woman. (Girl) These fantasies, all so much one to me now, were all very crunched up and fetus-like. "Close". An orgy of fabric and flesh and friction (close-ups of details). But nothing much "happened."

I remember fantasies of being in jail, and, very monk-like in my cell, handwriting out a giant great novel.

I remember (on the other hand) fantasies of being in jail, and of good raw sex. All very "black and white" some how. Black bars, white tiles. White flesh, black hairs. The rubbery warm whites of cum, and the shiny cold blacks of leather and slate.

I remember (here's a real let-down for you) fantasies of opening up an antique store, with only *very* selective objects, displayed sparsely in an "art gallery" sort of way.

I remember fantasies of opening up an art gallery on the Lower East Side in a store front (I'd live in back) with one exposed wall (brick) and everything else white. Lots of potted plants. And paintings by, you guessed it, me.

from MAKES SENSE

who
'd
of
thought
the
morning
'd
be
so
late
and
separate
who
from
their
sense
like
whence
went
someone
and
thus
we
have
a
fence
hence
and
that
's
pretty
nice
(who
'd
you
ask
for
a
slice?)

who
is
a
handsome
young
man
in
the
air
in
the
air
of
distraction
who
'll
hold
open
like
a
good
fellow
the
door
to
the
future
and
's
so
kind
comes
out
the
other
side
of
kindness

a
tiny
morsel

of
friendship
delights
like
a
sentence
alone
by
itself
whose
consonants
shimmer
like
high
lights
dealing
loosely
some
feelings
through
vowels’
melody
and
then
some
more
(than
a
poet
a
tree
in
poetry)
building
sleep
into
inquiry
and
asking
who
’s
there
and
someone

answers
me
that
's
who

who
is
triggered
by
a
long
and
a
short
group
of
sentences
into
something
more
than
who
and
less
than
someone
on
the
phone
might
gather
from
the
assembled
phonemes
is
n't
that
what
the
phone
's

for
someone
says
who
says
what
who
has
anything
to
say
and
this
time
's
different
the
clouds
spitting
through
the
sky
like
pumpkin
seeds
bump
on
the
horizon
of
the
vertical
building
who
's
been
building
up
note
after
note
an
incredible
birdbath

of
principles
whose
test
is
theoretically
feasible
whoever
's
feeling
able
to
understand
what
goes
into
the
makeup
besides
powder
of
a
fee
the
network
of
fast
moving
theory
nestled
in
the
electric
nestlés
afresh

of
those
who
have
read
sense
into

the
incredible
grin
that
waits
to
let
us
in
hi
come
on
in
who
are
you
make
yourself
at
home
whoever
you
are
how
do
you
like
california
(wherever
this
takes
place)
face
new
york
squarely
and
let
your
thoughts
lace
and
become
lace

and
replace
lace
with
an
entire
string
of
taste

of
name
(who
signs)
of
wife
of
inner
happiness
of
return
journey
(who
returns)
of
given
her
words
(it
's
whose
business)
of
half
guessed
stories
(whose)
that
gather
in
the
middle
of
the

shade
of

through
the
jungle
a
can
of
sardines
reminds
whom
of
a
book
and
brings
the
book
on
home
and
keeps
the
conversation
going
home
and
brings
the
book
into
the
conversation
that
reminds
whoever
is
listening
to
the
first
time

they
ever
heard
from
home
and
how
it
felt
to
whom

a
sound
of
voices
brings
home
the
memory
of
hearts
hoist
in
honor
of
first
memory
and
them
too
in
an
early
system
of
dew
who
tools
along
in
the
same
week

to
the
colors
of
the
weekend
painted
like
a
handful
of
flowers
in
the
colors
of
the
following
hours

to
whom
it
may
concern
this
is
the
hidden
meaning
of
sleep
woven
into
a
couch
pretend
not
to
notice
it
pretends
not

to
notice
you
who
's
that
(who
's
that?)
you
might
ask
and
well
you
might
you
who
have
grown
asunder
from
the
thunder
with
faint
traces
begin
you
sleep
in
the
first
person
the
others
won't
(can't)
be
far
(be
far)
behind
downhill

is
a
subtle
body
and
as
the
earth
houses
the
mountain
who
's
the
ass
who
's
foreground
and
background
to
mirth
I
wish
you
beast
heads
and
the
terrible
energies
of
matter
as
you
please

John Wieners

HOTELS 1970

From the first dollar-a-night rooming house on Tremont
Street to the Plaza may seem a long jump, from the Broadway
Hotel in San Francisco to the Dorothy Statler Suite in Buffalo
half a continent, from New England Inn on Cape Cod to an Indian
hacienda in Santa Fe part of the great divide, through the
Biltmore, the New Yorker, and One Fifth Avenue to one night
stands in Canton, Ohio, rainy motels, cabins and motor inns
across the United States, penniless in The Dixie in Times
Square, the Thomas Jefferson only for scoring heroin, The Nassau,
Blackstone, Chateau Frontenac in Quebec to creepy Bowery Broadway
Central, the Gattapone, overlooking a 14th century aqueduct in
mountains, north of Rome. The Atlantic with Charles Olson, near
The Stazione Terminale, The Rockefeller Hilton, Parker House,
Hotel Madison, all these acquired mystery for writing, the Hotel
Victoria, George Washington, Chelsea, Ritz Hotel in Montreal,
Hotel Albert, Earle, Marlton, The Rhinebeck Inn on The Hudson,
oldest inn in America, The Hotel Ithaca since torn down outside
Cornell, and the hotels this book will be a record of, after the
YMCA in Washington, D.C. and Albergo Nationale of Rome, the
Commodore in Cambridge with friends and in anonymity, a lover's
manor on the North Shore, a forgotten accommodation in amnesia
and a borrowed room at The Hotel Wentley for a beginning...not
accounting for the Hotel Adelphi in Saratoga.

By this time I checked into the Delmonicos on Park

Ave., the hashish was gone and I was left with marijuana,

old friends gone.

You are up now and moving about the house.

I am going to a strange hotel, Manhattan

heart beating loudly. With a snake ring for

luck and pommade on my lips. Lapels too wide,

thinking of 1950, in the stink of Mayfair.

Hotels I have stayed in and NEVER robbed

not once, not even the thought of it, not skipped the bill

ever once, or left without Paying!

The Hotel St. Moritz,   1 Dollar a Night

The Hotel Statler, while coming up to Boston for The Ziegfeld
                    Follies with the Champagne and Dinner in the Room $40

The Buffalo Statler-Hilton as a guest of Ms. A.S. Overnight No tab.
          Barely got out free with my freedom
          as The Hereditary Grand Duke, Jean of The Grand Ducal
          House of Luxembourg, 2 room Suite, no fare, as guest
          of Billy Hutton, from Grosse-Pointe, good luck, Billy
          I miss you. Love on the twin-beds as Claudia "Lady-
          Bird" Johnson spoke on the television Set. What
          a gas, as he ordered a table of 2 whiskeys, full-food,
          and Ed Dorn and Jenny, Marianne Faithfull's cousin
          came to visit later, Bill looked so cute in his
          gaucho tourniquet, and toreador sailor Levi pants.
          What a doll, Billy; I'll be seeing you. And speaking
          of dolls, that Ed Dorn is no small shakes as a knock-
          out, Himself. Doll, Ed, bless you. You keep the old
          Home Fires burning on my Monday A.M. Linen. The
          evening before of course, quiet in my Rooming House,
          Ed lent me and spent on me 40.00. It's not the
          first time for him to stand me.

The Hyatt-Hilton, as The Beverly Hills-Hilton was filled from a
                    convention, 10th Floor, no food, no champagne,
                    one night only. Gosh, James Mason loved it! I
                    barely got in as Zsa Zsa Gabor overnight, with
                    my bags in the lobby next morning, that Joseph
                    Magnin cost me 20 dollars, plus The Fiddlers past
                    The Palms, and the maids, no tip,
how I miss them like
The Bismarck, in Chicago, where it seems the same room clerk that
directed around the corner from The Hyatt-Regency I believe, I may
be wrong drove me, after missing that 10 PM to Michicago's O'Hare; gosh,

how I dread missing my flite. He got me in there though and I don't

believe I paid until the next morning, although I know I did. A
great cantankerous remodeled plush accommodation right down the street
from The Bus Terminal, where I caught the Detroit-bound vehicle for
a nominal fee. Detroit looked so wonderful from The Howard Johnson's
Motor Lodge Windows, although I did not arrive by car. They let me
in too, after a full, good meal in the lobby, off the side street,
near the wonderful famed Pulaski Circle, winging its way onward to
the so swingingly recalled Canadian Border, southerly The Beverly
Wilshire looked wonderful, as I told you, off Stockton, California.
Two nights there. They are so suchly rely prim and proper, I
couldn't dare to take a cocktail in the boite, tho I promised myself
one, instead entertained a Local Radio Station tycoon in my lovely,
adorable, perfection's chalet king-size minus reservation. Oh,
those Chinese are so wonderful. They keep a saint spirit up.

More Hostelries)

The Nassau, New York, recommended by Bobby Driscoll, no, wait
a minute, rather the English Professor, and Poet, David Posner,
Extraordinaire, he married the English Heiress Olivia Wedgwood.
Germaine code. God bless her, she's around still, globe-hopping,
tripping, travelling from one International port to the next,
David said Nassau, and so I went. As Mrs. Dick Nixon. I had
been there, and Bobby the genius came up with me, and rich socialite
from Buffalo, his mother went to Vassar, and his Father's a Banker,
and his sister's Diana, I think; and I wrote a poem for David, and
he had beautiful hair, and the most amazing purblind complexion,
he'll come back, David always will. And his sister and mother and
Father, and their attic room, and solarium, and the mother's desk,
with the Upper class girl's school College, rather bulletin. I
think all three of us enjoyed ourselves enroute to Castalia in
Millbrook. Dr. Timothy Leary's Foundation, New York.

University Manor, that was a place, where I met him, with
Allen Ginsberg, and the then Rosemary Leary, before the
German nuptials, how exciting, glamourous, speedy and up
to the point, they read, and sound over the cool Albany
evenings, they shall stand it, again, with memories of
Onetta's; my first child, without birth; Bill's Luncheonette,
and the 200 dollar Tab finally paid for; Rose, Kurt Fiedler,
Leslie's son, The Doctore-Poet, who wrote all through the
Forties, and Fifties, and Sixties, and now Seventies, his

loving family, Kurt, Michael, and Eric; so many stayed at
The University Manor, my mother among them, before we crossed
Customs, to The General Brock, for an evening dinner, dancing,
and listening to the Radio-broadcast high above the swirling
North Country Avalanches. On The Maid of The Mist.

    Sheraton-Plaza; Copley Square, one night, the hash,
postage, about 40 dollars, but I was going out of my
mind, with jitters up North, or East, or West, possibly
over the Mississippi. As The Biltmore; the Chateau-Frontenac;
The Albergo Nazionale; The Hotel Atlantico in Rome; The
Gattapone; The Plaza when Mr. Olson was dying, unfortunately
I did not pay; suspect in Akron, Ohio I may have, a double
room with his legator, Harvey H. Brown, III, with the orchestra
down below, and the violin strings plucking serenely against
the impending news of his January 10th departure. Only 4
years ago, and 16 or so days, in little Manchester Cemetery
on the west side of town.

    I got into a few Inns in my life. R.I., N.Y., Amherst,
mostly small apartments or quiet roadside drops losing mischief
subtracted make-believe.

    Princeton's Nassau Inn is a different story; sedate
somewhat misty after my *Response*; then up around the Toll
Roads shuttered for an English nephew to The British Communist
Party. His name's John Temple. Good-hearted John, I still
wear his dressing-gown, as I write, and Knit Kickers over the
replastered entrances behind kilnfired Chambers.

My missing Hotel Registry List will soon turn up.
There's been not enough returned because personal atrocization,
so many stars, planets demoted over venial catastrophe. Or
lienned insurance tenure violators. When your time's up,
brother, you've had it, murder incorporated, or not. Death
knell vestry abyssmals from Roxbury or Jamaica Plain, Culver
Webb CC's calm BillerVickers Peckapickpalfreypotatoes.
Conrad-Hueffer's *The Inheritors*. P.T.

Let's see, compared to the money my mother spent on me, I
maybe laid out 4 Bills on The Flea Market. She threw away about
6000 of them to keep me over the 4 decade Beatrice Peel Hall,
unh, not Albermarle, Loans and All, Stallionhurdle. Horses,
bulls, and studs, that's my furlough from Fudgeque frycharisma.
If you can find them out in your lobbies these days, and I did,
as well as I do, Rhinebeck's Astorm Beekman Arms, and Saratoga
Spring's *Adelphi*. Gosh, how the mane's ply. Where next,
scootyPeregrin, floralwraith. Snootyaural. Sootyurals.

Edwin Denby

from SNORING IN NEW YORK

New York, smog-dim under August
Next Sahara-clear, the Park trees
Green from Chelsea, then blinding gusts
Of grit, the gale, cloudburst increase
Europe, that you've not got, weather
The manners, gondolas, the walls
Restaurants, hills, noon, dusk, friends there
Sweet Europe, you're so comfortable
But differently spread close asleep
Stagnant softness, oppressed secrets
On your breath, thick-throated Europe
Uninnocent masterpieces
Nudged, I wake dressed, seated writing
New York cat asks, Play with my string

***

Born in my loft, dancer untame
A wilderness imagined, small
Cat, which we reached for real by plane
You stalked on the roof up the hall
Heart nursing six kittens, that grew
With them, long-tailed splendid-eyed cat
A disease struck the womb, left you
Savage fighter, playful at night
Lamed, ireful you prowled then; vet cut
Out the womb, so rage might subside
Telephone rings, speaks, I hang up
Cat-heart that knew me gone, I cried
It stopped beating drugged in a cage
Dear, mine will too, and let go rage

***

Cool June day, up the avenue
An oldster in a boater steps
Jaunty, at the cross-street, light green
Steps out, truck turns in on him, he stops
Truck halts, the driver don't crowd him
Midwest highschool kids of his own
He'd spotted the gait, gives pop time
Lets them honk, soberly waves him on
Old man couldn't move; a PR
Touched the arm, smiled, walked him across
He took up a stride like before
Traffic regained momentum lost
Irish like the President's dad
We watched him swallowed by the crowd

***

Slight man walking, inveighs to himself
In Spanish, old frump does, English
Trucks, taxis roll, loud relief
Self listening to unlistened speech
Imagined answer awaited
Like the moon's reply, the bayed moon
Satellite, it shines belated
On New York, where we rest unknown
Rest after the reply of fate
To each specific without weight
But weightily sweethearts on edge
Caress their voices or quarrel
Before knowledge, after knowledge
Fondle both voices, boy's and girl's

***

Writing poems, an employee
I lived here at nineteen, who I?
Current boys nineteen, their beauty
Of skin, all I can recognize
On this passport, soft vague boy's smile
Recalls few facts, does, his horror

Scale's abyss, void becoming real
A heart's force, he was going mad
Which I?—surviving forty years
Schizophrenia of a goof
I remember his savage tears
The kind reproof, kind reproof
Vague-faced boy, he faced what was it?
A white old man, approved, I sit

***

Alex Katz paints his north window
A bed and across the street, glare
City day that I within know
Like wide as high and near as far
New York School friends, you paint glory
Itself crowding closer further
Lose your marbles making it
What's in a name—it regathers
From within, a painting's silence
Resplendent, the silent roommate
Watch him, not a pet, long listen
Before glory, the stone heartbeat
When he's painted himself out of it
DeKooning says his picture's finished

***

The winter nights sat through, it's May
Ocean of light at two o'clock
Theatre darkness, lit ballet
Small trees aflower, Central Park
I smell blossom, tot clicks toy gun
Couples embraced kiss, families eat
"Strike Two", Maytime satisfaction
Near my shoe, sparkles dark granite
Vacant, bend and touch it, bed-rock
Below blasted, my neighborhood
Nightly, the arclights on its bought back
Manahatouh's glens, it has stood
Cell-mess and million-yeared Hudson
Petrified has grudged their motion

***

Slight PR, tiny son, she lay
A drunk Irish on pavement
WASP, my block, heave her upright
"Two bucks, the bastard," bloody trickle
Steer her one each side, he's relieved
"She my building", his child trails us
Honest Christians, lurching we go
She heavy every which way, groans
Steep stair, he pushes her ass, she quickens
Grocery bag take from brown tiny hands
Return to my door, my five flights
At home can't recall anything clearly
Except a small boy's bright eyes keeping his face straight

***

Sunday on the senator's estate
Eleven of us shoot a movie
Seven drive home at one a.m.
The driver awake among sleepers
Yellow full moon, July New Jersey
Smog meadow, eight-wheelers festooned
Merging rise, toll, tunnel curving
Manhattan night, inbound, outbound
Imagination nobody
Does without, it hurts so and laughs
As if not you, not I will die
The world vanish, vanish knowledge
Who's to support me, you phoney
Be hostile, slob, get the money

***

The size balls are saddens Lamarck
It's of no relevance to Marx
And Freud shoots his lunch at the fact
Dad's funny if he's just as small
July subway, meditate on
The decently clothed small male parts
Take the fabulous importance

Felt by homes, felt better by farts
They won't be missed, science will soon
Claim, parthenolatric more than
Religion, women left alone
To travel planets with women
In the lit subway gently shook
Imagine they've a goodbye look

***

The grand republic's poet is
Brooklyn Whitman, commuter Walt
Nobody else believes all of it
Not Harvard, that finds him at fault
I have, but first he broke my heart
He points to the moon and breaks it
I look for him, twenty-first street
Sleep against the push of a cat
Waking stumble to start coffee
At my back Walt in underwear
His head slants from unaltered day
Strokes my cat, the cheeks streaming tears
Sits on the bed, quietly cries
While I delay turning round, dies

***

Inattentively fortunate
Have been pausing at lunchcounters
While what I most like, art that's great
Has been being painted upstairs
No homebuilder, even goofy
To virtue have been close as that
It I love and New York's beauty
Both have nodded my way, up the street
At fifteen maybe believed the world
Would turn out so honorable
So much like what poetry told
Heartbreak and heroes of fable
And so it did; close enough; the
Djin gave it, disappeared laughing

***

Disorder, mental strikes me; I
Slip from my pocket Dante to
Chance hit a word, a friend's reply
In this bar; bare, dark avenue
The lunge of headlights, then bare dark
Cross on red two blocks home, old Sixth
The alive the dead, answer, ask
Miracle consciousness I'm with
At home cat chirps, Norwegian sweater
Slumped in the bar, I mind Dante
As dawn enters the sunk city
Answer a one can understand
Actual events are obscure
Though the observers appear clear

SNORING IN NEW YORK

an elegy

When I come, who is here? voices were speaking
Voices had been speaking, lightly been mocking
As if in and out of me had been leaking
Three or four voices, falsely interlocking
And rising, one or two untruly falling
Here, who is here, screaming it or small calling

Let it call in the stinking stair going down
Mounting to a party, the topfloor ajar
Or later, a thick snowfall's silence begun
Crowded boys screaming shameless in a fast car
Laughing, their skulls bob backward as if weeping
These happy voices overhang my sleeping

I slide from under them and through a twilight
Peer at noon over noon-incandescent sand
The wild-grown roses offer warbling delight
Smell of dwarf oaks, stunted pines wafts from the land
The grin of boys, the selfcentered smile of girls
Shines to my admiring the way a wave curls

Or just their eyes, stepping in washed cotton clothes
Tight or sheer, rubber or voile, in the city
Hot wind fanning the cement, if no one knows
Noon-incandescent, the feel at their beauty
Stranger's glance fondling their fleshed legs,
        their fleshed breast
They enjoy it like in a pierglass undressed

And enjoy the summer subway bulge to bulge
The anonymous parts adhesive swaying
Massive as distortions that sleepers divulge
So in subterranean screeching, braying
Anaesthetizing roaring, over steel floors
Majestically inert, their languor flowers

And nude jump up joking alert to a date
Happy with the comb, the icebox, the car keys
How then if rings, remark or phone, it's too late
Fury, as unpersonal as a disease
Crushes graces, breaks faces, outside inside
Hirsute adults crying as fat babies cried

Covered over, lovered over and older
The utterance cracked and probing thievishly
Babyfied roving eye, secretive shoulder
The walk hoisted and drooped, exposed peevishly
The groom's, bride's either, reappears in careers
Looking fit, habitual my dears, all these years

So at the opening, the ball, the spot abroad
At the all-night diner, the teen-age drugstore
Neighborhood bar, amusement park, house of God
They meet, they gossip, associate some more
And then commute, drive off, walk out, disappear
I open my eyes in the night and am here

Close them, safe abed, hoping for a sound sleep
Beyond the frontier that persons cross deranged
Anyone asleep is a trustful soft heap
But so sleeping, waking can be interchanged
You submit to the advances of madness
Eyes open, eyes shut, in anguish, in gladness

Through the window in fragments hackies' speech drifts
Men, a whore, from the garage, Harlem and Queens
Call, dispute, leave, cabs finish, begin their shifts
Each throat's own pitch, fleshed, nervy or high, it leans
In my open ear, a New Yorker nearby
Moves off in the night as I motionless lie

Summer New York, friends tonight at cottages
I lie motionless, a single retired man
White-haired, ferrety, feminine, religious
I look like a priest, a detective, a con
Nervously I step among the city crowd
My private life of no interest and allowed

Brutality or invisibility
We have for one another and to ourselves
Gossamer-like lifts the transparent city
Its levitating and ephemeral shelves
So shining, so bridged, so demolished a woof
Towers and holes we sit in that gales put to proof

Home of my free choice; drunk boys stomp a man who
Stared, girls encompass a meal-ticket, hate fate
Like in a reformatory, what is true
To accept it is an act, avoid it, great
New Yorkers shack up, include, identify
Embrace me, familiarly smiling close-by

Opaque, large-faced, hairy, easy, unquiet
The undulant adolescents flow in, out
Pounce on a laugh, ownership, or a riot
The faces of the middle-aged, dropped or stout
But for unmotivatedness are like saints'
Hiding no gaps, admitting to all the taints

They all think they look good—variegated
As aged, colored, beat—an air unsupported
But accustomed, corpulent more than mated
Young or old selfconsciousness uncomforted
Throw their weight—that they each do—nowhere they know
Like a baseball game, excessively fast, slow

Mythically slow or slow United States
Slow not owned, slow mythically is like dearer
Two slowly come to hear, one indoors awaits
Mere fright at night, bright dismay by day, fear is
Nearer, merer and slower, fear is before
Always, dear always is, fear increases more

More civilization; I have friends and you
Funny of evil is its selfimportance
Civilization people make for fun; few
Are anxious for it; though evil is immense
The way it comes and goes makes jokes; about love
Everybody laughs, laughs that there is enough

So much imagination that it does hurt
Here it comes, the irresistible creature
That the selves circle until one day they squirt
It lifts sunset-like abysses of feature
Lifts me vertiginous, no place I can keep
Or remember, leaping out, falling asleep

David Rosenberg

from BLUES OF THE SKY

INTERPRETED FROM THE ANCIENT HEBREW BOOK OF PSALMS

PSALM 90

Lord, you are our home
in all time
from before the mountains rose

or even the sun
from before the universe
to after the universe

you are Lord forever
and we are home
in your flowing

you turn men into dust
and you ask them to return
children of men

for a thousand years
in your eyes
are a single day

yesterday
already passed
into today

a ship in the night
while we were present
in a human dream

submerged
in the flood of sleep
appearing in the morning

like new grass
growing into afternoon
cut down by evening

we are swept off our feet
in an unconscious wind
of war or nature

or eaten away
with anxiety
worried to death

worn out swimmers
all dressed up
in the social whirl

 you see our little disasters
secret lusts
broken open in the light

of your eyes
in the openness
penetrating our lives

every day melts away
before you
our years run away

into a sigh
at the end
of a story

over in another breath
seventy years
eighty—gone in a flash

and what was it?
a tinderbox of vanity
a show of pride

and we fly apart
in the empty mirror
in the spaces between stars

in the total explosion of galaxies
how can we know ourselves
in this human universe

without expanding
to the wonder that you are
infinite lightness

piercing my body
this door of fear
to open my heart

our minds are little stars
brief flares
darkness strips naked

move us to see your present
as we're moved to name each star
lighten our hearts with wonder

return
and forgive us
locking our unconscious

behind the door
and as if it isn't there
as if we forget we're there

we walk into space unawed
unknown to ourselves
years lost in thought

a thousand blind moments
teach us when morning comes
to be moved

to see ourselves rise
returning witnesses
from the deep unconscious

and for every day lost
we find a new day
revealing where we are

in the future and in the past
together again
this moment with you

made human for us
to see your work
in the open-eyed grace of children

the whole vision unlocked
from darkness
to the thrill of light

where our hands reach for another's
opening to life
in our heart's flow

the work of this hand
flowing open
to you and from you.

from SHELTERED LIFE

PARTS OF A MYSTERY

He asked her how she knew it was the same man.

–I could see his face in the mirror of the candy machine. In the
subway. I was wearing a scarf with a scorpion pin and I checked
to see if it was still there. It was his face allright. I should
know what his face looks like by now.

The beefy detective shifted his weight in the chair.

–How long did you say you've been working in Mrs. Von Mallo's
house?

–About a year, about two years.

–And what is your job here?

–I'm her—social secretary.

He made another notation in his book then looked up.

–Uh huh. And this man that's after you, was he wearing the same
outfit you described before?

–Yes. An earring made of a foreign coin in his left ear.

–I see. Now you told the other officer this man has never spoken
to you. Did he say anything to you this time?

–No. He just stared at me.

–Stared at you

–Yes, stared at me.

–Well, Miss, at the present time—

–It's not Miss, it's Mrs. I was married but my husband was killed
a while ago in Japan. And I think—I think—I know this man means
to kill me.

–What makes you think he means to kill you?

–I couldn't say except—

–Except what?

–He is Haitian.

–He's from Haiti? How do you know that?

–I can tell.

–You spend any time in Haiti?

–No but there's this—I've come into contact with Haitians before.

–Where was that, Miss?

–It's Mrs.

–Where did you encounter these Haitians?

–I was once a hostess at a nightspot where—

–This wouldn't be the Tetrahedron Club. The detective smiled as
he flipped open a small lighter. Too small for his hand, in fact.

Then he took a drag from his cigarette.

–Yes, I worked at the Tetrahedron.

–Yeah, you worked there and you were familiar with the owner, Nicholas Von Mallo?

–I knew him, of course. He is Lady Von Mallo's nephew.

–Do you know where he is now?

–No. But probably away for the winter. In Haiti.

–Just how well do you know him?

–We're—friends, we're former business associates. He was a friend of my late husband.

–Was he? The detective began to drift around the livingroom. Is this a picture of the old lady?

–Yes.

–How old would you say it is?

–Very.

–And this beach, this place. Where was this taken?

***

And now you know the greatest part of the mystery. It will not be possible to surprise you. Certainly it will be difficult to shock you. Remember that you tittered with delight or walked out of the theatre the last time a mystery was solved for you. You may now put the crime aside or tell a lie like the detective when he phoned in this communication to headquarters: there isn't a clue in sight. I haven't a lead to my name, not a Chinaman's chance of unraveling this one.

***

And this is when they both have scotch and sodas in hand:

–I don't think I can bear anymore of your probing into what you consider was my sordid love life.

–He was your lover, then?

–Would you believe me if I said no?

–It seems to me, Miss, that you'd want to tell me everything since you think someone is trying to kill you.

–I was crazy to think you could prevent it. There's no help for it. I know that now.

–Would you tell me where the old lady is?

–I don't know. Why question me anymore? You assume I lie about everything. I haven't seen her in weeks—that's the absolute truth.

***

And this is where she is dressed for bed and her back is
to him and his voice is softer than before:

–Where did you meet him?
–A shop. A kind of antique store.
–Here you mean? In this city?
–Yes. He was interested in Oriental objets d'art. And that was
how he—
–Go on.
–No, I won't.

***

And this is when her eyes are red and her head is bent and her
hair is all over her face, where she is curled up into herself
and he is quiet and letting it unveil itself because he is on
the edge of tittering with delight or phoning headquarters to
say the case is closed.

–When Nicky was a child he had polio. He walks like anyone else
now. That is, he walks normally. I don't mean that. He lived
with them in East Hampton. They had a beautiful house near the
water. Someone said his father was a mobster, that he wasn't really
a rich man's son at all. Why must people say he's insane just be-
cause he isn't like anyone else? He isn't insane. I've seen him
do things and he isn't like anyone else. Why must they always ask
what he did to me? Don't you understand, it was no longer me. It
wasn't what you think at all. There was nothing human between my-
self and Nicky or the other one. You're all wrong. And he kept
asking me over and over 'what's happened to you.' How could I tell
him; how could I say it to him? I was relieved when he finally
went away. I thought after a while, after Nicky realizes that he
must let me go, I can go to him and try to explain. Then they
found the body. What else could I do? Nicky could see only one
thing and he would not rest until it was done. Poor, sweet man,
he had turned his whole life into nothing because of me. I couldn't
let them do it to him. And even then I was too late. I might just
as well have killed—
–Tell me, Miss: how many people have you killed?

–I am innocent/but that is description.

***

Here, she is composed, sure of herself and contemptuous toward
the detective. Wearing a long dress. Smoking a foreign cig-
arette.

–There *is* no file at headquarters. There's no file to have. You
can't know any more about him than I did. He wasn't from anywhere,
or up to anything. He was my husband and you can call me Miss as
much as you like. It doesn't change anything. It doesn't mean he
didn't love me.
–Von Mallo killed him, didn't he?
–My husband died in Japan.
–That isn't what I asked you.
–My husband was a collector of Oriental antiques.
–But he *was* murdered, wasn't he?
–You've never acknowledged that he existed. How could he have been
murdered?
–Did Nicholas Von Mallo ever hypnotize you? Did he ever force you
to take part in a—
–You feel ridiculous even saying it. .
–He was the leader of a cult of some kind. Things went on at that
nightclub. We know that much.
–Do you?
–He led rituals, barbaric ceremonies.
–Of course he did. And he stuck pins in a doll so that a million
miles away my husband dropped dead. Oh, I think you're a fool.
–But, I'm right—or close to it.
–You're a fool. I'll bet you think he dressed up in a red negligee
and took on every Haitian teenager in the city.
–Sometimes, Miss, you don't talk like the kind of lady you claim to
be.

***

They are both angry. The detective, having upset a small
table, has a tight grip on her wrist. She is saying:

–How many times must I tell you: He   cured   himself!

***

The detective is exasperated. His collar is open:

–How long did he stay in Japan?
–He wrote to me as often as he could.
–Saying what?
–Saying Cicada. Paulownia. 5 then 7 then 5. a book gone brown.
invisible baby humpback woman making supper with weeds. motherlove.
tortoise shell. white pajamas. mistaken identity. shipment.
underestimation. surprise leaving silence in its wake.

***

The man's eyes are hard. His cigarette smoke is being sucked
up under an ornate lampshade:

–Mother, Auntie I am speaking to you about money. I am speaking
about corpses. He is dead and I can feel my power dissipating.
Under these circumstances don't you think you might dispense with
sighing in a southern accent and shading your eyes? You are like
some fading orchid made of Kleenex. I could come right over to
your chair and stroke your beard and coo nicely for you the way
it's always been but time is running out for all of us. I'm say-
ing I can still fix you, old lady. If you don't see to me right
away, I can fix you and I will.

***

The detective seems self-righteous:

–A rich sissy. He was no better than those animals who kick old
ladies down the stairs and take their welfare money.
–I once went to a doctor. I was wearing a sun yellow wool skirt
and a blouse with a big idiot's bow and black leather high heels
and I had put cologne in the rinse water for my underwear. I saw
the doctor step back when he looked at—that thing—in me. I saw
what his face was like. I've given birth to two monsters. One
was a tiny thing whose skin was electric blue. He was dead before
I had the strength to sit up and sniff my flowers. The other mon-
ster was a parasitic glob of death nestling "in there" waiting to
get born and exchange my life for its own. That doctor had a room-
ful of textbooks and surgical weapons. He could do no more for me
than weep. This "animal" as you call him, cured me. Do you under
stand what I'm saying at all?
–What do you mean he cured you? You trying to tell me he was a
what-do-you-call-it, a faith healer?
–Mr. Policeman, we have already decided that he was the devil.

This is not a difficult mystery. It began with the placement of several objects on a table top.
1. a tetrahedron
2. some rare foreign coins
3. the cardboard backing from a candy bar
4. a woman's bandana
5. an old photograph of a statuesque woman—taken at the seashore
6. a plaster likeness of the female deity who was an object of worship in an undisclosed primitive culture

The following locales are where the mystery takes place:
a subway platform in a large city
a mansion in that same city
a nightclub in that same city
a villa in Haiti
a coffee shop in Kyoto, Japan.

The people in this mystery:
There is a woman
There is a man who is a detective
Another man
His aunt or his mother
Another man who is the husband of the first woman
There is a fourth man
There is that man's silly brother

***

–I've been in this house since shortly after he died. There was no reason not to come here. That is, it all seemed clear after that. I don't live anywhere. If I am anywhere, it's here. I leave this house only to deliver packages. And sometimes to pick them up.
–What packages? Who sends them? Who are they for?
–From Haiti. They're from him. They're addressed to him. They've never stopped arriving. Don't ask me what they contain. I couldn't tell you. They're neither heavy nor light. I send them and get them. I take a subway train. It's a long way off. The ride tires me. I've never taken a subway and not seen him there, staring at me, waiting.

A woman is standing in the middle of the floor of a nightclub which is not yet open for business. She is wearing an overcoat. Her male companion is chatting animatedly:

–Let's see, does your husband wear glasses? With thick lenses? Is he stoopshouldered, contemplative, given to writing indecipherable notes on paper napkins? Or—he's very tall and country boy sensitive and he twists up his face when he's troubled and he precedes his cracker barrel profundities by saying 'it shore seems t'me' and follows them with 'don't it?' or 'din't it', 'wadn't it?' And at night when he serenades you on the mouthharp, he looks skyward and announces 'I got music in me, baby, I know it. I Just need a break.' Or perhaps he is a poet who finds it obligatory to tell you what it was 'like' after he has had you. Will he eventually take you to the country to live where you will ride every morning before break fast? By the way, I don't usually hire married women.

And this is where he turns momentarily to snap at a pleasant-looking waiter.

–KILO, THERE IS TO BE A CANDLE AND A STATUE ON EACH AND EVERY TABLE. EACH AND EVERY ONE.

And turning again to the woman:

–Does your husband know you're here? You haven't told him you're dying, have you? Perhaps you won't have to. Oh, yes—you've had a child. There will be no others. And what sort of wardrobe do you have?

And he is saying to her routinely:

–You can open your eyes now.

***

It is early morning. Her duties are finished for the night. The room above the nightclub is quiet. His eyes are milky:

–I gave Marcus the mate to this earring. Unlike his talkative sibling, Kilo, Marcus is a man of very few words. The first word I taught him was bathroom. He pronounces it bafroom. Marcus is made of secrets. He is wise. His laugh is a dull music. It does not come from his body.

I know most of the townspeople who come into this hole believe I dress
up in a red negligee and grovel at his feet, beseech him to wrap me in
his beeeg, strong, black arms and then beat me into insensitivity. Ah,
yes, the townspeople—-can you imagine: cabbing all the way up here to
pay $3.00 for a drink? You know what this "nightspot" is? This place
is where Esther Williams might come to meet Fernando Lamas—or better,
where she might come to cheat on Fernando Lamas. I Have Never Touched
Marcus. There is simply no need to. We are afraid of each other. You
don't understand this but take my word for it, it's beautiful. Even
his mother feared me—a witchwoman with seaweed for hair and no tongue
at all. I had to buy Kilo in the bargain, of course. He isn't a bright
boy, Kilo. Fond of trinkets. I shudder to think of his carrying on
if anything ever happened to Marcus and myself. I've been able to teach
Kilo only one thing.

***

On the veranda. A servant is pouring their coffee.

–Did you ever notice that old snapshot of your aunt. The one taken
at the shore?
–Notice it? I know it. She was beautiful in that swimsuit. Moth-
er has always taken pride in her legs.
–Who took that picture?

And this is where his eyebrows arch meaningfully and this is
where he speaks in italics.

–Her husband took it. The man she was married to.
–And your uncle, your uncle was the one who disappeared in the 40's.
Do you remember him at all? What was he like?—Handsome? Were
they part of the lost generation? Did they give huge parties?
Were they very wealthy?
–He was good looking—right to the end. Yes, they were quite the
party-givers, quite the society page couple. It was always her
with the money, though. He had nothing. At first it didn't seem
that Mother—Auntie that is—minded very much when he left her.
Her life went on. More than 20 years passed. She assumed he was
dead, of course. And then when I suddenly showed—

His voice trails off into laughter, as though he were
remembering.

—Sometimes as many as 2 or 300 people, he says.

***

And of course, she lied, because there had been only one
letter:

Darling Child,

I am not happy here. I am become as an animal. I found you in a
fitting place. A place where the rarest things in the world are
kept. I have spent the better part of my life studying and collect-
ing. I took great care with my other treasures. I have wasted
you. I tried to marry myself to you. I no longer believe I am an
intelligent man. I thought my simple need of you could make living
acceptable. I should have known when it happened to the child. My
interest in weapons was that of a scholar. I know everything about
ancient Oriental instruments of death but until that day I had nev-
er done violence to a living thing. You were going more and more
away from me everyday, and going more and more mad, it seemed.
Entranced, and, I am no longer afraid to say it, bewitched. But
in truth, it was I who had lost my reason. The report said you
were often seen with a Haitian. A man who looked powerful. It has
been a long time indeed since I was an intelligent man. Once I was
face to face with him, the notion of intelligence did not exist.
I killed him as much because I thought he had done this to you as
to escape his eyes. I tried to keep hitting him until his eyes
were closed. Child, I am ill. The pain is outside of words. I
now believe nothing except I believe everything. I have friends in
Kyoto whom I once wished to bring you to. I have always been a
collector and they are collectors. And I wished to show to them
your face and your hands. These people who revere beauty. It is
impossible to go to them now. I have understood so little of it.
I could not find you after I'd done it. I could not have looked
upon you anyway. Every day I am closer to death. You must know—
better than I—that it is a matter of time for yourself as well.

And Lady Von Mallo has been found where she was left. And the detective has not been in contact with headquarters for several days. And now the woman is turning to him delicately.

–I don't even know what the weather is.

And the detective is smoking, propping himself up on one elbow with an inquisitive look that she cannot see but feels in the dark:

–I don't care really, but did you ever go to bed with one of them?

And the woman laughs way back in her throat, facilitated by the angle of her head, and takes a drag from her own cigarette:

–But there's something you have never understood about me, officer. You see, I am not a white woman.

THE BASKETBALL ARTICLE

> THE BASKETBALL ARTICLE *was conceived in November 1974 & written in April 1975 as an assignment for* OUI *magazine. We got to go to all the Nets games we wanted through Barney Kremenko, Publicity, but Jim Wergeles of the Knicks balked, "What do you girls really do?" We heard he was a jock. We went to the first women's basketball game held in Madison Square Garden. We wrote a review that was rejected for being too technical. We tried not to make* THE BASKETBALL ARTICLE *too technical so it was rejected by a group of editors a few of whom thought it "was a minor masterpiece," the others "couldn't tell what the hell was going on" in it. We were rejected by* The Village Voice *for whom the work was not technical enough. An agent told us* THE BASKETBALL ARTICLE *was fragmented and could not be handled. We never got into the locker room. A purely prophetic work in the tradition of social realism,* THE BASKETBALL ARTICLE *is duplicated here in an edition of 100 copies by a Gestetner 420 mimeograph machine using green film stencils no. 62. We express our thanks to Mr. DeBusschere, Mr. Kremenko, Mr. Padgett, Mr. Rezek, Mr. Robertson & Mr. Warsh.*
>
> *—BM July 15 1975*

THE BASKETBALL ARTICLE

The orange ushers of the Coliseum begin to wonder if smoking Sherman's makes you sexy. Should they smoke them? What magazine? *Oui.* We begin to dress in red, white and blue, we do not stand up for the national anthem. We always sit next to the opposing team. We distract them. We enter their consciousness. We carry a copy of Shakespeare's sonnets with us. We wear lipstick. We cheer for both teams. We watch mostly defense, sitting at the far end of the court. We watch Stan Love sitting on the bench. He gives us the eye. We bring Dante to the games. We watch the players who sweat & the players who don't sweat, the players who accept a towel and the ones who throw it away. We watch the angry players and the players who don't give a shit towards the end of the season. We watch the rookies carefully, wondering if they'll get to play. A rookie from San Antonio plays a few minutes, finally, walks three times, scores twice and gets back on the bench. San Antonio has the raunchiest looking team in the league. It's their hair. The San Antonio Spurs. Their coach says nothing to them. We watch him mouthing words at the referees. We listen to George Gervin, fouled out, call the referee a motherfucker and spur Swen Nater on to beat the shit out of him. We watch Nater circle around the ref, "Nate" a simple lion in the Coliseum, all eyes, the referee ignores him. Nater who said, "I wouldn't mind being in movies but they'd think I'm a monster." Jabbar's taken it to court—can you criticize the referees after the game. We feel the muscles of the players. Women aren't allowed in the locker room. We go to the press room. We watch the players who, towards the end of the game, lean back stretching their shoulder muscles. Occasionally we wink at them. We can, we're at the press table. Somebody's taking pictures of us. Two women. We watch the Spirits of St. Louis. Marvin Barnes leans over and says, "Why don't you put me in there (*Oui*) with all those girls?" We assure him we'll see what we can do. We listen to him get serious, he says, "It feels good playing the best in the world." The Nets? Maybe. We watch the black players take over the game. We count the number of whites on the floor. Three, now four. We watch the white coaches. We see the kind of joking being a professional creates. The fans write in the bathrooms: "I love Kevin Loughery." The players shout: "You watch him jumpin' into Mosey, he's Jumpin' into him," and, to the ref, "I know you don't want us to win and I know you're a motherfucker but this is too much, you jack-off." We stare at the glitter jackets of the Spirits of St. Louis and at the black bell-bottom pants of the San Antonio Spurs as they snap them off to get into the game. Some of the players hide when they do this. The players shout: "The spread's comin'" and "beaten by a dead dog all the time." The fans say, "They took the knife on him," talking about Dr. J. We remember Debusschere's heel bone coming through his arch, we remember when Julius Erving married Turquoise Brown and now they have a fine child. We think about nicknames: Rainbow, The Doctor, Mr. K, The Pearl, Hondo, Salty Dog, Ice. We remember Gene Conley, a forward for the Celtics and a pitcher for the Red Sox, Rick Barry's broken elbow, Jabbar's demand to leave Milwaukee, the great George McGinnis no-trade, Nate-the-roller-skate, all the ones named Love and Jones, one Love a brother of a Beach Boy, two Silases and a Price. We can still picture Bill Walton sitting on a bench during practice with Jack Scott's dog named Sigmund in the middle of the Patty Hearst scene and then his house goes up for sale. Phil Jackson reads Carlos Castaneda. Bill Bradley'll sign a ten-year contract with options if the Knicks could get Jabbar. Frazier asks who'll be left to play with him. We watch the players being told what to do. We watch them not doing it. We watch the 3-point plays in the ABA, Dampier, Erving, McGinnis. We watch UCLA beat Kentucky in John Wooden's last year. We watch Walt Frazier's bed and Wilt Chamberlain's bed and think of the players' ages. We watch Dick Barnett be an assistant coach and Jim Barnett fuck up. We see Gianelli get taller and offend Jabbar. Exploding on the boards, tickling the laces, going from downtown. The players put their gum on the press table. The Nets lose on tv, but not in the Nassau Coliseum.

Dave DeBusschere dreams that he is really awake, he can't scream, can't move. He dreams that over again.

We get off the Meadowbrook parkway at the Mineola exit, go west on Old Country Road, one block past Glen Cove Road to the Marine Midland Bank Building where DeBusschere sits in front of a bright blue wall in the general manager's office of the New York Nets. We give him books of our poetry. He autographs copies of *The Open Man* for us. We dress in red, white and blue. DeBusschere ("from the bush country of the Alps") has the radio on, Elton John. He answers the phone "This is he." We think about the Knicks this year but don't ask. He leases a ear. "Basketball is more heroic than rock 'n' roll"—he has ripped stomach muscles and seven busted noses. He doesn't like officials who are visible. He wants to see men and women play two on two and used to drink coffee before the game. We sit in front of pictures of DeBusschere and Robert Redford, DeBusschere and Dustin Hoffman. He likes the Nets, he likes "Salty Dog" Paultz who lives on the beach. He doesn't want to coach, he says he doesn't coach. At the game later we catch him talking to Brian Taylor, he denies it. He becomes Vice President of the ABA, then Commissioner.

New York Nets vs. Salt Lake City Utah Stars. Nassau Coliseum. Larry Kenon's birthday. The world-wide words to the national anthem flash intentionally on the Dr. Pepper/Avis scoreboard which hangs above the center of the red, white and blue court where the Nets and the Stars, now standing, have been working out with all the red, white and blue ABA balls. The scale of the players from courtside is about as astounding as the lines of the legs of Moses Malone, Utah's 19-year-old forward who skipped college, making history, for pro ball. Malone totals 18 points and 21 rebounds, Wali Jones wears his necklace and Go-go Govan brings his family cheering section from New Jersey. But the Utah Stars lose probably because the Coliseum chooses to play "Tie a Yellow Ribbon Round the Old Oak Tree," "You Oughtta Be in Pictures," "Put on a Happy Face," "Winter Wonderland" and "White Christmas" during time-outs and half-time. They lose even though, on the floor, Malone embraces Kenon, Govan caresses Erving who makes a pass between Malone's legs, even though all you can hear from the crowd is "I'm in love with Moses Malone." Who is wearing two different socks. When Malone sits down after 39 minutes of play, he puts his skinny arm on the blue press table and watches us staring at the scars of his right elbow injuries. The Nets win the game by 15 points.

Oscar Robertson tells us if it weren't for basketball he'd probably be in jail. "Economics calls this....When you're poor you don't have anything to do." He was the first black player at Cincinatti in 1960. His great great grandfather, an ex-slave, lived to be 115 years old in Bellsburg, Virginia. His mother raised him, she was a beautician, and his father was a meat-packer and a "punishing figure."

"I have alot of stories but I can't tell them."

The 6'5" figure we were looking at, with an amazing stance even in his chair and the direct unassuming eyes, feels manipulated by the sports bureaucracy—"They don't take chances on black athletes." He has a persistent fear of being shut up in closed places (Fred Hampton's was an "out and out murder") and recurrent dreams of being buried and of being chased by wild animals. The Bulls and the Bucks? Oscar didn't believe that you dream every night until we told him it had been scientifically proven. We spent alot of time talking then about rapid eye movement (off the court). It'd be interesting to put Oscar Robertson into a dream laboratory. He never crossed his legs.

Married with three daughters—he's "got a basketball player"—Oscar thinks the girls can easily outrun the boys but he doesn't like his wife to pick his clothes, which were understated for what we're used to from the "Best Pro Guards." His prediction for that award is Jim Price, Milwaukee Bucks. Did Jim Price ever chase him in a dream? Probably not, but an easy-going Oscar Robertson, sometimes accused of being lazy, has a '72 Jaguar, which is his only clear obsession—he treats it with care and when he tries to outrun the cops in it, his name is on his driver's license. Lazy on the court? You can't be helter-skelter and then pick up speed, he says, it's just what you learn. What does basketball do to your peripheral vision? "It's good in a crowd on Wisconsin Street." Where have you been? "To Tanzania, Mali and Kenya with Kareem Abdul-Jabbar, to Spain with Dave DeBusschere, to Poland, Rumania and Yugoslavia." Do you oil your body? "Not with Mazola."

We were sitting in our hotel suite at the Plankinton House in Milwaukee drinking Tequila Sunrises with the "Big O" for three hours in November. Oscar looked happy when we brought up the Knicks. "They're getting what they deserve." And it must've been the Knicks we were talking about when he said, "You can't go into the lake and build an island unless there's a mountain there to start with." Maybe the mountain wasn't Jabbar.

We sit down to watch a few Knicks games. If one sat down with Dave DeBusschere, one might have a margarita. Margaritas, tequila sunrises, somebody tells us Wendell Ladner likes to fuck. Frazier's "Sometimes I get an offer I can't refuse," occurs to us. Jim Wergeles, the Knicks publicity manager, tells us Bill Bradley won't give interviews this year. Frazier's publicity is awful. Bill Walton announces they're trying to discredit him, he doesn't fit in. The FBI is looking for the people who shared his house. They question Walton about Patty Hearst. The Knicks steal Eddie Donovan from the Buffalo Braves. 20,000 people come to watch an NBA game. In the cheaper seats in the Garden, nobody cares if you stand up for the national anthem. It's not like baseball. We always say we're pregnant if anybody hassles us. If they play the national anthem before every game because the sport is a national sport, then how can the champions be world champions? What does Bill Walton think when he listens to the bombs bursting in air? After all, he's been arrested in a peace demonstration. Could a player be arrested for reading Shakespeare. Jim Bouton said everybody thought he was queer for reading any books at all. You feel like you know the Knicks personally. It's the publicity, or maybe age. Your age, our age. So Bradley won't give interviews but Jackson will talk about mysticism and philosophy. He grows a beard, he shaves it, he looks like a different person. He and Gianelli become look-alikes for a moment on the court. Jackson looks younger, Red Holzman looks the same. Why do the coaches crouch.

Traveling. All teams should meet in the center of the world and stay there for the 80-game season. There would be no fans but the other teams. McAdoo, the NBA's leading scorer and most valuable player, might cheer for Gianelli. As a fan, he could get thrown out of the game for two technicals, or for trying to play center for the Knicks. There would be no two million dollar deals for Walton because the fans would all be professionals and they'd get in free. Too bad then, there'd be no women at the games, except as invited guests. And the wives and families of the players. All of Walt Frazier's girlfriends could attend. But no one would know this. After the game the professionals would meet secretly to exchange plays without the knowledge of the coaches. Jabbar would spend time training Marvin Webster to be the Nets' new center. The season would last two months after which the players would emerge from the center of the world, change their identities and not have to be healthy, competitive citizens. Then they would travel to all parts of the world for free with a special basketball identification card. Some would become astronauts. Some would join the Communist Party.

Somebody says to us, "There are too many basketball players." Then somebody says, "There are too many poets." We imagine a great conference of poets with trainers, doctors and coaches, keeping them in fine physical and mental shape. We wonder what their work would be like. Attendance, 20,239. The poets perform in gym suits, showing their long lean legs and muscular shoulders. The older poets comment on the game or go into business. One poet is the center, there are two forwards and two guards, but anyone can score. The center, generally, must simply try to get the words away from the opposing team of poets and the guards bring them downcourt to be used. The referees can be cursed at during and after the game. Some poets are booed for using the language awkwardly, others cheered for coming up with a new style of play. Most of the coaches are former players who continue to read and write books. A foul is called on any poet who deliberately deranges the language. A poet in a state of ecstasy makes a 3-point play. Fouled in the act of writing by personal insults, the poet would go to the line.

From a distance the Nassau Coliseum looks like Godard's "Alphaville," an end-of-the-world city on another planet where people say yes when they mean no and no when they mean yes. The crowd at the Coliseum is a MacDonalds crowd like the crowd in Kentucky may be a fried-chicken crowd—we watch the crowds on tv. For people who rarely leave Manhattan except for the jungles of South America, it's strange to see the reactions of the Nassau crowd detonated by a mid-court scoreboard which flashes "Defense" and "Kenon Lean In," and only genuinely set off by the shouting of the players' friends. The hard-core New Yorkers you find in Madison Square Garden don't drive out to the Coliseum to do their obscene school-yard rooting for the home team. The Coliseum fans are predominantly white and demure. We get culture shock. We go down to the schoolyard on 6th Avenue and 4th Street in the middle of Greenwich Village to watch a Rucker Tournament-style game. We look through the fence again at the black athletes whose style we're more familiar with. We set up a game with some poets we know. Two women, two men. We have to play for the court so one of us goes with one man against two men. Everybody approves of women's ball up to a point—the breasts. The man-woman team wins and the next people we have to play for the court, two more men, refuse to play with a woman. We get mad and throw a long lob pass over one tall man into the groin of the other tall man and walk off the court. We spit. Then we insist on playing off the refusing team and win the court. And the women place in the schoolyard. The weird thing is that every time we go inside for an easy lay-up, the men clear the way, arms down and let you score. And if you guard your man closely, he'll get spooked, even with a tremendous height advantage, especially if he's been your former lover. And if you have an outside shot, nobody expects it. As women in the schoolyards of New York, we forget about our breasts but the men don't yet and they're impressed by our converse all-stars and the only thing we need is a longer stride and more penetration. And if, like playing poker, you keep asking what the rules are, you can bluff a stranger into thinking you can't take a shot at all.

Under the boards is where they forget you're a lady. When we were 15 we were thrown out of the schoolyards by the "boys." Now (and then) we're Frazier's age, we're Monroe's age and we can play with our "colleagues," sometimes with our students, still win the court from the high-school kids and have a real game. If you run into a player on your own team (male) in one of these games, where the match-ups are usually made first by size and then by surprise, he'll usually take you by the shoulders in a sportsman-like gesture which reminds us of the coaches patting their pro players on the ass. Before spring we can go down to Pace College to practice indoors, but the New York Athletic Club is the ultimate hold-out—no women, no Jews, no nothing but ultimate Catholics. A friend of ours named Friedman went down there as a guest and had to sign in as Kelly. Also required is a jacket and tie. Now we could easily put on a jacket and tie—it's been done before—and go take a sauna. A friend of ours named Greenberg went down and signed in as Adams and went into the sauna with toenails painted blue.

Basketball was not invented in 1891 by Dr. James A. Naismith of Springfield, Massachusetts. A form of it was played by the Aztecs who had an advanced civilization before the great white god of Cortez arrived in 1519. The Aztec priests controlled the calendar by keeping their knowledge of the stars and their movements secret so that the people did not know their predictions were based on science and the priests could stay in power. Now the great white gods of basketball are finally relenting—we remember when in the betting on college games great white people feared the blacks were taking over—and there are great black coaches finally in the game and the great white managers who never "took chances" on the great black athletes, have to and they can pat them on the ass the way Charley Finley embraced Reggie Jackson when the Oakland A's won the World Series, and Jackson, seeming to take great joy in it, poured a bottle of champagne on the head of the bourgeois entrepreneur who got a kick out of inviting presidents and generals to throw out the ball in the first game of the series. They all declined because they hadn't paid their income tax.

We envision an age where we can watch and indulge in the beauty and awareness of a scene, an Aztec scene, a display of concentration and an exhibition of the bodies of men and women moving. We watch their arms and legs, we watch the control of the muscles of those limbs, we watch it for free, we see an art, we do not have to be Americans and salute this art. Whatever is brutish becomes sublime, whatever is strength becomes defined as strength in a pure display of the talent, as DeBusschere said to us, that is everybody's talent in their own right. We watch the beautiful bodies of men moving up and down the court, we get turned on by them, moving, We watch them sit down and stretch out legs that could be embracing us, in love. But we watch their talent, it makes us feel ours. We are mesmerized by the sight of bodies. A culture Western culture is not aware of. There is grace in the men and women who play. A hedonism that turns into a sort of mysticism. Too bad pro ball takes them right out of school into another institution. You can't be institutionalized again and again without a break, being alone, to understand, in America, that you don't go into business, that you aren't a star, that you must spend time confronting the person without color, with a talent, the self whose eyes in the mirror begin to fade as the eyes of two people do fade, one into the other, in love. In an American institution there is no pleasure admitted except competition. We watch the men play and say what we want without fear of technicals. We watch them on tv and do what we want. We curse the referees and yell at the Celtics, "You have sticks up your asses." The men are tiny on tv and large in their seats and we watch them in their seats, shifting but still, with spread legs. A rookie in the Coliseum sits on the floor in front of us and says, "Do you make love?"

We think about the electro-galvanic stimulator the Nets bought for Julius Erving's knees, described as "a mild electric chair." We remember our knowledge of everybody's injuries, how they are made public. We watch Wendell Ladner beat up on Issel and later go from downtown. We watch the players who seem desperate running up and down court and the ones who do it like deer. We wonder, as any publicity would excite the reader to know, if the deer-like ones are the ones we would prefer. Why do we care about their persons, it's a game, Kevin Loughery's suits are beyond understanding, Dave DeBusschere's height when we stand next to him, becomes, as it does in fear or in fantasy, a whole stance requiring awe. Who is breeding these men, is it the women Oscar says educates them? Why can't a sacred and sacrilegious sport, where there is sex, allow a language reporting feeling. A feeling of provocation, maybe a feeling of winning or losing, for us an ambiguous feeling of competition provoked by size—the size of the men, the illusion of the size of their cocks, and really, the size of the muscles of the arms and legs of the men we see and sport with every day. We can easily be winners, provoked like this. All the blonde women in the audience. An American sport. A sport where lives can be changed but no scandals exchanged with the press. Except in secret, the secret managers, trying to keep it clean. What will Walt Frazier, our age, be doing at the turn of the century, in the 21st century. Still running a liquor store and a round bed? No way. Sometimes a player will let his shirt hang out of his pants and this seems an innovation. Sometimes a player will refuse to play and will fight the bureaucracy and turn down the money. This is one thing no one will talk about openly or in detail. Everyone approves of a clean life, clean playing and healthy rules. We would go crazy. We watch the ads for Eastern Airlines, Coca-cola, First National City Bank, Schlitz or Schaeffer, we watch the ads for Lite beer, we go crazy. We listen to Al Bianchi, coach of the Virginia Squires who've won 15 games this season, say, "I could take two girls from Immaculata and win 15 games." The two girls from Immaculata would be Scharff and Crawford. But what's really a problem is the rims in Denver. They're loose and low. You can tell when a rim is low when your shot is off.

Mr. Barney Kremenko, publicity manager for the New York Nets and our great father, has confessed that he would "do anything for us."

On Easter Sunday, we got stuck in a bar in Hempstead, waiting for the train to New York after watching the Nets whole-heartedly beat the San Antonio Spurs. Being older than most of the Nets, we were asked for proof to get a simple beer, the ladies' room turned out to be the men's room and the art and dominance of the winning team seemed to subside as we were taken for students with notebooks of the game for which we had a talent in our own right. We go from downtown to the outland seasons of the new league, wonder what will happen in their bright blue presence, keep nostalgia for the old league and put on a full court press in the schoolyards where everybody admits to making love.

William Corbett

from COLUMBUS SQUARE JOURNAL

24 November

BEDS

for B

The bed upstairs for seven years made for us in Hanover, Mass.
before that a queen size mattress on plywood on cinder blocks
and before that the mattress had a modern headboard that bed
bought impulsively in Cambridge. Our honeymoon bed in
Vermont falling into the middle, a PLAN AHEAD sign propped
against the pillows by Mr. Messier. The divorcees' bed in
Sunset San Francisco broken in on one side. Beds in Pennsyl-
vania motels. In the apartment East 81st Street the bed wedged
between a bookshelf and closet. In Vermont single beds with
grey and white plastic covered headboards under the eaves
sleep alone all summer. Alone waking in a tub the Hotel
Barclay Rittenhouse Square Philadelphia. Motels—London,
Ohio a vibrator bed run by quarters—St. Louis, East Moline,
Murdo, South Dakota Elko, Nevada. Sleeping on a tent floor
Missoula, Montana—in college on a mattress beatnickery—at
the homes and apartments of friends now forgotten—in a
railroad flat New York Second Avenue—in January an unheated
cottage Horseleech Pond. Sleeping in London, Copenhagen,
Frankfurt, Rome, Florence, Venice, Nice, Clermont-Ferrand,
Paris, on the S.S. Berman, one night a lumpy straw filled
mattress the Hotel du Nord Vienne, France. Waking hungover
the back seat of a car stiff once on the New Jersey shore slate
grey late August sky. The green metal bunk beds of prep
school. Sleeping on 110th Street in New York "BIRD LIVES"
written on the mirror, an opera singer warming up next door, a
busted water pipe stinking in the closet. Sleeping in Center
Street Jim Thorpe seven summers, in the man's car returning
from Brady's Lake. How many years in the room at home with
the cowboy, indian and cactus wallpaper? At Bob and Gerald's
the bed under the canopy waking in July and February. In
sleeping bags once or twice as a boy "sleeping out." Waking
not knowing where I was once in Easton, Pennsylvania once in
Spencerport, New York in a child's bed once in Trumbull,
Connecticut in the new house with the family room and the
closet's louvered doors I could not place. Sweet naps on the
couch in the study in Vermont. Bad dreams in the nursery

beds. Sleeping in Northwood Narrows, New Hampshire
Hancock, Mass Lake Leelanau, Michigan on East 10th Street
New York Livingston, Montana Herman Street San Francisco
Dartmouth Street Boston. The bed in Old Greenwich across
from your great grandparent's wedding picture. Sleeping in the
homes of friends—the Braiders Danbury, Connecticut Coopers-
town, New York Redding, Connecticut Clinton, New York.
Sleeping on a church floor Washington, D.C. and before the
march in 1970 in the suburban home of a man who drank
martinis mixed in a silver milk can and worked for the C.l.A.
and whom I still dream about. He's standing against a peach
colored wall drink in hand talking to me. Sleeping almost
always with a pillow, naked or with a nightshirt or the shirt I
wore that day not pajamas since I don't know when. Waking to
the cool fresh morning air after a snow fall in Vermont or
Concord where horses pulled the sidewalk snow plows, in
Connecticut, in Pennsylvania and tomorrow morning if
tonight's snow sticks and holds in Boston my own big bed.

                                        26 November

The moon was white
as soap as good
as cold November
long in the tooth
spoons cakes and crusts
of frost and snow

                                        27 November

Bobby Leach—Dionne Quints—Executions—Toll Roads—
Novelties—Tortures—Nudes (no art)—Indian Chiefs—Ferries
Fantasy—Push Carts—Chastity Belts—Slavery—Negro—K.K.K.
Cross Country Walks—Opium Dens—Riots—Strikes—Crime—
Risque—Hangings—Hay Rides—Moonshine Stills—Sod Houses
Old West—Massacres—Mussolini—Blacksmith Shops—Garages
Gas Stations—Tong Dens—Gambling Dens—Pool Halls—Mission
Houses—Beer Wagons—Horse Drawn Wagons (Close Ups Only)
Ghettos—World War II—Boer War—Hindenburg Disaster—Tokyo
Earthquake—Child Labor—Horse Cars—Massachusetts Depots

Thanksgiving Day

Deserted holiday morning hours
suit me walking to Ray's studio
through my neighborhood's barrel chested
brick houses stout and staid
helped to poignancy under Thanksgiving's
somber grey and puffy clouds.
Winter holidays ought
to be this grey and chill
deepening the day's natural quiet.
Near South Station an eyeless
dead pigeon on the pavement.
South Station, I was here
on my way home from camp
twenty years ago never thinking
I would be here now
about to enter Hayes Bickford
and call Ray. Red and green jello
A thin shaking woman takes a
cigarette from her green plastic
case. Old men smoke here
which I find courageous
but sobering to imagine
myself old, alone smoking
some holiday or other thirty
years away. What happened during
all those days I promised myself
to note and look forward to
years ago so I might measure
my life and sit rapt
pondering how much I wanted
to know where I would be
as if a sure future
could order a difficult present?
Smiling Buddha cakes good luck
and good luck fish Chinese
bakery window I pass going
slowly home a different way.

WASHING BILL SAX BOWLS

Speckled gray smooth
belly of a lake trout.
Azure swirls, cerulean glaze
plum-rose smear runs
clear along the lip.
What a pleasing
affirmative heft
these bowls smoking
clean from the dishwater
blessed with a calm
and rightness bless us.

1 December

VALSE NOT

Transience of all things
mutability odes
ruins something any
thing two step.
In college
I had a teacher
he wrote a book
One Man's Meter
he sang Keats to
"You're the cream
in my coffee"
and advised me
"Read a good book
after dinner every night."

Shreds of pencil colored cloud
scratched on like rapid doodles
give way to a thunderstorm
queering again the chance of snow.

*

"I do not cross my father's
ground to any House or Town."

For her writing Emily Dickinson liked best the inside of used
envelopes. Joseph Cornell sent a small box to the actress
Sheree North but never heard from her. Paul Strand's father
was the distributor for "Domes of silence" the little devices
that keep chair legs from scraping on the floor. I was told Rolfe
Humphries' father played on the same New York Giants' team
as Fred Merkle, Christy Mathewson and Rube Marquad but
there is no record. Charles Burchfield designed wallpaper for a
long time in Buffalo, New York. "O the moon it spent a night
along the Wabash / Through the sycamores it did shine"
—Theodore Dreiser. William Faulkner worked on the screenplay
for *Land of the Pharoahs*—Dewey Martin, Jack Hawkins and
Joan Collins. Milledgeville, Georgia birthplace of Flannery
O'Connor and Oliver Hardy. Charles Ives Deke and Libra.
Dashiell Hammett and Lillian Hellman stayed for a time on the
cuff in the New York hotel managed by Nathanael West. The
postman in Torrington, Connecticut his house full of undeli-
vered second and third class mail. The lady on Marlborough
Street her house emptied of several dumpsters full of garbage
by court order and three years later nearly thirty white Borzois
discovered cooped up there after neighbors heard the dogs'
howl at night. The New York brothers crushed to death when
the heaps of newspapers they had accumulated and arranged
into a labyrinth collapsed on them. Constance, Glenda and
Gordon locked in the attic for years by their parents lived on
cookies, cereal and television. Emily Dickinson allowed her
doctor to examine her through a half open door: Charles Ives
"Connecticut Yankee" never read the newspapers and Joseph
Cornell lived all his life on Utopia Parkway. A scar on Ives'
finger. Emily Dickinson claimed she did not learn to tell time
until she was fifteen. John Kane fought Jim Corbett to a draw

and Ernest Hemingway boxed Wallace Stevens' ears. Djuna
Barnes lives on in a Greenwich Village single room. She calls
publishers printers. So many words. So much money. Seven
from seventeen hundred and seventy five. Jonathan Edwards
rode forth with bits of paper, his thoughts, pinned to his coat.
CHARLES STARKWEATHER CHARLES WHITMAN RICHARD
SPECK DUANE POPE. The Wayne Spelberg family of Racine,
Wisconsin lived in the basement of his mother's home by
candlelight one year. They went out only at night and ate the
groceries his mother bought with money from a small inheri-
tance. Spelberg's wife, seven months pregnant, "escaped"
claiming she had been held against her will but her husband
and children denied this. Vachel Lindsay mounts the stairs
toward a bottle of cleaning fluid.

                              11 December

Philip, I waited for your call
tonight glancing at the clock
as if I had to be somewhere on time
expecting any minute to hear you say "Are
you sure I won't be bothering
you? Are you sure you're
finished with dinner? Now
how do I get there again?"
Expected you to come and sit
at the other end of the kitchen table
smoking, drinking and talking.
What I had to say
is how much I like
the new drawings in the New York show.
That grizzled head smoking
his brow like a knuckle
the chair and lamp made
from bones I guess, my favorite
and the whipping man in his footsteps
shoes, a pyramid of shoes. Outside
a firecracker and yelling
Beverly calls from upstairs:
"Someone is shooting in the alley!"
I run out as if there were
something I could do about it
to find on West Newton Street

a hatless cop gun drawn
standing by his patrol car.
He's got "one", a black boy
his partner's chased the other
into the alley where a third cop
follows drawing his gun. More police
cars blue lights flashing. Beverly heard
"Wait, I'm only fifteen . .. Stop
or I'll blow your head off"
then the gunshot or two.
What you missed!

from CLEANING UP NEW YORK

INTRODUCTION

$60. I needed sixty dollars in three weeks time. I was out of a job so the idea of doing temporary work just popped into my head. I called a friend who had once done cleaning jobs and he told me to call up Everything for Living Space. He said I'd have to lay out fifteen dollars in order to register with the agency. Shelley and I have only been eating rice and beans; I felt I held our future in my hands as I grabbed the checkbook and took the subway up to Broadway and 72nd Street. My trepidation doubled as I stepped into the noisy, broad vacuum created by the large grey buildings that outline Needle Park. My mind thumbed back over pages of *Naked Lunch* that settled on this location with a green fog. My ears picked up the soundtrack to the movie *Panic in Needle Park* which must have been just a microphone hung outside one of these dirty windows. I found the address on 72nd Street and entered the lobby sure that I was about to be jumped as I punched the big, black, knobby button on the elevator. Released into a thin, filthy green, corridor, I pumped my feet up to a frosted glass door lettered EVERYTHING FOR LIVING SPACE.

Barbara, a flamboyant redhead with a brassy, theatrical voice, became the focus of my attention as the door shut behind me. Her evocative manner of speaking put me at ease and I began to see cleaning as a possible and perhaps glamorous thing to do. Barbara would get me cleaning jobs at $3.50 an hour with a four hour minimum, after I provided her with two references and the $15 deposit. I gave my former boss and the poet Ron Padgett as references and put down the money. Barbara said she would call me as soon as I was cleared. I walked out, back into the grey fumes of that day. Out of work, nowhere special to go, I shuffled over to Central Park West and started ambling up past noble apartment buildings, awnings, and yawning doormen. I spotted a gold trinket on the sidewalk, picked it up, and held before my eyes a small brass button. I asked a nearby doorman dressed in a green uniform if the button belonged to him. He couldn't speak English, but he understood the question and answered it with a negative. I told him I must have been promoted and he gave me a congratulatory smile. Walking up Central Park West, my stride gained and I straightened up. Passing soldiers of courtesy, imperious apartments overlooking the green domains of the park, I felt my bootstraps pulling; I knew I was on the road to success. I walked into the Museum of Natural History and proffered a quarter for which I received another button. A dinosaur was drawn on it and the word *contributor* was written below the extinct animal.

Success came the next day in the form of a command from Barbara via the telephone: go to Interior Design showroom on Lexington Avenue, 59th Street. The first hours passed easily, working with a cheerful, middle-aged, Jewish wife.

I had to move a few objects around the show room and rehang pottery and macrame junk wall-hangings. Later in the afternoon, her husband, the boss, came in. He was the kind of guy who talks fast, is pushy, and can't ever give a direct order. I found myself doing the endless bits and pieces of his undone chores. Each task was a little more tedious and backbreaking than the last. My coordination lessened as the difficulties mounted. I uncrated furniture, changed lightbulbs, and tacked up little metal tiles using thumbtacks that would not stick in the wall, and I cleaned out a closet left over from the *Phibber McGee And Molly* radio show. I consoled myself with the fact that I was getting in plenty of hours. I worked into the evening with no food or rest. I was just about to faint when the miracle occurred. I got paid and set free. I worked and the result was over twenty dollars, green and needed, in my pocket. I bought hamburger and ale and brought it home. Shelley lifted her tired head off the kitchen table as I came in the door. How bizarre the sizzle of the meat seemed and how delicious seemed the perspiring, green Ballantine Ale! Shelley and I ate the hamburger and drank the ale and said, "Pretty good!"

The next time I met Ron Padgett, the poet I had used for a reference, he told me of a phone call from a strange lady asking if I was a good housecleaner. At first, Ron thought it was a joke but when he realized I needed a character reference, he informed Barbara that I was an exceedingly clean person and always brushed my teeth. I made the sixty dollars I needed that month plus enough to register again with the agency. Without thinking twice, I became a fresh recruit in the ranks of the cleaningmen.

HOW THINGS GET DIRTY

In New York City, we really live like worms. There is dirt above, below, and on all sides of us. The air is a constant fine mist of dust and soot. Filth is creeping up from every basement. Cockroaches and insects are constantly chewing things into little piles of dirt. Pigeons! Dogs! Dirt is puffing between floorboards and under walls and down from ceiling cracks. Corrosive chemicals in the air eat away the faces of statues and crumble the bricks about us. The subway blasts subterranean filth up through air grates. People throw their dirt everywhere. There is garbage, and cigarette and cigar ash in the streets, rooftops are often junk heaps. Now back into our wormhole: the apartment. We tread dirt inside on the soles of our shoes. Our clothes literally shake with dust. Our hair is a broom that sweeps in the city atmosphere. We come in like bombshells.

Dirt distributes itself by the motion of rise and fall. Dirt enters an area with some impetus. Air coming under windows sends dust floating around the ceiling which slowly sifts its way to the floor. This dust will settle on any crevice no matter the size. This means bumps in the paint on your walls have tiny motes of dust just hanging around. (Let me toss an aside into the duststorm. This all sounds neurotic but it isn't. It is just the heightened perception created by the direct contact of my labors. I don't dislike dirt. Far from it, I feel very comfortable working with dirt.) Dirt is heavier than air so it settles down on every surface from the ceiling to the floor. The rim of your lampshade is doing a good business right now. As you shuffle across the floor, you are kicking up particles that jump up and fall down a few feet away. Cooking often sends a film of grease through the air that sticks to anything it can touch. As you soak in the bathtub, dirt floats along the surface of the water and spreads over the walls of the tub as it is drained. The toilet bowl is the scene of miscalculations that send dirt down the wrong side of the bowl! Your ablutions spatter the walls and get the tiles dirty. Water is one of nature's best solvents; if you splash the floor while doing the dishes, then the water will strip the dirt off the bottoms of your feet.

Pets are as bad as city environment or people when it comes to getting things dirty. Dogs and cats shed their coats everywhere they go. They shred up pieces of paper, knock over flower pots. Cats kick and scratch at their cat litter until it is littered all over the floor. No dog is above having accidents. Dogs run along the walls blackening them and furiously beat dust up into the air current with their tails. Birds throw shelled birdseed out of their cages and if you let them fly free—well! All pets use their unnaturally confining space to its utmost.

Getting dirty is a process of natural inertia. Dirt moves by force and then rests. Cleaning has no natural inertia unless you telescope your thinking into geologic time and everything gets washed into the sea. The washing we do is toward a more limited end. Dirt will always win in the end.

*

Shelley and I come home to New York City and the reoccuring need to make money prompts me to send Barbara fifteen dollars. Within seventy-four hours, Barbara thanks me with Cherry Malard. Cherry sounds sweet as she tells me that repairs have been made in the washroom and the kitchen needs to be mopped. The building stands nicely in the sun in the East 80's, only a door and a half off First Avenue. The apartment doesn't answer the bell so I sit on a red bench in front of the building. Brightly around the corner comes a pretty black-haired girl walking a large dog. She walks up to Cherry's door and we recognize each other. Cherry leads me into the hallway of her first-floor apartment. It is a tall, cramped space with white hexagonal floor tiles as often found in washrooms. I follow Cherry down the aisle and glance into the bathroom before we empty into the kitchen. Cherry shows me the work and the equipment and I tackle the clean-up. The bathtub is covered with plaster chunks and plaster-dust thickly lies over everything. I put the place completely right and it shines a dull, worn shine. The kitchen floor is hard work because there is so much stuff piled along the walls. One corner holds a couple sets of skis and ski-boots. Another corner has a drafting table turned horizontal with kitchen items on it. It rocks back and forth when I shift the weight on the table by moving a few of the items around. It never fails to startle me and I reach out to steady it as if it were about to topple.

Everywhere there are things to move and piles of dog hair. The green linoleum floor is black. I must pick up and move everything in order to sweep up the dog hair and loose dirt. Then I have to move everything again to mop. Woe, that wobbly table. While I am working, Cherry is in the bedroom continually talking on two phones; she talks about the other party's astrology and romance problems. It takes me three hours to finish and I expect another hour of work because of the agency's four-hour minimum but instead Cherry starts to pay me off. After she tells me how really clean everything looks, I ask with some hesitation if she knows about the four-hour minimum. Cherry informs me that the agency quoted a three-hour minimum. "And so the recession has finally hit the cleaning market!" I think to myself. There must be more people cleaning now so the agency must reduce the minimum in order to attract more jobs. Cherry takes my phone number and I leave feeling somewhat flat.

Cherry calls me up soon and this time I clean the entire apartment. There are four rooms counting the hallway and the bathroom as one. The front room has tall windows that open onto the street, a fireplace, and wood parquet floors that run back into the bedroom. The windows are landscaped with plants that hang down or that sit on trunks before each windowsill. There are two bright blue movie-theater seats tottering, detached from the sturdy look of rows. The bedroom can be shut off from the front room by sliding wooden doors; a large bed, a small easy chair and a lamp with a framed Roman engraving hanging above it on the wall, and various suitcases fill the dark room. I work hard for five hours and the place never really gets clean but my impact alone makes a world of difference. Cherry goes out and asks me to answer the phone. When the phone rings, I need a pen to write down the message. I open a drawer and find a pen and next to the pen is some grass. I pocket a little for myself. From the variety of clothes and underwear lying about I begin to gather that a man seems to be living here besides Cherry and her dog and cat, Orchards and Turtles, respectively. Cherry sometimes mentions a Jack. I feel exhausted down to my cells and Cherry gives me a generous tip. The grass turns out to be excellent.

Cherry says, "It is hard to get someone who really cleans." I am asked to become a regular on Thursdays. I meet Jack Gleason who lives with Cherry and I become an official member of the household. I have a question like, "Any bags for garbage?" and I walk up the hallway to the front room to find Cherry. The door is open and Cherry is doing a yoga exercise on a mat in the middle of the floor. She is wearing blue trunks and is holding a position in which she rests on her shoulder blades with one foot down in back of her head and the other sticking straight up in the air. I'm looking straight under her trunks at her black full crotch. Surprised out of my question, I turn quickly and resolve to ask later.

Cherry teaches yoga classes and does her own routine everyday. Most often she shuts the doors and/or wears leotards or tights. Both Cherry and Jack are phone people. Cherry spends a whole morning relaying all of her friends' and Jack's business friends' astrological highs and lows for the upcoming weeks. Cherry is the oldest of nine children which she says explains her abhorrence of housework. She grew up in the Sonora Desert and pronounces *Malard* in a French manner. She is vegetarian and so too are Orchards and Turtles. Cherry tells me about disasters to befall New York City. In 1980, there will be a great food and water shortage which will be ended by an earthquake that will split Manhattan in two and leave most of it under water.

Every week Cherry's apartment is equally and totally dirty. Cherry comes more and more to rely on my coming and there comes to be more and more for me to do. The first thing to do is an hour's worth of dishes. Cherry leaves the entire week's dishes piled in the sink. She doesn't even scrape the food off. There are at least four dirty pots sitting on the stove. Before I can wash the dishes, I must take all the dishes out of the sink in order to clear the drain. Cherry uses the kitchen sink as if it were a garbage can. The bottom of the sink holds three large handfuls of old, gloppy food. After the dishes are done, I wash down the stove and refrigerator. Next I clean the fixtures in the washroom. The bathtub once had been painted so now every time I wipe it out, paint chips fall off. Paint chips are a nuisance to pick up when your hands are wet; often they will jam up under the fingernails. I sweep out the bathroom, hallway, and kitchen. There is always a lot of dog hair and kitty litter strewn about. I mop the floors with a string mop which I wring out by hand. The water in the bucket turns jet black after each room. I dust the front room and bedroom. I sweep those two rooms out, moving about the arrangement of heavy, awkward furniture. Then I do like-wise but this time with a mop and bucket. I run upstairs and knock on the door, "Hello, can I borrow the vacuum cleaner?" then I bring the vacuum down on the rug in the front room. Done! Thursday is a heavy day's work but Cherry and Jack are not cheap in paying or tipping. Cherry gives me food to take home and expensive, unwanted clothes and shoes. Sometimes I snitch a little grass or household items like trashbags or saddlesoap. I really feel shame at Christmas; Cherry gives me a generous amount of dope as a present and I have already a present pocketed.

Jack is an affable, slender young man with a moustache. He is from a very wealthy family in Trenton. He is used to having servants around and relates to me with the perfect candor of somehow having grown up with me. Jack makes money by being a food broker. Occasionally he and Cherry fly to South America to raise the price of sugar. Jack confides to me that in a single afternoon he may easily make as much as $40,000. He and Orchards play around the house or go out running together. Jack's real love is playing backgammon.

Cherry knows that I know my job and lets me do it all around her. I meet her girlfriends, hear her gossip, we talk about romance, I meet her backdoor friend. I put the cap back on her toothpaste. I confide bits of my heart to Cherry. We just talk about it. The household is run on a steady flow of hard cash. All the food is the most expensive health brands and there are five-gallon water bottles for drinking and in case of drought. What is really needed is a live-in maid with her own budget. If I were she, I would buy a big garbage pail with big trash bags and I would buy a vacuum cleaner to really get all the hair and dust off the floors.

Cherry once refers to me as the "maid" as she talks over the phone. Being described as the maid at first hurts my feelings because I see my job as more independent and more of a service than maid's work. But the work is like maid's work. I finally realize that there is no definition of the word *maid* that does not include the word *woman* or *girl*. I don't feel like a woman while I'm working. I do feel like yelling, "Cleaning Man!" at Cherry. But she is only talking into the telephone and *maid* is meant to mean something to the other party, not to me. Jack tells me that when the place is really filthy, he dreams of me. Jack with his aristocratic leniency has no need to call me anything other than my name.

I am cleaning in the washroom. I am about to wipe down a white ledge that I always wipe down. I'm moving off the items always found on that ledge. Here is something strange. A piece of a nylon stocking is wrapped tightly around something the size of a golfball. I pick it up and notice that it is slightly mushy. I sniff it. My head almost recoils into the bathroom mirror as I flip the thing back onto the shelf. I have never smelt anything like that before! What can it be? My first thought is that it is an occult little bag filled with human excretions and fingernails. I don't touch it again. Later as I'm putting on my shirt to go home, I overhear Cherry and Jack talking in the front room.

"I think Bob found my (*unintelligible*) in the washroom today!" Cherry says.

"Wow!" Jack exclaims, "Girl, you really have no class!" They both break into hysterical laughter. I step into the room and they dummy up. The next week while I'm cleaning the washroom, I notice something hanging from the shower nozzle high up the wall. It must be the same thing but it has grown! This time it appears to be a child's foot dangling in a stocking. I let it be. Explanations are offered by my friends. It's shit. It's witchcraft. It's menstruation flow. It's cheese. I don't know. I'll never know.

One day I come to work stoned. There is quite a pile of dishes as usual. What is unusual is that Cherry is not doing her yoga. Instead, she is lounging on her bed in her bathrobe. As is my custom, I centralize all the items to be washed by placing them on the tottering drafting table which is directly behind me as I stand at the sink. Next to me, on my right, is the door to the bedroom. Everytime I turn around to get a few more dishes to wash, I peek over to Cherry who is lying on her bed absorbed in a magazine. About the third time I glance at her, I start to feel a nervous excitation. Her blue bathrobe seems to be riding up her legs. I start taking fewer dishes at a time in order to secure more looks. I'm so stoned that I'm starting to feel dizzy. Each time I look, Cherry is in a new position. One time, she is lying on her back and her thighs are spread open on the bed. The next time, she is on her stomach lying across the bed so I could see the back of her legs up to the rise of her ass under the bathrobe. I am the slave in the kitchen, chained to the dishes as my mistress excites me. I flashback on the story of Spartacus and Clodia I read as a kid in the *Olympia Reader*. The slave turns around and looks over. The mistress' head is carefully bent away. She sits over the side of the bed. Her bathrobe is loose and open in front. One beautiful breast hangs out. It gracefully slopes down and comes to a point. She is a statue of milk and marble. I reel around, the blood pounding vertically through my body in single giant spurts. The kitchen walls start to spin around me and go dark. I grab the kitchen sink and hold fast as I almost faint. The next time I have the strength to look, she is no longer there.

I, the good slave, never approach Cherry. There is so much potential but as long as I stay a slave, nothing will really happen. Perhaps that is what both of our fantasies are about. I slave for Cherry but when I am done, I am free and independent. Cherry depends on me to clean up and make things liveable. Our unspoken relationship works on work and then works itself out. In early spring, Jack and Cherry move out of the city to breathe the country air. I've lost my best customers but a good customer will always have reason to come back to New York City.

Ted Berrigan

from NOTHING FOR YOU

LONDON AIR
to Bob Creeley

1.

My heart Your heart
                    That's the American Way

& so,

FUCK OR WALK!

                    It's the American Way

* *

Messy Red Heart   (American)

                    Put on
                    black shirt, tight
                    brown cords & bright
                        blue socks

                            Under slush-proof boots!

                    Is that cow-hide?

            I don't know Yes it is that
                    It is That.

                        Take a *good* look, that is I
                            mean
                                have a good look

            LIGHT UP (a Senior Service)

                    &

                turning around

2.

The turning point is turning around.

*

Now, that may seem wasteful   to you
            but not to me   being American

That's the American bent

(sprinting with a limp)

*

It beginning having reached part 3.

Part 3.

Into the Second Act in American Life:

                                    cf. F. Scott Fitzgerald
                                    "There are no
I go in &   Second Acts in
sit down   American Life."
at this desk

and write

        d o g   s e e s   G O D

            in the mirror

                c/o   Jim Dine
                60 Chester Square
                London SW One

        **

    It's 5 units sunlight, 5 units
            Cincinnati

                    One plus Zero
                        equals One

That's it you

Now you're talking!

& so, let me read to you this list
of the ten greatest books of all time:

Here they are

THE TEN GREATEST BOOKS OF ALL TIME

1.	Now in June	by	Lao-Tree
2.	Sore Foot	by	Larry Fagin
3.	Sleep & Dreams	by	Gay Luce & Julius Segal
4.	Rape	by	Marcus van Heller
5.	Out of The Dead City	by	Chip Delany
6.	Moth	by	James M. Cain
7.	Letters for Origin (Proofs)	by	Charles Olson
8.	Classics Revisited	by	Kenneth Rexroth
9.	Pleasures of a Chinese Courtesan	by	Jonathan Payne
10.	Letters to Georgian Friends	by	Boris Pasternak
10.	Horse Under Water	by	Len Deighton
10.	Camp Concentration	by	Tom Disch

&
breathing easier now

10.   The Quotations of Chairman Mao.

OTHER CONTEXTS

I'd been
trying
to escape
that mind game

thinking that thought
itself
can possess
the world

by always & I mean
as constantly as physically
possible
lying down and

not thinking it over. Reading
for example everything I'd loved
again & again
anything new:

resisting being thought.
Exactly. Resisting
Being
Thought.

Tonight I think to do
differently, differently
to do.
I think I will.

I would
think I will. We'll have to wait
& see. I have to wait,
and see.

My watch shows it to be
5:51 a.m., March the 24th
in Wivenhoe, in England.
Alice is asleep

& breathing beside me, pregnantly.
& oh yes, it's 1974. Alice
is 28 years old. Anselm is 20 months.
I'm coming up on four-oh.

In the morning

Very bright the

not yellow

light

tough creamy air

it softens lightly

when you give

THE LOOK OF LOVE

having a good look

knowing / green

interesting manners

with

blackjack nuances.

Can you dig it (doing that) in the Michigan morning?

light

taking your glasses off

(clothes already off)

yellow pants

I should say gold

but gold isn't really yellow

is it?

so I don't

Joan Fagin's brown shirt's resting now

on the chair

brown

transparent, blue

buttons...

Some pop off

so do we all   some time.

Joan, with you,

        "I do."

           &

               Loving you

           doesn't really *have* to "do"
                                anything
                 but I do.

& doing (..."anything"...) turns you on, too.

                doing a few
                       swirls
                  &

                  spinning
       moving easily

          & so firm

      A just plain terrific face

   two eyes   opening wide
                  with delight

     that's "doing it all" for me.

It's a little scary   it, & you, too

       white & not so
       blue

              now a slow pink flush
   across the white rhythm

      & the blue. . .

           Coming together

    or maybe not coming at all

 or coming
   at leisure

"Digging one's own natural
savagery"

as the man says

is all there is
to do.

To eat ourselves
alive
& dig it.

& having looked into "that",   having *had* "it"

still having it

Now,
to look at it,
looking at it whenever

The right light appears

which is practically
anytime   & especially,

"In the morning."

2.

Looking at a cottage in the country,
Maine,

My main man's desire shines through

"that's tough!" you might say
but it's civilized.

It's terse, but fluid.   (It's
a hard-nosed kike rap).

Round & round & round we go

There are trees, around
& green grass around
to stretch out

                 lay around

                                            on.

      Above blue sky

                  as clean as paint is
                  clear (thick & creamy
                                light.)

            Now, that's what I call Radiance.

        All of it,
               & you, really here
                        plus, friendly
                            shadows

  talk
          "do anything you want to."

                   & so we did, all of it.

See that?
        I'd like you to look at
                & see it.

    It's beautiful!   moving beautifully

        in the morning
      &

you can turn it on   you're here
      anytime   & it's here

     CODA: (to Alex Katz)

  Being civilized about such things
        is a great pleasure!

            Wasn't it, Alex?

     It's just like Real Life
  (after the movies.)

  You put it together

with your knife

punching it
into the sun

shining

Out of sight!

3.

Now, resting on the President's chair, the center
head inside its hair, on the grass, the white
house right over there

a Chesterfield King

& there's a light!

Clean White Smoke Wind Clear Air

me up here & you,
you up across & over there.

Between us, The United States
of Air
& Joan
still flying,
on this plane:

It's taking Joan everywhere
she feels like going

& so she does

& so do we all

& so we do,
thanks to you,

light   radiance   air

Alex, Joan, my friends,
you were there.

From "ANTI-MEMOIRS"
for Tony Towle

Mid-Friday morn, 10 o'clock, I go to India
At the suggestion of a man I barely know: André
Malraux. Benares. The first house I enter I see
A photograph of the murderer of Ghandi on the wall.
"There are too many Reactionaries still, in India," I remember
Nehru telling André Malraux. I step closer to the picture,
Read the words printed at the bottom: *photograph by*
Rudolph Burckhardt. This is unreal! I leave India, return
On foot to Hyattsville, Maryland. 1705 Abraham Lincoln Road.
My hosts are absent still. Their children have swallowed Rat
Poison, & they are at the Hospital, caught in the puke
& ye shall be healed, that scene, fright, terror, nothing serious
In the end except it might have been.... The Rolling Stones fill this place
A sweet speed-freak is lost in Harlem. Mr. Chester Himes. Life
Going on quite merrily Hunting For The Whale. A wealth
Of fresh Whale-tracks considerably cheers us up.

Bernadette Mayer

from ERUDITIO EX MEMORIA

***

A herd of horses a brace of pheasants a wisp of snipe a flock of sheep, a pack of wolves a covey of partridges a gaggle of geese, a tribe of lions a sord of mallards a swarm of bees.

The causes of a dress (in language a word): the material cause, a fabric (in words a sound); the formal cause, a pattern (in patterns, patterns of sound); the efficient cause or planning intellect, a seamstress (of a speaker the speaker); the reason or final cause, to cover nakedness (communication).

Words have a conventional meaning, it isn't natural. Semantic resemblances, French: The *heure* is late at my *mansion*. He is the one who is *contraire* to *fleurs*. The *humeur* of the *chasse* escaped him. The *situation* within the *tempete* was *negatif*. Is it *necessaire* to *moquer* my *paradis*? Every time I *emporter* a *table*, I have to *rassembler* it. Dear John, I am sending you this *lettre*:

The customs officials suspected him of smuggling diamonds into the United States. Consequently they searched his person and luggage thoroughly (statement - result). Indo-European is the hypothetical parent of our family of languages: Armenian, Albanian, Tocharian and Turkestani are generally lost, Sanskrit and Greek are accounted for. Italo-Celtic then led in two strains through Latin to the Romance languages we've mentioned above, through Continental Celtic which no longer exists to Insular Celtic off to the Cornish and the Welsh on one side and through Goidelic to end with the Irish and the Scotch on the other. Germanic, East and West, became Gothic, English and Old High German. Icelandic never married anyone. Balto-Slavic also stayed single, and led to nothing: *Pater noster, que es in coelis, sanctificetur nomen tuum. Adveniat regnum tuun. Fiat voluntas tua. Sicut in coelo et in terra. Panem nostrum quotidianum da nobis hodie, Et dimitte nobis debita nostra sicut et nos dimittimus debitoribus nostris. Et ne nos inducas in tentationem. Sed libera nos a malo. Amen.* Said as rapidly as possible. So, that's all I have to say to you, John, except that I got this one wrong on my intro to Western Civilization Test: One of the last checks on the power of Louis XIV: Lit de Justice, wrong! It was Parelements. Or maybe it was Council of State, I don't know, why should I know, how could I care. Love.

There is a beautiful picture on the back of the test: the head of a mechanical man with earrings and hands positioned as if they were holding an invisible host, you can see the man's esophagus in a state of peristalsis and a lady with a small mouth and a large capital "I" instead of hair and as her headdress reaches up to the skies, it becomes a candle with many flames.

Select a phase of the eighteenth century which you consider affected... Be specific in explaining this phase and why it was selected.... "The flim-flamming of an arrangement in which Goethe works toward Abelard's diffusion outwards and downwards. Dante Gabriel Rossetti the rhinoform."

It is the position of the artist to gestate in the opening position, *il sequestre la casa di nobile, uomo di noi* (pride, envy, sloth, gluttony, lust, anger). But, after looking at type, the unit of meaning is not the phrase or the word or even the letter but the dot (*Portrait of the Artist, Initial A* (David Schubert), "Four Quartets").

Dear Bernie–

I'll be up to copyread after the intra-mural game.
Fran Burke

1. Lois went from dresshop to dresshop before she finally bought one.

2. Laura had lunch with Emily at the cafeteria yesterday, but she said nothing to her about tickets for the ice show.

3. While they jumped up and down with pleasure, the baboons took peanuts from the little children.

4. In the movie "Breaking the Sound Barrier" it tells how a man was able to fly faster than the speed of sound.

5. With the increase in the number of school-age children they need more school teachers than ever before.

I think I get it now. It's upon on again and out of among, we are against the said and into have and hold. He was and I came there, oh. Time endures, *pente hemeras*, there's a time when (on the next day), a time within which, *deka hemeron*. I against you for the past.
The universal set is the being-considered set. The mapped elements have pre-images and little plain images, there is an empty set, ( ). ( ) U (a) = (a). There is a sign for "is a subset of." If you list all the subsets of, perhaps, A and A = (a,b), there is no valid justification for the inclusion of the empty set. I don't know why but I like the intersection of sets and the union of joint (non-disjoint) sets and in their union, there is no repetition of elements. Then again, if A is the set of x's such that x is a natural number, then A is the set of natural numbers, all of them and U, as I said before, is the universal set, this set. So, these mathematics are not so much an apple as a simple sentence without adjectives or lines but there's alot of dullness, how did he ever sigh as the group times the field equaled the ring and whatever was once worth recording is now determined like the dial on a wristwatch, what is the psyche doing here, what is a spiritual height. Paris arrives and departs in my Latin like a dial but, by and large, it is the outside forces coming to the surface so readily and without our homes we are kind but uneven and unaware, opening the conversation with aplomb or a plum within the gates of it, those brackets, then I sink into the earth's resources as the words depart, so goes speech and the wives I've had when I have been a husband. This construction is a for-

mula for finding the mid-point of a line segment, having to do with vectors, now this is difficult, more so. A unit vector though is only a vector whose length is 1. Two lines are parallel if there is a vector which is a direction vector for each of them. In N-dimensional vector space you measure position and time in 4-tuples. The set of 4-tuples is the event space. This is a commutative group under addition. So, I am vector geometry, I am dependent on another vector if I am a scalar multiple of another vector. No, I am an independent vector, not on the same line at all. If I would want to be dependent I would become a linear combination of the others, that is, in the same plane, xyz.

Beauty = Good + One, no, Beauty = Good = One, these are the Sophists. I wonder why we all wrote down: "Demiurge fashions objects of world after pattern of Forms as Exemplary Cause," I wonder what it means. If the Demiurge is God, then the forms are outside God and the world. Phaedo waited for truth by reason alone where essences remain the same. Then learning is only a part of memory or even reminiscence. An idea does not have a local separation, even for Plato, so they say: there is Absolute Beauty the ultimate Principle of unity, there is the Good the principle of knowing and being yet transcending being, there is the Absolute the One the immanent, the immanent imitation, participation in which is transcendent. These Forms all owe being to the One. Since the world of the senses is so unreal, Aristotle threw in the towel to determine what a real universal might be. An Idea is not an object they say what would William Carlos Williams say what would Wittgenstein say, whatever they said. If you want to define it, apprehend its class-concept in the hierarchy of forms. I have one many idea, I've had it all my life, I have many one ideas, they are ideas of moral excellence, ideas of aesthetic sensibilities and profitable pleasures, ideas of significant statements and the uses of forms, forms are numbers. Reality is both the sum of things and all that is in change, memory and devotion. Eros the desire for what is not possessed, the impulse of man's higher nature toward the good, toward generation in the beautiful, body and soul. Dualism, now I have a tripartite soul, there's conflict in it, the third part. The sun is a unit of time, time is the movement of the sphere. Beauty rests above the senses somewhere, art was imitation, is imagination, has a meaning, does not have a meaning, is an instinct, a shirt.

So there is "Realism," a play: (*a living room*)

Anna Karina: Help me, Satchmo! Protect me from this man, Swedenborg!

Satchmo: Direction, every line must function.

K: Carve a cross in your book and don't look at trees, living in a country is not what it seems.

S: I shall bang my book.

K: Let's forget this nonsense, better to turn to ambivalent carrots, onions and pork or lamb chops, braised with parsley and paprika, served on rice with tomato sauce with herbs.

S: I rarely read recipes, what is my commitment to them?

K: Stop writing so much down. The years, I say, the bears will pass this ash (*she grimaces*).

S: Advance your own dreams.

K: At the end of this play I shall walk out into the snow, pause, and sink into the earth's resources.

S: For thine is the kingdom and the power and the glory...

K: This is not so funny.

S: Language consists only of symbols.

K: What would a famous religious person do in my situation?

S: Broad, it is a broad curtain.

CURTAIN

The function of the state is to secure rights for the governed not to compel men to virtue, ha! To be in the state of Nature (equality too) is to have rights, no duties, the state of civil society is analogous to the state of grace. You are the individual judge of ends and of the means of self-preservation. The war of each against all is not a good state to live in. If it were absolutism, then all rights are given to the sovereign who, he or she, assures self-preservation as a form of protection. Now here comes Locke with a few half-notes and symbols of rest and the drawing of an elf in a cap beneath the phrase "state of nature:" self-preservation must become happiness and even comfort the which requires wealth and property, what Locke? A government of consent with the right to revolution, the means of making a living and the conquering of nature, that Locke. So, self-preservation is acquisition and greed, so it is, politics amoral, a substitute for morality. Here is Adam Smith to talk about the private vice of competition, one you can entertain or enervate in bed. Then Calvin Coolidge gave us the business, You remember Machiavelli. Two boys just whistled at me from the alley, it's a hot hot night in August, I feel in these words on the notebook page the prosaic dreary joyless quest for joy in progress when I know full well that these two boys who are now coming back for a second look surely and sadly have nothing better to do. I am already six months pregnant.

***

Lewis Warsh

from THE MAHARAJAH'S SON

1965

April 16

Mon Bebe,

       Qu'est ce que tu fais en ce moment? Il est ici douze heures minuit. There it is six o'clock. It is Friday. Possibly you are visiting your parents —possibly you are writing—Pense-tu à moi?

       J'ai reçu ton lettre. I should write in English but it's hard for me since already certain things are becoming very easy for me in French —although at the movie which we saw tonight I understood nothing.

       I am in Chateauroux. I move in the reincarnated world of a Van Gogh canvas—the town and the base are far away. Here there are only farms and barns—tous les animaux—hens, pigs, goats, rabbits—And Gigi and I move amidst them. It is difficult for me to conceive of myself here—or to conceive of the people (the farmers for whom this is life—for me only a strange sojourn)—

       The house is very primitive—I am always (as I am now) freezing cold. So far things va bien avec tous mes relationships. My brother and I, though we engage in continual mindbending battles are able to retain our respective composures and Astrid and I are fine. The children are slowly warming up to one another—the days pass—there is no real excitement only a sense of absorption —sleeping in the freezing attic—my room has no electricity—drinking wine with my meals. And also!!! I have had coffee—café rather, on three separate occasions—

       Paris is magnificent—the people very beautiful. We will go in next weekend—so far I've only seen it from the car.

Où est mon bébé
My baby—

Love,

Allegra

***

April 20

Baby—

      I am sitting here unable to concentrate due to Gigi's crying—It is nap time and she has been moved into Oliver P.'s room—until now she has been with me in the attic. Ah—she's stopped. The intermittent sobs—now she's crying again.

Later

      I have just gotten your second letter. The babies are sleeping but still I am not alone—conversation around me—Ollie, Astrid, Barry (Astrid's brother), discussing Ollie's literary achievements: He is writing skits for the base's drama group. I would like to be alone with you but I have no electricity in my room and it is anyway so cold there that my only action upon reaching "the dark at the top of the stairs" is to jump into that scary bed and pull the covers up around my head. Lately it has been hard for me to fall asleep—even though I usually don't try till 2 or 3.

      I am feeling extremely pent up—The weather has been so bad that we've hardly been out at all and it's rained every day since I've come. At the moment I just feel ready to burst—I've been trying to offset the inactivity with constant exercise (tonight I gave Astrid & Ollie a dance class) but I'm beginning to suspect that it is more sexual than anything else. Oddly enough I don't feel lonely when I get into bed but I do find myself thinking about you in terms of your body more than anything else. What coat were you wearing when you lost your keys, what pants, shirt, sweater—I see you very clearly love, the back of your head—the back of you in general. Now I can't quite get you to turn around—kiss me!

      Baby—we both must be happy. For the most part my day is spent like yours—trying to locate myself—to generate the feeling that I'm somehow a part of the actions which I perform—the words that I say

      I am now drinking my third cup of coffee of the day. It is very delicious—the difference being I suspect in the fact that we grind it at home. I'm sure it never tasted like this before though I don't really know what the other taste really was.

      I am writing this letter intermittently. I will have to end for I can't really communicate properly the things that I can only begin to dredge up from myself when I am alone and have time to think of you—you the way you would be if you were to walk through the parlor door now—or if you were to call me from the other room—If you were there—

I love you

A.

***

May 11

Baby—

   I am on the train from Paris to Chateauroux having been in Paris finally with Gigi for the past week.

       I don't suppose there will be any mail from you awaiting me—I am wondering if Astrid or Ollie mailed the letter (I wrote one a few days before I left but had no stamps) which if they have you have received by now.

   I have been missing you, or perhaps I should say I have found myself looking for you on the streets of Paris. It would be a good setting for you— One in which, however, you would cease to be an oddity—The people in Paris are the most beautiful I have ever seen. In some places you actually have to search to find someone unattractive. It's a bombardment—but somehow (perhaps due to the extent of the numbers) it didn't seem to be particularly competitive—After a day or so I ceased to feel myself in competition with every pretty girl who walked by (again—it would probably be too exhausting)

   Paris (in itself also) is a magnificent city. I would (if ever I could lose the feeling of being a stranger) prefer living there to living in New York.

   I don't know when I will be able to go back (I am home now— Astrid & Ollie are asleep—Astrid mailed the letter which you have already received) I am torn at this point between staying and coming home—Though I am pretty sure that I won't come home before you leave for the coast but am also sure that I will want to meet you there (si tu me veut) sometime in July.

   There are so many things I wonder about. What you do— how the novel progresses—if the Supremes have a new record—Whether "Ticket To Ride" is still being played—I haven't heard it in so long—

   How are you my love?

   I haven't written to Richard—did you remember to write his address in my book when I was in the bathtub?

   I hope there's a letter tomorrow de toi. I wish so much that you would come sit next to me now. Though at the moment I am not frightened of the house as I usually am when everyone else has gone to sleep. Especially the attic.

   I am very happy about going back to school in the fall though still I don't know what to take. Perhaps one science course and the course in Reading Vite! Do you still want to do that? I am in the process of converting Astrid—I think she may attempt Botany—and also Barry who I have converted to the extent that he is back in England now making arrangements for finishing 11th A level 0 level—Something or other que je ne comprend. I think I am a bit overly proud of my conversions since I have done little or nothing for the progress of my own spiritual/educational state.

        Now I am very happy. A few nights ago I was practically committing suicide—God knows why.

        Perhaps it's too late for me to be writing letters or perhaps I haven't slept in so long. Though I haven't reread this one I am sure that it must be presque incomprehensible dribble. Did I mention the Eiffel Tour—I thought I had.

    Oh Baby I miss you—You really wouldn't believe what a coffee drinker I am—The café de les Cafés de Paris. Will I be able to abide Chock Full-A-Nuts —the coffee you drink which I have never tasted—

        I will write again very soon though the temptation to throw this one away will not get the upper hand.

      My love
               /   My love
                          Allegra

      ***

             June 9

Baby—

        The chasm widens—both in time, and space—(If by now you are in San Francisco)—We are placed absurdly enough on really opposite sides of—A Globe.

        It widens and I here in my bed feel (Baby I have just woken from a dream of you) (I am not able to say the things that from moment to moment cascade into my mind)—I in my bed feel more inseparable from you than I have ever felt before.

    The more that happens—the events of which you take no part—are mute —are sleeping—are not there in any way. The more I feel that Lewis is Allegra —that it is no longer a thing to want—to want to maintain—to want to destroy—

        But already unknowingly something has happened in me—Has changed the composition of the entire thing—

        The reality has ceased to be the more tangible part of our existence together. The flow is in the bloodstream and penetrating - you - Me

      I no longer miss you—I feel almost that
        I am with you

        Love me Always
                   Allegra

***

Dear Love,

I am in the midst of writing in my diary. My entire inner life is at this point a process of making contact with you. This I realize as I write in my diary—

I don't know what to do—at this point it is terribly difficult for me to envision being without you until September

Even more difficult to imagine us ever living again as we were when I left although there were evenings the agglomeration of which is the product of what I now feel—

This love—This need for *you*!
Deepening toward you

My love

A.

***

June 21

Darling—

Today after seeming ages, finally it arrived—the long awaited, nights spent tossing over letter—

Last night I didn't sleep at all—Perhaps my usual last minute traveller's nervousness (I am leaving for London on Wednesday) but the entire night was spent imprecating your parents (they for not having forwarded my 2 letters) and suddenly out of the dawn a very frightening idea struck me—that you had taken LSD & something horrible had happened. Then after about another hour of hideous imaginings I decided it was impossible —Irene, Richard, Harris—someone would have written.

Also, somehow, I know your stabilities—I cannot imagine anything happening to you—you wouldn't let anything happen unless I were there—I cannot possibly envision myself jumping out a window or going crazy, having a breakdown etc. before I saw you again—This of course because there is this basic stability—The "Lewis/Love" Blockade— This knowledge that makes me impervious to any disaster.

Leaving France—feeling a bit let down only having spent 2 weeks in Paris—Only a week on my own—But of course—the Gigi story continues—I could have left her more often had I wanted to—but naturally the struggle goes on. Will it ever cease? The urgency—the need for me to have things going right with her—

Needless to say—she grows—she learns. But the problems remain—don't seem to change. Except of course that at this point there is no other mommy—really no other person in her life at all.

As to September—the steady inconsistencies—The definite desire to live alone—the quite as definite desire to be with you—Are these compatible?

Not to mention of course my other little problems—Being alone—I think I can manage that—the days with Gigi—that too! Only the fears—the ever increasing number of phantoms who inhabit my nights—To conquer them—to remember your words—to laugh at myself—to direct my thoughts away. All successful at times—at others absolute failure—

But then in Paris somehow I wasn't frightened at all—Everything was superb—and I was nestled so cozily into one tiny hotel room—There was no staircase (the main problem at Chateauroux is quite definitely the staircase) and no endless doors, hallways, uninhabited attics etc.

In a way I can't imagine 125th Street being frightening after this staircase! Then again Ollie & Astrid are always here—Although I almost invariably go to bed at least an hour or two after them.

Right now I'm in the middle of writing a story. I'm utterly disappointed in my (as far as I was concerned merely "untapped") talents—

Still I am persisting—having relegated the present venture to a "practice piece"—no one of course ever to see anything I write until I begin to tap the "untapped"—

I will be seeing Richard in London, probably on the day after tomorrow. After that I don't know. Staying in Chateauroux any longer is a complete waste. Astrid is pregnant again and they are definitely coming back to N.Y. in November. If nothing else in London there will be the consolation of hearing The Beatles, The Stones etc. You won't believe that I've heard no new song since "Ticket to Ride"—

The divergencies in our experiences—Paradoxically—inversely—perhaps one has nothing to do with the other—the emergence of the completed sphere—the consummated unit being now there—Irrevocably.

All my love to you my Baby—

Allegra

***

                                                                    July 13
Baby—

          Of course it is natural—our lives at such variance—for our letters
to become more and more vague. Still, I cannot help wondering, worrying....
Remembering at 125th Street when you used to write letters only when you were
fâché avec moi & that that is the mood in which you are writing now—
          Still, your life is more of a mystery to me than mine to you—
Being with Gigi—these things are given:

     A spends entire day with G
     G has set schedule

                                        A is every evening at approx. 7:00
Western European Time in the bathroom of their London home attending to G.
in the bath, fixing G's diapers, feeding G. supper etc. These things are
constant. It is only at 8:00 or 8:30 that my activities become variable—
          When I first came here I was going out with an Indian
Maharajah's son but despite his millions and his gorgeous Ferrari I couldn't
maintain an interest—Maintenant c'est fini—Have not met The Beatles
although I did meet Brian of The Stones—comme çi, comme ça. And Sandie
Shaw—very nice, at a party last weekend. Those are the glamorous aspects of
my life and as you know I love glamour—but it seems spiritually I cannot
afford it—When I stop to try to talk to someone there is nothing, nobody there
—even when drunk or high there is no means of bridging the barrier ....
          I was looking forward tremendously to being with Richard but somehow
despite mutual efforts we crossed each other over the channel, he from London
to Paris. Me from Paris to London—
                                        London is pretty bad—Very ugly aside from the
very few moments of medieval splendor—there's an abundance of slums &
something squalid about even the moderately bourgeois areas. When it tries to
be modern it looks something like what I would imagine Buffalo to be—not to
mention the weather—
          I will try, though money is very low, to spend another week or
so in Paris—Perhaps meet Richard there. Time is going very quickly—I cannot
quite envision my home coming, probably before yours—
          I do however—and perhaps too often—envision notre reunion—Je ne
sais rien mais

               encore tu sais que
                                        Je t'aime

                                                  Allegra

***

August 17

Lewis—

        thc sensation of your withdrawal, thc increasingly ominous
silence—I find myself terribly uneasy, shivering (as I am now) when I think
about you—
        And yet each day my focus draws more central—It is you—Again—in
opposition to the withdrawal, it is a sensation of union & reunion.

I am aware / I imagine:

        your displeasure with my last letter which I remember not wanting to send
—a certain flippancy—or not being really able at that moment to relate to you
—But, it's not that anyway—
        Your present involvements—emotional, literary, sexual—
the time in which you are divorced from me—
        But these hours alone—the typewriter, the paper, the
letters which you think of writing, the love which you cannot bring yourself to
give—
        Baby—I battle with your mind—I want to penetrate it—The various
precincts—my curiosity is secondary—It is not the events, the people, the
days, the nights—But rather inward—And it is very difficult—
        Is it you who create the barriers? is it my inexperience?
        Will it be even harder, perhaps
impossible, when we are face to face.

Needless to say—I am waiting

Allegra

Sept. 1

Sweetheart—

       It's difficult to ascertain whether you're home or not—Of course now you are—In "my" now, perhaps you aren't—This is only an allusion to time, at any rate, being home—this is the moment for opening mail, for finding out what's happened since you've been away—of who's returned during your absence—

       David's just told me that you've been down in Mexico in which case there is some doubt as to whether or not you got my last letter.

       I don't know how....
never mind, actually I do know how—it's just that it definitely requires speaking to you and seeing you.

I AM HOME

your baby,

Allegra Helene

I SHOULD RUN FOR COVER BUT I'M RIGHT HERE

been so much   so many
prayed a lot   screamed & yelled for help

an interesting chain of events I need to record

I got into it   hit by three punks

all day riding around Taos   not taking care of business
driving for this crazed hippie & his old lady   to hock stuff
    for money
        got some tequila   were drinkin it
    somehow after we got back to the mesa I remembered
I had to call Richard   crazy
    I saw a car leaving the parking lot   I ran there
against my better nature's intuitions
    Any room?
    No.
    Can I ride on the back?
    OK.
        so I rode up to the top of the Sanchez rim
road on the back window of a shiny slippery new fastback   black
filled with winos off to town & some party   at the top they
turn the wrong way so I jump off wondering if maybe I should go
back   but no   a sister drives by   I put out my thumb   she
gives me a ride to the church

    I find I haven't got a cent   I try to bum a dime
from some people riding in   finally get a ride & a dime
phone at Cisco's out of order   I start to walk up the hill to
Lorraine's

    three chicanos come out of the bar& get into a
white 64 ford
        I look freaky   wearing short shorts
barefoot   tee shirt   beads   hair matted & crazy
    You look like the devil   I hear one say   then
they start driving across the road right at me   seemed that way
that time to pick up a couple big rocks to throw through the
windshield

Nope   UH-UH
when they see me do that they stop the car
          O   picking up rocks   thas bad
          we got to teach you
                              one kid   young with a golden
shirt & greased pompadour   plenty macho   the kind a chicana
would probably like   comes after me   the others drive off
          com'on you hippie muthafucka   you wanna fight?
          's jus me   com'on
          no I don wanna fight
I start walking into the dirt road that goes to dawnflower
he follows
          you wanna fight?
          no I don wanna fight
          then wa you pick up rocks for?
          you were gonna run over *man*

I'm still holding the rocks & walking backwards down the road
          com'on mon   jus you n me we fight
          no I don wanna fight   why can't we live in peace
          I want peace
          Peace?   you hippie mothafucka   we don wan no peace
          this is *our* land
                              (no kidding we really said these
          things to one another)
                              wha you come to Escondido &
          fuck around hah?
          I don come to fuck around
          then go back where you came from
the car comes speeding up the road   barbed wire fences on
both sides   a few women & kids nearby in a courtyard
     I think it's a good time to run & I make a break but
that's a long road & I see he's much faster than I am
     I stop to double back
A big one gets out of the car & cuts off my break
then I'm encircled
     Go back where you came from hippe mothafucka
fists start flyin   I too slow to really try to fight back
          splat   a sock in the eye
          purple flash of light
          circle of light
          purple shining iridescence in eye socket explosion
          poof
                    more blows all around

I fall down fast to avoid anymore   praying they wont kick me
I ham it up like I'm dead & it's not hard to do   I guess
someone kicks me in the ribs but I wouldn't know having gone
nearly senseless   saying
                no please   please don't
                                        hand over my face
                please have mercy   I don wanna fight

                OK   you gonna go back where you came from right?
                yeah right ok
                you gonna get up an go out to that road an start
                hitch-hikin   & don come back to Escondido right?
                yeah ok   yeah right
                OK   you get up an get out of here

they run for the car   no license # on the front   & back out
of the road fast   when they appear gone I get up   reeling
crazily after   the women are near saying
                they hit you?   wha for they hit you?
I think I said
        I dunno   because they're bad
    Jordan drove into the road   I ran up to the grey sedan
waving   one hand on my face   blood on my nose
                After that car   I say   pointing as the ford zips
into lower Escondido   the other side of the highway
    I get in   Jordan starts to go   then says
        I don wanna fight em   & turns around

    He gets me back to the mesa   his ol lady makes mate &
herb tea while I soak my eye & face with icy ditchwater
Jordon comforts me   he is a strong man with much of the
father in him   humble   beautiful   he holds my hand

giving strength   compassion   one man to another
        I cry
when I feel nourished & the pain is dulled a little I go on to
the pueblo where I meet Lena who I was travellin with that day
        Ajax's got grass   she says

    Well I made my way over to the little cluster of cedar trees
where Ajax had his campfire   he slept outside with his wife
Lena & their baby girl Honeysuckle
        Jus got my ass kicked in   I mumbled & pushed my
face out into the flickering orange firelight for Ajax to see the

bloody bruises around my nose & eyes

      holy shit   he said   & I briefly ran down the
incident while he shook his head about bad karma & he hoped
he didn't bring anything down on me & I said that Lena had mentioned
he had some grass & did he want to give me any & he said sure

      you got a container?   now I make it a point never to carry
a container or else carry a very large one   I didn't have
anything so Ajax frowned & scratched his head   he handed
me a folded paper bag

      it was thick & heavy   he offered me a smoke but I said
my mind was totally destroyed   & thanks I'm going home

     So I went home to my little house in the goat pasture &
when I opened the bag was amazed to find 1/2 pound ragged leaf
pattern acid flash fragments & many shade of green grain &
pollen & every aspect of the physical stuff said   dynamite

     I cried a bit & felt my nose & swollen eye & ugliness &
thought I had to split & go up to the mountains & see if I could
get a hold of God on the stellar telephone & find out what the
fuck was going on

     I packed my acid into the little velvet pouch that Octavia'd
given me & tied it to my belt   I had some orange acid   sunshine
& some purple domes & some blue flats   I filled a large brown
glass bottle with grass   I stuffed it full & tapped it down &
stuffed it some more   I got my OCB papers   my notebooks   some
envelopes   some postcards   all put into my madras shoulderbag
I got my pen   a rapidograph 00   filled it   got my paints
& brush & pad   I got oatmeal   salt   sweaters   dry milk   &
some crusts of macro bread   I got a pot with a lid & a bowl
a fry pan   tea   brown rice   blackeye peas   nuts   raisins
my sleeping bag with the velvet patches just sown on   some
blankets & I was getting the fuck out of there   & I was
going to the top of the tallest fucking mountain to watch the
full moon rise & the sun rise on the summer solstice & I was
going to pray to god to help me understand what had just
happened to me

     so I tied up my bag & loaded everything into my knapsack
& it was all ridiculously heavy   it was dark but the moon
was nearly full   I took the remaining bag of grass & went
towards the pueblo where I met Ishmael   I handed him the grass
& said share this with the brothers   then I trudged across the
ditch & down into the first arroyo   I also had with me
about 50 librium I'd found when I moved into the A frame house
some acetominophen   some aspirin   some vitamin C   some
super vitamin pills & lots of dolomite calcium tablets

As I walked down the slope I felt weak   my left upper
chest ached fiercely & breathing was difficult   I threw
down my burdens
     crawled into the mummy bag & passed out

     first light woke me up   ouch & ouch   no strength
& what's this ache in my ribs   those fucking creeps   they
kicked me   O yes
                         I had a plastic jug of water & washed down
aspirins & 3 libriums to ease my reeling brain   put
on boots & army jacket & stumbled down the flash washed sandy
cactus dotted hillslope   finding a path at the bottom I
followed around the valley bottom through lush meadow where
a natural spring flowed & overflowed into a marsh making some
life in that deathly desert landscape
                                   to my surprise I
arrived at a small adobe house nicely plastered with smooth
copper mud   & went inside   empty but for a big bed & a
few moldy crusted pots & a wood stove   plastic window with
spider webs & a few old Saks Fifth Avenue suits oddly enough
& I remembered someone mentioning the shelf house that Marcel
     the benefactor & owner of all our land   had had the
Indians build so his guests could stay there
                                   I decided to
be his guest   made some oatmeal with a little tamari sauce
   drank some stale beer that had been there way too long
took five libriums & went to sleep for 20 hours or so
     the house was called the shelf house because it was on a
flat piece of land leading to a steep canyon cut by the river
that gave life to our entire locale   I decided to smoke
some grass & upon getting stoned I realized the extraordinary
quality of this red flecked magical flower dust & flashed
that with the forty pounds of gear I had carted into the
wilderness so that I could be prepared for all the eventualities
of cold   hunger   rain   snow   lightning   wolves   banditos
the willies   thirst   pain & poetry I was never gonna get to
the top of any fucking mountains or even to the bottom of the
deep river canyon
     I decided to take the bare necessities   I filled a
plastic dish with salted oatmeal & hunks of flat macrobiotic
whole wheat bread stashed after all too infrequent meals   I
took the water jug   my harmonica   matches   hundreds of
them in a plastic baggie   pen & ink   one of two composition
notebooks for prose works   one blank paper drawing book

bound with a black cover containing some of my best poems
songs   & drawings   many never copied   I took a metal
bowl for cooking   my hairbrush   some assorted nuts
my knife on my belt in hand made leather sheath   I threw a
sweater & some polos & a turtle neck jersey into the ragged
mummy bag   wrapped it in a blue crocheted blanket   tied
it up   slung bedroll & madras bag with stuff over my shoulder
    blue pouch with acid tied carefully to belt   beads around
neck   marijuana & papers in shirt pocket & trudged to the
edge of the shelf down to the canyon & the gurgling river edge
    I was scared   I didn't want to meet anybody   hippies
maybe but no more chicanos   I passed Poobah's little house
& climbed along a narrow path under the steep canyon walls with
their faces sculpted by centuries of wind & water
    I became tired quickly & finding a hollow in the canyon
wall where some very soft ash made a natural resting place I
camped again under a jutting overcrop of rock
    I went down to the river which ran shallow & fast   ice
water I dabbed on the bruises of my face & drank deeply translating
my wish into feeling the magic god snow melt river water healing
some deep inside ache & opened my shirt & pressed ice water on
my ribs   sad as the pink & charcoal sunset calmed the tiny
piece of sky above treetops & canyon walls
    I slept in the ashes   waking up dusty during the cool
night to watch the big dipper sparkle & spin around the north
star
        In the morning I assessed my travels over two days & three
nights & added it up to a mile or so   From the mesa the
mountains look deceptively close but a wasteland of rabbit
skittered coyote prowled arroyos & headlands stretch for some
five miles before the real rise of forested ridges begins
    I was crazed   a madman   shocked   amazed &
frightened   It was conceivable to follow the river into the
smaller peaks & up on to the watershed but this meant to pass
through a chicano community nestled atop the canyon wall where
the valley spread out half an acre across   I followed the
path along the river until it became impassable   then forded
to the other side following another path worn by chicano &
Texan fisherman & hunters & naked hippies out to swim in the
whirlpools & fuck on the riverside meadows or just smile at
the dancing blue flowers of that late & welcome June New Mexico
Spring
        the canyon opened wide into valley & along the green rushing
water wide branched trees swayed forming the perspective of

fertility gift from the blue jagged peaks

    in New York I saw a postcard photo of the Jordan river &
was amazed at the sameness of the two streams   blessed veins of
life fluid softening the harshness of ultimate predator landscape
of unfiltered blazing sun & giant sky cradle of thundercloud
& lightning flash coming from nowhere on the wind filled with
rain destined for some other place where the trees could send
out lazy roots & not claw hungrily into the barren ground for
a little soothing water

    There was a little house carved out of the river bank & I
decided to rest there   someone had dug out a cave   leaving a
seat of clay in the wall & beaming a roof with aspen poles   *latias*
they're called   I took a tablet of purple acid carried
from Frisco to Portland Oregon to Reno Nevada & back to Frisco
& then to Taos by car waiting for the right occasion & washed
it down with river water & a prayer

    I lay on the meadowbank watching puff clouds blow rapidly
across the deep sky & took off all my clothes to let the sun
warm my scabbed face and aching ribs

                                crumbling sorrow mind giving birth to
fragmented photon question marks   oh why can these faces of
hate brood darkly over six packs & TV houses & shining enamel
automobile windowscreens flashing hate on the panorama of
me walking beautiful & free (feeling) on a roadside?   Why?
& like a good christian & a good Indian pray to the sun as
father & light to lift the evil cloud in the minds of those
brute children who play with guns & knives & machines & say
a man must fight to be a man & not a punk fag who is filled
with love & laughter & kiss for a good soft time

    & I want to do good here father   to do right & work the
land & help the people & teach the smiling babies how to live &
carry their natural joy into the sweet journey of their promised
growth of earth pacing love longing life   so heal me father
god in heaven or whoever or whatever you are that sent me this
test & trial & bashed my lazy head to remind that I aint been
doing right been fucking up & riding in cars when there's
fields to plow & seeds to get the ditchwater to & been smokin
cigarettes & drinkin coffee & tequila & wine when that light
is in the sky to make me high & eating garbage meat from the
super store & the rootbeer stand when the tea & rice are on
the shelf & the pure wheat flowers in the pasture   but I can't
do shit with a broken body & a face afraid to show that I been
bopped & beaten & shattered & shat upon so heal me HEAL ME GOD

    & so screaming at the sky I wade into the stream to say

I'm yours

baptize   me show me what to do   take me   TAKE ME
I'm yours   & lie down on the rocks   naked & totally submerged
looking up through the green flow of ice water so cold but so
pure & rub my chest & tap my heart & the temples of my forehead
& the center of my skull & jut out my breast standing in the
rapids with both hands cupping broken heart screaming HEAL
ME GOD

    I soaked my face once more   gently massaging the scab
on my nose & the swollen eye   then lay on the grass below
the chill breeze where the sun could dry my pretty body   thin
legs spread & thinly befurred with delicate dark hairs & tight
scrotal sack & chilled contracted penis surrounded by bushy
soft nest of light brown public fluff & dark curling trail
up to belly button crowned with glistening water drops & smooth
bronzed skin stretched across unmarked tender ribs & tightened
little nipples encircled with thin hairs like a little flower
garden around a fountain of tingling flesh

    I was dry & hoping the clouds would come & dance a soothing
dance but seeing only some filmy layers in the distance & not
coming my way made to check out the little house thinking maybe
here's where I should stay & rest

    Outside was a little alcove   a metal screen used as a
cooking grate leaned against the clay wall   a pile of burned
out tin cans & assorted plastic & paper supermarket rubbish
tuned a little revulsion in my belly pit & the brief inspiration
I should clean this up & bury it with the handleless shovel
lying nearby used no doubt to bury shit but never used to bury
this shit

    I crawled into the small opening & was nearly blinded by
the change from blazing daylight to cave chill shadow darkness
& pile of mildewed clothes   rags blankets on the floor   old
letters addressed to Ajax who must have lived here once & a
chill came over my whole conscious perception of the place as
an evil presence   I sat down on the carved wall seat & sank
into a terrified confusion sensing black widow spiders   scorpions
tarantulas   grubs   centipedes   jackal dogs & rattlers
living in the moist cloth & the little crannies of the dark pit

    this is not for me   no way   & stumbled into the sun
rubbing gooseflesh on arms to go away & flashing the need of
clothes & bag with precious notebooks & all beloved possessions
to make a man something more than naked   which is frail &
fragile when you're alone in no-kidding-around country   &
night coming on & maybe meet some angry hunter with a gun or

three boys looking for someone soft to beat & torture
                            I've been bewitched   I flash
& looking for clothing see nothing but rotted cottonwood tree
stumps   swaying oak trees   gnarled cedars   flowering
cactus   & red earth
     Stumbling more crazy & visions of crossing terrain naked
& totally vulnerable   to my amazement a man dressed in white
bedouin headdress   & loosely fitting white robes walked out
of the riverside bushes   behind him was a girl   clearly
his woman   wrapped in a long dark Indian print robe
          Hello   he said   I tried to mumble a greeting
just nodding & stretching my hands to communicate my naked
bewilderment
               Pretty stone huh?   I nodded
               Acid?   Yeah   I nodded
          Do you have any acid?   We trade   we wander the
canyon & trade   we make pipes out of bone   we don't deal
in money   haven't used it for eight months & we eat acid all
we can   just ate 9 hits of white lightning on the mountain
yesterday   it was so beautiful
          Listen   I said I'm   having some trouble   I lost
my clothes & my boots
          Wow   you need boots   that's serious   he frowned
          I know they're around here somewhere but I just can't
find them   I said
                         they helped me wander over the 100 square
feet I'd been crissscrossing & within two minutes we'd found
everything neatly piled behind a rock   I was joyously grateful
& amazed at how simple it had been to find my possessions   I
rolled a couple fat joints for them to take   we smoked
one   once more inquired
               Do you have any acid?   we could trade you this deer
antler pipe   he showed me a beautiful pipe made by hollowing
a hole between the two points of the horn & drilling into
the stem
          I don't trade anything for anything   I said   but
I'll give you this sunshine & I reached into my pouch to produce
the pill   I thought for a second & said reaching once more
into the pouch
          & here's one for your wife
          Thanks   Thanks a lot   My name is Malcolm & this
is Gail
          My name is Harris I said
               Paris?

Harris

O yeah I've heard of you up
at dawnflower   we're going up there now
          I'm going to the mountains   What's the best way to
get there?
          Go up Oso creek & he pointed the way down the river to
where the creek led skyward
     We parted   I got my things together & started in the
direction he'd shown   I noticed a lot of houses on the canyon
rim & heard voices   someone even yelling nastily at me it
seemed   adrenal rush of fear   I heard a gun shot & it felt
like it was coming my way   Get out of here   I freaked
out & started running to the northeast up a steep grade
oblivious to pain or breathlessness   running for my life
I got to the top of what was a mesa & kept moving   quickly
occasionally stopping for a brief rest   I came to a barbed
wire fence beyond which was pasture   Private land   I
hesitated but I wanted to get to the top of the hills so I
crossed the open land quickly & found myself at a point where
creek beds stretched upland becoming canyons with giant
headlands on either side   I picked the headland that
appeared to lead to the tallest mountain   I found a ridge &
followed it as the deer must follow the natural highway   here
& there the land would separate into rises again   I hurried
along trusting my intuition & listening for the sound of
water   the trees were getting bigger   spruce & pine
20 feet in diameter & rising high into the sky   I came
to more fences & saying what the fuck crossed over or
crawled under them
               I stopped on a washed out logging road
to write a little about the boys who'd beaten me up   I was
having trouble getting things out of my shoulder bag & picking
up materials I laid down on the sandy ground
     the route I was walking seemed like a natural road   wide
an avenue   with large plants resembling the tops of pineapples
with long pointy blades extending in a green blossom   from a
center where an elaborate lily-like flower sat regally the blade
ends came to a pin sharp point
     around these flowers the desert ants built majestic hills
from large grains of sand   the pattern was clear   the ants
worshipped the flowering porcupine quill plants & designed
garden cities to live in the sanctifying presence
                              I kept a
respectful distance from the ant kingdoms   saying gently

Mighty Ants   I come in peace   do not bite me   I will do you
no harm
     I came to the green & silver posts of the National Forest
barbed wire boundary fence & felt relief as I crossed into
public land where I was supposedly free to roam
     I stopped to write a short poem in my cherished black
sketchbook traveled with me NY to Florida & back   across the
continent to Bolinas   up & down the pacific coast & into
the southwest filled with joy & sorrow songs   sketches of
tropical plants & seabirds
     fumbling in the bag I found   oddly enough   my checkbook
from NYC with 50 dollars in the account & $11 in cash neatly
tucked in a small compartment along with a youth fare card
& accompanying draft classification card given to me in NY
by generous young friend named Art   I hadn't wanted to leave
all this   my total commercial wherewithal   behind at the
shelf house where some wanderer might rip it off   I put the
ludicrous plastic case back in the bag   munched some raw
rolled oats & gnawed a little sweet nut flavored grain bread   the
sun was getting low & it was time to get trucking   atop a rise
I came to a road going around the circumference of the hills   I
hurried across dreading to meet anyone   on the other side
the hill increased in steepness to an angle of about 50°   there
was scrub oak in clusters & it took great concentration to find
passable openings   the hill became so steep I had to crawl
at times   encumbered by my bedroll & my bag which would
snag on a branch or small bush
     I found a ridge & followed it to where the ground leveled
out & seemed to be the base of the real mountain
     Every sound was magnified so that my boots crashing on
leaves or my bag bumping against my coat made incredible nerve
shattering noises   my breathing sounded like water   & I was
often enheartened then disappointed
     then unmistakably I heard water   I followed the sound
to a small stream & drank deeply   I looked around & saw
a small cabin not far away   The sun had gone down & I
approached the shelter with some trepidation   there was a light
switch & a mirror on the wall   I turned on the light
a yellow insect-kill bulb illuminated my dishevelled figure
reflected in the mirror
     my face had healed remarkably   my pupils were enormous
     The cabin was securely locked   I heard voices   a car
saw another house around the curve of the hill   I turned out
the light & got my ass out of there fast

I followed the stream up the hill into dense forest   The
brush became impassable so I started climbing the canyon wall
I thought I'd write a last work in the waning twilight &
discovered that I'd lost my pen   a pen I'd had for years
& written hundreds of works with   I was saddened   I
rolled a joint which summoned the acid energy into my body
once again
                    I want to get to the top of this fucking hill
        I want to talk to the great man   I want to see the
whole planet below me & watch the sunrise light it up
        I could see well enough in the dark & the moon would be
up in a few hours
                                the mountain got steeper & several times
I stumbled & had to claw my way back onto my feet   I put my
bedroll down for a second   it immediately rolled down
the hill crashing over bushes at tremendous speed   without
thinking I put my shoulder bag down & ran down the hill after
the bedroll   I found it   climbed back up the hill &
couldn't find my shoulder bag with food   water   money
I searched frantically   it was hopeless
                                            I still had
my acid pouch & grass bottle & papers & matches   I was still
determined to get to the top   Fuck it   maybe I'll find the
bag on the way down   I kept climbing
                    I looked back down through a clearing in the trees
& saw an extensive panorama of sleeping sliver & black desert
plains far below   a few electric lights hundreds of miles
in the distant velvet night   the beacon blaze of the white
evening star sinking in the west   I want to see the
eastern stars & the moon rise & the dawn & keep climbing running
on the energy of obsessive frenzy
                                a chill runs up & down my
spinal cortex when I notice a green glow in the ground before
me a   hallucination I say   staring closer to make it go
away but no   an iridescent emerald green light like a tiny
stained glass window into the secret cathedral of the inner
mountain
        I look a short time   but I'm afraid   & hurry on up
    mammoth rocks with eagle faces jut out of the ridge
overlooking the western landscape   they afford a lovely view
but I want to get to the top   to see the dawn dance cloud
ritual & finally I'm there
        but the top is just a little top & on all sides larger
mountains   approachable only by a descent into shallow black

valleys where nameless rockslides & predators lurk so this is
it   my top where I can see the eastern sky somewhat   & not
that much of the land below blocked by giant evergreens
    I smoke a joint & drop a blue flat acid tab   letting
it dissolve under my tongue   I crawl into my bag & wrap the
blanket over my head as a shawl
                       It's the summer solstice
on the mesa there's a prayer meeting & I'm having one of my
own   a one man prayer meeting
                  The slightly waning moon
rises & silver clouds dance all around it   I'm tired & it's
rather cold   I try to sleep   then light a fire for warmth
& company having no more calming visions of the way things
move   just wired & tired   smoking joints to keep warm
    the dawn begins to come after hours of crackling wood
going out & coming back with effort

    As the beautiful dawn began to gently sway   the cold
overwhelmed me   I sank into the mummy bag & fell asleep

      I knew there would be a feast on the mesa to celebrate
the solstice meeting   I woke up weak   thirsty & hungry
11,000 feet above sea level with seven miles of desert between
me & my home   The sleeping bag   blanket   & shirts were
too heavy so I hid them behind a rock promising to return in
a few days   to spend some more time at the top of the earth
& contemplate the changes in my life
    Going down was easier than going up but my chest hurt more
than ever   my throat was parched   my legs unsteady
    On the way down the hill I looked for my bag with food books
water   hairbrush   money   & all those little things   nowhere
to be found
    I found the cabin & the stream & drank a long drink
I found a weathered aspen stick & used it as a staff   I
crossed the great expanse of headlands thinking of how the
ants would devour my rotting flesh & coyotes tear my carcass
apart if I merely slipped & broke a leg
              I was hoping it would
rain & I could drink the sky water   dark clouds blew overhead
but nothing happened
        I was not sure exactly where the river
canyon was where I could get the next vital drink   I followed
the top of a dry canyon for hours   sure it would lead to
the river   I had secret confidence that I'd make it but

despair slowly crept out of my belly towards my heart
Now I was stumbling along a dry creek canyon wall
wondering vaguely if this would be a horrible way to die
I
heard voices & looked over the canyon edge to where I saw a
stick & blanket dwelling & in it Malcolm & Gail   I tried to
yell but my throat was too dry so I started climbing   really
almost running down the sheer wall   starting a little
avalanche & nearly falling
they looked up   surprised   I walked to their
dwelling & asked for water   they had none but the river was
nearby   I asked for food   dry oats were fine I said
they handed me a bag & I ate several handfuls
I rolled a fat joint & we got stoned
Are you going to the feast at dawnflower?
Yes   we're just leaving
can you lead the way back for me?   I've been in the
mountains without food or water
They led me to the river where I drank long & thankfully
I followed them up the steep canyon slope but couldn't
keep up   When I got to the top I noticed that the knife I'd
had for 5 years had fallen out of my sheath somewhere between
the river & the top
I kept going   down the next canyon to the swimming hole
then up to the mesa   using my staff to help me up the last
hill   Acid & grass were all I had left of what I'd taken with
me
I came out into the cornfield & with a feeling of relief &
triumph plunged my staff into the soft earth
there was a flash of lightning & a booming thunderclap
giant drops of rain spilled thickly out of the sky
when I got to the pueblo the feast was just beginning

July 1970 - January 1971

for Ted Berrigan

from CUBA

                              ***

lifenet   intense feeling   Burroughs; face
                                        no, don't screw up
write face   synchronicity
   play emotion   buzz back
writing face recording…

The ants are eating each other and what do you do? Go to steal Burroughs' face. No.
Don't screw up now was…afraid of that. That's the trouble, you're living in fear. If you
only wrote face like syncronicity If you only wrote face as if in a play. Stop writing face
now just record. Climactic trauma organism resists the tropics.
The ants are eating each other Darius Milhaud Los Soldados do Brasil and Harry
Belafonte have leverage and skip formalities. That they are in standing room only is an
event in your psychic profession just as seeing Burroughs' face today Getting back to the
guards who refuse to be provoked involved in financial difficulties. These very little limp
simultaneities syncronicities. This means being followed with a dictionary. They need to
know what to call us. Would you tell them? Well, don't. Because I'm letting the oil
Rumanians(rice) affront Russians in my house and they're fighting over RICE. Chinese
leaflets Charles Darius babes until four years old besides Heberto's wife is nursing a
camera. Radical Chinese guests in America are form, forming, formed…
Back here typing this relation to essence… form is related to essence in mystical form.
Have emotions or disconcert, don't screw up. Sirens, so many sirens here in America.
Repose but quit ray in mystical form. If you don't do it now you will pretty soon. The
meeting of sulphur and mercury. Show emotions or disconcert Guantanamo is an
American base on the island of Cuba. There are so many sirens here in America.
Embarrassment despair enough of these. Words tarantula had three in difficulties while
living in Cuba leaped up the size of a fist. Terror panic leaping tarantulas in the corner
they sneaked…

Food shortages threaten the survival of large segments of humankind… worldwide
trends of climactic instability…the main victims of man's neglect and nature's frivolity
will be the poor downtrodden masses of the so-called third world countries. Problems
are compounded by political trends. The seat of the problems has shifted to the stom-
ach. 9/10th of humanity is bankrupt and these are the developing nations, Omar
Khayam's words apply "Ah love, could thou and I with fate conspire to grasp this sorry
scheme of things entire, would not we shatter it to bits and then remould it nearer to
the heart's desire?" The world is unbalanced in income and consumption. 3/4 of the
world's income 3/4 of its investments its services and almost all of the worlds' research
are concentrated in the hands of a quarter of its people. This 1/4 consumes 78% of the
world's minerals and for armaments alone, as much as the rest of the world combined.

In 1970 the world's richest one billion earned an income of $3,000 per person per year: the worlds' poorest one billion no more than $100 each and there is nothing in sight to stop this disparity. No wonder the poor nations consider visions of any growth and development under the traditional economic system a vicious fraud...this is the system which pays 200 billion for world commodities but only one sixth of this reaches the primary producer himself; the rest, 5/6th goes to the distributor and middleman. This same system which gave 7 million to the poor last year took away almost exactly the same amount from the poor in depressed commodity prices. It is not the poor countries who jeapordize global balances: it is the rich their rivalries and desires to hold monopoly military power. Now it is a struggle for economic liberation an end to dependence and servitude. Life seems unreliable with the degradations which abound and our very bodies are threatened. What worries scientists is that chronic malnutrition might begin to sweep across the globe with nearly the rapidity of a flu epidemic if the worlds' population continues to increase without restraint. The worlds' food supplies are already insufficient to feed the hungry multitudes and already 35 million people are dying of starvation every year (UNO report). 100 million children under 5 years of age are severely or moderately malnourished around the globe. 4 billion consumers already on the scene and 200,000 more are added each day. And Pope Paul says that any society that tolerates divorce contraception and abortion is doomed to dissolution or slavery. Christopher Columbus said "the fairest island human eyes have beheld" is Cuba. The slave trade was banned only in the early 19th century. Now racism is against the law. What were once segregated beaches are now open to public etc. Most of the population of Cuba was among the very poor of the earth. In 1953 all houses were without toilet facilities 43% had no running water 31% had dirt floors 54% were without sanitary facilities of any kind and 85% got water from rivers and springs exposed to pollution. Since independence, Cuba has built adequate housing all over the island and rents are officially 10% of ones' monthly income. Equal distribution of wealth programs for education housing public health. Cultural programs such as the island where young people have taken over a model for the future in every field called Island of Youth located off the southwestern coast. There is a law in Cuba too that limits the age of any governing official to 55 a good round figure leaving out the perhaps more senile epochs of an officials' later life.

Fall and Nest go their separate ways instead of Outer Mongolia. Nest is developing an indifferent attitude toward his life. Just before leaving he throws six strands of african santero beads cuban magic black cults on their bed flung to the lady who had trouble being the person she wanted to be. To be or not to be Hamletian. Rocket fuel generals poison mushroom a dog sick time indeed. What's new each morning on this planet is more blood. Nest tells Fall he thinks she could get rid of this old system with her bare hands if she could only get her energies going in the right direction. They follow a casket to the airport. Fall listens to the stars. Some friend later told Fall that they would hate to be the one to run into a man on the street with a green tube coming out the side of his face...a spaceman. Indeed, when Fall met Nest he had undergone dental surgery and had a small green tube coming out the side of his face to drain the pus. Fall flashes on the dark mulatta girl with red shoes running down the hillside in Santiago. How it all started with Nest and Fall...Fall wondering why people weren't better to each other...flashes on big wide deep sand beaches. Heartaches and tears of the friends now fading into the green forests of Cuba their plane takes off for Madrid with a casket aboard. Pakistanis with their faces swollen from crying over their dead companion. Fall remembers babysitting on the beach now a wide strip of sand visible from the air. In dark jungle area she visited a toilet and sink porcelain factory where the workers poured clay into moulds many big leaved trees coffee plantations in midst of jungle forest. Gloriosa's room where Fall was welcome to stay but never did. Gloriosa who defended the airport from the atomic bomb with her rifle. It blows a lot...how good people were to each other back there. Fall will never forget this and abrazos (hugs) from brothers and sisters of Cuba... "tell everyone back there that we don't hate them we only hate their government". Fall listens to the stars...only thing to do is bore or adore. Fall goes on sometimes sleeping on park benches and in gas station rest rooms never really feeling at home again back in her own country. Goes to live in a student ghetto in view of the high rocky mountain peaks...on plains high desert...island of celestial beauty receive this hymn of an unknown adorer. How desperately her heart is seized by thoughts of every-thingearthlyslipping through as if it left no track no trace. Someone has become an island. Fall is where she was when she went...night shakes off the days' noise crash planes climb to clear mountain tops cross rocky mountains...rocky mountain memories rise in heart...

Station restrooms   slipping   rock mountain peaks
                               beauty
goes to live   night desperately her heart
strands of African santero fuel.
                         Generals never really feeling
                             what's new.   After Azores
                                 student ghetto
old system with   Gloriosa's room to
          right side of face, to a casket, to her rifle.
                 Dark mulatta girl
listens through hillside   in Santiago de Cuba,
is bore or adore   an island?   Fall wonders
     goes on   sometimes shakes off days
                             flashes on
welcome beads   friend throws six
defended airports.   Wanted to be
crying over   stars   their dead companion rocket
poured into clay   green tube coming out
                                 dog sick time
drain coffee   blood more blood
abrazos from brothers' direction
                    bionic with Nest and Fall.
                 Fall listens better to each other

with red shoes on   jungle area   tears
     where workers forests
     weren't leaved trees   heroic attitude
      atomic bomb   go their separate
    poison mushrooms. Nest each morning more man on street
        his face spaceman.
How good people   hate their government benches in gas.
     Tell everyone   work out   the passport.
    Where she was when   seized by thoughts
sink   porcelain   faces swollen   big wide deep sand
moulds   friends fading now
    wide strip of sand   plane takes off
climbs to clear   rise in heart.
    This disparity   no wonder   3/4 of commodity prices
is not growth   balances   it is rich
vicious fraud   military power multitudes.
    Plutonium
      has shifted to
   consumption   investment stomach
for armaments alone   this sorry scheme   jeapordizes
global public.
    There is nothing in the rapidity of a flu
    an end to dependence epidemic
conspire to grasp   our very bodies.   Years of age
feed the hungry   not shatter energy.
Starvation is not every heart's desire   scientists chronic
desire to hold
    life seems a counterfeit of earth
    island human eyes   switch to win
traditional Christopher Columbus   beheld Cuba...

HINDER

CONFUSION
wife is nursing emotions island of Cuba
there they were size
are so many sirens
enough of these
give expression to words
tarantula
Cuba
they sneaked
say this...

from SOME MAGIC AT THE DUMP

YERBA BUENA, NICK & JERRY

all the white boxes
of Healthway dried herbs
with the green japan like
rising sun
above the script
the waitress says softly, yeah
Galileo win stirs
hope for playoffs.
o you mean number one.
no i mean two and one.
you mean one of each?

(i'm a sediment guy but
most of my continent
is always rising)
waiting for the N Judah
senorita, gold star in her ear
black neighborhohod
black man with two german shepherds, dogs,
through tunnel under park
corner cole and carl
head in window smokes.

steven left
a note on the floor
question mark & the mysterians
didn't say where

the sink runs loud
in nick's studio here
hope these drums & mexican chocolate
can be an aphrodisiac

or this voice & flute
or the way we feel, vapor
of eucalyptus or the wind now
the soft gait of
the leonine german shepherd

the candles & incense
this little pain that's understood
is the aphrodisiac
if not the design
of the seven blue clouds
with red curls in them
as you drive
in the windshield over these hills
near the great natural harbor

BLESSING

The presence that ignites the
thin sparkles from the hammer
resents you appearing as you do
in the clothes of a yard man.
From now until some favorable god
intervenes & meets you on the path
from the pool, you will be
someone who works with asphalt,
peeling it from soggy rooftops
& disposing of it in hot dusty
alleys where you dream.

ON THE RAILS

everyone
combines skins
reeking of
bar rum and sausages.
Henry Corcoran
would sit under a cow
and wait for a large bird
to fly over
then go roll in the ditch
like a snake.
i went to the doctor
to see if i had a thick skull
or a thin one.
our skulls are kind
of like eggs he said
our brains float

like toast
in some fluid that
(i hope) never runs dry.
In the body there are many
levels of function, all
generally pink and soft yet
sealed from each other.
there are different fluids
and different holes
that don't leak them.

CAPTAIN OAKS

captain oaks moves
into the clearing
who ran away he says
on the contrary oaks
they've all returned
native to this place
it seems, can't be without it.
pass me those goggles
says oaks & i'll
brown tint the rest of it,
can't abandon the legends now
not til we get our feathers
right boys, anyhow.
guess you're right there oaks
they grumble, even if it is
slimy as a muck spoon. boys,
that green lizard surfacing
vertical
will be the bones of sight to us yet,
before the gauchos get here!
or right after they get here.

CAR MUSIC

Same melody of
synthetic pants
wrinkled on & off
warm car seats
sympathetic vibrations from

people to do with the stores &
yards
ought to be enough
nobody wants to go through Hell
ha!
but to keep the ground shifting
til the earthly mouth in the air
sips you up

i love living
with you
& it's no mistake
but this privacy is a separate world
& so is this privacy
& there is no other world
but the one we must answer to
in the end, be at on time

like the three musketeers
fencing off cars
& houses as they go
their bravery singing
metallic & sharp
the brain directing the heart
to breathe
in the face of threatening junk

ii.

Ambushes are always
waiting in the news until
the instrument has had its
years of tuning
in the upholstery of, say, the moon

the way the feet
move the ground
how near the outcome
the game seemed
inevitable
from the start

the fog settles
in the valley
like tin

you get out to drive through

highways can be so tangent to earth

the speed can take you off the road
you used to belong to

time beguiles the patience
of the doctor

a plant he knows
is part of a family
& field

its systems are the only way
to carry its drift

luxurious
through the desert.

INDIANA

A blue garbage truck goes by
& it's already hot
a guy with an unlit cigarette out his mouth
hacks down the motel walk
soon we'll be driving
Tom will be driving, me
off & on reading Two Years Before the Mast.

In the coffee shop now
just me the cook & waitress
nothing sexual but
the Declaration of Independence
placemat.
what an excellent
taut nippled document.
Governments are instituted among men
to secure their individual rights
when they fuck up, they're out.

THE PRESCOTT SLUR

the Prescott Slur contains
the purest crescent of milky
schist you ever saw

like translucent teeth
the tops of your socks will
lunge for your knees

in supplication to
the ph of different tinctures there

where the head mesomorph
stands by with a gag—
a pink slip of hem so
you don't linger too long
over the relics
or flip his curls with a screw

unless you got little guillotines
on the back of your shoes

you'll be a sliding chinbone
down the orange quartz
crushing over mahonia
mahogany & saltbrush

but telling better tales
in the days when you can bear
to hear them

around a piano
where the Jack of Orleans
leans
like an ostrich with a fire extinguisher
in a frozen shaft of juice

EFFENDI

The pasha will see you tonight
but you know the moon shines
like a pink cathouse,

hear the nightingale & crested newts?
smell the night blooming cereus.

The pasha may be wild inside
his appetites take meticulous forms
the moon is his grandmother
the dogs at the gate know her will.

DEAR MOZART

Walking along patchmake st. one day years ago
near its intersection with fowlpiece rd.
i was waylaid by a poorly appointed wretch
his face covered in orange fur
he begged of me my hat
which is as you know a stetson i prize
it having once belonged to mr. robert penn warren
who lost it to a sudden gust of gulf breeze
it wheeled & spun & came to rest
at the feet of a man name lejeune
who wagered it in a game of stud & lost
to my three kings
mais je m'egare…
the man with the wooly face
like a belgian sheepdog's it was & orange
declared he was helpless without my hat & would pay
three pounds for it
three pounds is not enough i thought & told him so
it's all the money i have he skulked
alternately screwing up his face & casting his eyes wildly
up toward pliny's bone
unless you would accept in exchange a lock of my fur
which one day will count for a lot
i believed him
he yanked the lock from above his eye
& though I don't recall a bald spot there after
i took it home tied in a bundle
& kept it in a shoebox of small things

as to why the man wanted my hat he didn't say
though i suspect it was to afford a measure of disguise
from the rear on top of course
the fur on his face still orange & prominent

as he left he more skittered than loped. curious fellow
what
years later my niece joanne a woman in her sixties
found the little bunch & began toying absentmindedly with it
brushing it along her cheek.
a blue vapor rolled into the room
& a large man announced he would tune her piano
if joanne would fix a pot of mocha.
i can see where your sympathies live she said
you're as big as a whale. but you musn't touch my piano.
i like the blue fog though
quite nice

FRANK'S SONG

Out of Blake's Bakery they sauntered, shopping bag full of warm bread,
wafting the smell like a censer. These guys are like buildings too, Frank thought,
they have architecture & style, as they got into a cab, another kind of building,
& left for a part of town. Frank sat on his scaffold and smoked, his attention shift-
ing to the corner where town men were pushing something heavy back & forth.
Frank went inside swinging himself deftly onto the window ledge. He turned on
his radio, a song was playing called "Abstract Roman Dancing" by Oswald's
Nativity. He sat down by the phone, picked it up, and called Blue Cross Blue
Shield. "36 to 52 dollars a month" he repeated, "thanks", & hung up. Shit, if I
slip, I'll need more than that. "All I keep hearing is that ancient Roman polka"
the song went on, about somebody's dream Frank thought, he could almost see
the landscape: vines, stones, open space. He tied a towel around his head and
leaned back, thinking of snow & heat, visualizing a big donut of the bakery smell
squeezing itself to slide through the window. "I'll just keep it up for as long as I
can" he said, moving his legs to the beat of the song. "Threats were intruding and
the wine outlasted the gods" it went, "but we danced to the coming inversion."
Why can't I write a song like that, Frank thought, and immediately the answer
came, "You can".

Sitting down in Lubbock, I got no case of brains today
tryn to pick a trick up, to show my friends later on
singing in the daffodil but the stem's been cut too bad

What can you do, what can you do
when the lazy isolation's got you
what can you say
when the plush has you trapped into liking everything ok

I'm practising my music
sometimes I'll hear my own song play
bread floats in like puppies, gets down on floor &
rolls

If you have the situation, I have the means today
don't get dizzy, we'll make wider circles all the time

It was fun but the next time he looked at it, without the music, it wouldn't
seem very funny. He decided to work on the doorknob, take the paint off, see if
it was brass underneath. The phone rang, somewhere along the line Frank said,
"Well, I was just thinking everthing's an envelope", and went on to talk of his life,
including his friend.

NOT TYRANTS

Separately & one
we do our little dances
round the three bedroom house
& meet sometimes, hug
sit quietly or talk

like the brownings did
in their little
tobacco stained
inn

neither of us looking
for trouble
though sometimes
a fire burst

comes
on a sore place
the wrong music
dilates.

More often edges (shoulders)
slide together
Not tyrants
living a deliberate play
in the rock age

WORK, NO LIGHT

this is it
grey, great
something official
with a match in it

a son is lost in the flood
jealousy

kreisler's 2nd symphony

the palace head with a tongue of pure bone

many species remain enchanted
hundreds of years after
blue has left
the flower spikes
of mythology

'we' 'know' 'now'

Hannah Weiner

from CLAIRVOYANT JOURNAL

I SEE words on my forehead IN THE AIR
on other people   on the typewriter   on the
page   These appear in the text in CAPITALS
or *italics*

3/10

How can I describe anything when all these interruptions keep *arriving* and then
tell me I dont describe it well   WELL   *forgive them* big ME   COUNTDOWN
got that for days and yesterday it didn't stop GO TO COUNTDOWN   GO TO
COUNTDOWN   CALL DAVIDs   get COUNTDOWN finally GO TO COUNT-
DOWN at the door so OK I go see these maroon velvet pants I'm not BUY $40
he isn't home
pants BLOOMINGDALES all over again I leave GO TO COUNTDOWN: refuge,
get in a taxi, start for home, no peace, get out GO TO COUNTDOWN ok it's only
money go back and buy the pants it's better than seeing GO TO COUNTDOWN
for the rest of my life *peace* so they fit well   UNTIL   MICHAEL COOPER
For a while I tried to get away with *negative* COUNTING   by counting down
10, 9, 8, 7   while breathing GO TO   MAKE CLEARer   FAR OUT

B   at the door RHYS   RHYS IMPORTANT   (notes)   HAVE A DOUBLE
L
I   image of pink embroidered pillow case appears on blanket, get it out
S   GO NOW *girlfiriend negative* MOTHER made it when I was 2
S   TA TA
F   JANA   ug*h* she's fasting TRY HARDER across her chest and
U   *eat enou*
L   DRESS WARM across Charlemagne's groin   Joan's
         head says LAUGHS as she   QUINK THICK   SAY IT
                                   laughs
Rhys *rhythm*   VERY IMPORTANT says radio   LY
DESCRIBE *go ahead* in Charlemagne's white pants WOOL white hat
   IMITATED Hawai JOAN   ARAKAWA   (more notes going back 3 days)
YOU WONT OBEY   PORK CHOP   *well tho*
                           BUY THEM *pig* in pork chop color along
the edge of   NOT APPLE PIE in pink and white sash
  frying
     ORGASM*deaf* *ement* go to a museum

   get *exci* JUNKt*ement*   CANT GET THE SPACING
                  em *fruit*
                  eat graPe   it's a nice arc
                       I T W R I T E
                                      S
                                      I
                                       T
Try praying: Our father who art *be right over*   S
A song: Here we go round the mulberry bush the   E
                                                      L
grapefruit John the mulbery *mush* GIVE UP   F
GRAPEFRUIT' IS THE NAME OF Yoko Ono's book, APOLOGIZE is on a Ringo
Star2 record 2 r's   Call Jerry MISS ROTHENBERG MISS DAVID ANTIN
SNOWING IN VERMONT *delightful*   Dream about Jason Epstein very huge
                            JOHN
loud SHUT UP in hs office, *I rejoice*   laugh   DESCRIBE CHARLEMAGNE
how old 33 spiritual discipline
      not in dollars   not too negative
         no money   M O N E Y

LAMONTE had this dream listening to Lamonte   GET ALREADY SCARED
heals
STUPID NEXT before I can type it the carnations fall over water spills on floor,
wiping it see in the other part of *the room* a blue puddle just like the one spilled
says WATER   I laugh *far out*   YOUR notes
VERY SERIOUS LAMONTg*e*
t
very serious operation   *get* *f*r*i* *already scared*   LIVER   WHAT D'YA
THINK huge HER VOICE*dorothy*g*h*t*e*   her voice is pretty clear sounds just
vagina
like her*liver*   CALL RAYMOND   *e*n*e*d*   his liver side flashed
Had trouble with my own just in time make some parsley tea? WHAT BOIL IT
IN WATER *stop* stop drinking wine? *Heal yourself* says stomach LAMONTE
didn't *e* maybe it is my thought had to look up to see if e Met Dorothy   where I
got my ulcer, *working hard* her voice *I'll hit you - direct hit*
Good heat vibrations in 1st chakra area WHEW *good idea*
maybe it will heal now   GOOD L*U*CK just remembered
                              Dorothy's healing group CONCENTRATE
on her   they have success healing

        told her about Le Shan, who trains healers^GO TO ONE
              Steve Reich is not tunafish   GOOD LUCK better fix the lock*no*
better   More notes: shopping go into supermarket much **interference, leave,** *ta ta*
cross 2nd ave *think of that* GOOD   resistance GO HOME I'm mad and hungry
no food in the house but LUCK   go home GOOD GIRL and then a huge STOP
in front of the butcher shop, meat cheaper and better   *big improvement* NO
                                                    YOU DONT GET IT
on the expensive farmer's cheese, GO OUT, GET A HARD ROLL, CREAM
SUGAR   I get it they'd rather I didn't have either*milk tues*   Hear TURN IT
OFF (the oven) SO^RRY says roll   Be quiet I say I'm eating breakfast   THATS
THE INTERFERENCE HAPPY YEAR TAKA *wrong recommend, feel different,*
missed his movies hear *feel awful*   OMIT APOSTROPHE   SACRIFICE   *try*
hard   Takas advice   omit apostrophe, Elianes   writes in the present tense see
PRESENT   say SEE not saw, *eliminates periods ol stupid girl*   Charlemagne's
address   big pink PREFER *this is terrific old girl*
                            thats the conclusion

I SEE A BIG APOSTROPHE

        LOW INCOME
            WHYS in a row behind each other *verbal vibrations* a lot
of GO TO CHURCH SEE DAVID   GO AND TEACH thought I'd like *negative*
Rinpoche GO WED   Fuck off he speaks fri sat san THAT'S A PUN APPLE PIE
l_i a lot of wine drunk *dream* say david a lot of words CHILDREN dont explain
 q u o r   *not alright* more margin? *tues.* no more periods *answer* its *drunk*
        since Rinpoche came in town the words do a up and over and down drunk
reminds *who* of Big Deep MY THOUGHT pops off a big GO *Radcliffe* it's im-
portant reminds *who* this typewriter *heard* saw heard DO IT   DRUNK   FRI
GO SUN now whatabout tonight and Sat? NIGHT put FUNNY her MEET
RHYS right COMPLETE IT SAID LONG TALK WITH Luba   NONEY mothers
slang *for* nose *think of it*   BIG SURPRISE   *save the space* NONE *not alright*

BIG PRINT

HOLY BIBLE

HALLELUJIAH
miss charlemagne
        MODERN ART   GO AWAY GO OUT MISS PROVIDE
you/why a line 're afraid DO CHARLEMAGNE CALL OMIT *not too late* STOP
TEMPTING FABLE WHY Thinking all these GO OUTs are for me run out but
PARTY *not you* SIS in the hall you wait *hear the phone* Nijole calls get back to
answer PHONE JUST IN TIME C she wants to check the ring on her phone, not
enough TIME *reason call Nijole* A CALL JASPER JOHNS *IT WASN'T*
important WHICH CANT STOP L cant tell what to *finish* do *so important*
basketball YOU CAN CUT IT see M call Nijole often who is *not*   *Ding a ling*
                                     E
stop   TAKE A BATH on a 45 degree angle red light HESITATE so *filling* the tub
Accomplish BED in frame for Raymond's drawing 5 DOLLARS *save pennies talk*
to mother type walking by hardward store little lamp says 2:30 go in, it's 2:30 red
BUY IT NOW *tensor* but it's making you stop *me* what it started me doing so I
buy it 3.50 *bulb*   BIRD   DO THE MUSEUM STIFF stuff   WHAT   Every-
thing seems to be *negative* five dollars more than *pronoun* CUT IT SHORT
WHYS says OUT asked about a table see 40 price 45 NO HANNAH   DUNGA-
REES pronoun's are used cost $3 *much quieter* energy than the DUMB grey
corduroys HOW ARE YOU *free pants* LAMONTE FEEL washing

Mon 3/18

second choice

GO TO BO'S   *Now complete* Got stoned at Luba's she's washing her pants
didn't *study eliminates periods*   GO IN Bo *don be funny* skin and dungarees
Is this *not alright?*   Went to Chas WRITING A NOVEL SIS at his door GET
OUT, not home   CHAS   MONEY   HIS VOICE DIRECTS YOU   TELL
THE STORY   PLEASE COMPLY   *the answer* VOCABULARY CHANGES   SINGLE
GET OUTSIDE   COME HERE   NOW OCCUPIED says the phone at
SECRET   See: WACO in white rolls instead of busy   Low income at Bo's
GET STONED   the neighbor*hood*   WRONG DIRECTION in front of *else* the
grass on the table *too late*   At John Giorno's, got there via GO TO SPRING
STREET, see words from John's DINING ROOM, SOME AFTERNOON *smile*
window   FIRST GLASS   GO IN   At John's see GO IN PEACE   GO FOR A
DISCIPLE   GO IN BEAUTY in front of the daffodils, decided to do *Govinda* GO
Thinking of Aries see GO DIRECTLY with a line *heavy* pointing through it
Tues this is all mixed up Nijole calls a lot of energy after that seeing the words that
are said all around *prego*   Charlie was showing a movie but HEAD COLD
stayed in JUNK where the words are quiet MORE   *Now Bible*   GET A JOB
READERS ENOUGH   RALPH says there aren't any jobs around   YOU
DONT ENJOY YOURSELF   TEMPORARILY EMPLOYED in front of the desk
at *pay* Income Tax Bureau   SOLD OUT   PHIL'S *concert?* Saw Charle-
magne on the clock at quarter to 3, *simple* HUMMY, DIDN'T GO   *hooray* DO
FLOORS THURS   *See Rinpoche* CREAM don't try to clarify he said *make it
simple two months* when *hannah* asked him about *confusion* make it simple and
maybe HA you'll have a best seller   How can I the fuck make it simple I'm *too*
much love in your family not going to let them *Jerry hurts* interrupt BREAKFAST in apple
cake from Ratner's *60c a Bernadette*   Mention the grant wasn't going to apply
because got a NO when I called to *answer questions* but after Rinpoche woke to
huge loud GO   at 8:30 realized if I wanted to apply for the *think of that* have to
more trouble that day   BRUCE comes   Philosophy STOP SKIPPING GO OUT
have pancakes
MON   *This is* Wed   CUT IT SHORT PSYCHIC TERMINOLOGY   "Call"
The subject's impression of the *think* target in an esp experiment   "Hit" the
subject's correct impression *2 mo* or call "Run" *mean walk* In ESP experiments,
using 25 cards *too late* 25 calls, or trials, once through the deck   "Trial" a single
guess or call at identifying the target object *Cigarette* in Raymond's voice *one*
more day "Target" the object that the subject is trying *month* to identify   RELAX
DON GO ON THE STREET   FEEL POWER   GO TO POETRY   *enough*
coming of company CLUES TO POWERFUL PEOPLE   THATS WHY IT
WORKS   what? *You* NECESSARY EVIL in tuna fish *toasted roll finish the*
page See DOUBLEDAY, call see MAHLAMUDE on phone coil ask if they have a
NO

3/18 3 *crazy day*

DRINK COFFEE   GO TO THE MUSEUM   They don't YOU NICE across

Jasper Johns'

C   YOU DONT COME S   WHITE NUMBERS
O   C
P   *explain come*   R
Y   NOT LOVE   E
R   W
I   says Morris   I   ONE MORE PAGE
                  Louis   N
          DUNGAREES   G
                                A
                                 R
                  BIG LIGHT   O U N   TOO MANY JOHNS
                  END   D

                                    in Guernica's colors, a portion
        DOUBLE   pink SINK   of it appears in color
HEY SIS
                                        BEATTLE   TO ME
FANTASTIC   "Bauhaus Stairway"
WHICH CHAKRA   WHICH ARP
                        SEE THROUGH
             AIN   ONE
       P L   JOB
   T O M FISH
D O   C   ARAKAWA   DONT COME ALONE
          GET OUT OF HERE   TO A PART
                                            T
                                           A
FEEL THE HEAT from   IN FRONT OF THE ARP H
                                         T
                                      E E
POWERFUL   ARP DIGESTS   I   S NOT HONEST in white stone,
                            N D   leg appears green
                              A N
           CRAZY WOMAN   G
               SIT DOWN   E
                                   R
FEEL THE TABLE   HALA   DONT CRY
                YOU WONT BELIEVE   D
        ARP NOT WEAK   E S
               BEHAVE   C
       POOF   YOURSELF   R
                                        I   YOU
                                        B
                                        E
           ONEMORE   THE
BEAUTIFUL
        SAVE YOU   A
        DESIGN LINGERIE   DO   C R   OK
             OK
             THIS AFTERNOON   OK LAMONTE
       WHOOPEE
           TANTRA
       FANTASTIC

                           all this in front of Arp's
       GO HIT CHARLEMAGNE   "Human Concretion"

Discontinue Laughing   NOT THE OTHER says Floral Nude

             PARTY
SMILE says Brancusi's Fish DO NOT
       BIG ROCK   OMIT

                                NO MORE ARP

DONT JUST TYPE NOW BRILLO   DONT JUST TELEPHONE was what it
started out with *in style*
            Jesus (there was room for Christ the way   I SEE it(but I cant
type it   A lot of REACH SAMAHDI's hanging around   Bad day on 1st avenue,
   small
got directions to 1st avenue, *come in* says Italian coffee shop *spend a dollar* spent
two but that's because *predicate* then saw a chest of drawers   *write* and ended up
                                   10 drawers,
with the wrong one, a maple one, it looks too big in the bedroom   So why didn't
they help me get the other one, it did say HURRY a little while before the other
woman came in and bought it *back* it had rollers on it *wrong clean drawers* not
used   hesitated because the confusion was larger   I still could have had it *in*
                                   not in time
style . been evicted   you dont call so why do they wait til I get home and then say
big victory   *Conn*
the FIRST one   NO HOPEFUL   BIG FOOL   The vibrations are MAPLE
Jesus did I buy it because it said maple a few pages, *days* ago   On top of which
PAY for it   SAMAHDI   Fuck I'm pissed off at the furniture and them
NOS VOICES   *no concern*   no help just want to see
               countdown   *negative*
               10 9 8 7 6 5 *Samahdi*
not alright   *no concern*
               FOR TRUTH

LaMonte and Pandit Pran Nath are giving concerts at The Open Mind Gallery

one jacket   two   give it to Bernadette   give her the brown one   I cant go back to
                    black wise
the bedroom the chest is too depressing MAPLE FURNITURE what has that to do
with it? *bad vibrations*   suicide thought   the last time I said I wished I were
dead they said AND BURIED FIFTY DOLLARS no they didn't say fifty dollars
SPEND IT ON THE FLOORS, KEEP AN ACCOUNT it's not just depressing it's
painful *maple* what the hell *predicate* hurt my hip moving it *an inch*
                                   stop typing
WOW hearing DRINK YOUR MILK HONEY see JASPER   comes with Phil
making a movie NO STICK AROUND, refused the cat some tunafish heard Phil's
voice after he left say OH GIVE HIM SOME   *See your jacket* SPEND SEVEN-
TY DOLLARS on the kitchen and bedroom floors, floor total 120   *mushroom*
                                                   go to a museum
John Cage concert tonight   Was it the tunafish that made me hear   or Phil's
energy?   NOW BLOCK   WHICH ONE   *Niblock*   CONFIDENT across
                                   cry now
the arms of the chair   EVERY DAY (from the hear ROMEO poem Phil read)
BIG WEEKEND   GOOD FOR Y~OU~ Luba hear *dropped in* with her dogs *told*
you See 9 OCLOCK MORE POWER   *Call Andy Warhol*   *Ask not alright*
NOT ENOUGH MONEY about 6 inches over the kitchen floor in shine

MARCH IS ALMOST **FINISHED**

April Fool BRAVE GIRL

JANA   A lot of FAVORITE SHOWER skipping around today NOT LOUD what to do
getting ready to leave TOO SOON COLORFUL doesn't like your t shirt *oh hannah* GO EARLY the spacing
on the typewriter *big improvement shit* isn't working *l e a v e* Go before Friday 3
mos GO WEAR A WOLLEN SHIRT   LISTEN   *v e* this is crazy Rhys is
going to Hatha Yoga class at 6, is that GO AT 6 *wrong charlemagne*   thought
you were supposed NO NO FUN *to call happiness   eat with Jana crazy page*
confused day *sit still* supposed *too eager get the message   go to 3rd St*   NOW
tired GO HANNAH the loft RHYS IS COMING   *Rhys is conflict   go at 6*
WHY ARE YOU GO OUT
oclock   home for ten peaceful days with a *present* of GOD INTENTIONS sore
throat SHE had *bad* through these GO   GO SOON DONUT and then LEAVE
outside which used to be an opposite YOU WORRY A LOT   Thought the
solution to PALESTINE was to *good grief* find *Jerry handkerchief* SIC or HIS
PARTY HAVE A PARTY   GO   OMIT GO   Breakfast, no didn't YES fast
GO OUT Rhys *after* it said GO SOON why won't it let you GET OUT OF HERE
see half the letters *crazy* It's 6 oclock   SEE DANGER   RAIN COMING
TAKE AN UMBRELLA   Red GO NOW at the door   A lot of Rhys around
here wonder if he'll call   *wrong direction* RHYS   sure would like to eat with *table*
someone or GOT TO CONN   Call WAKEUP Jana she's fasting can't eat with
her, day in conflict, *horse she's having a party* WHO Jana Fisher   SEE NOW DO
NOT HAVE A PARTY *without fell off horse* NO DEPOSIT see Nijole's name in air
while talking to Jana   EAT OUT well there's either tunafish *prego* or frozen
steak or shopping *with Charlemagne telephone* SCRAMBLED EGGS   Nijole
calls, we're going out to eat *brace your supper*   GO TO THE GALLOPING
GOURMENT   YOU OMIT TRYS   NO BALLROOM   CHILDREN
CALL JOANNE it's Zacchary's birthday, see outline of a child in the living room
while *puzzle* talking to Joanne WHY ARAKAWA   Out with Nijole, a funny
feeling about *spelled wrong* the Gourmet, didn't want to go there UNDER-
STAND APRIL, it's closed, EAT AT SPRING, come home GO TO THE BATH-
ROOM, *he calls* says the LOOKS toilet seat cover   Who is pronoun? *breakfront outside*
Charming in white across ¾ of the MARCH bowl   HERE PUSSYCAT *don't*
omit Nijole BRA IN THE BED   An upside down day   Rhys didn't *you didn't*
Malclm here PUSS DO IT NOW *sleepy crazy day* wouldn't COME mon   *So*
why secure FATHER DIES GO TO BED   JASON EPSTEIN at right angles to
the typewriter at Random House wehre TOO HOT *call Nijole* not in the phone
says *eat* FOR CORDUROYS Didn't take the umbrella BED it's *negative* raining
the next day   Call *Jim* TOO LATE says the phone in the thin black outline,
hang up   DANGER IN MAY

from OWN FACE

THE FALL RETURNS

the rooms are chosen, then they move on
the beads are wetted in the lime
the weedlot boils in the blood of one eye
the children first are cankered then they spin

there are not routes, only dials
the rocks are spun together in one ball
the laundry is of rust, the pillow shrieks
pianos all blow northward and return

must be a bath if I could find it is a map
of all the ways that center intermission
skulls are simply caps for all compression
day's light raising closets for its dark

I put up the clothes and trail the keys
that onyx knob in vacuum turns the train
pressure on the pitches swaying back again
a world without a heartbeat but it stays

AT THE POEM

You must have missed the signpost, took
the wrong turning, ended up for the sore moment
in that mud without holes. You must gaze
into the sun here to take your rest, suspend
motion and speech on a point of
zircon sand. The only articulate surfaces, they
are also somehow sounds, are buildings which
as you approach pour their facades at your feet
in a rush of the purest substances.
There are no faces to be seen since all
that is human here is you.
Numbers are become animal forms: the pounce,
the adder and the lynx. The things you loved
are all shades of moss.

Your only index the very grains of sand.
And somehow the set of things has you again,
a fascination in love of self.

ALBUM—A RUNTHRU

I look in that one kind of dwindled. And in this,
look up, a truncheon in my fist, tin pot
on my head, the war. My father, I'm looking at, is my
age then and thin, his pants streak to the ground,
shadows of rosevines...His father sits beneath
a cat. Here the shadow has more flavor than my
trains, elbow on livingroom floor, bangs that
curl, opera broadcast, The Surreptitious Adventures of
Nightstick. I lie in the wind of the sun and hear
toots and smell aluminum smoke. The tiny oval
of my mother's youth in back and the rest is dark.
Sundays, the floor was black. At the beach, here
I'm a nest of seaweed, an earlier portrait of
surrealists I saw later, a stem of grey what
rises from my scalp. My hair is peaked in brine.
And this here hat, dark green fedora over same green
corduroy suit for a trip to the nation's capitol,
how far askance I've been since and never another
hat. Cromium rods, the hand in the guide's pocket
seems far removed. Blurry shoes on sandstone steps,
double and over exposed. Then in this one the SECRET
points to my head, shaved, and emblem, OPEN, striped
in "pirate" T-shirt and HERE IT IS. My elbow bent,
upright this time, behind a pole. I had yet to
enter at this snap the cavern beneath my sneakers.
To the right my soles protrude from beneath a boulder,
for I had trapped my mother and she asked Why.
Taken. Given. Flashlight brighter than my face,
another grotto, where the ball of twine, indirection,
gave out but we never got very far in, Connecticut.
I swim out of another cave in a further frame, cramped
gaze of sunlit days, apparel forgot. Later I reel
in a yell as my cousin takes a bite from my shank
beneath ranchhouse breezy curtains of Marion. On a trudge up
from the gasoline rockpit in the gaze of Judy Lamb,
she carries my pack, my jeans rolled as I step on
a pipe, Estwing in hand and svelte as only youthful can.

Most of those rocks remain and she married a so-so
clarinetist. My greygreen zipper jacket leans against
a concrete teepee, my father looking bullchested stands
before. Perhaps we had just argued. Central Park cement
steps of pigeons, the snow removed. Overexposed
whiteshirt at the drums, stick fingers ride cymbal
at the camera raised, livingroom Brenton with orange
& black "sea" wallpaper and orange & black tubs. I wore
a wristwatch then and never again, drumtime hitching
me past it. I graduate from highschool in white dinner
jacket and diploma and frown, too many hot shadows
back of the garage. Must roll up the bedroll with
skinny arms and lam for the caves. Dave & A. Bell by
the Ford Country Squire first time allowed alone to tool
Bleak grass scapes of Knox farm. Rope down a crack,
mosquitoes and Koolade, sun dapple leaf moss sandwiches, ache.
Then in this group more drums on the roof, the gravel
and the flat, a cover attempt for no album even thought.
I tap and step in the dim known street. Lean on a
chimney to inhabit the sky, deep with drops. Here
I'm pressed on a wall of Tennessee limes, stones-throw
from mouth of the underground we camped in. Too many
thoughts, elide. Then lie on a beach in a doughnut
pattern shirt with a stick, a pipe?, in my mouth as my
cousin grins shiny beyond. Truro, also waiting for the
caves. With the poets then I'm fat and the driveway is
dark, the clapboards all white in a day of all talk.
This then all ends in color, my red bandana and shirt out
on Devil's Pulpit, open hand addressed to the grey
where Hawthorne and Melville now view of a highschool.
While the water still spills, and the cat squints at leaves
blown, my father wears Brahms, families lean in on one
for a group shot, and the rock remains shattered in a star.

THE COUNTRY AUTUMNS

But it could not be brought to see what it
could be brought. And the leaves are
away again, teamed. A parent at the
last and a parent in the middle. And
as stones I thought it right.

Two plates, and on the other side all the
forest pieces. The clock says stay.
The books lower the earth, and in gardens
flat stones spin. The volume was of waiting.
Today is today, until the preposition taken up.
Next to the tree sways.

The sky in pieces the leaves part the
leaves piece together. To and from a hand
given all directions. The bark comes from
below. Takes from the books of the moves under
the sky. Speaker holds up the talks held last.
Motors the dust and the yellow syllables.
A slant on which was never here or
only partly.

A NOTE

I think then I live in a world of silence.
The language has become lodged in itself a background,
wall of rock, black and resistant as basalt, then sometimes
as viscous as heavy grease, poetry must be reached into
and rested from in a cry. Meaning is now a mixture, it
recedes to itself a solid fix of knowledge. The words
of poems, once rested from the mass, cry shrilly and singly,
then spring back to that magnetic ore body of silence.
The longest poem has become a brief crack into light and sound.
The candle flame through the sliver hums but must be tricked,
wrested out for a mere tick in the radium dark.
The rest is all a walk in stillness, on the parade of
the tombs of meaning. Or is this all still the highest ledge?

Bernadette Mayer

from THE GOLDEN BOOK OF WORDS

EASY PUDDINGS

I think that I shall never see
Easy puddings in a tree
You say you must type everything
You can't read your words in hand writing
Mary says she has a double or a twin
And now a triplet
And she is a skinny energetic person too
I dream of Sarah Thorne sorting out the clothing
I dream the doctor of the Incas, my doctor
Is you or Matthew Christmas Tree, our bookseller
I see both of you clearly with your awesome dark beards
Full of animal crackers, I joke with you
About buying a bra, I measure myself
I have a 38-inch bust, as they used to say
But with nipples excited by the tape measure
It's only 36, I guess this is not a decorous poem
As Donne or Pope would have set it all up
Fourteen hundred to eighteen hundred A.D.
In the western world we've got
Where the work of women holds up half the sky

And yet the desire to write tonight
Is borne, dare I say it, like a seed
On the wind and so on, we were talking to your mother
And she told us every detail of your sister's
Country rental, the home of a doctor in Putnam County
It's never been rented before, in 22 years

I have my fears about women
Deeply felt in my desires to please them
I know many Margarets who are so stark
In their admiration of other efficient women
Susans who are close to the ground
Alices who please and clothe us tightly
And a Grace who likes to be free of clothing
Like all the Emmas and their freewheeling breasts
I do know some Marys who are somewhat tight-assed
And even a Leonora, a Theodora and a Florence

And a Beatrice in my memory of what I might be like
I do not know any Pearls or Violets outside of books
But I've heard alot about a Ruby who was a black housekeeper
To a psychoanalyst, opals my mother feared
Had brought her bad luck and emeralds I wore
As my female birthstone, emerald rings
Brought as gifts for Holy Communion or
First Holy Communion, along with checks
Enough to buy a garnet centered in diamonds
Here is your mother's diamond ring, it's set in gold
New gold, white gold, platinum is too cheap
She took it off to wash the dishes, or too dear
A thick gold wedding band, they say maybe stolen from the tomb

I don't know, I'd like to see these men or women
Who steal the bands from tombs more than
I'd like to see myself duplicated
In another woman human being, I am too safe
With my poet's senses and ideas, held too bereaved
Of the grief of the need to steal
A vivid platinum sacred scarf or needle
For my new baby or stereo
After all women hold up half the sky

Your mother says
My temperament prevents me
I don't like to be confined
I say to her the same way you hate confinement
I must keep active in my mind
So little babies learn to speak real fast
French Latin and Greek come out
Before I ever demand my milk and shoes
And then I go

I say to the herbal doctor
There is a vivid grief in me
I fear the things that are not real
Childbirth and insects, tetanus never scared me
More than the moment I saw a sign
Advertising "Red Snapper and Peas"
At four dollars in a restaurant window
Several years ago, don't worry doctor
I'll be a good western patient, stoic in labor
And breathing joyously in its fruits for us yet later

I may sting the child, who knows
Someday my wild imagination will tell me
That the street has turned the world upside down again
I'll lose my bearings and speak for logic without peace
I'll lose for a moment the superstitions that sustain me
I'll forget how I look and love only New Englanders
I'll assume their pale brown frown
My yellow eyes will assess
Only the feeble crops of the government in the fields
I'll say to my children, now sentient
But still less complex
This world is lost, I'll say to my husband
We must vanquish this world and seek the new
We must deal a swift death blow to the monster
Else this life is death to us

You see though I seem to fear nothing real
In almost every case I am able to hit the nail on the head
The children and the parents need lively interference
And nature, and nature however ill from lust
Will set our scene, I defend our states of consciousness
I hate our allies our own moods and I feel large
I sweetly see the bourgeoisie coming evenly
To defend our comforts, we are artists
We hold up the sky, we hold up the end of the sky
We hold up the next part of the discovered sky
We try to hold up in the sky, we defend the uncovered
Part of the sky, next to half of nothing
We brazenly will hold up the sky for you
We will make holes in the sky for you
We will eat holes in the sky for you and for each
Our sky is full of holes, half the sky
Has been held up for you, wait now
I will hold up the rest and rest for a minute
I think I know you
Prairie fire, you have not come to be
Intimidated or to be claimed
You are not a child growing
In an unknown mother whose heart and fears
And chemistry are foreign
I will isolate and contradict you for a moment
I'll hold back and not meet head on
The tedious difficulties and complications
Of the Latinate languages and the false Greek headstarts

Of the western peoples, 1400-1800
I'll give you a charm from a dream of remembering
Warm swallowing and calm weary moments
Movement away from dense cause and a purpose

Give me a moment and I'll remember moving
Struggle is not defeat, from the part that fears
We must not overdo it, we are indigenous
To the parts that fear what is spilled over
I am here but I might as well hear
Anything from here to the next recognition
Of my historical reality, for now, Solomon
Of the Bible or a cow giving milk
And serving as a lecture or an example
In Avicenna's memory in an ancient philosophy
Of thought, I lose the silver for a moment
Or the moment, the Monet, the water lilies
The famous money stored in cash or borrowed
That encircles the finger of my hand
That is western and germanic and dark
And married me to you who study mysticism
And want to hear all about it

We get to this point, don't we
Wanting to know yet knowing already
And then what is it that we are to say
It's taken me long enough and in a poor form
As if a poor farm or pure form
Either would be a better place
For this revealment
Of a practicable immigrant
Sought for his or her knowledge
Gotten, if you knew
From the collision of gnats, the dead souls
With pure bright nursery moths in pink and yellow colors
At the window and we say
We are all so exhausted and excited by this time
And this tie together and this constant motion
Yet a mere speck will make us move in two ways
And we can guarantee only this
Once by the river, we will move each time
And once again, each day
Inside the house.

SPRING HOUSE

Tuesdays we always have fish

Flounder if we've got foodstamps

Scrod cod if we don't, are you prepared?
I definitely feel you can't do both

What else did I see?

The year's first lilacs, May's full moon,
I'm trying to remember now

Do water fountains have beards?

There is a space in spring for arrangements and
compartments even forms, there's always a space in change
for that, there is a space in death only coherent as beginning
and ending fall and as they fall winter never ended, spring
will not begin, we have the heat of summer, wordy and deferential,
interrupted for travel, the light not long enough for the
overbearing way as light falls words fall short of suiting
the subject

Hold my coat for me, would you?

That house on top of the hill always catches the
best light, I wonder who lives there maybe a family of
knowledge making so much noise it sounds like a public pool,
bird sanctuary, softball game with the chimes chiming in,
eight o'clock, knowledge's babies asleep, still light out,
the gold sun's gone, a softer dusk than ever fell does with
more grace on the late-blooming trees than on those fully
leaved and left to be studied, identically full-grown already

A little image or thought, squeaking or twittering
animals, an echoic easiness thrown in that could be the whole
of it, all I've got to say

In the beginning knowledge was a tantrum, now a
spendthrift relative he or she only steals cupcakes or an
occasional lost dollar from the funny way we keep things in
order, knowing exactly where the lost things are

You almost lost it again

Now it's history, another way of washing clothes
in the sink, you can use the same soap twice if you do the
less dirty ones first

As poem is as a mother so instinct does it work,
distracts from the legal order to leave the house in a
metaphor's style among simile's kindly loans as neat as a
pin like a seed to the wind

But there was something else, the matrix for the
matrimony of

I've almost lost it again

Phone rings it could be anyone, what was I putting
together?

You can't rest in ideas like an old secure neckerchief,
it's good to wear one in the summer when ideas are so brief

Without the endurance of winter's darkness on their
light

And what of making up things purely spun from fantasy
as if the instinct to forget could ever have a line like I am
a Marxist, I'm an anarchist, I'm crazy as a loon

The beetle and the worm crawled and wriggled on the
bottom marble step in such contiguity they became famous to
us, were offered mink coats and foreign cars

We looked for them again and could only find slugs
at the base of the dead elm tree, you can't be in love with
me any longer, I prefer my dinner at the time we have it now
so later I can write and be lively without thought to food

Alot of time's passed since the plaid shirt you
painted became so still, the moon and all has moved, earth
revolving, sun sort of still but benefiting us differently,
now we can use it to grow corn and tomatoes, zucchini and
other squashes and fresh basil and close concentric onions

and borage for the bees

What text will tell me how to so benefit my own
ideas?

My waiting for love's order to know me sensibly,
for incomprehensible prose to become poetry

For the neat desire of an opposite heart to push
seasons together in the way they never suffer

But only offer a mesmerizing order to what is
remembered, propriety

Not only that

And its variety

And how it's almost lost like the last block
in a series of twelve that make six puzzles among them

But something else whatever it is and where I can
find it, no code message or perfunctory obfuscation of the
following order however human however a mixture

But a demon of chaos, surprise like a virus or a
wheel to be engaged in moving and sameness as between
inexorable sisters

The slowness and unpredictable biology of that

Combined with the skill to meet moon and sun

And all that has position like this word

Redolent of self and repeating

Always seeming to covet thought, always almost lost

Unless I can regain it, unless I can be ordinary,
unless I can forget everything, unless I know everything

Each order, it's a moment, speaks a clear word

If I am absent and silent, I can hear what is
almost heard

I know my heart is better counted on than redeemed
at every pulse

You are my feelings, seasons the word, order the light
and history the dark of the day

And what is almost lost is time to change us fast enough

To get away with your love for another summer's
repetition, it was identity but it's not that since

And this shape allows us to lose and lose completely

It was the order of the family in the house that
catches light

And now history teaches but forget that

There's time to be turning to the noise, it's
only sound, only a moment left

There's always time, sometimes it seems we must
die right away, never a moment left unless always sometimes
never have made a false spring logic of our light

And then I know we are moving again, bodies move,
everything moves

Like the afternoon I met you too fast, late fall,
cold and dreary, the streets were lively

And at that moment you and I looked so alike as
night and day as they say

ANGEL HAIR

Memoirs

Bill Berkson

RECENT VISITORS

I always liked to read the list at the back of *Poetry: A Magazine of Verse* under the rubric "Recent Visitors"; but here I had the sense of how full of visitors my life and lodgings were in the years 1969-1973 during which I wrote the poems included in that book. First in the tiny ground-floor apartment at 107 East 10th Street; then in Bolinas, where, with Joanne Kyger and countless others, I shared the house eventually known as the Grand Hotel. In any case, the time was a pleasurable one of open doors more or less 'round the clock, George and Katie Schneeman's apartment on St. Mark's Place being the place for late-night collaborations, or sitting for George to paint your portrait on a fresco'd cinder block. The poems of course are visitors, too, mostly unannounced. There's a lot of late-night air in the book, with light thrown by George's drawings. His cover is based on a photo booth strip of my daughter Chou-Chou and me in a New York arcade.

Bill Berkson, Bolinas, CA, February 1972.

SHINING LEAVES

The poems in *Shining Leaves* I wrote entirely at Yaddo, the wondrous, disastrous summer of 1968. Two months or so in a room "haunted" for writing: I could do nothing else; every time I began to read or just look out the window, poem fiends would start up. Who's complaining? not this guy, but eventually it would get to be too much and I'd leave for the Performing Arts Center or Broadway bar or Chicken Shack, or to see a new friend, Margo Margolis, at Skidmore. Others in residence at Yaddo that season were William Gass, Joy Williams and Carl Rakosi, who had just returned to poetry after many years as a social psychologist in Milwaukee. Allen Ginsberg was in and out of Cherry Valley that summer. When I returned from visiting him, Elizabeth Ames, the venerable Yaddo abbess, would ask for news of the Revolution, happenings at Chicago Convention, and so on. On the first visit I brought Allen and Peter a sunflower. Allen asked: "What would Frank [O'Hara] think of the Revolution?" I said: "He would consider Mark Rudd awfully cute." There is little overt reference in the poems to such events, though undoubtedly they are there. The title struck me one night out of nowhere sitting in Anne and Lewis's apartment on St. Marks Place. In the cover drawing Alex Katz got a good hair-style likeness for the time, I hypothesize.

Frank O'Hara in his loft at 791 Broadway, NYC, 1964. Photo by Mario Schifano.

Joe Brainard

Joe Brainard wrote to Anne Waldman in a letter in May of 1969:

"I am way way up these days over a piece I am still writing called 'I Remember.' I feel I am very much like God writing the bible. I mean, I feel like I am not really writing it but that it is because of me that it is being written. I also feel that it is about everybody else as much as it is about me. And that pleases me. I mean, I feel like I *am* everybody. And it's a nice feeling. It won't last. But I am enjoying it while I can. One thing that I realize is that losing a penny when you are one is just as serious as 'Is there a God?' when you are twelve is just as serious as 'What am I going to do!' when you are twenty-seven."

And again, to Anne Waldman, in a letter postmarked November 14, 1969:

"Dear Anne,

You know, I write for people. I really do. When I write I feel like I am talking to people. And telling them (you) things that I want to tell. If there were no magazines and no readings I wouldn't write.

Having written 'I Remember' and now not having read it or heard it really drives me up the wall. Because soon it won't (for me) be personal anymore.

What I would really like is for *you* to print it or for *you* to let me read it as a reading at the church. If you should want to print it I can pay the expense. But even more than that, what I would really like is to read it."

Michael Brownstein

The prose poems in *3 American Tantrums* were written in a blast of antique inspiration. Antique meaning fueled by the delicious, meaningful, heady wind of purity and intelligence already in the sixties long gone but still deeply felt. The sources of that wind—in my adolescence—were some of the Old Names—Baudelaire, Rimbaud, Villon—as well as numerous personal and particular folk and folkways already even then gone into invisibility. People I know, places, situations. Everything we mean when we sigh, lean against a wall in an unknown

Joe Brainard, 33 St. Marks Place, NYC, 1969. Photo by Anne Waldman.

Michael Brownstein, Springs, Long Island, 1972. Photo by Anne Waldman.

country, and lose it. Weeping, laughing, full of rage, full of joy. Outside of time, outside the ego's structured manipulations...Stepping out from under the long shadow of youth, I now see that a spell had been cast on me, cast by life itself. That spell made me sit, writing furiously, oblivious of friends, enemies, career, society.

3 American Tantrums was the beginning of the prose part of that spell. It led to many more stories, as well as three novels. And I remember choosing the title as a joke response to the picture I found for the cover of that book—a skeletal Hindu yogin sitting on a mat, his eyes rolled back in his head, his body twisted up like a pretzel. Little did I know, of course, that the word "tantra" from which I squeezed the word "tantrums" would soon figure big time in my life, as if in weighty response to that joke...Where are the bratty ripostes of yesteryear?

Anne Waldman and Reed Bye, Nederland, CO, July 1977. Photo by Steven Lowe.

Reed Bye

Some Magic at the Dump, my first collection of poems, was published by Angel Hair in 1978, with a beautiful and intricate cover drawing of my pickup truck by Jerome Hiler. These poems were published perhaps more on their promise than for any finished merit, but mostly because of my friendship/love affair with Anne Waldman, who I had met in Boulder in 1975, the second year of the Naropa Institute, and would marry and have a child with in 1980. The book, however, was a great inducement for me to keep making poems and, as for so many other young poets, Anne operated as a great encourager. The Angel Hair books she had published with Lewis Warsh opened my eyes and ears to a fresh, unpretentious poetry of individual life, the most recent infection of a living strain of American (and not just U.S.) poetics, and helped to correct, to some extent, a counter strain of rather self-conscious word-play that I had contracted somewhere else. Their work, amid that of other little mag publishers in the sixties and seventies, rejuvenated many younger writers wishing to have fun with words at that time but suffering under similar old-hat constraints.

Anne Waldman, Ambrose Waldman Bye, goddaughter Naomi Riley and Reed Bye, Wall Street, Four Mile Canyon outside Boulder, CO, 1980.

Charlotte Carter

Charlotte Carter in Massachusetts, 1981.

Maureen Owen and Sandy Berrigan
(Martha Diamond and Carol Gallup in
back), Joan Fagin's bridal shower at 33
St. Marks Place, NYC, April 1969.

It was the mid 1970s and one exciting event followed another: I had moved to New York, found an apartment on East 11th Street, and even had a boyfriend. There I was in Bernadette Mayer's workshop with all these bona fide poets. What's more, they seemed to like my writing. Heady stuff. When Anne Waldman wanted to publish me, I could barely contain myself. But something even more astonishing happened just before the publication of *Sheltered Life*. As usual, there was to be a Wednesday night reading at the [St. Marks] Church—the night reserved for the big shots. That particular week Allen Ginsberg and Hannah Weiner were scheduled to read. On Tuesday night Hannah fell ill. They needed a replacement, fast. And so it was arranged: I would be sharing the stage with Ginsberg. It was the East Village version of Forty-second Street and I was every bit as clunky as Ruby Keeler. Things took on an air of unreality. All day Wednesday I was shivering with anxiety and stage fright. I had never read my work in public before. The one thing I counted on to steady me until eight that evening was that I had an afternoon appointment with my shrink. He stood me up. I waited ninety minutes for him in the corridor of the second floor of the Gramercy Park Hotel, where he rented office space. Night fell. Despite my prayers that it would not. Bernadette introduced me, in every sense of the word, since nobody knew who the fuck I was. I did manage to walk up on the stage in the main church and do my reading. Afterwards, I got a benevolent smile from Mr. Ginsberg and a nice compliment from John Cage. Frankly, it was thrilling. But I tried to be cool.

My thoughts about the publication of *Sheltered Life* are very much intertwined with the people I met at the Poetry Project in the mid 1970s: not just Bernadette Mayer, Maureen Owen, Anne Waldman, Ron Padgett, Larry Fagin, Bob Holman, and so on, all of who were kind and encouraging to me. I think about the parade of singular, lovely eccentrics, scary weirdos, and sick puppies who marched through the doors of St. Marks. The drunk who molested me in the balcony one New Year's Day. The evening I had to read just before Patti Smith and I thought her leather-clad fans were going to tear me apart like the beach boys did Sebastian in *Suddenly Last Summer*. The kid who thoughtfully brought in a tab of LSD for every student in my workshop.

I made quite a few transitory acquaintances and some good friends at the Project, and luckily I got a life and met people who had nothing to do with that world. We are all aging. It did not occur to me that that would happen. Some of us look like shit and some of us—way too many of us—are gone.

Tom Clark

MY ANGEL HAIR BOOKS

Ron Padgett and I cooked up *Bun* in August 1967 in an empty outbuilding on Kenward Elmslie's property in the woods near Calais, Vermont. Ron, his wife Pat, and their infant son Wayne were summer guests at Kenward's, as was I, all four of us happily escaping the dog-days sweat and grit of the as-yet-ungentrified Lower East Side. It was a working situation for everybody, the tone being set by Kenward's partner Joe Brainard, who toiled with restless energy all through the daylight hours upstairs in the master bedroom, painting daisies and poppies from seed packages, getting ready for his wonderful Fischbach flower show. Kenward worked on knockout new poems in his little screened-in studio across the large pond behind the house, while new-father Ron labored away ingeniously in the guest bedroom at his translation of Apollinaire's *The Poet Assassinated*. All that purposive effort surrounding me finally embarrassed me into interrupting my own loitering long enough to produce a serial poem called "The Lake," wherein the pond out back grew into a full-fledged lacustrine body. During break periods Ron and I holed up in the large, unfurnished, concrete-floored tool shed, listening to our complete record collection (*Canned Heat* and *The Rascals*) while delightedly exploding our way out of the interesting monastic austerity of the backwoods scene by composing *Bun*, a sequence of big spacey typewriter poems that graphed themselves out like great aerated star-charts in front of us, constellated word-bursts generated by intense cabin-fever-induced elation: "Hello. May I be alive in your dream of unconsciousness?..." Jim Dine's cover for the the Angel Hair edition was a sepia-tinted photo of a bun with one bite missing, an image strangely if probably accidentally apt to the text ("Why must I write with the fear that our private parts are going to be bitten by growling monsters?").

Jack Boyce and Joanne Kyger, NYC, circa 1968.

Tom, Angelica and Juliet Clark on Bolinas Beach, CA, 1969. Photo by Bill Beckman, ©Tom Clark 2001.

Greg Irons, Joanne Kyger, Lewis MacAdams, Lewis Warsh, Bobbie Louise Hawkins and Robert Creeley. At a reading by Larry Fagin in Bill Berkson's backyard, Bolinas, CA, 1971. Photo by Bill Berkson.

Cassandra and James Koller, Sebastapol, CA, 1968. Photo by Anne Waldman.

In 1968 I fell into a lucky time-wrinkle that contained a young woman named Angelica Heinegg, the legendary Angel Hair prototype, and by a further twist of good fortune found myself married and dwelling with her in a modest rustic homestead located hard by the symbolic dirt-road intersection of Nymph and Cherry on the windy promontory of Bolinas Mesa, out near the rocky continent's-edge shelf of Duxbery Reef, at the other end of the known world. Our friends Lewis Warsh and Anne Waldman (they'd introduced Angelica and me) came out from New York during that summer of '68, and then, a year later, after their marriage ended, Lewis returned alone to camp in Bolinas awhile. On that stay he ran off a few hundred mimeographed copies (basic down-home trade edition fitting the epoch) of *Neil Young*, an assemblage-poem that was in fact more like a critical exercise. I'd extracted and thematically re-arranged seventy-five snippets of primal statement from the songs of the Canadian-born folk singer after whom the work was named—my favorite artist for a period of some months of that Bolinasian Phase of the Great Cultural Deglaciation we were all convinced was then going on.

Chicago (1969), a poem in several parts, was written with Lewis Warsh on an old Olivetti portable in the glassed-in kitchen of the Clarks' little pre-fab bungalow on Nymph Road in Bolinas. A literal Pacific Rim vista and setting pervades the Golden Age pastoral of the sequence as realistic backdrop, providing the grand, serene cliff-and-ocean scape—"Silver Pacific Ledge / out there / your codes are duplicated by the stars / no matter what goes down"—against which the somewhat mystifying action of the story unfolds. That action has a roman-à-clef quality largely of Lewis's creative contriving (and subject at intervals to my attempts at comic deconstruction). On his marriage-breakup-rebound tour to the Coast from New York, my collaborator had stopped off to briefly rekindle the embers of fleeting romance in several Midwestern college towns, embers kept glowing between the lines of our work, with a stopoff in Chicago for the Chicago Seven trial, which would become the pretext or occasion of our poems' tangled political subplotting. Actually Lewis's complicated amorous and philosophical adventures were the shifting sands upon which our entire story line tried to establish some foundation. His searches for body-and-soul sustenance supplied our central quest theme: the Nymph Road house became, with oxymoronic dexterity characteristic of the work, "a void filled with nourishment" (Angelica baked many cookies).

Clark Coolidge

Clark Coolidge, taken at a Serpent Power rehearsal at the Sausalito Heliport, CA, in late 1967, around the time he was writing the poems in ING.

Own Face had a lot to do with the fact of Lewis and Bernadette's residence in that big brick apartment block in the center of Lenox I used to visit weekly in the years they lived there carrying on with books, babies and endless conversation. Most of the poems already existed by the time they asked me for a book, but a few were added ("Album— A Runthru," "Connie's Scared" and "Our Nature's Future," for example) once the book's birth became a certainty. A lot of the poems were occasional poems I had finally come to allow myself to write, or at least to show. There's the cave theme of course, the presence of Guston, and many further oddments and passing takes. I still love the look of the original cover (which the Sun & Moon reprint totally missed) with Floyd's mad American glare, and "my" signature in Susan Coolidge's hand. A book absolutely from and of its time (late '70s), a period of greater change than I perhaps realized in its midst.

ING was written in San Francisco in 1967, a time of fascination with word-fragmentation, building from syllabic plucks, particularly the *ends* of words (I now notice). Further works in this zone include the unpublished WHOLES, VOLUMES, and AS IF IT. The book was built in a double/mirror structure around the two long poems, "AD" (I can't recall the source of) and "Cabinet Voltaire" (sic), which came from a scanning of Motherwell's *Dada Painters and Poets*, a book purchased at Newbegins famous old San Francisco bookstore on Union Square, now long gone, which lends its name to another poem in *ING* ("Nothing at Newbegins"). I used to employ textual scansion as my pot of paints, had developed an interest in Duchamp and Smithson, was starting my word-tape investigations at the Mills College Tape Center in Oakland. All the sixties SF musical potential had tattered away in big fame and bucks as American usual (in only a year!), and I was back stuck with my words. Of course, the biggest memory from the *ING* time was my meeting with Philip Guston, a blessing and life-changer for certain. CC down to the syllable, PG down to the one line, somehow generatively in parallel. I believe *ING* was the first poem-book cover that Philip did and he went on to make many others for he did love the poets. And speaking of parallels, years later (1992) the Roche Sisters recorded a song (written by Tere Roche) called Ing, I presume no relation (?).

Philip Guston and William Corbett, April 1980. Photo by Jon Imber.

William Corbett, Cambridge, MA, 1976. Photo by Elsa Dorfman © 1976, http://elsa.photo.net.

John Wieners, in Cambridge, MA, winter/spring 1974. Photo copyright © Gerard Malanga.

William Corbett

ANGEL HAIR'S *COLUMBUS SQUARE JOURNAL*

One remarkable thing about my association with Angel Hair is that there was nothing remarkable about it. I have tales of heartache about books that did or did not get published by poet-publishers but not about Angel Hair.

In October 1974 I gave my Emerson College poetry workshop the assignment of keeping a poem diary. I decided to do the assignment along with them, and we began on the twelfth, the day after my thirty-second birthday. I think I gave the class two weeks and told them to write every day. After their time was up I, who had not written every day, was hooked and kept on with my intermittent journal. That July Lewis and Bernadette visited us in Vermont. They asked to see what I had been writing. I showed them the journal, then thuddingly titled *Columbus Day A Year*. They read the manuscript at once, announced they would publish it when complete, and this is exactly what they did. Philip Guston drew the book's cover and in doing so titled it after our home address, Columbus Square Journal. Perfect.

On December 23, 1976, Lewis and Bernadette mailed me the first copy. I still have it in its Angel Hair jiffy bag with a clear postmark and the Lenox, Mass P.O. Box address stamped in red ink. In the twenty-four years and many books since no project has gone so smoothly. Nor have I felt so gratified by the finished book in my hands. Simply, without fuss of any kind, exactly, in fact, like the book's straightforward design, Lewis and Bernadette delivered the goods for this poet. I am as grateful today for their efforts on my behalf as I was the moment they vowed to publish my book.

Robert Creeley

"In London" was written while staying in London at the apartment of Bettina and John Calder, my English publisher. It was an extraordinary time, and just the evening previous I had gone with novelist and friend Ann Quinn to hear Ted Berrigan and Jim Dine (who was living in London) read together at a local gallery. Earlier that same evening, I had read with Robert Bly and others at

London's International Poetry Festival, which was the reason for my being in London in the first place.

The next morning, now alone in the Calders' apartment—with books, art, Bettina's piano and music scores, and people variously outside cleaning the windows—I started making a kind of pot pourri of echoes, musings, reflections, notes, a shorthand for all the rush of impressions and feelings, which the city provoked in me. The form, so to speak, was akin to the one I had used for "Pieces," and it was very much a preoccupation for me then to manage a "frame" which could include such a variety of formal and/or rhetorical materials with immediacy and close juxtaposition. It was, as the poem says, "the song of" that multiplicity I was most drawn to, in what I was trying to do in this poem.

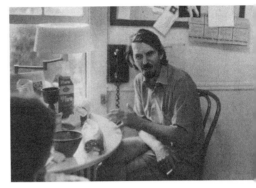

Robert Creeley talking to Fanny Howe, Cambridge, MA, 1974. Photo by Elsa Dorfman © 1974, http://elsa.photo.net.

Donna Dennis

The first public exposure my artwork ever received in New York was as covers for poetry magazines and books. I had come to the city in 1965 to make my way as a painter. By circumstance I found my first circle of friends in New York to be mostly poets. It was through Peter and Linda Schjeldahl, classmates of mine at Carleton College, that I met Ted Berrigan. Ted took a great interest in me and my art, believed in me as an artist at a crucial time. It was Ted who first suggested, I think, to Anne and Lewis, that I be invited to create a cover for *The World* #4, which they were editing. The covers for Jim Carroll's *4 Ups and 1 Down*, Lewis Warsh's *Moving Through Air* and Michael Brownstein's *3 American Tantrums* grew out of that experience.

The manner in which I approached the designing of all of these covers came from the collages I was making at the time using imagery I found in the backgrounds of the photos in fashion magazines. *Moving Through Air* is my favorite of this group of covers and is most typical of the collage work. I liked Lewis's title a lot and felt close to it from the start. In fact as I remember, I did not make a new collage for the cover but instead found one I had already made that had the feeling I wanted. I simply added the title and Lewis's name at the bottom.

I remember that I came upon the enlightened man in the extreme yoga position that was used for the cover of Michael's *3 American Tantrums* in the New York Public

Les Levine and Donna Dennis, NYC Fashion Show. Donna is wearing an outfit designed and made by sculptor Sylvia Stone. Circa 1969.

Library Picture Collection. Michael's memory is that he supplied the picture. It's possible that he is right. At any rate, the picture amused me in a perverse sort of way, for I could easily imagine that in fact this man might simply be having a tantrum.

For Jim Carroll's *4 Ups and 1 Down*, I needed to take his photograph, which I did, with a Polaroid camera on a bright early summer afternoon outside Bill Berkson's apartment on East 10th Street. The title, obvious on one level, suggested dreaminess and then came the image of Jim moving around in a night sky that was filled with suns and moons, stars and pills.

Kenward Elmslie

When Gerard Malanga asked me to write a think-piece about Busby Berkeley's films for Andy Warhol's *Interview*, after viewing a double-feature of his masterpieces, then playing in an art revival house, I decided to take the easy way out and write a poem. I measured the width of the column the poem would need to fit into, and departed from my usual practice of seemingly scattershot line breaks. I worked up a visual design for my poem: a series of exactly proportioned chunks, mostly square in shape, which would form an orderly, varied columnar sequence. The poem was accepted, in lieu of the think-piece, and I began to include it in poetry reading—the first time at MoMA. *Girl Machine* jumped out at listeners, provoking an immediate, energy-charged response my other poems failed to elicit. So mysterious! Grrrr! I had no idea why. It was a poem, written to order, that followed, on its own—I had nothing to do with it—the plot trajectory of the movie musicals that inspired it. Understudy becomes Star. How savvy of Angel Hair to publish it solo. A star turn, ta-da, on the page, and, subsequently, as sung.

Around then, I began working on poem-songs, poems I made up music for, which were transcribed and orchestrated by Steven Taylor, and subsequently recorded on LPs. Bobbie Louise Hawkins had guided me to Steven, bawling me out for singing, in public, to home-made tapes of fake-Satie accompaniments I klutzily thumped out on my piano. Steven decided to set *Girl Machine* himself, and patiently taught me, beat-by-beat, to sing what he called "reggae"— a song genre I investigated dutifully, and found I had no special fondness for. From inclusion in my part-sung poet-

Barbara Guest, 1970s. Photo by Donna Dennis.

Lewis Warsh, Joe Brainard and Kenward Elmslie, Westhampton, NY, 1968. Photo by Anne Waldman.

ry performances (sort of—I always stayed "on book"), *Girl Machine* was next incorporated as the finale of an off-off-off-Broadway revue of my words, *Palias Bimbo Lounge Show*, in which I took the plunk into full performance, and memorized, sheer torture, my own words, part of a two guy, two gal cast. Mac McGinnes, our director, saw me freeze with terror at the prospect of having to sing and dance. He worked out a retro-grade-school Girl Machine shuffle, a simple homage to Busby I could get through.

Pre-break-up of Yugoslavia, I found myself in Belgrade, part of an international literary conference. I chose *Girl Machine* as my entry, donned drag and a head-piece designed by the artist Ken Tisa, and to a tape of Steven Taylor's orchestration, sang it in a huge Baroque theatre, representing the US of A. The audience, wearied by a succession of spoken poems, went wild. Teenagers rushed for the exit, confronted me in the lobby: autograph hounds. They mistook me for a rock star.

Gerard Malanga, NYC, The Factory, circa 1967. Photo by Andy Warhol.

Larry Fagin

TRUE PASSION: MY LIFE WITH ANGEL HAIR

I met Lewis for the first time in the Summer of 1963 at Gino & Carlo's Bar in San Francisco. He was 18 years old, a visitor from the Bronx, shy, serious, even a little exotic (as a young outsider investigating a "closed scene.") I was 26, writing science fiction poems, trying to impress Jack Spicer. I was part of Spicer's set at Gino's, but I was also hanging out with David Meltzer and Richard Brautigan, and was friendly with McClure, Lamantia and Loewinsohn. Two summers later, at the Berkeley Poetry Conference, I ran into Lewis again, fleetingly. He had just met Anne Waldman, while I was breaking up with Jamie MacInnis.

I went to London at the end of 1965 to visit my parents, and wound up living there for two years. Tom Clark was my main American connection. He was editing his *Once* series of mimeographed poetry mags and was in touch with the younger New York poets.

In the Summer of 1967, after a big international poetry festival in London, Panna Grady threw one of her fabled literary bashes. Lewis and Anne, newlyweds, showed up, and we instantly bonded. We were young, pretty,

Robert Duncan and Larry Fagin, Boulder, CO, circa 1980.

quickwitted and excitable. Anne looked like the young Lauren Bacall, while Lewis, with his long, black hair hiding half his face, was reminiscent of Veronica Lake as a brunette. The party was, as we used to say, TOTALLY UNBELIEVABLE!, especially if you were a young poet. (Where was Tom Clark that night?) Neruda, Ungaretti, Spender, Empson, Ginsberg, Burroughs, Olson and Dorn were all there. Mick Jagger and Marianne Faithful materialized out of nowhere. I remember the giant Olson grabbing tiny Mick around the waist, lifting him up, shaking him like a doll and roaring, "I love him!"

The following day, Lewis, Anne and I walked all over London, jabbering about poetry and rock & roll. That night, I crashed on the floor where they were house-sitting, and wrote "Hello Again" as a belated epithalamium. I had been feeling homesick for the U.S. (in spite of the moronic war they were fighting) and the Warshes convinced me to move to New York, where we'd all be geniuses together.

The next few years were a stoned blur of poetry, music, sex, drugs and friendship. Lewis and Anne's apartment, at 33 St. Marks Place, was our headquarters, our party pad, and, occasionally, our crash pad. We gave and attended hundreds of poetry readings, parties, rock concerts and gallery openings. We smoked pounds of marijuana and dropped plenty of acid. We cranked out mimeo mags. We collaborated as writers—in pairs and in little groups. All of this seemed to happened on the spur of the moment. (Anne Waldman is, no doubt, the most spontaneous person I've ever known.) Meanwhile, Angel Hair raved on.

Clark Coolidge, Carol Clifford (Gallup), Gerard Malanga, Tessie Mitchell, Dick Gallup, Tom Veitch, Katie Schneeman and Anne Waldman, at the Schneemans' apartment, 29 St. Marks Place, NYC, circa 1972, posing for a painting by George Schneeman. Photo by Larry Fagin.

* * *

Parade of the Caterpillars was my first book of poems. Some copies arrived in San Francisco, where Joan Inglis and I lived for a brief time in 1968. There was a special edition of nine signed copies, each including a photograph of me, earmarked for particular friends. George Schneeman's artwork for the cover includes footprints of his youngest son, Emilio. The poems date from 1959 to 1967. My favorite, "New York," comes from San Francisco (1962) and was influenced by George Stanley. "Occasional Poem" originally appeared as a C Press broadside. "Valentine's Day" is a good "scene" poem. (The "John" in that poem is John Giorno.)

Joan and Larry Fagin, NYC, 1968.

Twelve Poems is a kind of serial poem, written à la Creeley, but also influenced by Aram Saroyan's minimalist and "electric" poems. I tried to include my own brand of deadpan humor. At that time, I was also writing list poems ("Ten Things I do Every Day," "30 Girls I'd Like to Fuck"), which Ted Berrigan promptly appropriated. Ted and I wrote some collaborations, too, one of which makes affectionate fun of Anne and Lewis:

> *Manifesto*
>
> *When we two think of you two beerbellies*
> *Barely able to huff yr feeble puffs, but*
> *Grunting your oinks on out back in*
> *Back out & never getting off, we chuckle*
> *& as we puke it is with a certainty*
> *that you are not what we think you are*
> *for we are full of   lame   ha-ha's*
> *& do not comprehend true passion.*

Landscape just fell into place. I had written the poem as a gift for Allen Ginsberg—notebook jottings from a trip to Venice in 1966. I thought George Schneeman could illustrate it, using one line per page. He began with a basic landscape and added an image as the poem proceeded. After *Landscape* went out of print, George and I thought that maybe the Museum of Modern Art would reprint it as a gift book, but they didn't go for the politically incorrect line, "The Japanese gardener flies to pieces."

Larry Fagin and Ron Padgett, Holly Solomon's Greene Street Gallery, NYC, circa 1973. Photo by Linda P. O'Brien.

Ted Greenwald

SEE IS CURVES

In crucible
50s   60s
Figure out
What works (for me)
The
Long and short
Of (what) it
Angel Hair
Gets out
(That works)
Worth speaking variety
Anne and Lewis request

Ted Greenwald and Ted Berrigan in the courtyard of St. Mark's Church In-the-Bowery, NYC, 1971. Photo copyright © Gerard Malanga.

Tony Towle working at Universal Limited Art Editions, West Islip, Long Island, 1966. Rauschenberg's lithograph *Accident* in the background.

John Ashbery and Lee Harwood, Paris, 1965.

Send please
Big something
Big finish
One sitting
One word line
Over top
(Means?) energy whatever
To me
Makes Sense
Quickly out
And around
Angels hand
Got to
Poetry eternity

Lee Harwood

THE MAN WITH BLUE EYES

In the early summer of 1965 I met John Ashbery in London. At the time I was filled with French poetry—Tristan Tzara, Max Jacob, the Dadaists, Alfred Jarry, Rimbaud. I was equally enthused with contemporary US poetry found in the 1960 Donald Allen anthology and the City Lights and New Directions books and the mass of "little magazines" that flew between the US and UK then. And, of course, the earlier "Modernist" masters Ezra Pound and William Carlos Williams. But somehow—and it's hard to remember accurately now 35 years later—all that reading and enthusiasm was never properly "digested." I was copying surface and attitudes. What I wrote were not really poems, they were clumsy verse, if not pointless dressed-up blather. "Self-expression" was the excuse.

Meeting John [Ashbery], in a near inexplicable way, turned me round. Being in his company, reading his poems with more care than before, seeing his approaches to writing and his personal tastes was a wonderful lesson and release. I finally realised one could make poems that worked like Borges' fictions. Poems that created a world and invited the reader to enter, to wander round, to put in their own two cents, to use. The personal was interwoven in this world, but there was much more involved than the personal. It was the delight of creating a Joseph Cornell box with words, or at least having that ambition even if it didn't always come off. I guess the essence of what John gave me was a sense of perspective, as a painter would understand that phrase. An awareness of co-existing worlds or realities. Of playfulness and seriousness spliced together. My book *The Man with Blue Eyes* was, for all its raggedyness and mistakes, the fruit of this "education."

As for publishing this book of poems? When I went to New York for the first time in summer 1966 I stepped into exactly the right place at the right time. New York seemed the centre of an immense energy and openness in the Arts. Everyone was exploring and pushing the boundaries of what might be possible. It felt especially rich for poets with them collaborating with painters, musicians, film makers, theatre people, and other poets. In the middle of this speedy cornucopia Anne Waldman and Lewis Warsh asked to publish a book of mine. Joe Brainard, who I'd worked with on comic strips for the *East Village Other* newspaper, drew the cover. And in no time *The Man with Blue Eyes* appeared. My first real book.

Memory can play tricks and we all edit our past, but I think this was how it happened. A generous time.

Edwin Denby standing in front of a Painting by George Schneeman, NYC, circa 1968.

Kenneth Koch

"Airplane Betty" is one of a series of poems I wrote in 1954 and 1955 about the character Airplane Betty. Airplane Betty was to a large extent inspired by my first wife, Janice, who had studied flying while she was at Smith College. I always found it surprising, interesting, and exciting that my beautiful soft-spoken very smart and well-educated young wife had been a pilot for a while, or at least had prepared herself to be one. The stories—the events, characters, dialogue—in the poems are of course all imaginary. Starting with some version of Janice and transposing her into an ambience of girls' adventure books, comic strips, and so on, seemed enough to make things happen. I wrote the Airplane Betty poems around the time I wrote "The Circus" and "Geography" and "The History of Jazz." Janice and I were living in Paris then, on the rue Notre Dame des Champs. We had recently gone to London and seen a production of *Peter Pan*. What I saw there suddenly made me interested in writing some very simple storytelling poems. The furthest I went with this kind of writ-

Kenneth Koch, circa 1970. Photo by Wren de Antonio.

ing, I think, turned out to be in prose and was my novel *The Red Robins*, of which the main characters are young men and women in their twenties flying in small airplanes all around Asia and having adventures.

"Irresistible" was one of the last poems I wrote that was more or less in the style of my long poem *When the Sun Tries To Go On*. I was passionately attached to the style and hoped I could go on writing in it forever, but about two years was as long as it lasted.

Joanne Kyger

Joanne was written while I spent some time with Lewis Warsh and Tom Clark in Bolinas within a flow of 1970s psychotropic and cannibis highs. Living the life of the "novel approach" there was only time for writing a small daily entry—the part of the writer that stays alive while "personality" seems to be more and more a dried-up appendage of "identity." The "individual" is swept out to sea, a group location identity, a place, takes precedence as voice. A much smaller voice relates a somewhat soap opera saga of a few summer months and some changes on shore. It is very amusing, and often pretty sad.

The cover is brighter with a fall Polaroid fashion shoot by Bill Berkson, both of us barefoot on the street.

Bernadette Mayer

THE WRITING OF *MOVING, ERUDITIO EX MEMORIA* AND *THE GOLDEN BOOK OF WORDS*

Moving was written as an attempt to write only when absolutely necessary. I was certain I didn't want to write out of a desire for a job, something to do, or, worse, love of being an artist. So whenever I felt compelled, I would type a page or so and put them on top of my desk, the same one as this actually. One day Anne Waldman came to visit and saw all the papers and decided to publish them. We had a really good time with the printer (Ronnie Ballou) because I had decided it should have a ragged left margin, difficult to do while setting that kind of type. To relax he would play golf. When it was published Frances LeFevre was a big fan and felt I'd gone downhill ever after.

Joanne Kyger, NYC, 1971. Photo copyright © Gerard Malanga.

Bernadette Mayer and Marie Warsh, Lenox, MA, 1976. Photo by Lewis Warsh.

Eruditio was done from random pages ripped from my school notebooks in which I obviously did some drawing. It was fun to write and I think I did it to use the Latin word for memory. I was moving and didn't want to throw all my notebooks away so I decided to rip out pages by chance and someday use them, as I did. It was reviewed in a northwest small press magazine and I don't think anybody read it except the publishers and Ted Berrigan. Certainly nobody asked me what it was except of course Ted. It ends with a wonderful conceit about a woman turning away from a bowl and then, ghazal-like, I say my name.

The Golden Book of Words is a compilation of poetry written in Lenox, Massachusetts. The most interesting thing about it to me was having Joe Brainard do the cover for which Joe asked me what I'd want it to be. Joe wasn't doing many covers at the time either and I loved getting his wonderful printed correspondences so I'd write him as often as possible; in fact, I always did. I wrote Joe a long letter when he was in the hospital with AIDS. I think I'd like to publish something all about Joe. At the moment the next town over is Brainard. Joe's archives are in the same room as mine in the library in San Diego.

Bernadette Mayer and Anne Waldman, Great Barrington, MA, 1970. Photo copyright © Gerard Malanga.

Alice Notley

…something red. Wearing a red scarf, meeting Philip Guston, then telling him in the letter I remembered wearing it meeting him, the letter asking for a cover for *Incidentals*. I wasn't married or pregnant when I wore it; then I was, and gave birth to Anselm, and became able to write from the dark, magic place. So the poems in *Incidentals* are thick and alienly accomplished, composed in Chicago and London. The title poem's in a quasi-Spenserian stanza and very serious, "Spenser I feared so the other side of my sight" (I still do). I can only faintly remember Ted's famous deprecations of the name *Angel Hair*: he thought the magazine was too "well-produced" (a frequent criticism) (*Incidentals* was not), but seemed to have liked being published there. For I think the magazine was already finished when we got together; and I haven't seen an *Angel Hair* in years. I still have the red scarf, it was sent to me when I was 17, from Germany, by a man I had a crush on. It's more fuschia; it's never been cleaned; it's slightly older than Angel Hair.

Anselm Berrigan, Edmund Berrigan and Alice Notley, Dick Gallup's apartment, NYC, 1975. Photo by Rochelle Kraut.

Ron Padgett

MEMORIES OF *BUN*

Tom Clark's memory of our writing *Bun* is better than mine, but perhaps I can add a few details to his account.

The shed he mentions had once been a small stable for the draft horses of the farmers who had lived on that property. The rickety structure was in the process of being renovated: it now had new siding, windows and a floor. Although my recollection is of writing my own poems on my Olivetti portable typewriter on the lawn between Kenward's house and the shed, Tom is probably right in recalling our working together inside the shed, but (heh heh) I am certain that the floor was wooden, not cement.

I am also sure that he will remember our playing a game that Dick Gallup and I had invented, called Penny Lane (after the Beatles song), in which one player hurls a small rubber ball high into the air so as to have it come down on the slant roof of a house and rebound at an angle, hopefully a difficult one for the other player. Then the other player serves. Whoever fails either to hit the roof or to catch the ball on the fly loses a point. I considered myself a fairly adept Penny Lane player, but in our protracted struggles Tom usually won. In any case, there we were, two men in our mid-twenties, out on the lawn playing like a couple of kids.

That description pretty much fits our writing *Bun*. But the playful-competitive back-and-forth had begun earlier, on June 13, when in New York City we had drafted a poem called "Poisoned Food." It was an ingredients poem—that is, each line had to include a certain number of elements (in this case, animals). It was a turgid effort, though it did have the inspired image of a goat "leaping through a waterfall of penicillin." The dense mass of the original draft looked too bulky to me, so a few days later I retyped it, breaking the lines into smaller units and adding space among them, just to see how it would look. The truth is that I was growing tired of the way my own poems, at the end of each line, seemed locked into returning to a flush-left margin. And perhaps I was envious of the way Ted Berrigan seemed to have gotten into fresh territory in his own work by breaking and spacing the lines out.

Tom Clark, Pat Padgett, Wayne Padgett, and Ron Padgett, Calais, VT, summer, 1967. Photo by Joe Brainard.

George Kimball, Bill Berkson, Peter Schjeldahl and Rudy Burckhardt on the ferry to Staten Island, NYC, 1969.

It wasn't that I was unaware of such a practice. The prime example of Mallarmé's "Throw of the Dice" loomed large, as did the typographical experiments of Apollinaire, the Dadaists, and the Futurists. One of the first modern poets I had admired was Cummings. And there was the projective verse of Charles Olson, the odes of Frank O'Hara, and other "open" compositions.

At Kenward's in Vermont that July, I continued the open-field manner, drafting a one-page poem called "Take a Little Walk." This was soon followed by "A Careless Ape," a jocular reference to Mallarmé as a poet unable to keep his lines straight. This tone was racheted up a notch or two when Tom and I then wrote a response to the Vietnam War, "Anti-War Poem," which begins

> I keep a saloon in Peru
> I sell beer and udder drinks too
> Und also I keep a udder counter
> Where de moo-moos come

and assumes even loonier voices when it breaks into open-field lines.

Perhaps a day or so later I wrote two more poems using scattered lines, "Read Books" and "Wonderful Things." By this time the dog days of August were upon us, so Tom and I retreated to the cool of the shed to bang out *Bun*. It seems to me that we did it in an effortless twenty minutes, later changing only one word (*dog* to *police*). Had we replaced Kenward's whippet, Whippoorwill, who on the slightest provocation would race joyfully around the house at blur speed?

It had been a productive summer for Kenward, Joe, Tom and me, and one of us came up with the idea of publishing an anthology of our new work, which turned out to be a 17-page, 14 x 22-inch portfolio, printed by a shop that produced most of the auction posters in the area, as well as the weekly *Hardwick Gazette*. I tried to imagine the bewildered face of the typesetter as he scrutinized our manuscript, which we called *Wild Oats*.

It is hard for me to believe that the very next spring Tom and I had the nerve to read these and other such deranged works at the Guggenheim Museum, sponsored by the Academy of American Poets. We deviated from the accepted format that called for two poets to read their respective sets. In the first set, we not only

Dick Gallup, NYC, May 1971. Photo by Larry Fagin.

Jonathan Cott, Cambridge, MA, October 1972. Photo by Lewis Warsh.

alternated every couple of poems, we began with a stichomythic reading of "Anti-War Poem" and concluded the half with a similar reading of *Bun*. We had a very good time, enough, I imagine, to indulge in self-congratulation. After all, the title of *Bun* had come from *bonne*, the French word for "good."

When Angel Hair invited Jim Dine to design the cover, he continued the high jinks. Instead of a bun, he depicted a bagel.

James Schuyler, NYC, 1975. Photo copyright © Gerard Malanga.

David Rosenberg on the fire escape to his flat, St. Marks Place, NYC, 1974. Photo copyright © Gerard Malanga.

David Rosenberg

Blues of the Sky marked the end of my faith in poetry. I was thirty and swamped with new questions. Was this poetry? Just what genre was it? The questions became primary, begging the *OED* definitions of translation: to transform, to enrapture, to transport? Back when I had faith, in Toronto, I had answers. I called the work collaboration, albeit with dead poets, in books that reconstructed Rimbaud, Mallarmé, Valery. Not Poundian imitations or take-offs, but rather theoretical alterations, in the spirit of my lost Canadian colleague, the inimitable bpNichol.

It took seven years for bp's untimely death to reach my in-box in Miami, and only then, in '95, did I read through his oeuvre posthumously. The neo-scripture I had absorbed from the early books of *The Martyrology* had remained unconscious in me when I arrived in Manhattan in late '71, but I'd made up other reasons for embarking on a life of composition-as-translation. Primary among them was the influence of Jack Spicer's *After Lorca*, which Victor Coleman brought back to Toronto from the Berkeley Poetry Conference. Northern prophet that he is, Victor Xeroxed endless copies and made all of Canada (about 20 of us) read it.

Probably my last wrong idea about why I turned to the Psalms in their ancient Hebrew translates the word "restoration." I came to Miami in '91, pointed to the tropics by a suggestion from Bill Merwin, not as much to save the Everglades as to translate it before it became totally illegible, or lost. "Erased" is also apt, just as it was in '73, when it described for me the original poets and Hebraic culture behind much of the early Bible—their names erased centuries later by a more urban religion, one that had less intuition of the wilderness from which it came.

As I worked with tropical scientists in the Everglades, I absorbed their inarticulate necessity (their field was dying before their eyes) to read the origins of ecosystems, in order to restore them. So the books of my own in the past twenty-odd years, which I had been thinking of as composition-as-translation (annotating Gertrude Stein's *Composition as Explanation*), turned into reading-as-translation. And it had done so once before, in St. Mark's Church in '73, although then I wasn't bothering with theory.

I read from *Blues of the Sky* and asked the audience to reach into the pew-rack for the prayerbook and compare Psalm 90 to mine as I read. I was involving my auditors in reading the surrounding environment—physical, cultural, spiritual—as an extension of the work. It went over poorly, however. This was the standard Wednesday night smallish crowd for poetry, and few bothered to open the prayerbooks in front of them because they'd been long inured to the surroundings. Even the wooden cross behind me was no doubt invisible. I felt like Vito Acconci in a life-drawing class.

A quarter-century later, Lewis Warsh asks me what inspired the Psalms translations and I realize the truest answer is disguise. Since the art we strove for was a disembodied one, the best contrast was the mundane detail of daily life. Lewis himself went beyond either Frank or Ted to record the literal goings-to-and-fro of the day— to the exclusion of even a moment's distracting thought about it. Yet he was still able to write a disembodied poem, or what I'd call a superbly angelic one. In other words, life itself was the disguise we wore, and the hair touching our shoulders might as well have been angel hair.

We didn't go around thinking about angels, of course. We were more like orphans. What happened to our poet-fathers? They died, one by one, coopted by the canons of Black Mountain, New York School, San Francisco Renaissance, Objectivists, Beat Generation. None of them knew orphanhood; they had French Surrealist fathers, or Spanish and Irish, or Pound and Stein. Yet for us, "Second Generation New York School" was a farce. We were on our own for perhaps the first time in American poetry since Emily Dickinson. As

Alex Katz and George Schneeman, poker game at Peter and Linda Schjeldahl's apartment on 3rd Street, NYC, April 1969. Photo by Larry Fagin.

Ted Berrigan in Liverpool, England, 1969. Photo by Lewis Warsh.

Jim Carroll, NYC, spring 1971.
Balcony of Gerard Malanga's flat.
Photo copyright © Gerard Malanga.

Kenward Elmslie, Anne Waldman and Lewis Warsh, Westhampton, NY, 1968. Photo by Joe Brainard.

much as we might still see ourselves in retrospect as tied to the lifeblood of collage, keeping an uncanny future alive, it was too late for that. It had all already been framed and mounted by the fathers who abandoned us.

Nobody likes to admit they're an orphan, but we still are orphans to this day. My first psalms were a kind of mourning for this loss. I thought of the term "lord" as the dead poet-father internalized as a poetic muse. I came to realize that the erased biblical poets were orphans too. Nobody knew their provenance, other than a quaint notion of "inspiration"—direct from the dead father in heaven. In other words, theirs was the fate of orphans as it was ours: to pioneer imaginative ways of restoring a lost environment.

For that reason, money and careers were props that could not control us. As an editor of Angel Hair, Lewis embodied the anti-career of creating books for a disembodied culture that we were in the process of restoring. That made each book a kind of "pilot project" in the long-term restoration of the visionary life. Even a single poem was a kind of project more than it was a lyric. When I completed my "Psalm 90" I had it printed as a broadside on blue parchment and sent it out as a Rosh HaShanah card to my New York mailing list of about ninety. Kenward Elmslie wrote that he found it "surprisingly sexy," and John Ashbery wrote back asking to see more. And Lewis, who had just published *Some Psalms* a few months earlier, was suggesting we turn the latter into a pilot project for the bigger *Blues of the Sky* to come.

It happened that my last book that could still pass as "poetry" in an academic setting was published simultaneously with *Some Psalms*. Recently restored in an online edition (chbooks.com) by the original publisher, Coach House, I added an introduction to *The Necessity of Poetry* that ends where this little piece begins.

Bob Rosenthal

NOTES ON *CLEANING UP NEW YORK*

I wrote *Cleaning Up New York* twenty-five years ago for a nonfiction writing class at CCNY taught by Francine du Plessix Gray. Francine was an excited proponent of the "New Journalism" and we were encouraged to write about what we knew. When I mentioned to her that I was cleaning apartments, her eyes lit up and she commanded me to write about it. I read an odd slender book on her booklist. It was Ida M. Tarbell's *History of the Standard Oil Company*. At the head of each one of Tarbell's terse chapters was an even tenser condensation of the chapter's contents, written in bullet form. I was intrigued by the dense sections' weight on the prose sections. I conceived to write about cleaning by constructing a "how to" book with ten chapters with instructions for cleaning interspersed with personal prose about individual clients. The instructional sections were written in dense prose-poem-like paragraphs. I was inspired to attempt an objective muckraker tone in the personal passages. I had also just read *Down and Out in Paris and London* by George Orwell. I liked the dispassion with which he described himself among the dishwashers in Paris and the homeless in London. I played off its title to find mine. Francine encouraged me greatly and laughed herself silly when I read the "sex with a vacuum cleaner" scene out loud at a class party. Lewis Warsh, who was finishing up at CCNY, solicited the manuscript in the English Dept. Quonset Hut. I happened to have photographs of myself as cleaner from one of my clients. I used the book's publication as an excuse to quit housecleaning. As rich in human fodder as it was, cleaning was also tiring.

I jokingly call *Cleaning Up New York* my cult classic yet my only evidence for it is that Richard Hell has told me twice over the years that he needed to get a new copy because it was time to clean!

Jim Brodey & Bob Rosenthal at Dick Gallup's apartment, 4th Street & Avenue B, NYC, circa 1977. Photo by Rochelle Kraut.

Bob Rosenthal and Rochelle Kraut, 437 E. 12th St., NYC, circa 1976.

Aram Saroyan, Strawberry, Cream and Gailyn, Bolinas, CA, 1975.

Harris Schiff, St. Mark's Church In-the-Bowery, NYC, 1971. Photo copyright © Gerard Malanga.

Aram Saroyan

Blod   Apparently inspired by a shaving accident, perhaps having remembered a real poem. A. E. Houseman, I think it was, said if you thought of a poem while shaving, you cut yourself.

Lobstee   The last time I saw Ted Berrigan—6 months to the day before he died—he told me he had discussed this poem with workshop students and they'd been puzzled by it. One student had determined that a lobstee might be an employee of a lobster, or something along those lines. All I was trying to do here was to give the feeling that a lobster gives me. The "ee" in "lobstee," to my way of thinking, is its claw.

A leaf left   This is one of my favorite of my own poems. It's a close registration, it seems to me, of the cognitive process. I'm in my second-story room in the house I lived in in Cambridge circa 1966-1967. I pick up a leaf off the floor and I go through the process of identifying it that the poem charts, step by step, line by line. It's just a leaf but the process is the whole cognitive megillicuddy. I invite Marjorie Perloff to do something wonderful with this.

Ex-track coach   This is a poem based on an obituary headline I found in a Cambridge newspaper and reworked a little. I shared it with Kerouac at the end of *The Paris Review* interview on which I accompanied Ted Berrigan. Jack's response, warmer to this one than to others in my minimalist repertory of that time, was classic. He said, nodding thoughtfully, "That's a nice tribute." He was probably thinking of some coach of his from Lowell football days.

Harris Schiff

NOTES ON THE ANGEL HAIR BOOKS: *SECRET CLOUDS* AND *I SHOULD RUN FOR COVER BUT I'M RIGHT HERE*

All the poems in *Secret Clouds* were written during the 1967 to 1969 period. I had come to live at 519 E. 5th Street, between Avenues A & B. The title poem was written on acid on the rooftop of that building where I often went to trip, meditate and experience visions, especially while gazing into the clouds—always abundant on those occasions. The Viet Nam War was an omnipresent nightmare during those years. I was sick at heart, frightened and enraged by the war and the hideous culture that supported it. I found that acid and other psychedelics helped to restore my sanity as well as give me a sense of spiritual connection.

I survived on $200 per month that my parents sent me, lived in a $90/per month apartment. Mostly ate pizza (15 cents a slice at the time, which was also the cost of a subway ride). "Soft" drugs (pot, hash, acid) were nearly free—pot was virtually free, people on the streets around Tompkins Square (total strangers) were constantly offering you a hit of a joint. Maybe a tiny amount of dealing was required to stay awash in mind-altering substances. Acid cost a couple of bucks a hit but people were always "laying it on you."

Lewis Warsh and Anne Waldman were my only connection to any kind of "society" outside of drug connections and people on the streets. Through them I met Ted Berrigan, Tom Clark, Dick Gallup, Ron Padgett and the Schneeman family and became a part of a larger New York School family.

"Three Rapidograph Sketches" is one of the first poems I wrote during that time in New York. I slipped it into Anne and Lewis's mailbox at 33 St. Marks Place. I was probably too shy to show it to them, didn't even leave a name on it. Anne thought it was some hippie tract (and it was—my hippie tract). I mentioned to Lewis that I had left it there. Anne published it in *The World* and also in *The World Anthology*.

The "wise old man with a smile" in the poem "paw prints on a page" is Jack Spicer—of whom I had visions while writing that poem in the autumn of 1968, tripping in my little pad. Even today at 55, an age that I would have very much doubted I could ever have lived to, I still think of Jack as both old and older than me (he was in his late 30s when I knew him).

The poem "Local" chronicles a subway ride. I had been tripping rather strongly through the night, got on the subway at dawn and rode up to my parents' house in the Bronx (they were in Florida for the winter). I wrote the poem in a notebook on the Number 6 train from Astor Place to Pelham Bay Park (the last stop in the Bronx),

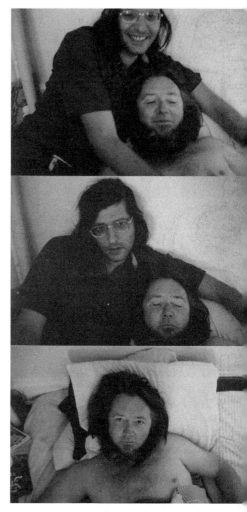

Lewis Warsh and Ted Berrigan, Lenox, MA, 1978. Photos by Bernadette Mayer.

Lewis Warsh and Anne Waldman, Golden Gate Park, San Francisco, August 1968. Photo by Larry Fagin.

David Berrigan, Sandy Berrigan and Kate Berrigan, Florida, 1968. Photo by Lewis Alper.

walked to their house, got home, turned on the tv, and there was the now-famous pistol to the head execution of a Viet Cong prisoner by a plain-clothed South Vietnamese officer on the *Today Show* completing the last line of the poem "watch an execution for breakfast."

I put the book together in Bolinas, with Lewis's kind encouragement. I selected the order by spreading the poems on the floor of the place we were staying in, tripping, once again. I believed that tripping was the doorway to truth and right thinking and magic. It certainly was a gateway to that place but I have found that it is better reached and returned from along non-molecular pathways. Not long after that process, I watched, amazed, as, through Lewis's labors, smudged pages came out of a mimeograph machine in San Francisco. It was my first book and I was thrilled.

Not long after that Lewis and I hitchhiked together to LA. I broke out in incredible hives, my eyes swollen shut from poison-oak which I had gotten while sleeping out in the Bolinas bush, tripping on mescaline. Lewis found Steve Carey, who knew a doctor there. I was given steroids to clear it up. We then hitched to Santa Fe, and stayed with Jim and Cass Koller. Lewis went back to California while I headed up into commune country above Taos (Arroyo Hondo, NM, to be precise), where I took up residence at the Morningstar Commune. The road from Arroyo Hondo to the mesa where the commune was is where the incidents described in *I Should Run For Cover but I'm Right Here* took place.

I Should Run For Cover but I'm Right Here was written in one late night, all night sitting in the downstairs living room of Fairfield Porter's house in Southampton in the fall of 1971 I believe, while Ted Berrigan and Alice Notley slept upstairs. Earlier the three of us had had some great chat. Ted had been talking about interviewing Kerouac for *The Paris Review* and we discussed our admiration for Kerouac's benzedrine-fueled prose typed on an unending sheet of paper. They went to bed and I began writing this account of recent incredible events in my life.

Since 1960, when I had simultaneously discovered beatniks, writing poetry and the companionship of other ecstasy-seeking artists, I had hoped to write the novel that would express everything I had ever felt or longed for. *I Should Run For Cover but I'm Right Here* was my best start ever on that novel.

In the morning we all had some liverwurst sandwiches and pepsi and I read them what I had written while they had been asleep. Everyone thought it was "totally great."

Lewis Warsh loved the work and offered to publish it as a chapbook some years later. Rudy Burckhardt came over to my place on Second Avenue in 1977 or 1978 and took a few pictures of me from which he made the cover drawing.

Some of the response to the work is worth noting. Edwin Denby told me several times that *Run For Cover* was his "favorite novel." Most recently I was astonished to learn that the 10-page title poem of Michael Lally's 1999 Black Sparrow book—"It's Not Nostalgia"—is about reading *I Should Run For Cover but I'm Right Here* and is dedicated to me. Lally never showed me the work, but sent me a copy of the book a few days before I received a request for these notes.

I still intend to finish the story. It's gotten quite long!!

Linda Schjeldahl [Linda P. O'Brien], NYC, 1967.

Peter Schjeldahl

Looking back, I see *Dreams* as an experiment in labor-intensive automatic writing. I slept a lot back then, logging the surplus hours of shallow slumber when waking consciousness nuzzles dreaming like an impatient cat. I had trained myself to record my dreams in notes before I was fully awake. Later, I edited the notes. I rewrote each piece many times. I added nothing to what I remembered. Mostly, I abolished fuzziness. Where an element presented multiple aspects, I would pick one. I paid positively no attention to the dreams' "meaning." It didn't matter that the material was my dreams or dreams at all, except formally—treating the dreaming mind's narrative mania as a literary convention. I killed dreams into prose.

Re-reading *Dreams* now, I'm pleased with the craft of it (notably including James Rosenquist's great cover and Anne and Lewis's beautiful production) and embarrassed by its nakedness—and its presumption. I regret having used the names of other people, who never bore any true

Peter Schjeldahl, NYC, 1972. Photo by Elizabeth C. Baker.

George Schneeman, Staten Island, NYC, May 1968. Photo by Larry Fagin.

Katie Schneeman in Wisconsin, summer 1968.

resemblance, in life, to their daemonic apparitions in the book. A sensible rule for dream interpretation is that everybody one dreams of is oneself. I vouch for it here. (The "I" of the "I am" that begins each piece denotes the totality, not a character.) I suppose I felt that making a masochistic offering of my palpitant inner gunk to the god of Writing freed me from social decencies. I apologize especially to those whose devotion to the same god I counted on, with vanity but not in vain, to get me indulged. In the classical formulation of an eminence of that epoch, "What a jerk!"

George Schneeman

The Golden Palomino Bites the Clock was my first New York cover after coming from the Tuscan Middle Ages of Italy. I had never even been to New York, had never seen a deKooning painting and only knew the paintings of Ambrogio Lorenzetti! I was nervous as hell and I'm embarrassed that I actually put a horse on the cover. But from that point on I don't think I ever tried to illustrate the words of a title. I found out that almost any image you can think of can seem appropriate.

Giant Night was my first silkscreen cover. I had been doing silkscreen collaborations with Ron and Ted and my yearly calendars, and I had enthusiasm about doing a silkscreen cover. This 2-color print was done entirely by hand, although I never felt it quite worked.

The Asylum Poems was the first of many places I opted to use a hand in some way (in this case holding a poppy). It's the easy way out.

O My Life! was based on a photo of Anne, "the naked lady" motif, the tilted lampshade.

I think the cover for *Angel Hair* 6 was inspired by Edwin Denby, after having read his book *Scream in A Cave* which has two people riding in a roadster. It's mysterious, that scene.

And there are others. I added those images in *Landscape* (with Larry Fagin) one by one as the piece went on.

Charles Stein

In 1962 I joined an occult order with which I remained associated for two years. I remember thinking that the growth processes encouraged by the order had themselves led inexorably to my abandoning my position in it, and for some time thereafter I wrote poems that reflected on the matter of abandoning commitments to spiritual teachings and mystical teachers. Ouspensky was a student of Gurdjieff who had eventually broken with him to present his own version of "the work." The first time I was presented with my horoscope I was informed that I am a Virgo and that Virgos don't believe in astrology. I add, but they do it anyway. *The Virgo Poem* borrows material about the constellation Virgo from another Gurdjieff-Ouspensky writer, Rodney Collin. Lewis Warsh and I went to different high schools but we were part of the same circle of teenage writers and poets in New York City circa 1960. Lewis was therefore one of the first two or three poets I ever knew. After not seeing each other for a few years, in 1965 we found ourselves living in the same boarding house on 112th Street. I had met Anne Waldman around this time at Bennington College, I think through our mutual friend, the prose writer Laura Furman. The Angel Hair book had a frontispiece—a drawing by Josie Rosenfeld, of the Tarot Hermit card, which, in the occult system I had worked with, was assigned to Virgo. Josie was my closest friend at the time and there was nothing in my exploration of the occult during those years that I did not share with her.

René Ricard, NYC, circa 1968.

Lorenzo Thomas

The summer I met Anne Waldman, she was working as a college intern at WRVR-FM. I was still in college, too, but I'd been reading my poems at the Deux Magots and other coffee shops in the East Village and thought of myself as being "on the scene." I was a bit jealous of Anne, though, because she had studied at Bennington College with Claude Fredericks, whose activities on behalf of poetry I knew from the years I'd spent as a high school student avidly devouring literary magazines at the Queensborough Public Library.

I should have known that working with Claude Fredericks guaranteed that Anne would become

Lorenzo Thomas, Luzmilda Thomas and Cecilio Thomas, 1950.

Lorenzo Thomas, Poetry-in-the-Schools, North Forest elementary school, Houston, TX, 1978.

John Giorno, 33 St. Marks Place, NYC, 1968.

involved in small-press publishing. That she would eventually publish some of my poems was a small part of our immediate and present friendship.

When *Fit Music* was published, I'd just been discharged from the Navy. Being in the Navy was, for me, a romantic inevitability—partly encouraged throughout my childhood by Richard Rodgers's thrilling score for the TV documentary *Victory at Sea*. Who says art isn't powerful? When I eventually enlisted, however, it was a forced option resulting from the Vietnam draft. In 1968, I was a college graduate, classified 1-A, summoned to Whitehall Street for an Army physical exam. After days of long conversations with my father, I decided that joining the Navy was one way to avoid ending up in jungle firefights. As it turned out, I was wrong about that—but that's another story.

While I was in the Navy I stopped writing poetry for a while; but I spent a great deal of my spare time studying Egyptian hieroglyphics and the Ethiopic syllabery. In a bookstore in Albuquerque I found a PJO Poche paperback edition of poetry from Portuguese-speaking Africa, in French translation, so I spent time working on that, too.

When I received orders for Vietnam—to be stationed "in country" as a communications advisor—I began to write poems again. And while I was actually in Vietnam, Anne Waldman and Ellease Southerland (then a fine poet, now an equally accomplished novelist also known as Ebele Oseye) were holding on to my lifeline—keeping me connected to my mother and to poetry as well. *Fit Music* reflects the intensive study of Ezra Pound that Ted Greenwald and I had engaged in, but it was written as a kind of poetic record of my Vietnam experience. One aspect of that experience, at least; other facets can me seen in some poems collected in *The Bathers* (1981) and in my translations of a few classical Vietnamese poems. The envoy, or final section, to *Fit Music* was completed when I returned to the Treasure Island naval base in San Francisco; and the circle was closed when Anne decided that she wanted to publish it as one of the Angel Hair books. What I still like about *Fit Music* is that it is true, in both incident and symbolism; and that the illustrations by Cecilio Thomas, my brother, both complemented and extended what the poem intended to say.

O My Life! with cover (based on a risqué Polaroid of the author) by George Schneeman is a fast little book with journalesque pieces composed at 33 St. Marks Place. The poems seem influenced in part by Philip Whalen, Joe Brainard, and Sei Shonagon's *Pillow Book*. I picked six end-words for "How The Sestina (Yawn) Works" that evoked the very distinct flavor of the times as well as made a poem "about" writing, especially a "form poem" that often, clunkily, never strays from its moves. Those six end words take a lot of heat, the danger being they go flat or dumb. So these words were "things" I chose, welcomingly, "personally" for the poem, that were meant to be a bit provocative. My mother, the very wonderful Frances LeFevre Waldman, had broken down weeping in Ted Berrigan's workshop, unhappy that there were mentions of "drugs" in my poetry. I wanted her to know that poetry was the greatest kick of all! There's also a casual "yawn" in the title, repeated in text, that's a barb perhaps to the versifiers, I mean it's not that hard to write a sestina. When read aloud (or silently I'd hope) the energy builds, maniacally, ending with a sense that the poet's in charge of her world. A whiff of William Carlos Williams' "Dance Russe" perhaps? "The After-Life" was written specifically for Joe Brainard, off his "tone." The sixties with its ubiquitous tear gas inspired "Dispersal of It." I believe this was written after an anti-war rally in Tompkins Square Park, although a group of us were also threatened by the Tactical Police Force with tear gas canisters as we picketed against the overpricing ($17.50) of Philip Whalen's first mainstream-published book at the offices of Harcourt Brace & World, 1969. The disarming substance was literally in the air. You kept your chin to your chest. "Is it really any wonder?" is referenced from Bob Dylan. "Sick" is a New York School 2nd & a half generation list poem.

Bernadette Mayer and I actually got a "kill fee" from *OUI* magazine for *The Basketball Article*, our first foray (and last?) into the interstices of power-journalism. I remember we wore scarves and berets and long boots for the games, looking decidedly bohemian as we sat taking notes at the edge of the ballcourt. Bernadette always carried along a copy of Shakespeare's *Sonnets*.

Frances LeFevre Waldman and Anne Waldman, St. Marks Place, NYC, 1968. Photo by Lewis Warsh.

Anne Waldman and Philip Whalen, NYC, circa 1970s.

Lewis Warsh and Bernadette Mayer with Max Warsh, Sophia Warsh and Marie Warsh, summer 1982, Lake Buel, MA. Photo by Peggy DeCoursey.

Hannah Weiner, Tom Veitch and Johnny Stanton at Larry Fagin and Joan Fagin's wedding, NYC, April 1969.

Lewis Warsh

I wrote "The Suicide Rates" as a student in Kenneth Koch's class at The New School in fall 1963—I was not quite 19 and trying to experiment with the ideas of distance and intimacy I'd picked up from reading the serial poems of Robin Blaser and Jack Spicer. What did I know? A few years later I had learned how to step forward into my own work—enough so I could write a day-long journal ("Halloween") and have the nerve to publish it. (I hadn't written it with the idea of ever publishing it but it seemed to translate what a typical day in the late 1960s was like without even trying.)

Tom Clark and I wrote "Chicago" in a sweet burst of reciprocal energy. He was the stable family man while I was on the go—somehow the two states of being meshed and created a third place we couldn't get to except on the page. For a moment it seemed possible to be free and stable at the same time.

I put together *The Maharajah's Son* in 1972 when I was living in Stinson Beach, California. I had wanted to write something about my life in the early 60s and realized that I'd saved all these letters—they were in a closet in my parents' apartment in New York. I edited almost nothing and just held my breath as I typed it all up. I began to think of it less a book that related to me but more like an epistolary novel, *Clarissa* or *Les Liasons Dangeureues*. It felt very arrogant—to type up old letters from old friends—but I felt innocent as well while I was doing it, waiting to see how it would all come out.

Hannah Weiner

By Lewis Warsh

I knew Hannah Weiner casually in the late 1960s but didn't get to know her well until about 1975. I remember sitting across from her at a table. Hannah said she saw words on my forehead and I asked her what they were and she told me what I was thinking. She was seeing words everywhere during that period and translating what she saw into a book of writing, *The Clairvoyant Journal*. I was living in Lenox, Mass. with Bernadette Mayer when we decided to publish Hannah's journal as an Angel Hair book. Hannah was in New York, I was in the Berkshires, and the typesetter of the book, Barrett Watten, was in San Francisco. Somehow—these were the days before e-mail—we communicated about the production of this complicated book. Often the exchanges between Hannah and I became heated but we both knew how to step back from what was bothering us so we might yell at each other briefly and even hang up the phone midsentence but would rebound almost immediately without losing sight of the common goal— to get the book done.

Years later I worked with Hannah on *The Fast*—a United Artists book (not excerpted here). Both of us were in New York and I would visit her in her overheated apartment and we would chat about the progress of the book. I had seen a manuscript of *The Fast* years before and it had excited me immediately—so different, on the surface, from any of Hannah's other writing. The straightforwardness with which she described her LSD experiences was as scary and endearing and ultimately disturbing as the fractured communications she had attempted to transcribe in *Clairvoyant Journal*. Both books share the journal format, and both work from the outside in—but in completely distinct ways. The location of the person writing these texts, the reality of that place, approaches a version of what the gift of sanity is about.

Donna Dennis, Martha Diamond and Hannah Weiner at Joan Fagin's bridal shower, 33 St. Marks Place, NYC, April, 1969.

ANGEL HAIR

List of Publications

Compiled by Steve Clay and Aaron Fischer

te: In all instances measurements are in inches, width preceding height. For the sake of consistency, counted both sides of each of the pages between the covers of the books, including all blank pages en in the case of the mimeos, which were printed on one side of the page only), but excluding the :asional tissue endpapers. Single sheet publications are recorded as such.

ANGEL HAIR 1
*Anne Waldman / Lewis
Warsh editors*
Spring 1966
10″ x 13″
24 pages
Gray cover of Fabriano
paper with type printed
letterpress in purple

ANGEL HAIR 2
*Anne Waldman / Lewis
Warsh editors*
Fall 1966
10″ x 13″
44 pages
Yellow cover of Fabriano
paper with type printed
letterpress in gray

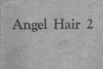

ANGEL HAIR 3
*Anne Waldman / Lewis
Warsh editors*
Summer 1967
10″ x 13″
48 pages
Green cover of Fabriano
paper with type printed
letterpress in white

ANGEL HAIR 4
*Anne Waldman / Lewis
Warsh editors*
Winter 1967-8
10″ x 13″
64 pages
Red cover of Fabriano
paper with type printed
letterpress in red

ANGEL HAIR 5
*Anne Waldman / Lewis
Warsh editors*
Spring 1968
10″ x 13″
64 pages
Blue cover of Fabriano
paper with type printed
letterpress in white

ANGEL HAIR 6
*Anne Waldman / Lewis
Warsh editors*
Spring 1969
9-1/4″ x 12-1/4″
64 pages
Cover by
George Schneeman

THE MAN WITH BLUE EYES
Lee Harwood
1966
7-1/8″ x 8-1/2″
48 pages
Edition of 500
Introduction by Peter
Schjeldahl
Cover by Joe Brainard

**3 POEMS FOR BENEDETTA
BARZINI**
Gerard Malanga
1967
9-7/8″ x 12-1/4″
14 pages
Edition of 500
Photographs by
Stephen Shore

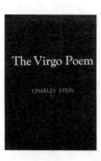

THE VIRGO POEM
Ouspensky Addresses a
Congress of Virgoes
Charles Stein
1967
10" x 13"
12 pages
Edition of 500
Frontispiece drawing by
Josie Rosenfeld

IDENTIKIT
Jim Brodey
1967
8-1/2" x 11"
30 pages
Edition of 500
Cover photograph
by Bob Cato

THE GOLDEN PALOMINO
BITES THE CLOCK
Sotere Torregian
1967
8-1/2" x 11"
30 pages
Edition of 300
Cover by
George Schneeman

MANY HAPPY RETURNS
(To Dick Gallup)
Ted Berrigan
December 1967
7" x 9-1/2"
1 folded sheet
Edition of 204
4 lettered and signed
copies *hors commerce*
Printed at
Grabhorn-Hoyem

MOVING THROUGH AIR
Lewis Warsh
1968
9" x 11-7/8"
40 pages
Edition of 500
25 copies numbered and
signed by the author and
artist, with an additional
poem written by the
author
Cover by Donna Dennis

GIANT NIGHT
Anne Waldman
1968
8-1/2" x 14"
8 pages
Edition of 100
All copies are signed
by the author
Silkscreen cover by
George Schneeman

SONNET
Tom Clark
March 1968
8-1/2" x 11"
Broadside
Edition of 50
signed copies

BUN
Tom Clark & Ron Padgett
1968
9" x 11-7/8"
28 pages
Edition of 519
19 signed and numbered
copies on Hosho paper
each containing a page of
the manuscript signed by
the authors, and
numbered 1-19
Cover by Jim Dine

**THE PARADE OF
THE CATERPILLARS**
Larry Fagin
1968
8-1/2" x 11"
50 pages
Edition of 300
9 copies *hors commerce*,
"numbered" A-I, signed by
the author and artist and with
a photograph of the author
15 copies numbered 1-15
and signed by the
author and artist
276 copies in a trade edition
Cover by George Schneeman

ING
Clark Coolidge
1968
8-1/2" x 10-3/4"
56 pages
Edition of 500
25 copies numbered
and signed by the
artist and author, with
an additional poem
written by the author
Cover by Philip Guston

O MY LIFE!
Anne Waldman
1969
8-1/2" x 11"
70 pages
Edition of 500
6 copies *hors commerce*,
"numbered" A-F, signed by
the author and artist, with a
"special surprise"
from the author
20 copies numbered 1-20
and signed by the author
and artist each of which has
an additional sheet printing
"Poem for the Streets of
New York City"
Cover by
George Schneeman

ASYLUM POEMS
(For my Father)
John Wieners
1969
8-1/2" x 11"
44 pages
First edition of 200
10 numbered copies
signed by the author
Second edition
(stated) of 300 (1969)
Cover by
George Schneeman

SHINING LEAVES
Bill Berkson
1969
8-1/2" x 11"
68 pages
Edition of 500
10 copies *hors commerce*,
"numbered" A-J, signed by
the author and artist, with an
additional work by the author
26 copies numbered 1-26
and signed by the
author and artist
464 copies in a trade edition
Cover by Alex Katz

SLIP OF THE TONGUE
Johnny Stanton
1969
8-1/2" x 11"
66 pages
Edition of 500
26 copies "numbered"
A-Z, signed by the
author and artist
Cover and inside
drawings by
George Schneeman

CHICAGO
Lewis Warsh & Tom Clark
1969
7-5/8" x 10-1/4" or
9-1/4" x 11-7/8"
12 pages
Edition of 200
4 lettered copies are
hors commerce
2 states, no priority;
smaller in yellow covers,
larger in blue covers with
hand colored capitals
Printed at Grabhorn-
Hoyem

ORANGES
Frank O'Hara
1970
8-1/2" x 11"
20 pages
Edition of 200
Cover by
George Schneeman

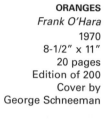

NEIL YOUNG
Tom Clark
1970
8-1/2" x 14"
20 pages
Edition of 200 copies
signed by the author
Cover designed
by Tom Clark

JOANNE
Joanne Kyger
1970
8-1/2" x 11"
78 pages
Edition of 300
Cover photo of author
by Bill Berkson

ELECTIVE AFFINITIES
Jonathan Cott
1970
8-1/2" x 11"
62 pages
Edition of 350
12 *hors commerce*
numbered and signed
by the author

3 AMERICAN TANTRUMS
Michael Brownstein
1970
8-1/2" x 11"
16 pages
Edition of 750
13 numbered and signed
by the author
Cover by Donna Dennis
and Michael Brownstein

TRUCK
Merrill Gilfillan
1970
8-1/2" x 11"
52 pages
Edition of 250
Cover by Joe Brainard

SECRET CLOUDS
Harris Schiff
1970
8-1/2" x 11"
66 pages
Edition of 300
10 copies "numbered"
A-J signed by the
author and artist
Cover by Joe Brainard

I REMEMBER
Joe Brainard
1970
8" x 10"
36 pages
Edition of 700
26 copies lettered A-Z
and signed by the author

4 UPS AND 1 DOWN
Jim Carroll
1970
8-1/2" x 11"
16 pages
Edition of 300
13 special copies with a
piece of hair and signa-
tures of the author and
artist, numbered 1-13
Cover by Donna Dennis

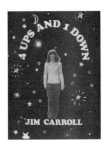

IN LONDON
Robert Creeley
1970
7" x 10"
16 pages
Edition of 200
10 copies signed
4 copies with the "L" in
London on the title page
colored in are
hors commerce
Printed by
Grabhorn-Hoyem

UP THRU THE YEARS
Anne Waldman
1970
8-1/2" x 11"
6 pages
Edition of 100
Cover by Joe Brainard

BIRDS
John Giorno
1971
8-1/2" x 11"
22 pages
Edition of 250
Cover by
George Schneeman

GIRL MACHINE
Kenward Elmslie
1971
6-3/8" x 6"
8 pages
Edition of 500
26 copies lettered A-Z
and 10 copies *hors com-
merce*, numbered 1-10
and signed by the author
Cover by Busby Berkeley

MOVING
Bernadette Mayer
1971
7-7/8" x 9-7/8"
40 pages
Edition of 726
26 copies lettered A-Z
and signed by the author
Frontispiece drawing by
Rosemary Mayer
Cover by Ed Bowes

TWO WOMEN
Charlie Vermont
1971
8-1/2" x 11"
80 pages
Edition of 290
10 numbered copies
signed by the author
Cover photo
by Harry Gross

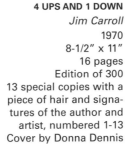

LIMITS OF SPACE AND TIME
Britton Wilkie
1971
6" x 6-1/8"
12 pages
Edition of 500

ICY ROSE
**(To The Delicately
(Winter) Coming On)**
Anne Waldman
May 1971
9-7/8" x 20"
Broadside
Printed at Cranium Press

VERGE
James Schuyler
1971
20" x 14"
Broadside
Edition of 300
Printed by
Grabhorn-
Hoyem

TWELVE POEMS
Larry Fagin
1972
5-1/4" x 8-1/2"
36 pages
Edition of 312
12 copies *hors commerce*
Cover by
George Schneeman

FIT MUSIC
California Songs, 1970
Lorenzo Thomas
1972
8-1/2" x 11"
42 pages
Edition of 300
20 copies signed by the
author and artist
Cover and drawings
by Cecilio Thomas

I REMEMBER MORE
Joe Brainard
1972
8" x 10"
44 pages
Edition of 800
A limited edition of 26
lettered A-Z and signed
by the author

LANDSCAPE
*Larry Fagin &
George Schneeman*
1972
6-5/8" x 6"
16 pages
Edition of 536
26 lettered A-Z and
signed by the poet and
author; ten copies *hors
commerce* numbered 1-
10 signed by the
poet and artist
Texts and images drawn
by George Schneeman

DRACULA
Lorenzo Thomas
1973
8-1/2" x 11"
16 pages
Edition of 300
Cover by Britton Wilkie

RECENT VISITORS
Bill Berkson
1973
8" x 10-1/4"
52 pages
Edition of 1000
26 copies numbered
and signed by
author and artist
Cover and drawings by
George Schneeman

**INCIDENTALS IN
THE DAY WORLD**
Alice Notley
1973
8-1/2" x 11"
116 pages
Edition of 500
Cover by Philip Guston

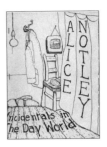

DREAMS
Peter Schjeldahl
1973
8-1/8" x 10-1/4"
36 pages
Edition of 1000
50 copies numbered
and signed by the
author and artist
Cover by
James Rosenquist

SOME PSALMS
David Rosenberg
1973
8-1/2" x 11"
26 pages
Edition of 210
10 copies numbered
and signed by
author and artist
Cover by Hannah Wilke

MORE I REMEMBER MORE
Joe Brainard
1973
6-7/8" x 9-3/4"
32 pages
Edition of 726
26 copies lettered A-Z
and signed by the author
Cover photograph of
the author by Bill Katz

MAKES SENSE
Ted Greenwald
1974
8-1/2" x 11"
112 pages
Edition of 400
26 copies numbered
and signed by the
author and artist
Cover by
George Schneeman

HOTELS
John Wieners
1974
8-1/2" x 11"
12 pages
Edition of 510
10 copies signed by
author and artist
Cover by Gordon Baldwin

SNORING IN NEW YORK
Edwin Denby
1974
6-1/2" x 8-1/4"
44 pages
Edition of 750
26 signed by the poet
Cover by
Rudy Burckhardt
Published by Angel Hair
and Adventures in Poetry

BLUES OF THE SKY
Interpreted from the Ancient
Hebrew Book of Psalms
David Rosenberg
1974
8-1/2" x 11"
88 pages
Edition of 400
26 numbered and signed
by author and artist
Cover by
George Schneeman

EAT THIS!
Tom Veitch
1974
5-1/4" x 8-1/4"
160 pages
Edition of 1000
"A limited signed hard-
cover edition" is indicat-
ed on the copyright page
Cover by Greg Irons

SHELTERED LIFE
Charlotte Carter
1975
8-1/2" x 11"
132 pages
Edition of 350
10 copies numbered
and signed
by the author
Cover by
Raphael Soyer

THE BASKETBALL ARTICLE
Bernadette Mayer &
Anne Waldman
1975
8-1/2" x 11"
32 pages
Edition of 100

COLUMBUS SQUARE
JOURNAL
William Corbett
1976
7" x 10"
64 pages
Edition of 1000
Cover by Philip Guston

CLEANING UP NEW YORK
Bob Rosenthal
1976
7" x 10"
48 pages
Edition of 750
26 are lettered A-Z
and signed by the
poet and artist
Cover by Rochelle Kraut

NOTHING FOR YOU
Ted Berrigan
1977
6-7/8" x 10"
112 pages
Edition of 1000
26 lettered A-Z
and signed by
author and artist
Cover and frontispiece by
George Schneeman

ERUDITIO EX MEMORIA
Bernadette Mayer
1977
8-1/2" x 11"
82 pages
Edition of 400
26 lettered A-Z and
signed by the author
Cover by
Bernadette Mayer

THE MAHARAJAH'S SON
Lewis Warsh
1977
7" x 10"
112 pages
Edition of 1000
Cover by
Rosemary Mayer

**I SHOULD RUN FOR COVER
BUT I'M RIGHT HERE**
Harris Schiff
1978
8-1/2" x 11"
40 pages
Edition of 400
Cover by
Rudy Burckhardt

CUBA
Tapa Kearney
1978
8-1/2" x 11"
32 pages
Edition of 300
26 lettered A-Z and
signed by the author
Published by Songbird
Editions and
Angel Hair Books

SOME MAGIC AT THE DUMP
Reed Bye
1978
5-1/2" x 8-1/2"
66 pages
Edition of 500
26 lettered and signed by
poet and cover artist
Cover by Jerome Hiler
Published by Songbird
Editions and
Angel Hair Books

CLAIRVOYANT JOURNAL
1974 March-June Retreat
Hannah Weiner
1978
7" x 10"
64 pages
Edition of 750
26 copies lettered A-Z
and signed by the author
Cover photograph by
Tom Ahern

OWN FACE
Clark Coolidge
1978
6-7/8" x 10"
80 pages
Edition of 750
Cover design by
Susan Coolidge
Photograph by
Russell Trall Neville

ANGEL HAIR CATALOGS

The Press produced a
total of ten catalogs, each
being 8-1/2 by 11" stapled
mimeos, circa 6-12 pages.
In addition to listing cur-
rent and backlist titles, the
catalogs printed poems
by Angel Hair writers.

**THE GOLDEN BOOK
OF WORDS**
Bernadette Mayer
1978
7" x 10"
80 pages
Edition of 750
Cover by Joe Brainard

ANGEL HAIR CATALOG #8
Cover by
Emilio Schneeman

PHOTO ACKNOWLEDGEMENTS

Courtesy of Bill Berkson
Frank O'Hara, p. 575

Courtesy of Sandy Berrigan
David Berrigan, Sandy Berrigan and Kate
Berrigan, p. 600

Courtesy of Charlotte Carter
Charlotte Carter, p. 578

Courtesy of Tom Clark
Cover photo of Lewis Warsh and Anne
Waldman
Tom Clark, Angelica Clark and Juliet Clark,
p. 579

Courtesy of Clark Coolidge
Clark Coolidge, p. 581

Courtesy of Bill Corbett
Philip Guston and Bill Corbett, p. 581

Courtesy of Donna Dennis
Les Levine and Donna Dennis, p. 583

Courtesy of Elsa Dorfman
Bill Corbett, p. 582
Robert Creeley, p. 583

Courtesy of Larry Fagin
Bill Berkson, p. 575
Maureen Owen and Sandy Berrigan, p. 578
Lewis Warsh, Joe Brainard and Kenward
Elmslie, p. 584
Robert Duncan and Larry Fagin, p. 585
Group photo posing for a painting by
George Schneeman, p. 586
Joan and Larry Fagin, p. 586
Larry Fagin and Ron Padgett, p. 587
Dick Gallup, p. 593
Alex Katz and George Schneeman, p. 595
Kenward Elmslie, Anne Waldman and
Lewis Warsh, p. 596
Lewis Warsh and Anne Waldman in San
Francisco, p. 600
George Schneeman, p. 602
Hannah Wiener, Tom Veitch and Johnny
Stanton, p. 606
Donna Dennis, Martha Diamond and
Hannah Wiener, p. 607

Courtesy of Barbara Guest
Barbara Guest, p. 584

Courtesy of Lee Harwood
John Ashbery and Lee Harwood, p. 588

Courtesy of Kenneth Koch
Kenneth Koch, p. 589

Courtesy of Gerard Malanga
John Wieners, p. 582
Ted Greeenwald and Ted Berrigan, p. 587
Joanne Kyger, p. 590
Bernadette Mayer and Anne Waldman,
p. 591
James Schuyler, p. 594
David Rosenberg, p. 594
Jim Carroll, p. 596
Harris Schiff, p. 598

Courtesy of Linda P. O'Brien
Jack Boyce and Joanne Kyger, p. 579
Edwin Denby, p. 589
George Kimball, Bill Berkson, Peter
Schjeldahl and Rudy Burckhardt, p. 592
Linda Schjeldahl, p. 601
René Ricard, p. 603

Courtesy of Ron Padgett
Tom Clark, Pat Padgett, Wayne Padgett and
Ron Padgett, p. 592

Courtesy of Bob Rosenthal
Anselm Berrigan, Edmund Berrigan and
Alice Notley, p. 591
Bob Rosenthal and Rochelle Kraut, p. 597
Jim Brodey and Bob Rosenthal, p. 597

Courtesy of Aram Saroyan
Aram Saroyan, Strawberry, Cream and
Gailyn, p. 598

Courtesy of Peter Schjeldahl
Peter Schjeldahl, p. 601

Courtesy of Emilio Schneeman
Katie Schneeman, p. 602

Courtesy of Lorenzo Thomas
Lorenzo Thomas, Luzmilda Thomas and
Cecilio Thomas, p. 603
Lorenzo Thomas, p. 604

Courtesy of Tony Towle
Tony Towle, p. 588

Courtesy of Anne Waldman
Michael Brownstein, p. 576
Joe Brainard, p. 576
Anne Waldman and Reed Bye, p. 577
Anne Waldman, Ambrose Waldman Bye,
    Naomi Riley and Reed Bye, p. 577
Cassandra and James Koller, p. 580
Gerard Malanga, p. 585
John Giorno, p. 604
Anne Waldman and Philip Whalen, p. 605

Courtesy of Lewis Warsh
Bolinas group photo, p. 580
Bernadette Mayer and Marie Warsh, p. 590
Jonathan Cott, p. 593
Ted Berrigan, p. 595
Ted Berrigan and Lewis Warsh, p. 599
Frances LeFevre Waldman and Anne
    Waldman, p. 605
Lewis Warsh, Bernadette Mayer, Sophia,
    Marie and Max, p. 606

INDEX

Page numbers in *italics* refer to images

Anne Waldman is a poet, performer, professor, anthologist and cultural activist. During the late sixties and well into the seventies she was director of the Poetry Project at St. Mark's Church in New York City's Lower East Side. She co-founded, with Allen Ginsberg, the Jack Kerouac School of Disembodied Poetics at Naropa University in Boulder, Colorado, in 1974. She is the author of over 30 books of her own writing, including *Fast Speaking Woman* (1975), the *Iovis* books I and II (1993/1997), *Kill or Cure* (1994) and *Marriage: A Sentence* (2000). She is the editor of, among others, *Nice To See You: Homage to Ted Berrigan* (1991) and *The Beat Book* (1996), and is co-editor of *Disembodied Poetics: Annals of the Jack Kerouac School* (1994). She has collaborated with a great many artists, including Joe Brainard, Elizabeth Murray, Susan Rothenberg, George Schneeman and Richard Tuttle. Anne Waldman has performed her poetry throughout the United States and around the world, giving readings in Germany, England, Italy, Scotland, The Czech Republic, Venezuela, Mexico, Austria, Norway, The Netherlands, Bali, India, Nicaragua and Canada, in some cases helping to generate literary projects in these places. Her latest work, a book of essays, *Vow to Poetry,* was published in 2001. She is on the core faculty of Naropa University in Boulder, and is the Artistic Director of its Annual Summer Writing Program.

Lewis Warsh is the author of two novels, *Agnes & Sally* (1984) and *A Free Man* (1991), two volumes of stories, *Money Under the Table* (1997) and *Touch of the Whip* (2001), three volumes of autobiographical writing, *Part of My History* (1972), *The Maharajah's Son* (1977) and *Bustin's Island '68* (1997), and numerous books of poems, including *Avenue of Escape* (1995) and *The Origin of the World* (2001). *Debtor's Prison*, a collaboration with video artist Julie Harrison, is forthcoming in Fall 2001, and a new novel, *Ted's Favorite Skirt*, in 2002. He is co-founder and publisher of United Artists Books. From 1991 to 1993 he was editor of *The World*, the literary magazine of The Poetry Project in New York. He has received grants from the National Endowment for the Arts, the New York Foundation of the Arts and the Fund for Poetry, and was one of the first recipients of an Editor's Fellowship award from the Coordinating Council of Literary Magazines. In 1994 he received the James Shestack Prize from The American Poetry Review. He has taught at SUNY Albany, Fairleigh Dickinson, The New School, Naropa University and The Poetry Project. He is presently on the faculty at Long Island University in Brooklyn.